THE FINAL DAY

BOOKS BY WILLIAM R. FORSTCHEN
FROM TOM DOHERTY ASSOCIATES

We Look Like Men of War
One Second After
Pillar to the Sky
One Year After
The Final Day

William R. Forstchen

THE FINAL DAY

A TOM DOHERTY ASSOCIATES BOOK New York

THE FINAL DAY

Copyright © 2016 by William R. Forstchen

A Forge Book
Published by Tom Doherty Associates
175 Fifth Avenue
New York, NY 10010

www.tor-forge.com

Forge® is a registered trademark of Macmillan Publishing Group, LLC.

The Library of Congress Cataloging-in-Publication Data is available upon request.

ISBN 978-0-7653-7673-2 (hardcover)
ISBN 978-1-4668-5190-0 (e-book)

Our books may be purchased in bulk for promotional, educational, or business use. Please contact your local bookseller or the Macmillan Corporate and Premium Sales Department at 1-800-221-7945, extension 5442, or by e-mail at MacmillanSpecialMarkets@macmillan.com.

First Edition: January 2017

Printed in the United States of America

0 9 8 7 6 5 4 3 2 1

For Robin

ACKNOWLEDGMENTS

It has been more than seven years since the publication of *One Second After*. Much has happened in the time since, as it of course does with all our lives. My daughter has matured into a fine young lady and graduated from college. Two and a half years ago, after giving a talk at a "prepper" conference, I met the true love of my life, my "Twin Flame," and we were recently married. Many new friends have come into my life because of what I write, and a few have drifted away. New lives have joined my world, and some old friends have slipped away, in particular a beloved veteran of Omaha Beach, Andy Andrews. There have been great surprises, the biggest one being that what started out as a relatively unknown book catapulted to the *New York Times* bestseller list and some even claim it helped to trigger the Prepper Movement. If so, I only see my work as a small part of a phenomena now embraced by millions.

There have been disappointments as well, and the biggest one is that I wrote *One Second After* at the behest of close friends in politics who believed that even though it was a novel, it would lay before the American public the existential threat to national survival. I had an optimistic belief that the book would trigger political action to harden our electrical infrastructure and have a far more robust foreign policy to prevent such weapons from getting into the hands of those who would willingly launch an

EMP attack. That has proven to be an utter failure and leaves me, and should leave all who read this, asking a most fundamental question: Why have our federal and state governments ignored this threat? In my own attempts to raise awareness and press for a political solution, I have, at times, been met with mocking disdain. It does remind me of the hypocrisy of those who lecture us about guns, and do so while surrounded by professional guards who are indeed well armed, while extolling us to strip ourselves naked. The analogy between those two issues is apt and you can project what I mean from there.

It is why I now believe that the only response left is for "we the people" to be prepared individually, then turn to neighbors, friends, and so forth until we as an entire nation can indeed take care of ourselves. I write this only days after the tragedy in Orlando, Florida. The casualty list is over a hundred. I fear that soon it could be a thousand, ten thousand, and, in the event of an EMP, into the hundreds of millions. Being truly prepared, individually and as a nation, is the only way we can ever ensure our survival against the forces of darkness and hate.

Anyhow, this is supposed to be an acknowledgments, and if you have read this far, it is time to get on with my many well-deserved thank-yous. Without the support, trust, and efforts of my friends at Tor/Forge Books, you would not be reading these words. Thirty years ago, when first entering this business, I met Tom Doherty at a conference and decided even then that someday I hoped to work with him. He and his team are the ideal of a publishing crew that every author should hope for. Thanks must go as well to my agent, Eleanor Wood of Spectrum Literary Agency, and her son and daughter, who are now part of the firm. We've been together more than twenty-five years, watched our children grow, and she has always been by my side as a friend and advisor. A special thanks as well to my friends with Ascot Media Group. They are a public-relations firm second to none and have played an instrumental role in getting these stories about EMP out to the public and media.

If I tried to name all the friends who have stood by me, offered advice, and impacted my work, these pages would run on like an Oscar acceptance speech. Those of you reading this bought the book to get to a story! Therefore, as Lincoln used to say, "I shall keep this short and sweet like the widow's dance." Thanks must go to my friends, neighbors, and coworkers at Black Mountain and Montreat College. They have accepted and even embraced my setting of a story in our community with grace. Whether a crisis comes one day or not, this truly is the best place on earth to call your home and where I have spent nearly a quarter of a century teaching. Shortly after *One Second After* came out, I was asked by newfound friends at Carolina Readiness to speak at a prepper conference they were sponsoring. I was expecting fifty guests or so, and I found instead over six hundred packing the room! That was just the start, and across these seven years I have met thousands of preppers . . . people of common sense, ideals, and faith in their God and their country. I am honored to count all as friends. And finally, the teachers in my life, going back to Ida Singer, then Russ Beaulieu and Betty Kellor, to Gunther Rothenberg, and at my college men like Don King and William Hurt. I hope I have lived up to your expectations.

In closing, I wrote in *One Second After* that it was my fervent prayer that thirty years hence my books would be forgotten, and if recalled at all, it would be that the darkness I feared never came to pass and my daughter went on to a life that she would live in peace. I still pray for that. I once believed my government would act to ensure our safety when it came to threats such as EMP and attack by radical groups around the world. I now have my doubts, at least short term, that such will be the case. I now place my faith of a peaceful future in your hands, my fellow citizens, it is up to us to act proactively so that this nation of, by, and for the people does not perish from the earth.

William R. Forstchen
June 2016

THE FINAL DAY

PROLOGUE

This is the BBC News. It is 3:00 Greenwich War Time, broadcasting to our friends in the Western Hemisphere on this the 920th day since the start of the war.

Later in this program, we will provide an in-depth report about the tragic aftermath of the full-scale nuclear exchange between India and Pakistan, followed by a report about the situation in the Middle East where the conflict continues to rage between Israel and its neighboring states—except for Jordan, which today reaffirmed its alliance with Israel against the Caliphate and its allies.

But first the news from the United States:

Today the self-declared federal government based in Bluemont announced that the former states of Virginia and Maryland have been brought up to what the government defines as "Level One" status, meaning that all forces allegedly in conflict with the "Reconstituted Federal Authority in Bluemont," as it now describes itself, have been pacified.

The Bluemont government announced earlier in the year that it has abandoned its plans to establish the Army of National Recovery, more commonly referred to as the ANR. Today's announcement of the completion of establishing stabilized status in those two mid-Atlantic states has been attributed to actions waged by the traditional armed forces of the United States. The Bluemont government declared that the victory was achieved by units withdrawn from

*confrontation with China's occupation of states in the West and other units that
were in service overseas on the day the war started.*

*After our reporting of other news of the day, a panel of experts will discuss
the apparently changing status of the situation in North America.*

*But first, this message for our friends in the western provinces of Chinese-
occupied Canada: "The chair is against the door." I repeat, "The chair is against
the door."*

CHAPTER ONE

"Do you remember the opening line of that book by Charles Dickens, 'It was the best of times, it was the worst of times'?"

John Matherson whispered the famous line with hands wrapped around a warm mug filled with, of all things, coffee—*real* coffee. He looked over at his friend Forrest Burnett, who had arrived bearing the precious gift. Where it had been looted from John had learned never to ask.

Forrest's crooked face, twisted up by his old Afghan wound, left eye socket covered with a patch that certainly gave him a pirate look, smiled in reply.

"Wasn't that from the movie where the guy gets his head cut off by the French mob at the end?" Forrest replied.

John chuckled. "Yeah, something like that."

"That guy was crazy, stepping in to take his friend's place at the guillotine, and to top it off, the guy who gets rescued escapes with the girl. Never did like that movie. Why mention it?"

John sighed, standing up and walking over to the window of his office to look out.

The first snow of late autumn had arrived early this year, blanketing the Montreat College campus with half a foot or more. Old-timers prognosticating over woolly caterpillars and nut-gathering squirrels had predicted

this was going to be a tough one, and this early November snow appeared
to be the first proof.

Before the Day, a first snow, for John, was a time of relaxation and happy
memories. Classes were usually canceled, forewarned by the Weather Channel on the Internet. He would have stocked in extra firewood, and it would
be a long day of reading by the fire, Jennifer and Elizabeth outside playing,
coming in soaking wet for some hot chocolate, and later in the day board
games like Clue or Monopoly. If the power went out, so what? It added to
the cozy feel, at least for the first few days, camping out by the fireplace and
watching the woods fill up with snow.

Before the Day . . .

Jennifer is dead. His eldest daughter, Elizabeth, all of nineteen years old,
was a mother with a two-year-old son and had finally taken a further step
away and moved out of the house in Montreat. She had married Seth
Robinson—the son of his old neighbor and close friend Lee—and was
living with her new husband, and they were already expecting a child.

How that as well had changed after the Day. Only a few years back, the
line had become that twenty-five was the new eighteen. Most kids were expected to go to college, get a degree, start their first job on the career ladder,
date for a while, at last find the right partner, settle down, and around
twenty-eight to thirty finally start a family. It was again like the world at
the time of the Civil War—to marry at sixteen, seventeen. An unmarried
girl at twenty-one was seen as already becoming an old maid.

No longer, and the historian in John read it as something that was primal, that after a tribe, a city, an entire country had lost so many lives in a war,
the paradigm shifted to marrying young and starting families young—the
so-called baby boom of the late '40s and '50s a recent example.

At the other end of this age spectrum, Jen—dear old Jen, mother-in-law
of his first marriage to Mary—was gone. Perhaps in a different time, her
life might have gone on for another five, even ten to fifteen years. But gone
now as well were all the hospitals and medications that extended life, and
thus something primal occurred with the elderly. Once they had seen too
much tragedy, the will to live for so many was simply extinguished.

She had quietly slipped away in August. He had seen it far too often after
the Day—the elderly one day calmly saying that they had experienced

enough of life with all its vicissitudes and it was time to leave. He found her one evening sitting "alone" out on the sunporch, happily talking with her husband, young Jennifer, and her daughter—his wife, Mary, who had died long before the Day. She was talking to ghostly presences. He stood silent, eavesdropping as she talked and laughed softly to replies that were silent, at least to his ears.

Makala had slipped up to his side, listened as well for a moment with tears streaming down her face. Makala then guided him to the far end of the house, telling him to leave her be, that, as a nurse, she had often seen such, a clear sign that the beloved who had already crossed over were gathering to help in the final journey.

Jen insisted upon going to sleep that evening not in her own bed but out on the sunporch that looked out over young Jennifer's grave. They found her there in the morning, as if just gently asleep.

They buried her next to Jennifer. Yet another thread that connected John to a former life severed that day.

Even his old familiar office was gone, burned out in the fight with Fredericks back in the spring. It was decided to move what was left up to the Montreat campus and set up a new town office in the basement of Gaither Hall, a logical decision after it had served as the backup command post during that fight. It had been suggested to actually move it into the now-empty office of the college president, but John could not concur.

That office complex held for him a deep symbolic significance. When a special meeting involving representatives from across the ever-expanding "State of Carolina" took place, he would unlock that room for use. Centered on the office wall opposite the desk of the college president was the famed painting of George Washington kneeling in prayer at Valley Forge. It was a reminder of his friend Dan Hunt, who once occupied that room and died in the first year after the start of the war.

His own office downstairs in the basement of Gaither was an easy walk from his home and just down the slope from the college was the new "factory," christened "the Dreamworks." Within the walls of what had once been Anderson Auditorium, full-scale production was under way, assembling new electrical generators complete with wirework for drawing out copper wire for the generators and the stringing of power lines.

The electrical light that illuminated his office regularly flickered as power fluctuated up and down; the system was, after all, jury-rigged, very much a learn-as-you-go process.

The snow was picking up again, swirling around the small campus commons below Gaither, the tattered American flag that had flown during the air battle with Fredericks's Apache choppers standing out stiff in the northeasterly blow.

Watching such moments with the first snow of autumn falling had once indeed been the best of times, and he tried to not let melancholy take hold. He was actually drinking real coffee, the room was illuminated by an actual electric lightbulb, and the woodstove that students had installed in the room was radiating a pleasant heat the way only a wood-fired stove could.

"Why so depressed, John?" Forrest asked.

John heard a match striking and looked over his shoulder and saw Forrest leaning back in his chair and of all things actually lighting a cigarette. Merciful God, how he now longed for one as well, but the promise to his dying daughter and the potential explosion from Makala if she ever detected the scent on his breath was enough to restrain him, even though he did step closer and inhale the drifting smoke.

"Just the snowfall triggering a lot of memories this morning," John replied, settling back into his office chair, his gaze still lingering on the snow dancing on the wind. The sound of laughter echoed, and he caught a glimpse of a couple of his students sliding down the slope on a makeshift sled. Kids, long ago hardened by war and backbreaking labor to repair the damage of the spring battles to Gaither Hall before the onset of winter, were taking a break and again being kids. Their unit commander, Kevin Malady, would soon be out with a shout for them to get back to work, but for the moment, he was glad to see them enjoying themselves.

"Yeah, same here," Forrest said, gaze drifting off as he absently reached over with his one hand to scratch the stump of his missing arm.

"Feeling it again?" John asked.

"Ghost limb, they call it," Forrest said with a chuckle. "Yeah, it feels like it's still there and itchy as hell. Memories of snow for me get all screwed up by this." He motioned toward the missing limb with his good hand and then up to the eye patch.

"I loved to hunt as a kid; we always got a lot more snow over on the north side of Mount Mitchell than you did here. Easy to track deer, fox, bear. Friends and I would even camp out in it, get a deer, and then just stay out in the woods for days living off the venison and some potatoes and corn we packed along." He smiled wistfully. "And more than a few mason jars of shine and a bit of homegrown weed as well. A lot better than sitting in a damn boring history class in school, and given the way the world is now, a better education for our futures as well."

"For someone who apparently hated history classes, you sure know a lot about it," John said with a smile.

"Oh yeah, you were once a history professor. What good did that do you when it came to surviving in this mess?"

"It helps at times, Forrest."

"Okay, I guess it did when it came to running things and getting that 'Declaration,' as you folks call it, written. Lot of good that will do, though, if the BBC reports are true."

"Gave me the idea for how to face off against the Posse."

"You mean you used Hannibal's plan for the Battle of Cannae?"

John smiled at that and nodded. "Seems you know more history than you let on, Forrest. Often the mark of a good leader, which you sure as hell were and still are."

"And it should have told me not to volunteer for that extra tour of duty in Afghanistan. The way it was being fought by the time I shipped there, it had turned into another Vietnam. Build laagers, hunker down, can't shoot even when shot at, and the bad guys own the rest of the countryside while we wandered around like fools trying to win 'hearts and minds.'"

Forrest shifted his gaze to the storm outside as he took one final drag clear down to the filter and let the cigarette burn out. He stood up and went to the window, pulled the flimsy curtain back, looked out, and sighed.

"When I copped all of this in Afghanistan it was a day like this one." He motioned again to the eye patch and the missing arm. "It was a freeze-your-ass-off day. Still haunted by the memory of all that pink frozen slush where the rest of my squad lay, blown apart, the crunching sound of footfalls on snow as the bastards who ambushed us came in to make sure we were all dead and loot our weapons and gear. That's my memory of snow now."

John was silent. It was the most detail his friend, who but six months back had been an enemy who had damn near killed him, had yet said about the day he was torn apart in a war all but forgotten now.

Several minutes passed as they silently sipped their contraband coffee, a gift Forrest would show up with occasionally with a clear "don't ask, don't tell" understanding between them. Forrest lit another Dunhill, smoked it halfway down, and then pinched the flame out, sticking what was left into his breast pocket.

"To what do I owe the honor of your visit today?" John finally asked, for it was a very long trek over the mountains, requiring several gallons of precious gas for Forrest's Polaris six-wheeler.

"You've heard the BBC reports about Roanoke being pulled in with the government up in Bluemont?"

"Yeah, I was about to suggest the state council getting together here this weekend to talk it over. It is only prudent to expect we might be next on their list."

"I expected an immediate response after the way we trashed their ANR unit back in the spring, and then nothing. But I think something has got to be stirring by this point."

"Why I said, 'Best of times, worst of times,'" John replied, watching as the last wisps of smoke from Forrest's cigarette coiled toward the ceiling and then disappeared.

"'Best of times, worst of times,'" and this time it was Forrest. "I was hoping for a winter of peace after so much crap these last few years."

"You think it will go bad?"

"If you expect shit to happen, John, you'll never be surprised when it does."

"Thanks for that cogent piece of advice."

"The price of a good cup of coffee and the offer of a cigarette. Anyhow, beyond bearing potential bad news, I thought I'd hang around here for a few days. With the storm, it'd be a good time to teach some of your kids winter survival stuff."

"Good idea. What made you think of it?"

"Because before it's done, I think they'll be fighting a winter campaign, my friend. Up in the mountains of Afghanistan, it was colder than Valley

Forge, the Bulge, even the Chosin Reservoir in Korea. The Afghans understood it; more than a few out there with me did not. I don't want to see that again."

"You think it will come to that?"

"Don't you?"

John did not reply. There were far too many other worries at the moment. The harvest was barely adequate to see his rapidly expanding community through the winter, especially with this early onset of autumn snow when there should have still been time to gather in additional forage. Two years ago, his worries extended only as far as Montreat, Black Mountain, and Swannanoa, but in the exuberant days after the defeat of the forces from the government at Bluemont, dozens of other communities had allied in, as far south as Flat Rock and Saluda, north to the Tennessee border, east to the outskirts of Hickory, nearly sixty thousand people in all. A tragic number when it was realized that more than a half million had once lived in the same region.

The city dwellers who had survived in the ruins of Asheville were of course welcomed, but few came in with any kind of resources, having lived hand to mouth on what could be scavenged from that once upscale new age–oriented community. It was the backwoods communities like Marion, even Morganton, with groups surviving like the one led by Forrest who joined with a quid pro quo of skills and even access to food that really counted in what all were now calling "the State of Carolina."

Forrest was usually not the talkative type, and John remained silent. Something else was up with this man, and John waited him out.

"Someone came into my camp yesterday," Forrest finally offered. "I think you should come back with me and meet him."

"Who is he, and why?"

"Some of my people found him wandering on Interstate 26. Poor bastard is pretty far gone—several ribs broken, bad frostbite, and coming down with pneumonia. He got jumped by some marauders on the road and took a severe beating. Chances are he'll be dead in a few days, so we decided he should stay put and you come to him."

John did not reply. Forrest was not given to extreme reactions; months earlier, he had come into Black Mountain, leading nearly fifty of his community, after they were hit by an air attack from Fredericks's Apaches. The man had been gut shot and kept refusing treatment until those with him were treated first. If he judged their refugee to be too sick to travel, John wouldn't question the decision.

"Who is he?"

"Says he's a major with the regular army. Claimed he served alongside you years ago. Name of Quentin Reynolds. That he was with the army that took Roanoke."

"Quentin?" John whispered. The name struck somewhere, but if they had served together, that was close on to a couple of decades ago.

"Claims he was an adjutant to a General Bob Scales who's in charge up there."

"Bob Scales?" And with that, John sat bolt upright. It was Bob whom he had been speaking to at the Pentagon when the EMP hit. It was Bob who had been his mentor during his army career and who had arranged through the good ole boy network his teaching position at Montreat when John left the military to nurse Mary through her final months in the town where she had grown up. "Bob is alive?"

"He didn't say that—just that he served with him."

"Still, I got to talk with him," John said excitedly. He looked back out the window; the storm was picking up. "Think we can make it now if we left today?"

"If it's like this down here, I wouldn't want to venture crossing over Craggy Gap and the Mount Mitchell range with night setting in. It was really blowing in as I came over this morning. Best let it settle down first."

"Damn it." John sighed. "This Quentin, think he'll make it?"

"Can't say, to be frank. Just had a gut sense I should come over and tell you. Anyhow, who is this Bob Scales?"

"I served with him years ago and thought he had died when things went down. If he is in charge of things up in Roanoke, my God, I got to find out."

John's worried thoughts were interrupted by the sight of Paul Hawkins running across the commons, head bowed low against the storm. Paul barged into the room, bringing with him a cold blast of air, Forrest cursing for him to close the damned door.

"John, you gotta come see something now!" Paul cried, features alight with a broad grin, made rather comical by the mantle of snow dripping from his broad-brimmed hat.

It was Paul and his wife, Becka, who had discovered the nineteenth-century journals of the Institute of Electrical and Electronics Engineers, known as the IEEE, in the college library's basement, the trade magazine for the new industry of electricity. Filled with discussions and debates about the new science of electrical engineering, complete with detailed patent applications by the likes of Edison, Tesla, and Westinghouse, it was a discovery that ignited the plan to restore electricity, a "blueprint," to bring their community back online.

"What is it, Paul? I'm kind of preoccupied at the moment with some news Forrest brought in." He nodded to his friend sitting in the corner.

"Can't explain it; you just got to see it now. You too, Forrest."

John looked over at Forrest.

"You sure we can't go back over the mountain today?" John asked anxiously.

Forrest shook his head. "Maybe first light tomorrow."

John knew better than to second-guess Forrest, and he sighed. It would have to wait. He looked over at Paul, forced a smile, and nodded.

"Well, let's go see what has you all fired up."

If Paul thought there was something worth going out into a blizzard for, it had to at least be interesting.

The two pulled on jackets and, with heads tucked down, followed Paul out into the gale, Forrest cursing all the way as they followed Paul on the walkway that led up to the old library. The storm was of such intensity that John realized Forrest was right; to cross over the six-thousand-foot-high mountain range in this weather, no matter how urgent the mission, would be suicide.

The library, a building that architecturally had never fit into the classic native stone construction of most of the other buildings on campus, had always been a source of woe. It had leaky ceilings, and even before the Day, it had been sealed off for a semester because of the dampness and mold.

Once into the building and his hat and scarf removed, John took a deep breath and knew his allergies would soon nail him. The main part of the building was dark, the sound of dripping water echoing. A single light shone through the swinging doorway leading into the back office, where Paul and his young wife had taken up quarters, preferring to live there rather than in so many of the well-built and now-abandoned homes and cabins that surrounded the campus. At least this part of the cavernous building was warm and cheery, a large woodstove providing heat. Becka was there, balancing a newborn twin on each arm, and John smiled at the sight of them, going up to kiss Becka lightly on the forehead.

"How you doing, young lady?"

"Feeling better thanks to Makala's attention and help." As she spoke, one of the newborns stirred, whimpered slightly, and then nuzzled back in against her mother.

As is too often common with twins, they had been a month premature. There was a time when that was not much of a concern with nearly all hospitals providing intensive care neonatal centers. But now? The babies had come into the world in what was the community's local hospital in the old hotel, the Assembly Inn, on the far side of campus. John's wife, who was due herself in another two months, had taken charge, and rather than let them return to their makeshift home in the library, she had ordered the three to stay at their home, setting up a nursery in the sunroom and hovering over all three during the first crucial weeks.

It had been an emotional experience for John, his home again echoing with the late-night cries of newborns, the sight of a very pregnant Makala up with them every night, in the morning holding one of the girls while an exhausted Becka nursed the other.

The sunporch had been the final sickroom for his daughter, Jennifer, who died there. It was also where his mother-in-law, Jen, had slipped away. He had tried to balance all, death and new life in the same room, and in some small way, it had helped to ease his grief and heartrending memories.

John fought down the temptation to ask to hold one of the twins for a moment. Makala had repeatedly warned that in this now heavily germ-laden world, the less exposure they had to others over the next few months, the better. Paul, after a quick kiss to Becka's forehead and a fond look at the girls, was already pointing the way to the basement door.

John and Forrest followed him down into the darkness, and at the bottom of the stairs, Paul flicked a switch and a single fluorescent light flickered to life. It was definitely something John and Forrest were still not really used to—a flick of a switch and a light comes on. The town's electrical grid was still slowly expanding from its first base at Lake Susan, and half a dozen other hydro projects were under way across the State of Carolina, but electric was still strictly rationed to public facilities and even then only ran for half a dozen hours each day. Paul and Becka had a special exemption for the cavernous library basement, able to illuminate their work area by recharging old flashlights while the power was on and suspending them from the ceilings so they could continue what they called "mining the past," and from the way Paul was acting, he must have hit pay dirt again.

John looked around the storage area in wonder. The air was heavy with the disquieting scent of mold, mildew, mouse droppings, and tens of thousands of slowly decaying magazines and books. He paused to look at one pile that Becka said she was sifting through, a vast stack of *Life* magazines going back to the 1930s. The sight of it triggered memories of when he was a boy down with a bad case of the flu when his mother would come home from the library every few days with magazines from the Second World War era and the ones from the Civil War centennial of the early 1960s, inspiring his lifelong interest in the subject.

Life, Look, Saturday Evening Post, Newsweek, Time, even a pile of *Mad* magazines created a nostalgic smile and also a sadness for the lost world—not just of his childhood but for everyone's loss.

"It's back here, you guys!" Paul cried, pointing the way, and John felt pulled away, resolving that someday, if there ever was a someday without all his worries and concerns, he'd come back down here and perhaps just spend that day with *Mad* and the zany artwork of Don Martin, or dig through the stack of *Boys' Life* for short stories by Ray Bradbury, or just look at the cover art for *Saturday Evening Post* and the lost world of Norman Rockwell. He looked over at Forrest, who was smiling as he thumbed through an aged copy of *Playboy*. John wondered why anyone would ever donate that to the college library book sale.

Forrest shrugged. "I used to get it for the articles," he said a bit defensively, and John laughed. A pleasure since laughter was now so rare in his life. "Really, I loved Jean Shepherd—you know, the guy who wrote that Christmas movie about the kid with the BB gun. Here's one of his stories."

John looked over Forrest's shoulder, a bit disbelieving, only to see it was indeed a story by "Shep," whom he used to listen to on the radio when he was a kid and had once used the identical excuse when his mother had found his stash of the infamous magazines hidden behind his desk.

"Come on, you two, and leave that magazine there." Paul stood, pointing the way farther back into the rabbit warren of the basement.

John followed him, going past a table stacked with educational tools discarded decades ago: old Dukane machines, which were thirty-five-millimeter projectors rigged to a record player, the slide changing every time there was a high-toned beep from the record—students were forever trying to imitate the sound of the beep to throw the projector off for some show for health class; overhead projectors, abandoned when PowerPoint came along; stacks of eight-track music cartridges; old classical 33 RPM records, which were useless, though older 78s were sought after thanks to those who had found hand-cranked record players in their attics and basements; mimeograph machines, which even he had tried to fiddle with after the Day, but the copying solution with its unique alcohol smell was nowhere to be found or reproduced. Just the sight of those old machines triggered a memory of the smell when a teacher handed out an assignment or bulletin, the blue ink smearing at times if still wet.

There were IBM Selectric typewriters, a dozen or more; John had looked those over as well after the Day, hoping that maybe the ribbons could be looted for his long-ago worn-out Underwood manual typewriter. There were several Singer sewing machines, from back in the days when the college was a female-only institution and students were most likely taught home economics. Of all things, a grandfather clock caught John's eye, something that might be worth salvaging until he saw that the weights and pendulum were fake, an electrical cord draped up over the top of the machine. And back in a corner, of all things, a pinball machine, a classic Black Knight, which he remembered was still in use in the student lounge when he had first come to teach at the college.

Paul had stopped at a workbench in the far corner of this moldering gold mine of lost memories and lost technologies. He was smiling like a guide in a cave who was obviously proud of his domain as if he himself had created it.

He was pointing at a tan box, the corporate logo just above the keyboard—a more than thirty-year-old Apple IIe computer.

"You found an antique computer and . . . ?" John asked, voice trailing off.

"Behold," Paul said, still grinning, and with a flourish, he clicked the On button for the fourteen-inch monitor and then the computer.

The screen flashed to life, the room filled with light as the screen warmed up and came into focus, displaying the Apple logo in glorious RGB color.

John actually stepped back in amazement, almost feeling like some tribal primitive, a flash memory of the teddy bear characters in one of the *Star Wars* episodes, which he hated since militarily it was so absurd, going near crazy with wonder and then worshipful awe at the sight of C-3PO, floating around the tribal gathering thanks to Luke using the Force.

"My God, it works?" Forrest gasped.

"Hell yeah, it works!" Paul cried. "Watch this!"

He put an old five-and a-half-inch floppy disk into one of the disk drives; it started to whirl and click, and all three stood silent as the seconds passed, and then a tinny familiar tune barely audible echoed from the monitor's speaker and the logo for Pac-Man flashed on to the screen.

"Oh my God," John whispered in awe, a deep, almost tearful nostalgia filling him. When Elizabeth was five and recovering from a long bout of the flu, his wife, Mary, had pulled their old Apple computer out of the attic, set it up by Elizabeth's bed, and entertained her for a long rainy spring day with Mary's favorite games the two of them had played while they were students at Duke.

He had written his master's thesis on that computer, needing over twenty floppy disks to store his paper on proto-computers created for gunnery control prior to World War I. He was the envy of many students and even some of the professors who were still on electric typewriters or just beginning the transition to the first IBM Micros, as they were then called. Just running the final spelling check had taken several days, which at the time seemed like a miracle versus having to pay some English major to manually check your work one final time and then hand type it yet again.

Using a brand-new, expensive 2400-baud modem, he had actually managed typing in lengthy string codes via a system called the Internet to try to access data from a British library without success, but it was still a fascinating adventure at the time. Printing it out had taken half a day on their tractor-feed dot-matrix printer. He could still recall the speed and buzzing sound of it as it glided across the page, a momentary pause as the tractor feed advanced the paper up one line, and then the printer head running backward across the page.

"Mind if I join you three?"

John looked back to the darkened staircase and forced a smile of welcome. It was Ernie Franklin, the man who saved his life during the final confrontation with Dale Fredericks. He was grateful, of course, but at times Ernie could be more than a little domineering.

"I sent word to Ernie about my find," Paul whispered.

"Why?" Forrest asked.

"He worked for IBM back in the days of *Apollo* and the shuttle—figured the old guy might know a thing or two."

Ernie stepped up to the workbench, gazed at the screen for a moment, and snorted. "It would have to be one of those damn Apples. Damn toys."

"I did write my master's thesis on one," John retorted.

"And then they screwed everyone over when Jobs dropped the operating system and went running off with those dinky nine-inch-screen Macs. We laughed our asses off over all you Apple fanatics stuck with the IIe system."

"Wait a minute," Paul interjected. "I asked you over here to explain something, Ernie. We can argue about which system was better later."

John nodded, looking back at the image on the screen of the Pac-Man character, the tinny theme playing over and over.

"Could you turn that damn music off?" Ernie asked. "My daughter was addicted to that damn game, and it drove me crazy."

Paul looked at the machine, not sure what to do, and Ernie just stepped forward and flipped the switch, turning it off. All three gasped as the screen went dark, as if he had pulled a curtain back down over a returning to the past from before the war.

"If it turned on before, it will again," Ernie replied calmly, "but before we do that."

He reached into his jacket pocket and pulled out a small flashlight and clicked it on.

If anyone in their entire community was prepared for life after the Day, it was Ernie Franklin and his family. After more than three years, they were still living off long-term rations stockpiled years earlier. His all-terrain Polaris was still running, and John had learned not to ask just how much gas he still had stored and treated against degrading. The old guy was always proud to show off his solar-powered flashlights like the one he had flicked on now, and without bothering to ask permission of Paul, he popped the lid off the top of the old—one could even say antique—computer.

This basement was Paul's domain. John waited for a response from Paul, the young man who had designed and brought back to life the electrical system of the community, but Hawkins said nothing, obviously deferring.

Ernie peered inside the guts of the old Apple like a dentist poking around in the mouth of a victim in the chair, grunting with disapproval.

"Inexcusable," Ernie whispered. "You educators never knew how to take care of a computer. Look at all this dust, and what the hell is this?"

He pointed down at the motherboard, and the three leaned forward to look over his shoulder.

"Looks like dog or cat hair! This is a mess. For now, leave it off; I'll take it back home and blow it out."

"What?" John asked.

"I'm taking it back with me. I still have some canned air."

"Canned air?" Forrest asked. "What the hell are you talking about?"

"Pressurized air in a can for cleaning computers."

"Just blow on the damn thing," John whispered.

Ernie did not even bother to reply to what he thought was such obvious stupidity. "Let's wrap it up; I'll take it with me."

"No way," John stated quietly and forcefully. "It stays here for now."

Ernie braced himself back up, ready for a good argument, something he always took delight in.

"Look, Ernie, it stays here. This thing is pure gold. Transporting through a storm back to your place, that's crazy. Just go get that canned air, whatever else you need, and come back here."

"That will take at least a gallon of gas," Ernie replied with a cagey smile. "Will the town provide it?"

John sighed. They were scraping the bottom of their gas supply, his dream of somehow going over to steam power for transportation and the running of precious farm machinery still at a cold start for now. But this was too important to argue about at the moment; the curiosity about this discovery and all that it implied was overwhelming.

"Give me the bill tomorrow; I'll make good on it."

"Sure." And without further comment, the lid off the computer, he reached to the side and flicked it back on, and again the three standing around him gasped as the screen flickered to life.

"I thought you said it needed to be blown or something," Forrest said, and there was a bit of a grin as he spoke, for Ernie was infamous at times for going into off-colored repartee. Paul cleared his throat and nodded back to the stairway where his wife, having tucked the twins in for their nap, was standing and watching the goings-on.

Ernie nodded, backing off, and continued to peer into the machine. "It's okay for the moment," he finally replied, continuing to examine the motherboard and other boards slotted in for the video and sound, chuckling with delight.

"Damn, I gotta admit, in its day, it really was something, even though it was a toy compared to what we were developing with IBM. A 64K machine for under three thousand bucks—and that was in 1980s money, no less. You know, I helped design the operating systems for the space shuttle. Five computers not much bigger than this thing ran that entire spacecraft. That's when we had to squeeze out every byte of usage in the software. No gigs and terabytes around back then, even with the big Cray machines the military had. We were still storing data on ten-inch magnetic reel-to-reels when I first started."

He sighed, and for a moment, John could sense the inner sadness of this man who had been viewed as a crazy Jeremiah by some when he would publicly warn about the fragility of the nation's infrastructure. He had retired to these mountains with that exact thought in mind, that it was all about to come crashing down.

"Ernie, the question is how and why?" John asked, interrupting his musings.

"What?"

"How and why is this computer working?"

Ernie stepped back and looked around the semi-dark room, illuminated only by the single fluorescent light overhead and the softly glowing television screen.

"Easy enough. I bet this machine was dumped down here fifteen, maybe twenty years ago when you guys finally decided to leave Apple behind and upgrade to a Pentium. Someone stuck it in a corner, and—the key thing— it was totally off-line. The EMP pulse and its impact has a lot of variables. Intensity, line of sight from the weapon burst, how much shielding this basement provided."

Ernie shined his flashlight around the room, chuckling sadly at the sight of all the piled-up magazines, books, and electrical tools that were once part of the business of teaching at a small college. He walked over to where several white and black boxes were stacked under the workbench.

"Now these babies," he announced with delight, "those are mine; I helped write some of the software. IBM 8088s, our competition for the Apples, which you educators loved to cling to. Bet the administration at least had those; they always were smarter than professors when it came to this stuff."

John bristled slightly at Ernie's jab as he squatted down, wiping dust and mildew off the front of one of the boxes.

"Yup, a tower box model. We gotta take a look at this next."

"Wait a minute," John interjected, "let's not get ahead of ourselves here. Ernie, how, why, and what do we do with it?" As he spoke, he nodded back to the Apple.

"Like I said, it survived the EMP pop and then just sat here undamaged. Nothing unusual about that."

"How come we didn't know before?" Forrest asked.

"Well, because we just didn't have the juice," Paul replied. "Once we've got at least some electricity going, why, we just kind of . . ."

The question was so damned obvious, John realized. Why didn't any of them come running down to this basement the day after they got a few kilowatts of electricity running and start trying to hook things back up?

"I never really thought about it," Paul said woodenly. "Too busy with getting lighting, juice for the sterilizing autoclave and hot water in the hospital, high-intensity lighting for the surgery room, more juice for the chemistry lab, stuff like that. Any of the computers sitting in faculty offices and such were just dead hunks of toasted boards and wires and tossed into a basement or Dumpster after the Day, figuring they were all fried."

"Because they were all wired in and got zapped by the full overload," Ernie stated.

"Ernie, a question?" John asked.

"Sure, what?"

"You of all people, didn't you think to stick a computer into your base-ment inside one of those faraday cages folks were later talking about?"

Ernie looked off, now obviously embarrassed and caught off guard, his silence answer enough.

John remembered how a few months before everything hit the fan, how Paul and others with the IT team for the school had finished remodeling the computer center because the school was creating a new major in cyber-security. The old machines, in an age where a computer aged faster than Detroit-built cars of the 1980s, were just simply tossed into the Dumpster after the hard drives were downloaded for anything of value and then wiped clean.

Truly a throwaway world that now seemed a thousand years away.

The fluorescent light overhead began to hum and flicker.

Ernie quickly reached behind the Apple and pulled the plug, the screen going dark.

"This power supply isn't clean at all," he growled, glancing over at Paul.

"What do you mean, not clean?" Forrest asked.

"Just that." Paul sighed. "Someone throws a switch on in the hospital, it sucks up a few kilowatts, the voltage to the rest of the grid fluctuates, and that can be death, especially for these older machines. It's exactly the thing that can kill this computer while we're gazing in wonder at it. I'll bring some surge protectors along."

He hesitated.

"All right," Ernie sighed, "I got a couple of portable solid-state solar-charging battery systems at home. Gives clean, steady juice for electronics—I'll bring that over as well to power these computers."

"You got one of those?" John asked sharply. "Nice to know now."

Ernie shrugged. "Be prepared, as the Boy Scouts used to say."

"But you didn't have a computer stashed off, did you?"

"You accusing me of something, John?" Ernie snapped back.

John held up a hand in a calming gesture. "No, but still?"

"Look, we all got caught with our pants down in different ways. My wife Linda kept complaining that I was trashing up the basement with cast-off computers, so, like everyone else, I tossed them out when I upgraded every year or two."

He sighed, and John could see that the memory troubled him. The old guy had most likely spent many a night kicking himself with that memory of all the computers he had once owned and then thrown out rather than storing away. Again, the throwaway society before the Day. At least some of the old-time ham radio operators had hung on to those precious devices and had them stashed away "just in case." Some even took pride in the niche hobby of actually operating old ham radios with vacuum tubes rather than "newfangled transistors."

Such a lost world, John thought sadly, looking at the darkened screen of the computer, symbolic of all that they had allowed to slip out of their grasp. America in an instant plunged into darkness and wondering at this moment if the few small flickering lights of hope were going out now as well.

He remembered Sir Edward Grey's heartfelt cry when midnight struck on a warm August evening in London of 1914, and war with Germany had come to pass. "The lamps are going out all over Europe, we shall not see them lit again in our lifetime."

In a way, how prophetic his words had been. That first war ending a hundred years of peace. The prophetic H. G. Wells predicting it truly was the beginning of the end, complete with atomic weapons. The steady, peaceful advance of the Edwardian era did indeed die in the trenches of Ypres, Verdun, and the Somme, with civilization taking a step backward to unleash poison gas, flamethrowers, bombs tumbling from the sky into undefended cities, and millions tearing at each other in the squalid mud of the trenches in primal rage with knives and bare fists. It led to a second war of death camps and brilliant flashes of light delivered on August mornings, thirty-one years after Edward Grey spoke and H. G. Wells uttered his prophecies, as entire cities were incinerated in a blinding flash.

Then the long years of what was called a Cold War, civilized nations ready to unleash a thousand such flashes of light over their enemies, no one realizing at first that when they created those first such bombs, it was not the blast, the fire as hot as the heart of the sun, that could destroy; it was something subtle, a mere microsecond of a massive gamma ray burst ignited out in space, that as it raced to the earth's surface at the speed of light would free off electrons in the upper atmosphere's oxygen and nitrogen—and as it did so building up to an overwhelming static discharge that could cripple the greatest nation in the history of humanity and leave 90 percent of its citizens dead two years later.

It was something he had long ago learned not to allow himself to dwell on too much, for surely it would drive him to impotent despair. Here he had been asking Ernie the how and why of this one computer surviving when the far greater question still was how and why his entire nation, his entire world, had allowed the unthinkable to happen. Who was responsible? Surely someone must have known it was coming. And with that coming, his youngest daughter became marked to die.

"John, are you okay?"

It was Becka, who was standing behind him, reaching up to touch him on the shoulder with a soothing gesture. He realized there were tears in his eyes, and he forced a smile.

"Yeah, sure. The babies asleep?"

"Like kittens."

It was hard with just those two words to hold back long-suppressed tears. Those were exactly the same words Mary used long ago to describe Jennifer when she was tucked in and asleep. When they had learned she had a highly aggressive type 1 diabetes, they could not help but hover watchfully over her. The memory of it was made even more poignant after Mary learned she had something aggressive as well, breast cancer that would finally take her, leaving him with two young girls to raise. Nights when he would look in at her asleep, the two girls asleep to either side of her, knowing their mother was ill, and with childlike instinct sensing that she would soon go away from them forever.

And he would think of them as two kittens nestled in against their mother.

He struggled for control, turned away from the others, and walked off to the other side of the basement, absently picking up one of the old *Life* magazines as if studying it, his friends having the instinctive sense that he wanted to be alone.

The magazine was from right after World War II, falling open to an article "Our Boys Are Come Home"—pictures of the old *Queen Mary* being escorted into New York Harbor, fireboats around it up sending up a salute of red-, white-, and blue-colored water, the Statue of Liberty in the background. Joyful mothers, wives, and children embracing young men, young men with dark, haunted eyes, age far beyond their years etched into their faces, in tears as they returned embraces. On the following pages, an article about the new homes to be built a thousand at a time in a place called Levittown.

Gone, all of it gone. The young captain from the ANR he had taken prisoner back in the spring and who was now part of his inner core of advisors had briefly served with that force on the Jersey Shore, facing Manhattan, a deadly island now quarantined with reports that bubonic plague and cholera were still endemic with the few thousand survivors still living there, scurrying and scrounging in the vast, abandoned concrete canyons.

No nuclear blast had leveled what was once said to be the pulsing heart of the Western world . . . just quietly turn off the switch, and in an instant, it was as uninhabitable as Antarctica or the searing Gobi Desert . . . its once fertile lands that had greeted Henry Hudson and Peter Stuyvesant long paved over—except for Central Park, where it was rumored that feral dogs, once tamed and loving golden retrievers and spaniels, had been wiped out, replaced by breeds of mongrels who again hunted in packs and would kill anything, including a man foolish enough to wander into that overgrown forest.

He closed the magazine and set it aside. It was too much to bear, feeding this sudden surge of depression. He again could hear the other four talking among themselves, a bit of a friendly argument that did have an edge to it as to why no one had thought to check on old computers and other electronic devices earlier.

He wiped the tears from his eyes and took a deep breath. "Galileo and the telescope," he said.

The others fell silent and looked back at him.

"What?" Paul asked.

He forced himself to smile—at least there was still a touch of the college professor in him—and as he looked at Paul and Becka, there was a flashback to when they were students in his History of Technology class, more often than not paying slight attention to him as they gazed lovingly at each other in the back of the classroom.

"You remember our discussion about Galileo and the telescope?" he asked, taking a few steps back to join them.

"Not exactly," Paul replied.

"It's like this, and it applies to us now," John said, taking a deep breath, feeling a bit of calmness coming back with this diversion. Grief was a luxury in this world, especially for him, the one that far too many looked to for strength. Later, if still troubled, he'd let it back out when alone with Makala, though even after their more than two years together, he still felt uncomfortable when memories of his long-departed first wife troubled him. He had loved Mary deeply, but it was different from what he now felt for Makala, where there was a more mature intensity and a sense that she was truly his equal partner in all things.

"I'm all ears for this history lesson," Ernie interjected, and now he did smile. It was at least one area where Ernie really did defer to him, and there was no sarcasm in his voice.

"Think about it," John continued. "It is an unanswered question I find to be fascinating. Modern eyeglasses were being manufactured by glassmakers in Italy as early as the fourteenth century. They could even grind them for each individual's needs. They used to be given as a symbol of achievement to scholars at universities of that time, since most of them had gone half-blind after years of studying manuscripts in dark rooms like this illuminated only by candlelight.

"Across three hundred or so years, lens grinders were making glasses, and the question is, how come not one of them, even by accident, one day held up one lens in front of another and had the 'oh my God' moment that the two lenses, one in front of the other, were a telescope?"

He fell silent and now smiled inwardly, the grief of a moment before pushed aside. It was almost like being back in the classroom again—and this time, even Paul and Becka were listening.

"Then some guy in Holland, can't remember his name, actually does that and does go 'Oh my God!' He put the lenses into opposite ends of a leather tube. Thus the first telescope."

The four were silent for a moment, and he wondered if they were caught up as he had always been with the fascination of this question of why three hundred years had passed when the tools were there literally on any lens maker's bench.

"So you're saying that that stuff for telescopes lay around for three hundred years and nobody thought to do it?" Forrest asked.

"For starters, yes."

"I remember this Italian girl in the dorm across the commons from my room when I was in college; we had a telescope aimed at her window 24-7," Ernie interjected. "You'd think one of those Italian glassmakers would have figured that out."

John sighed. There was always someone in a class to blow away a teaching moment, and even Becka laughed, commenting that was exactly why every girl in Anderson Hall always kept her blinds down.

"You're losing the point," John finally interjected, a bit exasperated.

"Please continue," Becka replied, though there was still a touch of a smile as she looked over at Paul.

"So this guy in Holland makes the first telescope, and—typical then and now—the government gets wind of it and tries to clamp down a security lid on the whole thing."

"Why?" Paul asked.

"Military secret," Forrest said, and John nodded. "In Afghanistan, we were under strictest orders to smash our night-vision gear if we ever thought we were going to be overrun. They had stuff they had captured from the Russians years earlier, but nowhere near as good as ours. He who sees first or sees farthest wins."

"Exactly what happened," John continued. "Holland was fighting a bitter, decades-long war with Spain—actually, the Hapsburg Empire—for their independence. A ten-power telescope at sea gave them a huge advantage, when from miles away you could tell if that ship on the horizon was friend or enemy, to run or to fight. But like with all weapon systems, the secret doesn't remain secret for long, and soon the word was out."

"Same as today," Ernie said softly. "I still want to get my hands on the damn idiots who allowed North Korea and Iran to get the bomb."

"So do we all." John sighed, and again the thought . . . surely someone knew before they were hit. Surely someone knew it was coming.

He let the thought drop for now, for it most certainly would take him back to his melancholia of but minutes ago.

"Anyhow, to finish this little class," he said, clearing his throat. "And this is the really interesting part. Galileo receives a circular letter, sort of like the trade journal of his day, from a friend describing this new invention. Being Italian, in Renaissance Italy, he goes to a lens maker and shows him the design, and he now has his own telescope to fool around with and then starts making his own. But here is the fascinating part. He actually plays around with it for some time until one night he points it at Jupiter."

"Checking out the girl bathing in the river down the street until then," Forrest interjects.

John just sighed and pressed on. "That night changed everything. He was the first to observe what we now call the Galileo moons and in doing so presented proof that the universe is not geocentric."

The four just looked at him, and he could sense his old students were now prepared for and would politely endure his launching off on some professorial run of thirty minutes or more about just how fascinating this moment was.

But he stopped there, aware that they were standing in a cold, dank, mildew-laden basement, and if Makala found out that a young mother still recovering from giving birth to twins had been forced out of politeness to stay and listen, there'd be hell to pay. Besides, with all the rush of emotions this experience had triggered, he was suddenly very tired.

"The point is that apparently every computer in use on the day we were hit got fried. We go without electricity for over two years until you two"— he nodded gratefully to Becka and Paul—"bring us back at least to the late nineteenth century world. But then in all the rush and excitement that created, none of us actually thought to look at the old electronic tools stashed away and forgotten in places like this. So thank you, Paul and Becka, for this discovery; you two are our Galileos."

He was pleased to see that his words had hit; both of them were smiling at each other, Paul's arm slipping around Becka's waist as he kissed her on the forehead.

A thought struck him.

"We lost our house in the fight with the Posse, but my mother-in-law, Jen,

God rest her, was a regular pack rat. Beside the old cars, she hung on to everything. I remember when we moved in, there must have been half a dozen old cell phones in a desk drawer."

"No good without the towers," Ernie interjected authoritatively.

"I know, but just curious. We all used to joke how we could remember phone numbers from when we were kids, but once the cell phone craziness hit, and then the smartphones, one simply just said a name or tapped a screen and the number was there. We lamented all the photos lost, all the text messages that touched our hearts and were saved being lost. Just curious now—I'll dig them out and bring them into the office tomorrow and see if they light up again."

"No good in that," Ernie replied, "other than nostalgia. The question really is what to do with this computer and any others we might get running again."

"Go on," John offered, for it was indeed the question that had hit him the moment the screen had flickered to life and he was staring at that damned grinning Pac-Man.

"Databases," Ernie replied. "Lone computers, like this Apple IIe, are nothing but toys."

John was silent, not leaping to the defense of an old friend of a machine that had enabled him to write a master's thesis in near record time.

"It was linking them together. The Internet back in the mid-'90s that truly launched the revolution. A machine alone, okay, it's entertaining, and kids can play that dang Pac-Man and Mario on it until the motherboard finally fries off, and the way this one is smelling, I don't give it very long unless I take it apart and clean it. I'm thinking about databases—uplinks, for example. Those guys up in Bluemont, don't tell me they don't have systems up and running. I'll assume the low-earth orbit sats got killed off when the war blew, but the ones up at geosynch? I'd give my left—"

He paused looking at Becka.

"Excuse me. I'd give my left arm to be able to tap into that data flow and they don't know I've hacked in."

After mentioning losing an arm, seconds later, he realized the faux pas he had committed in front of Forrest, who had indeed lost an arm. He looked over at the veteran anxiously, and Forrest forced a smile.

"At least it wasn't the arm I use for important things."

Ernie offered a weak grin of thanks.

John, however, was looking at Ernie wide-eyed.

"Could you actually do that? Eavesdrop into Bluemont's comm system?"

"I already knew the story about Galileo, Professor Matherson. And yeah, maybe I could."

John looked over at Forrest, remembering the reason his friend, a former enemy, had ventured over the obstacle of the Mount Mitchell range in what was becoming a driving blizzard with word that someone who had once served with his closest friend in the prewar army had trekked two hundred miles to eventually reach them.

"I'm giving you whatever gas you need, Ernie, to move whatever you want here, to this basement. If you can get any of these machines up and running, do so ASAP. I'll put the word out in a town announcement for folks to start rummaging through attics and basements to see what can be found."

"I'd advise against that," Forrest interjected.

"Why?"

"We learned that our old bastard friend Fredericks had one or more people of his planted here. Let's assume the same. For now, I'd suggest keeping this nugget quiet, and let's talk to that Quentin fellow first."

John took it in, hesitating.

"Galileo, don't you think he regretted blowing his mouth off about his discovery?" Forrest interjected. "He should have stayed quiet a few years, done his research, gotten it out to a trusted few others; instead, he invites the church officials in, and bango, he's on trial for heresy and under house arrest for the rest of his life."

John looked at his friend with surprise.

"Hey, a lot of long nights when deployed, plenty of time to read history, same as you, even if I didn't get a fancy degree."

John smiled and nodded in reply.

"Until this storm lets up, we'll focus on what Paul and Ernie are playing with," John said, though at this moment his thoughts were far more focused on who Quentin Reynolds was, if indeed Bob Scales was alive in Roanoke, and what portent that was for the future.

CHAPTER TWO

It was two days before the storm finally abated, the morning of the second day dawning bright, clear, and still. John was up first, shivering as he pushed kindling into the woodstove, the sole source of heat for the house, watching it flare to life as the kindling ignited from the hot coals from the night before, and then carefully feeding in split lengths of seasoned hickory and oak.

Memory of another time hit him every time he did this. His abandoned and burned-out home up by Ridgecrest had a fireplace. Of course everyone wanted one when they moved to the mountains, and it was a source of comfort for Mary in her final days, wrapped in an old family quilt and nestled in an overstuffed chair pulled up close, John making sure the fire was blazing cheerily. The fireplace was purely psychological for Mary, though young Elizabeth, fed some propaganda in her middle school classes, would sniff, saying it was inefficient, polluted the atmosphere, and contributed to global warming.

She was right on at least one point—the amount of heat generated when compared to the warm air sucked up the chimney all but equaled out—but there was something about crackling wood in the fireplace, the radiant heat striking a primal chord that just made one feel comfortable and content on a cold, snowy day.

Now it was different. The wood was not delivered as it once was—by one of his neighbor's friends at a hundred bucks a truckload, at least some-what seasoned and stacked by the back deck. During the first winter after the Day, it had been a mad scramble for heat, any kind of heat, and more than a few had died, not from freezing—though that did happen—but more often from pitching heart attacks while trying to hand cut and then split firewood, complete to chopping down decorative dogwoods and cherry trees in the front yard. Long forgotten was the time when nearly every home and farmstead had its own woodlot of a couple of dozen acres, up on the side of a mountain slope too steep to be cleared for plowing or even grazing.

Preparing for the next winter started even before the last snows of spring had melted off and was why a farmer cherished having several sons, whose daily chore was to spend a few hours every day cutting down trees, bucking them down to stove length, splitting the stove-size wood by hand, and stack-ing for curing, not just for warmth come next winter but for daily cooking, heating water atop the kitchen stove for the occasional bath . . . all of it accomplished by hard labor.

Gone as well was the essential knowledge of anyone 150 years back. Sea-soned hickory and oak put into the fire would last through the night; maple was easy splitting; pine was good for a quick start-up fire but didn't last for heat; locust became fence rails; the now-extinct chestnut could be burned but also made excellent furniture; in a pinch with the wood pile running low, unseasoned ash could be harvested and used; and, if out on a cold, rainy day, one could carry some rolled-up strips of birch bark, which would burn like a torch to get an emergency fire going. Information essential for living, which nearly all had to relearn to survive.

The Melton brothers, after months of backbreaking work, rebuilt a long-ago dam face while the rest of their family labored for weeks to shovel out the silted-up marsh behind the remnants of the dam. Dams long ago built to block off once bubbling mountain creeks often fell into eventual disuse as decades of summer storms and the floods of springtime thaws trapped hundreds of tons of silt, the narrow valley pond behind the dam turning into a marsh and then eventually abandoned . . . and besides, who needed a water-powered mill dam with all its labor and headaches when first steam, and then a twenty-horsepower electric motor, could do the same amount of labor?

In this new world gradually being rebuilt, the Meltons were the first in the valley to actually get a water-powered sawmill up and operating just below Ridgecrest, along the aptly named Mill Creek, because down its tumbling length, there had once been a dozen small mills for wood cutting, grinding corn for—among other things—making mash for a still hidden nearby. They built it on a site where a great-grandfather had once run a similar mill, which, when the "revenuers" were not poking around, supplied mash to stills up and down the valley.

Ernie and family tried to argue they now owned the land and had the surveyor plats to prove their modern legal argument. It had nearly turned ugly until John helped negotiate a deal that whatever logs Ernie dragged down to the Meltons with his old reliable Polaris off-road vehicle the Meltons would cut up for free. And if a few mason jars were mixed in with the returned firewood as well, no further questions would be asked.

The historian in John loved the sound of that mill, knowing he was hearing the echo of a long-ago age of waterpower . . . the creaking of the slowly turning waterwheel, the rasping of the saw driven by the wheel, the redolent scent of fresh-cut wood and cool mountain water cascading over the waterwheel. And although corn for actual food was still a "national" priority, in this the third year of harvest since the start of the war, he was learning to turn a blind eye toward the thin columns of wood smoke rising up from nearby valleys and the occasional whiff on humid fall mornings of corn mash fermenting. He would ease his sense of duty with the thought that "as it was in the beginning, so it is again . . ."

Farther downstream, Paul Hawkins's team was waiting for the community of Old Fort to finish rebuilding what had been their original dam for a water-powered turbine so that he could set a generator in place and get the small community of survivors down there back online. The villagers of Old Fort, all but wiped out by the Posse attack, planned to run a wire along old Route 70 toward Marion and sell the power for trade items and food.

In this the third year since the Day, an economic trading system was again back in place, and it did include white lightning brewed in remote mountain valleys , but now included much else as well. Those with foresight to stockpile some precious metals found they indeed had real worth again; in fact, by the standards of this terrible new world, they could be counted as wealthy, the silver and gold not just something to be locked away in a safe for "just in case"—"just in case" had indeed arrived at last.

Increasingly scarce was .22 ammunition so that it was hardly on the trading market anymore, worth far more per round than the rabbit or squirrel it could put on the table. The weapons to be valued for hunting were the old flintlock rifles, once the realm of history buffs, reenactors, and muzzle-loading hunters. Lead salvaged from dead car batteries and saltpeter from manure pits provided two of the ingredients. Sulfur came from the old re-sort spa of Sulfur Springs down in Rutherford County, which long ago had provided the crucial element for gunpowder manufacturing from the colo-nial period and the Civil War. The Peterson family, old man Peterson once a good friend of John from Civil War roundtable days, had set up the family business, which tragically killed his daughter and grandson, who had made a fatal mistake several months back out in the mixing shed, blowing up themselves and the entire building.

There was even talk of scrounging up enough bronze or brass to make several small cannons for defense, a strange thought given the town had endured air attacks from Apache helicopters and now had a precious Black Hawk in their possession, a world of retro weaponry mixed with surviving remnants of a prior age.

Beyond the trade in gunpowder from Rutherfordton, and networking out to other communities struggling to come out of a dark age, a viable economic system was indeed emerging.

It was not until after Fredericks's defeat that John had learned that within Asheville, Fredericks had actually attempted to impose a mandatory con-fiscation of all silver and gold coins that had once been government minted. Unknown to those areas outside of Fredericks's brief period of control, he claimed a decree from Bluemont had ordered such, with a so-called fair trade of a hundred dollars in printed money for each silver dollar and a thousand dollars of paper money for each one-ounce gold coin. Only those caught with silver or gold on them complied under duress, meaning, "We caught you; give us the coins—here's your paper, now go and keep your mouth shut, or you are under arrest for illegal trading."

Those thus caught referred to the paper as being "not worth a damn Frederick" or to a more direct scatological reference as its only real use. Yet another troubling bit of information that had come to light after that vain-glorious man's bloody defeat.

The paper currency was even how those serving with the ANR had been paid. Those who had survived and surrendered after the battle to take out Fredericks were expecting execution and thus were stunned by the offer to stay and join the community.

All of them were young, generally in good health thanks to the rations they had lived on for months, and were then divided up and assigned to different units within "the State of Carolina's Militia."

There was some resentment for the first few days on the part of his own people—for, after all, over thirty from the town had been killed fighting against these young men and women. There had been one tragedy when a young man from the college murdered one of the ANR troops, blaming his victim personally for the death of his fiancée in the fight to take the courthouse in Asheville. It proved to be an extremely tense day, the nearly hundred ANR prisoners fearing that they had been lulled by John's promises and that Fredericks's warnings that to be taken alive by "those mountain rednecks" would mean torture, rape, and death. Some had gathered together, ready to fight or flee, when more than a few locals supported the young man's vengeance killing as justice, plain and simple.

It proved to be just about the most difficult day John had ever faced. The community had yet to stand down from a state of military emergency; therefore, John was deemed to be in command under military law. Reverend Black had insisted upon sitting on the tribunal since the accused came from the college where he now served as chaplain, rather than a civil trial since the crime had occurred while the community's troops were still "in military service." Reverend Black, when he pronounced his vote with tears streaming down his face, startled everyone, declaring it had to be done, quoting Old Testament verses, that killing in combat was a tragedy that had haunted mankind from the beginning, but this death was cold-blooded murder, using the translation of "murder" rather than "Thou shall not kill."

John realized he had to carry out the sentence himself as he had done with others; it could not be delegated, though he spent hours praying over it, hoping to find a personal way out. At the end, the young man took it stoically, forgiving John for what had to be done and appealing to the dead man's friends for forgiveness as well. Memory of it, along with so many other memories, still woke him up in a cold sweat in the middle of the night.

As to the regular army prisoners, especially the helicopter crews that had slaughtered many in Forrest Burnett's community, there had been outright calls to execute them. But John had had enough of executions, even though many—especially Forrest's community, which had endured the atrocity of being strafed by the pilot—cried for blood. In the end, John ordered them banished, pushed to the far side of the barrier on Interstate 40 at the top of the mountain and told to start walking. Chances they would survive a week were nil, and it was decided by all that the punishment was just.

The aftereffect? The ANR survivors witnessed something they had never expected, even expressing regret for the entire tragedy and its end result, and thereafter, no mention was made—at least publicly—of having been on one side or the other in the battle for Asheville. The ANR commanding officer, who had grown up near where John originally came from, now served as a platoon lieutenant in the militia, and what she and others had said about life outside of their valley added more fuel to his worries.

All the ANR personnel had told him, along with reports by the BBC, served to fuel his suspicions and concerns about what exactly was taking place at Bluemont, and he was eager to get on the road to Forrest's community on the far side of Mount Mitchell.

The fire within the stove was now crackling hot, radiating warmth. He remembered an old favorite author who wrote on Americana, Eric Sloane, his works filled with wonderful detailed sketches of life long ago, stating that a wood fire heated you twice—from the labor it took to cut, split, stack, and haul the wood and again when it finally burned as it now did before him.

All well and good, John thought with a smile, *if one was young and twenty and had grown up with life being such.* There had been offers, which he always saw as little more than attempts at bribes, to provide him with wood and so many other things, but it was a point of honor that he worked and traded for it like everyone else. Before she passed, Jen, almost as if it were an afterthought, had revealed that there was a stash of several hundred dollars of face-value silver filling half a dozen mason jars tucked away in a corner of the basement. When the government had gone over to clad coins

back in the '60s, her husband, George, had denounced it as a damned conspiracy and had taken to emptying out the silver dimes, quarters, and occasional half dollars into a jar on his nightstand at the end of every day and
then stashing them in the basement when filled.

The find had truly made them rich, and the historian inside of John had
of course been fascinated by this first step back to a "real" money-based
economy when he started offering a quarter here, a few dollars there for the
essentials of survival. Silver and gold had disappeared from the economic
flow long ago, and now finds like his were reintroducing them. Throughout the various communities that now made up the State of Carolina, there
was hardly a basement or attic that had not been ransacked by surviving
family members—and more than a few looters going at abandoned prop-
erties in search of such stashes. One such prowler, a drifter who had slipped
in past the security posts guarding the approaches to Black Mountain, had
been caught just a few months ago. Murder and rape were of course capital
offenses, as was the case with one of his militia killing a former member of
the ANR. Stealing food had been added to the list as one for which one
could possibly face capital punishment. Some said it was little better than
the obsessed policeman in *Les Misérables* hunting down a man who stole a
loaf of bread. But after the starving times of that first winter, people did die
for lack of a loaf of bread or the pig they had been raising on scraps to provide meat for the winter suddenly disappearing.

There was no jail in the town, except for an overnight lockup for the
occasional drunk and disorderly. In such a time, to punish someone by
locking them up in a warm jail, feeding them, and then having to feed
and compensate someone to watch over the offender was absurd. An in-
fraction of stealing other than while mobilized for military service resulted
in a civil court. If the theft was not crucial to the survival of a family or the
entire community, the standard punishment had finally become a sentence
to labor in the communal farmlands. Thus it was for that looter in search
of a stash of gold or silver, who labored for a month and then disappeared
the night his sentence was completed.

A supreme irony was for all those who had secured their precious metals
in bank vault safe-deposit boxes. With the failure of electricity, the vaults
were automatically locked, sealed as tightly as some long-lost ancient tomb,

owners of what some claimed were hundreds of ounces of gold only able to stand outside the empty buildings and stare forlornly. John and the town council had even agreed to divert power into the old Fifth Third Bank on Montreat Road, a surviving employee then attempting to unscramble the locking systems, to no avail.

Those standing outside watching the attempt, growing frustrated, started to suggest just blowing the entire thing up, which was of course vetoed. So the bank still stood, as did the other banks in town, the treasures within as remote as if lost in the hull of the *Titanic*.

Inwardly, John breathed a sigh of relief, for if successful there would have been a rush to crack into or blow up every bank in western North Carolina, and the flood of coinage pouring out triggering that age-old nightmare of inflation.

As for those who had purchased gold and went along with it being stored at "a safe and secure location in Switzerland," they were truly out of luck.

John sat by the open door of the woodstove for a few minutes, dwelling on all the events and changes taking place, willing to bet that Ernie had awoken the Hawkins family at dawn, tool bag in hand, ready to continue probing the computers found in the library basement. He watched the flames dancing, enjoying the radiant heat blossoming out, the fire, as it always does, weaving a hypnotic spell, the iron sides of the old stove cracking and pinging as they expanded from the heat.

"How about some eggs and grits for breakfast?"

He felt Makala's warm touch on his shoulder and looked up at her with a smile.

"Sure. But sit down with me for a few minutes first."

She laughed, pulling her flannel robe in tight, revealing just how pregnant she truly was.

"If I sit on the floor, it will take a forklift to get me back on my feet."

"Come on, I'll help you."

With a groan, she sat down by his side and snuggled in close, extending her hands toward the glowing fire.

"Sleep okay?" he asked while brushing a wisp of her golden hair back from her forehead and then kissing her.

"Little badger must have woke me up half a dozen times. That baby wants out."

He laughed and put a hand on her bulging tummy. He waited and a moment later was rewarded with a kick. Laughing, he kept his hand there and kissed her again.

"Wish you'd wait a few more days before trying to get over the mountain," she announced. "It's still most likely snowing on the north slope, and the wind up there can kill. You ever read Jack London's *To Build a Fire*?"

John smiled and nodded at the memory of a scoutmaster when he was a boy, getting the troop out of Newark and up to what at the time John felt was the true wilderness at High Point, New Jersey, for a three-day winter survival trek. Shivering around the campfire at night, the scoutmaster had read that tale to his group of frozen city kids, most of them convinced their leader had gone crazy to drag them out on this trek. John remembered reveling in the adventure of it, all the time imagining that it was like being with George Washington's troops at Valley Forge or the midnight march through a blizzard to take Trenton.

Romantic then, but Makala did have a point. Temps could be twenty degrees colder up at the crest line at Craggy Gap, and though calm down here, it could be a thirty- to fifty-mile-per-hour blow up there.

He had approached Billy Tyndall yesterday with the thought of using their Aeronca L-3 to fly him over the mountain range, a short twenty-minute hop by air, so he could meet this Quentin Reynolds, and Billy had replied with two words: "You're crazy." He then went on to a lecture about the killer weather conditions to be found around Mount Mitchell, pointing to an old FAA map of the region pinned to the wall of the makeshift hangar, where a specific warning was printed about the dangers of severe turbulence in the area.

"You ask any pilot who's not crazy and thus still alive about flying around up there, especially in an old underpowered tail dragger, and they'll tell you that you are indeed crazy. We damn near got killed last time you and I flew there; it wasn't the bullets and Apache helicopters that scared me half as much as getting slammed by a downdraft and sending us right into the side of a mountain. So no way."

So waiting for a crystal-clear and very calm day was out.

"It can't wait," John finally replied to Makala. "Forrest said the guy was in bad shape. If he slips into pneumonia, he could be on the edge of dying unless we can get some of our antibiotics into him, and that alone is reason enough to at least try to get to him. There's something about the name of this guy that rings a bell somewhere in my head beyond the fact that he claimed to have served with my friend Bob Scales. I gotta go."

"All right, help me get up, eggs and grits, something to stick to your ribs."

John never could figure out the Southern obsession with grits, but when one has gone through a starving time, the memory lingers.

"Did I hear *grits*?"

The two looked back to see Forrest coming out of the guest room, pulling up his suspenders over his shoulder, deftly doing so with his one hand.

John stood up, helped Makala get to her feet, pushed a few more split pieces of hickory into the stove to ensure a good, long, hot fire, and closed the door. A moment later, Makala had the iron skillet resting atop the woodstove. She'd also set an old-fashioned percolating coffeepot filled with water—which was again coming out of a faucet tap thanks to the electrical pump that soaked up a significant part of the town's electricity but again provided safe, clean running water to most homes and another item of the past—ready to put in some chicory roots and an herbal concoction.

"Oh, damn it, wait a minute." Forrest sighed at the sight of the coffee percolator and disappeared back into the guest room.

They both knew he had some, the scent of it as seductive as any perfume, and both of them had silently hoped he still had some left. Etiquette was never to ask people if they had a secret stash of some precious item like chocolate, honey, coffee, or cigarettes. One waited to be offered, and while visiting with John and Makala, coffee—wherever it had come from—was part of breakfast again. After the meal, Forrest would step outside, at Makala's orders, to enjoy his one cigarette, Makala keeping a watchful eye on John so that he didn't break his vow to Jennifer.

Forrest returned, and in his open hand he held out four small plastic K-Cups—hazelnut, no less—fully caffeinated.

Makala all but snatched them from his hand. Along with rare .22 bullets and silver coins, the once ubiquitous K-Cups had become a cherished trade item, the coffee within still fresh even three years later.

Makala carefully cut each one open, not letting a single grain fall to the floor, and emptied them into the percolator before putting it on the stove.

"Now tell me you got some of those creamer cups and packets of sugar, and life will be complete," John interjected, breaking a golden rule of good manners. Forrest smiled, reached into his pant pocket, and produced three of the creamer cups as well.

"Sorry, but sugar is out."

"Apologies for asking," John replied, but Forrest smiled. "Who'd have thought those darn things would one day be worth so much?"

Within minutes, the grits were simmering atop the stove, and heaven of heavens, the scent of coffee brewing filled the room. The sound of the coffee percolating was a flashback to childhood, cold winter mornings, still dark outside, coming down to the kitchen, his father nearly finished with breakfast, letting John have a few sips of the warm brew before bundling up to take the train over to the gas plant in Harrison. It was a breakfast sound that disappeared with the advent of the Mr. Coffee machines, a sound he still missed, and all the other nuances of that time and place: his father's insistence on heavy cream and to hell with the cholesterol count, fresh bacon at least three times a week, or even the dreaded winter breakfast for kids—hot oatmeal—with a slab of butter and perhaps a sprinkling of cinnamon.

There was something about the quiet of breakfast time that triggered such nostalgia for John, particularly on a cold day—the sky a sparkling blue, the freshly fallen snow reflecting the morning light, the trees, especially the pines, still blanketed from the storm just passed.

John helped to set the table, appealing to Makala to get off her feet while he placed a single egg on each plate, doled out the grits, and then carefully poured cups of coffee for each, as a proper host shorting himself slightly while making sure the provider of such largesse had an extra gulp in his cup.

Sitting, they joined hands, John reaching over to touch Forrest's empty left sleeve, said grace, and then wordlessly dug in, savoring each bite.

Meal done, there was several minutes of silence, each one enjoying their cup of coffee while gazing out the window, until Forrest finally stirred.

"Time to get going."

John nodded, helping Makala to clear the table and clean the dishes in a pot of hot water that had been set atop the woodstove. Even now, after three years, people were still falling ill because of the lack of hot running water. The Saturday-night bath was again a nineteenth-century ritual of heating water on the stove and standing in an old washtub, soap again a mixture of lard and wood ash and crushed mint leaves to at least create some kind of pleasant scent.

John pulled on a tattered snowmobile suit that hung loosely on his lanky frame, followed by ski mask and gloves, and hoisted his emergency travel pack stuffed with winter survival gear, including a small tent, dry clothes rolled up inside a plastic bag, some dried beef jerky, and matches with a twisted-up piece of birch bark packed in a waterproof container. He picked up his M1 Carbine, which had become his preferred weapon, checking to make sure it was cleared, holstered a Glock, and waited for Forrest to suit up in the guest room.

Makala looked at him anxiously. It was still all so ironic. They were only traveling twenty miles up over the Mount Mitchell range and down to where Forrest's community had decided to remain even though there was plenty of vacant housing in Asheville and right here in Black Mountain and Montreat. John had argued repeatedly with Forrest before winter closed in to move, but Forrest always rebuffed him, that he and his friends preferred to stay on the land that had once been their home; none of them were cut out for what he still sarcastically called "city folk," and he did have the logical point that by staying north of the mountains, his community kept an eye on the northern flank of their world.

The year before the Day, several of John's students who owned jeeps had offered an adventure ride for his two daughters and himself, and it had turned into a day the girls adored, traversing fire roads and trails clear up to Mount Mitchell and back, soaking in the splendor of a sunlit autumn day. Now they were suiting up as if going into combat; there was still always a remote chance that perhaps some marauders following the old Blue Ridge Parkway were in the area and would gladly kill for Forrest's old Polaris 4×6.

Forrest came out of his room wearing heavy winter camo, left sleeve cut off and sewn closed. A hunting rifle was slung from one shoulder, and a military-grade M4, taken in the fight with the ANR, was slung around his neck and across his chest.

"Ma'am, thank you for your hospitality," Forrest said, nodding politely to Makala, old mountain etiquette coming to the fore, extending his hand, giving her half a dozen K-Cups—which she tried to refuse, John watching the exchange and of course inwardly hoping that the game would play out with Makala reluctantly taking this incredible gift, which could mean coffee in the morning for nearly an entire week.

"Take care of my husband," she finally replied, kissing Forrest on the cheek, and he actually blushed slightly. He had long ago come to accept that his scarred, twisted face with one eye missing gave him a deadly looking demeanor, and rare would be the woman who kissed him, even in a friendly gesture of politeness.

"He can take care of himself, ma'am; otherwise, I wouldn't salute the son of a . . ."

"Bitch? Yeah, can be that at times," she said with a laugh and then turned and looked John straight in the eyes. "I know you've got to go, your damn sense of duty and all that. But, John Matherson, if you get yourself killed and leave me seven months' pregnant, I'll never forgive you."

He looked around the room. More than enough firewood was stacked by the stove, the fire within radiating a comfortable glowing heat, augmented by the brilliant sunlight streaming through the sunroom window. If all went well, he'd back by midday tomorrow . . . if all went well, something that in this world no one ever took for granted.

They went down to the basement garage, the place where there had once been a lovely blue Mustang convertible, destroyed in the fight with the Posse. The old, battered Edsel still ran but was rarely used now since it was such a gas guzzler. When time again permitted, he planned to go into Asheville and prowl the abandoned automotive shops, finding a set of tires to match up with a 1958 Edsel, the tires on his nearly bald. The engine as well needed a major overhaul, and trying to find new rings and valves would be another challenge.

They opened the garage door, and it took a minute for Forrest's open-air vehicle to start and keep running. John put his gear in the back well, double-checked the two jerricans, making sure they were filled with gas, waited for Forrest to ease the vehicle out of the garage, closed the door behind him, and climbed into the open-air seat. Just sitting there made him doubt the wisdom of this trip. It was freezing cold; the old-fashioned thermometer next to the garage door, mounted to a faded tin frame advertising the "new" 1958 Edsel, registered fifteen degrees. His wife was right; chances were it would be below zero up over the pass. He tightened up his jacket, made sure no flesh was exposed, looked over at Forrest, and nodded.

"Let's go get Lee Robinson and hit the road."

CHAPTER THREE

"Still alive?" Forrest asked, looking over at John, who was shivering like the last leaf clinging to a tree in a hurricane, though John realized it might be that he was still scared witless.

Going up the mountain range wasn't too bad, though the snow depth gradually increased. There was little wind; the sunlight was sparkling with such intensity that John cursed himself for not bringing along sunglasses. It was a journey through what he could only describe as a world out of the old tourist calendars that used to be sold in town of the splendor of the Black Mountains on a winter day. Pine and spruce branches were bent low under the weight of snow, forming tunnels along the old fire road as they crept up toward Craggy Gap.

But as they neared the summit, harsh reality suddenly closed in. The pass at Craggy was concealed by low-scudding clouds racing up the north slope of the mountain range. Gaining the Blue Ridge Parkway for a short run westward to the paved road that led down to Forrest's community, they drove into a true whiteout, visibility barely beyond the front hood of the Polaris. The unrelenting wind had stripped the trees bare of snow, to be replaced with a thick coating of rim ice that actually stuck out horizontally from the bent-over branches.

The roadway itself was blown nearly bare of snow, but around the first bend they encountered a six-foot drift, created under the lee of a cliff. Forrest actually sped up, laughing as he plowed into it, John and Lee both cursing him, Forrest with but one hand clutching the steering wheel while shouting for John to shift the vehicle into four-wheel low drive. They nearly stalled out and then broke through, a few seconds later skidding sideways down the ice-covered road until they hit a patch of snow and thus gained traction again.

At least the parkway was two lanes wide with crash barriers to stop them from tumbling into a gorge, but once off the parkway and onto a paved road that led down the north side of the mountain, John felt his nerves beginning to snap. The road was a series of ice- and snow-covered switchbacks, the clouds lifting enough to reveal the terror ahead.

"We'd better think this one over!" John cried, but Forrest, laughing, just hit the gas.

It was a long, white-knuckled toboggan ride of several miles, speed building up, John convinced they were going to crash or flip, Lee cursing madly from the backseat, but just when death seemed inevitable, Forrest would shout for John to shift a gear, and the Polaris would skid around a curve, straighten out, and then descend toward the next switchback.

John realized that the twisted-up, battle-scarred veteran was one of those types that after coming so close to death had just simply lost his fear of it and even enjoyed challenging and taunting it, the adrenaline far more addictive than any drug or booze.

They finally reached level terrain, Forrest skidding to a stop and without comment getting out of the Polaris to relieve himself by the side of the road.

"You crazy bastard!" Lee shouted. "You could have killed us all back there, and for what?"

"Afraid of dying?" Forrest asked, looking back with a sardonic smile at Lee. "We're alive; we had a hell of a rush. What more could you ask for?"

"I'm walking back," Lee muttered, looking over at John, who was shaking so hard he could barely unzip his ice-coated snowmobile suit to relieve himself as well.

"Five more miles from here, we'll take the fire lane over there; cuts the trip in half and saves on gas."

At least the last few miles were somewhat more tranquil, except for one steep-pitched turn, John hanging on to the roll bar overhead to maintain balance while looking down at a ravine to his right that dropped fifty feet or more, where he saw poking up out of the snow at the bottom the wreck of a long-ago lost jeep.

"That one killed a cousin of mine five years back," Forrest announced casually. "Freaked out that his fiancée had broken their engagement, he got liquored up and went out night hunting for deer, missed the turn, and went over the cliff. He always was a stupid bastard. Took two days to find him, and we just decided to leave the jeep there as kind of a memorial."

"Crazy must run in the family," Lee grumbled.

At last they came out to a paved road, and suddenly the land looked familiar, the exact same spot where Forrest and his community were camped when they had taken him prisoner back in the spring.

Smoke wafting up and streaming away from a stove rigged up inside the community firehouse promised warmth; the ragtag array of old RVs and camping trailers ringed in tightly around the firehouse, which was the community center.

Why these people still elected to stay here again filled John with wonder. Half a dozen miles away, there had once been a luxury resort of million-dollar vacation homes, complete with its own airstrip, all of it abandoned. He could see their side of it, though, for this, after all, was their land going back 150 years or more. Forrest and his friends had grown up in these valleys, knew every trail, and though game was all but completely hunted out along the south slopes of the mountains, over here a skillful hunter, especially when tracking in winter, could still find deer and bear, as clearly evident by the two bucks, gutted and skinned, hanging up outside the fire station.

Forrest pulled up in front of the fire station, a small crowd of well-wishers coming out to greet him. John recognized more than a few, former enemies who had joined their side in the confrontation with Fredericks. There were polite handshakes, a few inquiring as to his wife and her health, and thanks for the help she had extended when so many had been injured.

John peeled off his ice-covered ski mask, unable to conceal that he was still shaking, and someone immediately led him into the fire station, an elderly woman shouting for the crowd to let him warm up while she handed out hot mugs of—what else—yet more coffee, which, though scalding hot, John downed in several long gulps, sighing with relief, luxuriating in the warmth within the building.

"How's our guest doing?" Forrest asked.

His question was greeted with silence, and John felt a wave of dread. The old woman who had handed him coffee finally spoke up.

"He died during the night."

"Son of a bitch." Lee sighed, looking over at John, who sat down, shaking his head.

"We should have gotten him to the hospital," Forrest finally said, "but with the storm coming on . . ."

His voice trailed off into silence.

"Have you buried him yet?" John asked.

The old woman shook her head and nodded to a side room of the fire station. John stood up and followed her while unzipping his snowmobile suit; being inside felt stiflingly hot after so many freezing hours to get to this futile conclusion. He inwardly cursed. If Forrest only lived next to I-26, they could have easily transported him in a truck down to Asheville before the storm set in.

The old woman opened the door, and John felt a slight wave of nausea. How his wife ever handled the daily exposure to all the scents of a hospital ward was beyond him. It smelled like a sickroom, and he wondered if there was the first faint whiff of decay in the air. The body still rested on the bed the poor man had died in, covered by a sheet.

John drew the sheet back. No matter how many times he had seen the face of death, it still struck at him. It was said that pneumonia was "the old man's quiet friend," but it was obvious that the final hours must have been a terrible struggle; the man's face was contorted, eyes still open, features ashen gray.

"I'm sorry. I should have taken care of him, washed and laid him out proper before I let you in here," the elderly woman escorting him whispered, and she reached over with gentle fingers to close the dead man's eyes and tried to wipe away the grimace, though rigor mortis had already set in.

"I know this man." John sighed, gazing intently. "I remember him from the War College. I think he was on my friend's staff."

John pulled up a chair and sat down as Forrest and Lee came into the room.

"I knew him," John said again, "not well, just one of those staff types always standing a few feet behind and to the side of a general."

He struggled to dredge up more of a memory. The world before the Day was filled with so many memories, so many of them now hazy, distorted, washed over and replaced by the trauma of the last three years. The dead man before him was one of thousands of memories. Perhaps they had sat in on a conference together, maybe shared a drink with others. Wasn't there a military history conference at the War College where he had given a lecture?

If so, it wasn't noteworthy enough to remember right now, and that in itself struck him as tragic. Another life had disappeared; who and what he was John could barely remember. Did he have a family still alive that treasured him and would want to know his fate?

"Did he have any papers, military ID, anything like that on him?"

Forrest shook his head. "No wallet, nothing. The guy was pretty well beaten up when we found him, muttered something about getting jumped by marauders on the far side of the pass for Interstate 26."

"He had several busted ribs, a lot of bruises, cracked jaw, and nearly out of his head when Forrest brought him in," the old woman said, and as she spoke, she gently reached out to smooth the man's hair back from his forehead, a maternal gesture that touched John.

"Janet here was a nurse; you remember her sister Maggie, who took care of you when you first came to visit us?" Forrest said

Visit. John smiled at that. When he was captured, with a busted rib as well, Maggie was the first person to show him sympathy. Maggie was gone, killed in the air strike back in the spring.

"Your sister was an angel," John said, "and thank you for seeing to this man. Did he say anything to you about how he got here and why?"

"Not much I could understand. He kept asking for you, sir. Said he had served with a friend of yours—Bob Scales."

There was a sudden leap of hope. On the Day, John had actually been talking to Bob, who had called because it was Jennifer's twelfth birthday. In the final seconds of that conversation, Bob began to cut the friendly chat short, his tone changing, saying, "Something is going on here," and then the connection went dead.

For nearly three years now, he'd wondered what had happened to his old friend. Was he still alive? Did the man lying on the cot know the answer, and perhaps even more important, why had he come here?

"Had served with Bob Scales"—and John hesitated—"or was now serving?"

"I'm sorry, sir; he kept drifting in and out."

"Janet, it's John, please. Now try to remember everything he said."

Forrest left the room and returned a moment later carrying a couple of folding chairs, deftly opening them.

"Could we leave the room?" Lee whispered. John looked back at his friend and could see that Lee, with a stomach even weaker than his, was getting queasy.

Janet nodded in agreement and drew the sheet back over the body, and Forrest motioned for them to head into another room. The three men stripped off their winter gear, Janet coming in a few minutes later bearing four cups of coffee, black.

"I'm sorry, but I gotta ask, and hope I'm not being impolite," Lee said. "You guys always have coffee. How?"

Janet looked over at Forrest, who, in spite of the gravity of the moment, actually chuckled.

"I always said don't ask, don't tell, but this time? Okay, I'll spill. We found an abandoned truck, gone off a ravine up near that rich folks' resort you keep wanting me to move into. The dang truck was loaded with cases of these K-Cups, cases of them. Sorry, I kind of forgot to tell you about it."

There was a tense moment of silence. There was an understanding among all that "finds" that could help the entire community should be shared. But it was not mandatory; the few who had tried to press the issue as an actual statute once the initial state of martial law was over with were denounced as thinking like commissars. Medical supplies, a truckload of preserved meat or canned fruit that children needed, and such were one thing, but tens of thousands of K-Cups?

"Finders keepers," John finally replied, and Forrest visibly relaxed.

"Sorry, John. There were half a hundred cartons of high-class cigarettes in there as well."

"Don't even mention those," John replied sharply, not even wishing to contemplate his struggle with that addiction that still haunted him, for like nearly all ex-smokers, years could pass and yet still the urge to try "just one" could hit. The only thing that kept him straight was his promise to Jennifer.

John looked over at Janet, who was sipping her coffee.

"Try to sort through it all, even the trivial, which might be really important."

"Like I said, he was brought in here badly beaten up, half-frozen to death, frostbite to fingers and toes; if he had survived, he might have lost those anyhow. Three ribs staved in—wonder that his lung wasn't punctured; that injury was certainly no help when it came to the pneumonia already setting in—cracked jaw as well, which made it even harder for him to talk and understand what he was saying. Fever was up over 102 when I got to him, no way to check blood oxygen level, but I could tell it was dropping. I was praying you'd get back with some antibiotics, but by last evening, I knew he was over the edge. He slipped into a coma and died at around midnight."

"What exactly did he say?" John asked, pressing for something, anything.

"He came somewhat clear for a brief period just before slipping into a coma; I've seen that happen before. Said to tell you that you've got to get to General Scales up in Roanoke and stop them." She hesitated, looking to the door as if to make sure no one else was listening. "He said, 'EMP might be on the table.'"

"What? Were those his exact words?"

"'EMP is on the table,'" Janet said.

"Whose table?" John interjected, leaning forward, eager for an answer.

"He never said who, what, or when. Was he remembering how the war started, talking about now or the future? I kept trying to gently prod him when he was conscious, but like I said, he was feverish and pretty well out of his head when he was brought in. I think if he had been out in the open even a few more hours he'd have died from exposure and would be lying under the snow rather than in the next room."

John wearily shook his head and sipped his coffee. "Anything else? Please try to remember his precise words, ma'am."

"Just that you, John, had to get to a General Scales."

"Was he talking like General Scales was a memory from the past? I think I recognize Quentin. We might have served together while at the War College. Was he talking like that, rambling about our past or that I had to see him now?"

There was far more to this for John than just the urgency of a question about a garbled message from a dying man. If Quentin was speaking in the present tense, that meant that Bob Scales, one of his closest friends from before the war, was still alive—a prospect that could profoundy impact his responsibilities as a leader of his community. It meant a respected and beloved friend had somehow survived the Day. He had heard about the reports on the BBC that Virginia had been "pacified" by forces of the regular army. Was Bob the general in command?

Janet was silent for a moment, obviously carefully going over her memories. "Forgive me. I should have had a notepad with me and written it all down as he spoke. I'm sorry."

"Don't blame yourself, Janet," he replied, though inwardly he wished she had indeed done just that, for memory of a conversation with a dying man that one was trying to nurse at the same time could indeed become garbled.

"There was something." She sighed. "Again, I'm sorry; I should have written it down as he was whispering to me. He rambled about going to Roanoke. 'Find Bob there' or something like that."

John looked over at Forrest and Lee, who were taking it all in but wisely were remaining silent.

"I got to add—maybe call it a perspective—sometimes he was talking as if it was before the war, kept saying he had to get his wife and kids out. When he talked of them, he would cry. It was terrible to see him like that; poor man was such a tortured soul."

"Who isn't?" Lee said softly, gazing out the window.

"He said something about looking up H. G. Wells's epitaph, that the guy was right and will be right again."

Why would he mention H. G. Wells's epitaph? John wondered. He had read Wells as a kid, but all he could remember was *The War of the Worlds* and an old movie, *Shape of Things to Come,* Wells wrote the script for back in the 1930s predicting the coming of World War II.

"And you checked over everything he had on him?" John asked.

"Everything. Forrest and I stripped him down to check for injuries. He was in military fatigues but no winter overcoat, weapons—something about the marauders after taking him had stripped him down and joked they were going to sell him." She paused. "You know, there are still some hide-away groups out there that won't hesitate to take someone as food."

John nodded. Fragments of groups like the Posse were still out there in remote valleys and on mountaintops. They had learned to stay clear of his communities, but like jackals, they did linger on out on the fringes of a slowly reemerging civilized world.

"What he still had on was soaking wet. We stripped him down and found no paperwork or anything like that. All we could do then was to bundle him into warm blankets, give him aspirin and a few shots of moon-shine, and hope for the best. I told Forrest to fetch you; the poor man kept saying you were the one he had to speak to. Sorry, but that is all that I can tell you. Whatever answers he had rest now with his soul."

John stood up and went back into the temporary morgue, respectfully pulling the blanket back to gaze at the battered corpse as if somehow an answer would emerge or, like Lazarus, he might rise up "to return and tell thee all."

He sat by the body for several minutes, the others not entering the room, as he gazed at the mortal remains of a major he could barely remember.

The dead offered him no answers, just silent wondering. He covered the body and returned to the room where his friends waited in silence.

"Forrest, can we get home before dark?"

Forrest sighed and nodded.

CHAPTER FOUR

"So that's it," John said, leaning back in his chair after reciting the adventure of the previous day and the mystery it now presented.

The small office was crowded, representatives of the "Senate" for what they defined as the State of Carolina packed into the room. The body heat from so many people, along with the woodstove, made the room hot, the scent of the air all but overpowering with its warm, musky smell of unwashed men and women.

The long-ago paintings of the Founding Fathers gathered in debate made them always look all so clean. He now understood far better why old films would at times show an effete French or English nobleman daintily holding a scented handkerchief to his nose. With the onset of winter, even the weekly bath had become a laborious chore. Makala was one of the few who still insisted upon a Saturday-night bath for both of them, and during the summer a skinny-dipping jump into Flat Creek on a near daily basis, even though it was freezing cold throughout the year. But at least in the summer they could lie out in the backyard to sunbathe and wistfully talk about a day to come with electricity restored when they might even scavenge up an old Jacuzzi and somehow get it running again.

Most had reverted back to the nineteenth-century practice of putting on

long johns when the cold weather set in and not taking them off until spring
arrived.

John often wondered if the Founders had smelled as bad; hard to picture
the brilliant Jefferson or Washington himself smelling like those gathered
in the room, even when at Valley Forge.

He tried not to breathe deeply, but Makala, who was impervious to such
things, noticed his discomfort and cracked a window open, letting a gust of
frigid air into the room. A few shifted uncomfortably, but others nodded
a thanks.

"I've reached a decision as to what I think we should do—or, to be more
precise, what *I* should do," John said, "but we are no longer under martial
law. It will require significant resources; therefore, it is up to you."

"It's precious little information to make any kind of decision on," Reverend
Black said, starting off a debate that John feared might run for hours. "A
stranger who you think you recognize wanders into our region, claims he
wants to talk with you regarding something that involves an old army friend
of yours."

"Yes, that's basically it."

Black sighed. "When a man's time is drawing to a close, he often drifts
back years, decades. A good friend of mine, a colonel during the Second
World War, climbed out of bed the night before he died and started to
wander about the hospital corridor, yelling at the staff to put their helmets
on and get ready because a banzai charge was coming in. The poor guy
had to be restrained. He kept yelling and cussing at everyone, this from a
man who until his final days you never heard a foul oath from." Black
smiled wistfully. "It was good old soldier cussing at its best."

Forrest chuckled softly. "I can teach some new ones any time you want,
Preacher."

Black gave him a bit of a baleful glance but then smiled.

"Even the way he was talking, the turns of phrases sounded like something from an old movie rather than the way we talk today. My point, he was
back in 1944 up until the moment his last breath slipped out of him with me
holding his hand and praying by his side. His last words, though . . ."

Black's voice faded to a whisper, and he was obviously struggling to hold back on his emotions. "His last words: 'Let us cross over the river and rest under the shade of the trees.'"

That put a lump in John's throat. "Stonewall Jackson's last words," he said softly.

"Precisely my point," Black replied. "He was in a different time and place, perhaps remembering that quote from a class in West Point when he was still a plebe. I think it might be the same with this poor tragic Quentin. Therefore, John, I have serious doubts as to anything he said."

"Tell A. P. Hill he must come forward," Lee Robinson interjected.

John looked over at his friend and nodded with understanding.

"What?" Ernie asked.

"Some of the last words of both Robert E. Lee and Stonewall Jackson," John said. "They were back on the battlefield calling for a trusted general to bring his troops into the fight."

"So the whole thing could be a hallucination?" Ernie asked.

"It could be," John replied.

"Then take it as such, John. We' got way too many other things to worry about—that report that a new band of marauders is camped in what is left of Charlotte, the chatter we're picking up from BBC and other sources that the Bluemont government is officially ceding all territory west of the Mississippi to China and Mexico, the fact that we have to face the reality that as we incorporate more isolated communities into our state, food supplies through spring are coming up short. Let's stick with what we know."

There were nods of approval from several others gathered in the room, including Makala.

"Wish I could agree," John said, looking out the window, a light flurry of snow swirling down outside. First a blizzard and then this so early in the year. He hoped it was not a portent of a hard winter to come. Before the Day, such winters were a source of pleasure for a college professor, usually resulting in a relaxing day off to play with his daughters or just sit by the fireplace and read. Now it was a reinforcement why not too long in the past, hard winters were referred to with dread with names such as the *freezing time* or *starving time*.

"John, there's nothing new on the BBC," Ernie announced. "Actually, something of a shutdown with their reporters, all foreign reporters being expelled from Bluemont—or, for that matter, anywhere else within areas controlled by that government."

"Precisely why I am worried, *really* worried. After we beat the hell out of Fredericks and then the far-too-public announcement that we were forming a 'State of Carolina' until such time as the nation came back together, you remember the BBC report just a few days after we took Fredericks out, that this entire region was being declared as a 'Level Five,' meaning in control of terrorists and rebels? But then after that? I thought they were going to hit us hard and fast as an object lesson. Instead? Zero response from those who claim to be the central government."

There were some nods of agreement.

"I still want to believe the bastards simply gave up on us," Maury Hurt interjected. "Their failures with trying to make some sort of military force out of their ANR, the way they got the crap kicked out of them in Chicago, Cleveland, Pittsburgh, or whatever is left of other cities up there, knocked Bluemont on its heels, and they've backed down. And now with winter setting in, I want to believe that we have nothing to worry about, at least until spring."

"Want to believe? Or know for a fact?" John replied.

Maury sighed and shook his head.

John gestured to the faded map of the United States that adorned the wall to his left. Doing so triggered a memory of Fredericks doing the same to him just six months back with his grandiose talk about a reunited America. "These reports from the BBC are that Bluemont is in negotiations with China and Mexico. They've already conceded all territory west of the Continental Divide and south of the Red River."

"And word is as well that Texas and others are putting up a hell of a fight about that," Ernie interjected angrily. "What the BBC might say is one thing, but the reality on the ground?"

There was a breakdown of any semblance of an orderly meeting as others interjected that it would indeed be a very cold day in hell before those living in Texas or any other state along the Continental Divide would tamely submit to outside occupation.

"Food and security can often trump any argument about national identity," Reverend Black finally interjected. "Besides, how many actually survived out there? In the first summer after the attack, chances are more than 90 percent died in Tucson without air-conditioning or any source of water. Where does Denver get its water from? Again a major die-off. Sure, maybe some ranchers know what to do, but fifty raiders like the Posse show up at their ranch to steal cattle, what's left a day later? Forget about the old fantasies of life out west with everyone a self-reliant cowboy. Sadly, I'm willing to bet chances of survival out there were far less than in our secured valley here."

His grim pronouncement silenced the room.

"Let's stay focused on what John is talking about here and now," Black said softly. "I, for one, have to admit I'm changing my views somewhat and seeing his side of the argument."

"I might agree," Makala said, her voice controlled and cold. "But not John this time. Yeah, this is personal for me. We've got a baby coming in two months, and I want that child's father alive and here. Call me self-centered, but I claim the right for it after everything we went through back in the spring."

The others looked over at her, and John could not make eye contact with his wife, whose anger he knew was barely contained. When he had first talked with her about his thoughts after returning with Forrest the night before, it had triggered the first real shouting match of their marriage.

"Just let me go over the facts one more time," John replied, avoiding his wife's malevolent gaze. "Someone who apparently is what he claimed to be, a major who either is or was serving with General Bob Scales, tries to reach me with a message. He dies before reaching his goal. He says something about an EMP."

"And no one is sure if in his delirium he was talking about what happened," Forrest snapped. "John, I held a lot of buddies as they died." He looked off, his already twisted face contorted. "They usually babbled about a woman, a wife, a girlfriend, their children; more than a few younger ones cried for their mothers. Damn all war." Forrest sighed and then fell silent, withdrawing into memories too intense to show before others.

"Precisely the point," Makala snapped. "I've sat through many a death-watch, and so have you, John."

He lifted his gaze to her and from deep within that gaze held a warning for her to go no further. Yes, he had done as she said, and a day, barely an hour, did not go by without memory of his daughter dying, whispering to take care of her beloved stuffed animal Rabs.

Makala fell silent and then silently mouthed, "I'm sorry."

Perhaps tragically, her action now firmed his resolve, the paradox of so many loving relationships where when one challenges the decision of another in public, they often become even more determined to see it through, while a quiet word whispered when alone could have so easily worked and swayed the decision in the other direction.

"I have to go to Roanoke," John said, and he looked over at her as if anticipating a response. But she was silent, though he could see tears clouding her eyes.

"Something is up, and we would be foolish not to assume after the way we wiped out Fredericks and his gang that there would not be some sort of response. Throughout the summer and up until this early advent of winter, I dreaded suddenly hearing helicopters coming in. That or just the flash of fuel-air bombs going off as a reprisal. If anything, the lack of response has made me even more anxious, as it should have for the rest of you gathered here."

He looked around the room at the representatives from the Asheville City Council and Hendersonville; the storm and need to conserve precious fuel had prevented the other members of the Senate from such outlying regions as Morganton, Weaverville, and Waynesville from attending. An old-fashioned handheld telephone lay on his desk, off its receiver, their definition of a conference call so that those representatives could at least listen in over a crackling phone line.

"There are only two ways of getting there," John continued. "The first by road. We have the captured Bradley to do that."

"And Lord knows how many landslides, fallen trees, downed bridges, marauders like the ones that poor Quentin ran into, and, for that matter, the government garrison that is reportedly still in Johnson City to block you," Ernie replied. "And we all know anything beyond Hickory is still a no-man's-land, so that way is out too."

"So the only other way is by air."

He looked first at Billy Tyndall, the pilot for their precious L-3, who firmly shook his head.

"It is 140 air miles to Roanoke. I already looked it up. And sure, give me any open field and I can land, but after this blizzard, who knows? But we'll have to haul our own gas to get back, and that all but maxes out the weight load. So my vote, no way in hell."

"I already figured that, Billy. The L-3 is too precious to risk, its duty tactical to keep an eye on the interstate approaches, and you are doing a magnificent job, my friend."

"And I for one am telling you—wait until spring."

John shifted his gaze to Maury Hurt, whom he had not apprised of the plan he was formulating and the reasons behind it.

Maury, who had been leaning against the far wall, stiffened. "You got to be kidding me," he snapped.

"Just hear me out, will you?"

"I already know what you are going to say next," Maury replied. "We've got a captured Black Hawk helicopter that we took from Fredericks, and you want to use it to go to Roanoke?"

John simply nodded.

"You're crazy."

"Like I asked, just hear me out."

"Oh, I'm all ears, John."

"As Billy already pointed out, it's 140 air miles to Roanoke. The Black Hawk has a combat radius of around 350 miles, a ferry range of over 1,000 if we keep the weight load down —which means we can fly up there, scope things out. If we get a clear indicator that my old friend General Scales is there and in command, I would venture a landing to meet with him. If not, we just turn around, haul out, and return without even landing."

"And who do you mean by 'we'?" Maury asked.

"You're the designated pilot now."

Maury shook his head, laughing nervously. "I had a couple of hundred hours as copilot in a Huey over twenty years ago." He did not add that his career in the National Guard as a chopper pilot had been cut short by a nasty crash, a few cracked vertebrae among other assorted broken bones, and a lifetime of swearing off flying since then, until this current situation when they snatched one of Fredericks's Black Hawks in the fight for Asheville.

"I've got a total of ten hours' flying time in that damn thing, and it scares the crap out of me. Sure, we captured a helicopter, one without any manuals, or servicing routine other than what Billy, Danny McMullen, and I can guess at. Damn it, John, a chopper isn't like that old plane of ours where you change the oil, do a compression test once a year, and that's it."

"It is a bit more complex than that," Billy interjected, "but yeah, Maury's right on this."

"Maury, yes or no, can you fly me to Roanoke and back?"

Maury hesitated.

"Yes or no."

"If I plan to see my grandchildren"—and he paused before the next jab—"or your child that's coming, all bets are off."

John sighed with exasperation. "Let's get down to the bottom of this and why I feel I have to go. I think this Quentin Reynolds was carrying some information way too important to ignore and to let disappear in the frozen ground with his dead body. He died for a reason, and that was to somehow get to me with a message. What, I don't know, but for him to set off over land to reach me means it must have been damn well important."

"Or the excuse of a deserter who got jumped on the way—then, delirious, had some made-up story to worm his way into our community." Ernie sniffed. "You yourself said you still aren't even sure if he is valid or not."

"Look, damn it. There is one fact that can't be disputed. I served under Bob Scales during Desert Storm One. Without his help, I would never have moved here." He hesitated, looking at Makala. "When my first wife was hit by cancer and wanted to be close to her family in her final months, it was my friend General Scales who networked me into a job at Montreat. If he is still alive, I owe him a hell of a lot. If he is still alive and sent this Quentin fella to find me, it must be important, damn important."

Makala offered a sad smile of understanding, and he nodded his thanks for that.

"Quentin Reynolds, I believe, just might have been sent by my friend to contact me. Just to know he is alive means the world to me."

"And you'll risk your ass and the only helicopter in our entire state to find out?" Ernie interjected.

John wanted to shout yes in reply but thought better of it. If he turned this personal, the council would vote him down, and frankly he could not blame them then if they did.

"The question of why has to be answered and answered now. If it is about an EMP, another one, we had damn well better find out and quick. It might have been the ravings of a dying man remembering the tragedy all of us endured. Or was it a warning that we might get hit again?"

The low murmuring in the room of those he could sense were about to tell him to just calm down, relax, go home with his wife, and take a few days off after the stress of his trip over the mountain now fell silent.

"Are we going to be hit again?" John asked.

"By who?" Again it was Ernie. "Why bother? America is finished as we know it. Sure, we flattened Iran and North Korea. India and Pakistan are turning each other into radioactive wastelands, the same in the Middle East. We still have the nuke boomers at sea. Why would anyone want to hit us again?"

John looked at Forrest, and though he felt the demonstration would be absurd, perhaps it was the only way to get his message across.

"Forrest, you got any of those K-Cups of coffee on you?"

Forrest, who had been listening intently to John, recoiled slightly. "What the hell is this, a shakedown?"

"Just yes or no—you got any on you?"

"Yeah, why?"

"Give me one."

"Why?"

"Okay, loan me one; I promise I'll give it back."

Forrest reached into the side pocket of his battered fatigue jacket and pulled one out and reluctantly tossed it over. John snatched it and looked at the lid.

"Hazelnut, my favorite," he whispered, and he put it on the desk in front of him. "Okay, my friends, who's gonna grab for it first?"

"Come on, John, what kind of game is this?" Reverend Black asked.

John could see the hungry gazes of those crammed into his office. His own indulgences with Forrest these last few days he had not discussed with anyone else in this room, Makala and Lee the only ones present who had enjoyed the largesse of Forrest's secret hoard.

"To my point. You all want it; I know you do. But let me just add this one caveat in."

"You and your professor's Latin." Ernie sniffed, his gaze locked on the small, white plastic cup.

"One chance in ten—no, make it one in a hundred that coffee in there is laced with cyanide poison. A one in a hundred chance it turns into you drinking the Kool-Aid—Jonestown kind of stuff. Some of you remember that insane day. Still want it?"

He could see the confused glances.

"Hell, you might risk it for yourself just for the taste of coffee again. But share it with your spouse, your kids? Who wants to try it?"

No one spoke.

He scooped up the white plastic cup and tossed it back to Forrest, who looked around a bit suspiciously, reminding John of Gollum the way he clutched at the One Ring, and quickly slipped it back into his pocket.

"Point made," John announced.

"What point, damn it?" Ernie snapped.

"One chance in ten, maybe one chance in a hundred, that the message that Major Quentin Reynolds was carrying was a warning of things to come. Last time we got hit, no one here knew it was coming, and look at us now. Suppose someone somewhere is planning to do it again? Suppose my friend General Scales is still alive and wanted to get a warning to us?"

"Then why all the mystery?" Ernie retorted. "If your buddy is still alive out there and has this big secret he wants to warn you about, just fly in and tell us, or get on the radio and announce it. The whole thing is screwy, John, and you know it."

"I agree in part, Ernie. Yeah, it is strange, a lone guy claiming to have served with the general showing up half-dead. But we definitely live in a screwy world. Maybe my friend has reasons for not doing what you said. I can think of a dozen of them."

"Name one."

"He knows something he can't let anyone else know for whatever reason and wanted to get word to me. Send it out on a radio and the entire world can listen in. Fly here? That draws notice as well. I could go on, but there's a couple, for starters."

Ernie took that in. "Or the whole thing could be a trap to lure you out of this valley by claiming a friend is still alive with some sort of secret message. You take the bait, and Bluemont gets payback for Fredericks with you dangling from the end of a rope."

John could see Makala go tense over that one, nodding in agreement. It was exactly what she had said within minutes after he returned from trying to see Quentin. It was a setup to entrap him.

"Think about it," John pressed in, avoiding eye contact with his wife. "We are just starting to get back on our feet. We've got electricity back, a lab here on campus making antibiotics and anesthesia; they even think they'll get one of Doc Weiderman's old x-ray machines he had packed away down in the basement of his office on the day things hit back online soon. Think of what that would have meant after our fight with the Posse and with Fredericks. We've got water pumping again through the town water mains. We are starting to crawl back out of the darkness. But if we are hit by another EMP, again without warning, we might as well just bury the last two and a half years of struggle, dig a grave for the rest of us, and crawl into it."

"Who would be crazy enough to do that again?" Maury asked.

John shrugged. "Who was crazy enough the first time? After the fact, we finally figured out it was North Korea and Iran handing off nukes to terrorists who launched them from container ships in the Gulf of Mexico and the Pacific. There are still terrorist cells out there, maybe wanting to this time provoke a full-scale global nuclear war. Could be China wanting to push us down even further but stand there looking innocent and then suggesting we need more aid east of the Mississippi. Ultimately, it doesn't matter who."

He paused for a moment.

"Did it ultimately matter who did it last time? The result was the same; it took us to the edge of extinction. If it might happen again, and there is a chance we can get a forewarning, I want that chance for all of us."

"There's one other reason now," Ernie said.

John looked over at him, ready to let fly with an angry burst for him to remain silent but then realized the secret would soon be out anyhow, and laying it on the table could help with his argument.

"Okay, this is classified, and I mean *strictly* classified; it has to stay in this room." John paused, looking at the telephone receiver on the table in front of him, tempted to hang it up. But those listening in were now part of the government as well. "Do we all understand each other? What I say next can go no further."

There were nods of approval, all now obviously filled with curiosity.

"We've managed to get a few computers back up and running."

"A few computers?" Billy said. "So what? Play Pac-Man, or some dumb-ass flight simulator on them? The Internet is gone forever, at least here, and unless linked up, they're useless."

"Didn't AB Tech in Asheville once offer a course on aircraft maintenance?" Ernie asked.

"Yes, why?"

"How did they teach it?"

"Computers, of course, and anything hooked into the net and plugged in for power got fried."

"Maybe the maintenance manuals for the L-3 and the Black Hawk were on CDs. I got another old PC up and running over in the library yesterday while our hero John and company were trying to kill themselves going over the mountain. Give me a computer, give me data stored on a CD, and I'll get the machine to run it. You want it?"

Billy could only nod.

"And fiber optics, my friends, were not cooked off. They're dark now, but give me enough machines and the juice to run them, and I'll get a network—at least local—up and running again."

"So we can play games and send those damn tweets," someone snapped.

"No, damn it. Data transfer was the lifeblood of what we were. Medical libraries, technical data beyond the magazines moldering in the school basement . . . find a way to hook me in, and we can even eavesdrop on Bluemont."

Though John was growing increasingly frustrated with Ernie taking the topic off the point he was trying to close in on and talking about more than he should, this did catch everyone's attention.

"After I left IBM back in the late '80s, that was the business my wife and I set up. We wrote the software and provided some of the hardware for those big array dishes. Not the crap units you all started to get with your televisions; I'm talking about the big stuff used by governments. Chances are the LEOs were most likely taken out in the war, but the geosynch stuff I bet is still definitely online."

"Translate, please?" the Asheville rep shouted from the back of the room.

"Oh, jeez. LEO, low-earth orbit. Companies like those direct television networks, their satellites were high up, twenty-three thousand miles up, what we called *geosynch*. The comm sats up there were heavily proofed against any kind of electromagnetic pulse. Had to be in order to survive solar storms, or coronal mass ejections, as we called them. Chances are Bluemont and other surviving governments are still using them for chatter and for encrypted stuff as well. You give me enough juice, some fairly recent computers that some rich kid tossed into his basement when Mommy and Daddy gave him an even faster unit for his damn stupid games, and I know how to start listening in."

"You mean hacking?" Maury asked.

"Yup. Hell, my wife is a pro at that. Some years back, we installed the tracking software for a Middle Eastern country to link into a geosynch satellite."

"Which Middle Eastern country?" John asked.

Ernie just smiled and replied, "Classified."

No one interrupted as Ernie smiled expansively, pleased that he had obviously taken over the meeting for at least a few minutes.

"Well, the bastards welched on the last half of a payment of around a million bucks. Figured they had the system we installed, so why bother to pay some Americans once they had it in place?" Ernie started to laugh.

"They hadn't counted on my wife, Linda. She sent them the usual notices and finally a warning, and they basically told us to screw off. Anyhow, they didn't reckon on her. She had a Trojan in the software, hacked into it on day 121 of overdue payment—after all due proper notice and warning, of course—and fried their entire system off. We lost a million bucks but laughed our butts off." Ernie chuckled at the memory of it.

"We have another resource as well," John chimed in. "This college was starting up a cybersecurity major just before we got hit. We have some kids here that were getting top-notch training in how to keep systems secured from hackers."

"Which means that in order to stop a hacker, you have to know how to hack," Ernie interjected. "Put those kids to work doing something useful rather than having them dig for roots and who knows what we might find out, not just about this rumor regarding an EMP but a lot of other stuff we haven't even considered. It's out there; it's time we started listening in, and if there is another EMP that hits without warning and the machines I've got up are running when the hit comes, we're back in the Stone Age, this time with no hope of return."

"What Ernie told us is another reason I have to go to Roanoke," John quickly announced. "We are coming back online. Ernie, if another EMP is popped today, or a few months from now, what happens to your work?"

Ernie looked at him and finally nodded. "I change my vote, John, even though it will eat up a hell of a lot of our reserve fuel for that chopper. I say go and get your answers."

John looked around at the others. "Let's say Ernie's statement is a motion. Those in favor?"

All but two raised their hands—the pilot who would have to take him . . . and Makala. And he knew there would be hell to pay once back home, but like it or not—and though the thought of a helicopter flight did turn his stomach over—it had to be done.

CHAPTER FIVE

John finished packing in total silence. There had been no cross words between him and Makala after the meeting and the decision to go, and the silence was indeed deafening. He scanned through his checklist of extra clothing and winter survival gear one more time. He had added in old-fashioned auto maps once put out by Exxon covering Virginia, Tennessee, and North Carolina, just in case they went down and had to hike back. The backup plan if such happened was to try to raise radio contact with Billy Tyndall, who would attempt to fly out and pick them up one at a time, but if that could not be done, it would be at least a two-week hike, in winter, to get back home.

He had carefully cleaned his Glock and was packing along four extra magazines. His shoulder weapon would be drawn from the community armory, an up-to-date M4 with half a dozen magazine loads.

He heard Maury's jeep, driven this time by Danny McMullen, pull into the driveway. Rather than come in, Danny wisely just tapped the horn a few times.

John shouldered his backpack and walked out to the sunroom, where Makala sat by the window. She was clutching Rabs, his daughter's much-battered and beloved stuffed rabbit, and the sight of her brought tears to his eyes.

She looked up at him. She was crying. He walked over and knelt by her side. She turned away from him and began to shudder with sobs.

"I've got a bad feeling about this one, John," she gasped. Then she turned, holding Rabs, and threw her arms around his shoulders.

"I have to," was all he could get out.

"We've all lost too much. Jennifer became like my daughter, poor old Jen like the mother I never really had. And now this. I never knew I could love a man with such intensity."

She broke completely, holding him tightly, and as she did so he could feel their baby quaking within her. He loosened her embrace, leaned down, kissed her distended stomach, and tried to force a laugh through his tears.

"Little bugger just kicked me in the face!"

"And if I didn't love you so much, I'd kick you too!" Makala cried. "Haven't you done enough? Everyone in town feels the same as I do, even Ernie. You damn near got killed more than once this spring. You've done enough. Forrest is eager to go; so is Ernie. You've already written out a letter to this Scales person, if he is even real and still alive. They can carry it and just drop it. Please, John."

Her tears were coming so hot and fiercely she couldn't talk for a moment.

He did not reply. He had stated he was going, what was now defined as the Senate for their so-called state had reluctantly voted in agreement, and there was no backing out now.

Chances were she was right; he was acting on an assumption, and though he had not articulated all of it openly, he fostered a deep-seated fear that Quentin had come as a warning, that something terrible was about to unfold, and he might be the only person who could find out what it was and act.

He had argued with himself in the hours after the meeting that he was simply being paranoid and taking too much upon himself, but his decision had been made, and long years of training and experience still told him that so often a first hunch, a gut feeling, carried with it the need to act.

He could only pray that Makala's gut feeling came from emotion and was wrong. At least he could hope that was the case.

Danny tapped the horn again. John reluctantly stood up, easing out of Makala's embrace. She stood up and threw her arms around him.

"Damn it, John Matherson, if anything happens to you, I think I'll kill you!" She began to laugh through her tears. "God go with you and bring you back safely to us."

"**Clear** rotors!" Maury shouted, leaning out the window. It had been agreed that Billy Tyndall would stay behind in case he was needed with the L-3. Danny McMullen was therefore in the copilot seat. He had zero flying time in a chopper; his military experience in the air force was working on the big stuff—B-52s, KC-135s—but at least he had a sense regarding the Black Hawk's power plant, and it was better than no one.

A security team of three was going with John, led by Forrest and accompanied by Kevin Malady and Lee Robinson. They could have taken half a dozen more, but each additional man was another two hundred pounds of weight, which equaled more fuel being needed. Besides, Maury's few hours of flight experience were with an empty load, and Danny in the other seat would have to learn on the job, so the less weight the better.

Side doors were opened for liftoff at Maury's insistence in case something went wrong and they had to get out quickly. The twin turbine engines above and behind John were whining up, rotor picking up speed, icy-cold air whipping in around him. He looked over at Forrest and Malady, sitting opposite him. John had of course endured many a chopper flight while in the army and never liked them; more often than not he had his puke bag out within minutes. Those two, though, were grinning, Malady shouting it felt like old times; Forrest, M4 slung across his chest, raising his one hand in a thumbs-up.

They are actually enjoying this, John thought, struggling to maintain a calm outward appearance. Several hundred from the town had turned out to see them off, for this, after all, was a major event for the community, with their police chief, Ed, struggling to keep the crowd back a hundred yards. Maury might have some idea about flying, but John knew that getting a helicopter up and away safely was a hell of a lot more difficult than taking off in the L-3.

They lifted off, nose pitching high, rolling as well to starboard. He could see Danny frantically pointing at something on the dash. The chopper then lurched forward, almost nosing in, Danny cursing so loudly that John could hear it even over the roar of the engines. And throughout it all, Forrest and Malady seemed unfazed. Lee Robinson, for whom this was the very first flight, had a nervous deathlike grip on John's shoulder and was cursing as well. Glancing out the open side door, John could see the horizon tilting at what must have been a thirty-degree angle. In a light plane at takeoff, it would surely be a stall, but Maury nosed back over and gradually like a yo-yo, going up and down, they started to gain altitude, lose it, pitch back up again, and finally, nose tilted down slightly, began to move forward, still rising up, clearing the Ingrams' parking lot.

Maury finally managed to gain some directional control, nose pitched forward a bit more, speed relative to the ground picking up, and he spared a quick glance over his shoulder, motioning for the side doors to be closed, blocking out the frigid blast.

The flight path was shaky at first, nose oscillating back and forth as Maury gingerly worked the controls but at least was putting more distance between them and the ground.

He nudged the chopper into a northeasterly direction, dipping the nose a bit more to gain bite with the rotors and forward speed. They crossed over the Swannanoa Gap, now up five hundred feet above ground level. It was the place where the great battle with the Posse had been fought out. Looking out the portside window in the door, John could see the steep slopes around what had been the Ridgecrest Conference Center, the woods still evidently flame-scorched from the battle. They hit a burble of turbulence as they cleared the gap, while still picking up speed. Down below were the twisting turns and tunnels of the Norfolk Southern railroad, an engineering marvel of the nineteenth century, the longest and toughest mountain grade east of the Rockies that had taken half a decade of labor by thousands to traverse those eleven miles to the top of the pass. He caught a glimpse of the Meltons' sawmill, in spite of the cold the water still flowing with enough energy to turn the wheel and the saws within, while a mile farther down was the clearing where the power dam for Old Fort and beyond was being installed, work stopped for now.

They continued to climb. Danny had handed him an old FAA aviation sectional map of their route. It would skirt along the northeast flank of the Appalachian Mountains to just south of Roanoke and then cross over the range to sweep down on the Virginia city located in the southwestern corner of the state.

With a stiff northwesterly wind still coming down into the South in the wake of the blizzard, both Maury and Billy had warned them it would be a bumpy ride, but at least on the way up, by gaining altitude up to eight thousand feet or so, the wind quartering on their tail would help whisk them to their goal and save on fuel. For the return flight, if they did not land, the flight plan was to get down low into the valley to avoid the stiff upper winds.

As they reached their cruising speed of 140 miles an hour, a mile and a half up, they were soon sweeping past the majestic sight of Linville Gorge, formerly known as "the Grand Canyon of North Carolina." It was a flash of memory for John, who had taken Jennifer and Elizabeth on a hike all the way up to the top of Table Rock. It had been an exhausting trek, made even more memorable because of the fright all of them had due to an encounter with a rattlesnake on the way back down. Jennifer had been terrified to the point where John had to carry her the last half mile down to the car, while more adventuresome Elizabeth wanted to go poking around in the brush with a long stick to find another one.

Snakes were definitely one of the major negatives in his life, and during the previous summer, perhaps because of the radical decline in human population and snakes' natural predators—such as possums, which some residents trapped as food—they had become a plague in the Montreat Valley. Regardless of his city-bred fears, some of the kids at the college had taken to eating them, a thought that turned John's stomach.

As they soared over the gorge and Table Rock, he hoped all the snakes down there would freeze to death with this early winter.

They shot over Brown Mountain, that mysterious place with strange glowing lights that locals claimed were lanterns carried by long-departed native spirits, and then past the once popular tourist attraction of Grandfather Mountain, abandoned, carpeted in a deep blanket of snow.

More turbulence and then the stomach-churning scent and sound of Lee getting sick, heaving into a plastic bag, spilling some as he cursed and fumbled to try to seal it shut. Forrest and Malady, sitting across from them, chuckled at Lee's distress, Forrest fishing into the pocket of his winter fatigue jacket, pulling out some salted beef jerky and offering it over, shouting for him to chew on it. John could not help but smile at Lee's scatological response even though he was fighting down nausea himself. In spite of their disagreement, Makala had set out some ginger tea for John to drink before leaving, a tonic she claimed actually did work with motion sickness, and perhaps it did so at this moment.

They soon crossed over Interstate 77 up near Mount Airy, the highway twin ribbons of white, the snow-covered humps of long-abandoned cars still cluttering the road. As they passed over villages and small towns, here and there he could see a plume of smoke from a chimney. Mount Airy, which had claimed to be the role model for Andy Griffith's Mayberry, actually showed signs of life; a cluster of homes in the center of town had smoke pouring from chimneys, and a few farmhouses on the outskirts of town showed signs of life as well, with even what looked to be several horses out in a snow-covered field.

But so much of the landscape was empty, barren, devoid of life. No roads were cleared, of course, the landscape below, once teeming with life, now a vast dead world that was once bustling with the activities of man. Near the interstate, except for Mount Airy, village after village appeared to have been burned out and abandoned.

John unbuckled from his seat and, crouching low, went up forward to squat between Maury and Danny.

Maury looked over his shoulder after struggling for a moment with the controls, nose pitching down slightly.

"Damn it, John, you moving around throws off the center of gravity on this thing."

"Sorry, just wanted to check on how we are doing."

"Fine, but just don't move around now."

"We on course?"

Maury had yet to figure out what must have been the built-in navigation screen during the few hours he had practiced with this chopper and decided not to waste battery and fuel to figure it all out, so they were navigating by dead reckoning and an FAA sectional spread out on Danny's lap.

"That's Interstate 81 off to our left on the other side of the mountains. We're crossing into what was once the state of Virginia."

The way Danny had said *what was once* struck him.

"About twenty minutes out, I'd reckon; the wind up here is giving us a good fifty-mile-per-hour boost."

After Mary died, John had taken the girls on several trips up to the War College at Carlisle to visit Bob Scales when he was commandant there and then would bore Elizabeth to death spending a few days visiting and hiking around Gettysburg and Antietam. Jennifer, however, loved the trips because of the Boyds Bears shop just south of Gettysburg. He pushed that memory aside; it was far too poignant. The drive up and back was a long one—it usually took four hours or so to pass Roanoke—and here they were approaching it in little more than fifty minutes.

"Anything on the radio?" John shouted.

Maury shook his head. He had barely mastered that system as well, knowing enough to have it tuned to 122.9, the old frequency for general air traffic in what had once been defined as uncontrolled airspace, and alternating it with the frequency for what had been the civil airport at Roanoke as listed on the FAA map.

They started over the mountains, turbulence picking up again, Danny shouting off waypoints he had marked on the map with a grease pencil, while working an old-fashioned circular slide rule, once the standard tool of all pilots, to check on relative ground speed and rate of drift from the quartering tailwind, giving course corrections to Maury.

John looked over at his friend and could see that he was relaxing a bit. If anything, this first cross-country flight was instilling some confidence in his friend, who had only practiced locally since the capture of the chopper, carefully conserving their limited supply of jet fuel with each practice flight. John scanned the gauges, figured out which one was fuel, and was pleased to see they had consumed little more than one-eighth of their load.

More buffeting as they dropped through three thousand feet, airspeed up to 170 miles an hour, a whiff of an unpleasant scent produced by Lee mingled in with the exhaust from the turbines.

"That's Roanoke," Danny announced, pointing ten degrees or so off to their port side.

In the cold winter air, it stood out clearly just beyond the low range of hills surrounding it, larger than Asheville. Plumes of smoke were rising up, not for heat but rather buildings that were burning.

"Think it's hot down there; something's going on," Danny announced, looking over at John, who nodded.

The airport was located just north of the city. To reach it, they'd have to fly directly over the city and whatever was going on down there.

"Swing us west, Maury," John said. "Circle us out a half dozen miles or so; don't go directly over the city, and we'll approach the airport from the other direction."

It came up quickly with a ground speed of well over three miles a minute, John scanning the air around them. There was a flash of light from a building at least ten stories or so high, smoke rising up an instant later.

"Damn it, there's fighting down there!" Danny shouted.

John felt a hand on his shoulder, looked up, and saw that Forrest was leaning on him for support, joining them to look forward.

"Looks like a hot LZ to me!" Forrest shouted. "Where's the airport?"

Danny pointed to the right and forward. John picked up the binoculars resting in a flight bag between Maury and Danny, knelt up, trying to keep his balance, and finally got a close-up glimpse of the airport on the far side of the city.

It was packed with aircraft, nearly all military. Half a dozen helicopters, a mix of Black Hawks and Apaches, and two old C-130s. Friend or foe? Like the choppers Fredericks had brought with him back in the spring, nearly all the aircraft lined up below were painted in faded desert camo scheme, military equipment brought back to the United States after the Day.

"Someone's calling us," Maury announced, slipping one headphone back and looking at John. "Demanding we identify ourselves. What should I do?"

This was not exactly what John expected. But then again, what did he expect? A deserted city? A destroyed city? A war going on that they were blundering into? But certainly not a welcome mat with a big sign scraped out of the snow: "Welcome, John! We were expecting you."

"John, what do we do?"

"Just state we're from Carolina and if General Scales is available to put him on the line."

Maury did as requested, waited, and then shook his head.

"They're ordering us to land immediately."

Maury gazed intently at John, who mulled that over for a few seconds while looking toward the city that was now off their starboard side half a dozen miles away. There was definitely a fight going on in the downtown area. It looked similar to Asheville, a cluster of taller office buildings downtown, suburban sprawl stretching out for several miles in every direction.

"Tell him we'll comply."

"What?" Forrest shouted. "Are you flipping crazy, John? There's a fight going on down there. We land and Lord knows what we'll be getting into. Whoever is down there will keep this bird, and if we're lucky and not shot on the spot, we might just be allowed to walk home."

"Just tell him we'll comply," John shouted again, "and then be ready for a low-level pass so I can drop a message pod and then get us the hell out of here!"

He looked back up at Maury, who now had approximately eleven hours of stick time on this chopper. He was asking for a maneuver that nearly all pilots loved to do, legally or when no one was looking, illegally. Before the Day, the mountains around Asheville served as a practice range for pilots preparing to deploy to Afghanistan or wherever there was mountainous terrain, and he always got a kick out of watching their high-speed passes, sweeping in low through the Swannanoa Gap, skimming up over his house, at times nearly at rooftop level, and weaving in and out across the mountain passes. And all of them most likely had hundreds of hours of airtime before trying such maneuvers.

Maury grimaced, Danny looking over at the pilot and forcing a smile.

"John, get aft, make sure everyone is strapped in, and open the door!" Danny shouted.

John staggered back the few feet to the aft compartment, sparing a quick glance at Lee, who truly fit the definition of green faced, shouting for him to tighten his belting. Forrest strapped in across from John and then shouted instructions as to how to open the side door, which John had to struggle with as the helicopter pitched back and forth, the door at last sliding open, the cold blast of winter air whipping by at 140 miles per hour stunning him.

He reached into his backpack and pulled out the message pod, a plastic torpedo-shaped container with a thirty-foot red streamer attached to it, snapping off the rubber band that held the streamer in a tight ball, letting several feet unravel.

He glanced up and through the forward windshield and saw that Maury was banking in toward the airport but was now caught in a strong crosswind, struggling to crab the chopper so they could fly down the length of the main runway. There was a hell of a bounce as Maury nosed over, Lee looking at John wide-eyed and a second later disgorging what was left of his breakfast and dinner from the night before onto John's lap.

"They're threatening to shoot if we don't land!" Maury shouted, barely heard above the roar of the slipstream racing past the open door.

"Tell them to screw themselves," John shouted, "after we get the hell out!"

They crossed the threshold of the runway, going flat out, Maury, nervous at running so low, bobbing up and down, tail rotor assembly swinging back and forth as he fought to keep control at such low altitude, with a variable crosswind sweeping across the open runway. John glanced up again. They were a hundred or so feet up, crossing over the paved runway, a large white number 12 flashing by underneath. To their right, he could see the airport terminal, the building burned out, collapsed, a couple of dozen private aircraft, long ago abandoned, pushed off to one side of the tarmac and jumbled together. Next to it, the control tower was still intact. He wanted to shout for Maury to try to get closer to the control tower, fearful that the dropped message might not be noticed.

He waited a few more seconds.

"They want us down now!" Maury shouted.

John ignored him, leaning out the open door, message cylinder and red tail ribbon bunched up in his hand, anxious at the thought that it just might get wiped aft and tangled into the tail rotor.

They swept over a grounded Apache, several personnel on the ground craning to look up—or were they pointing something—and in answer to the thought, he caught the flash of a tracer round snapping past the open door.

He threw the message cylinder out, arm getting whipped back by the slipstream, slamming it against the outside of the chopper, the wind sucking the glove off his left hand, shoulder feeling as if it were about to break.

More tracers, a metallic crackling sound behind him, like someone punching a hole through aluminum or titanium, which was exactly what was happening as several rounds slammed into their Black Hawk.

The impacts startled Maury, who instinctively pulled the chopper into a steep banking turn, and if not for the safety harness, John would have been pitched out. Gasping for breath in the violent crosswind, he caught a glimpse of the message cylinder already down on the ground, the red tape attached to the tail still spiraling down, someone running toward it, while at least two others with weapons raised were continuing to fire at them.

"You damn fools!" John screamed, making a universal rude gesture as Forrest, one-handed, stretched out and grabbed the back of John's harness to help pull him back in. Even as he did so, Maury pitched the chopper hard to starboard, causing John to tumble back in, landing hard on the floor, which was splattered with Lee's vomit.

Kevin Malady unbuckled himself from his safety harness, half crawled over Forrest, and slammed the portside door shut.

"We okay?" John shouted.

"Sons of bitches!" Forrest yelled and pointed to the side of his helmet. It was dented in, a bullet having creased it.

John looked at it, a bit shaken. A couple of inches farther down and his friend would be dead, and he realized that for the bullet to have entered thus, it must have snapped past him by a margin of only a few inches as well.

"We okay?" John shouted again, Danny looking back at him.

They were past the perimeter of the airport, heading east. Danny returned his attention forward and was obviously saying something to Maury, pointing toward the instrument panel. John unclipped the safety harness and crawled up between the two.

"Problems?"

"Yeah!" Maury shouted. "I think we've been hit. And look off to your right. An Apache that was up in the air is peeling off toward us."

He looked to where Maury was pointing and caught the flash of rotors. The narrow profile of the Apache was hard to see, but he could discern it was headed their way.

"They're ordering us to come back, land, or we'll be shot down."

"Can they?"

Maury was silent for a moment, attention focused to where Danny was pointing at one of the gauges.

"One of the turbines might have taken a hit; it's heating up a bit, RPM dropping. They're designed to take punishment; let's just hope it holds together. Supposedly, you can fly this thing on one engine, but I wouldn't want to try it right now."

Maury banked again to port, taking them on a direct easterly heading, away from the Apache.

"Can he catch up to us?" John asked.

"Don't know!" Maury shouted. "I remember the Black Hawk is a bit faster than the Apache—at least it was when I was flying these things. Wait a second."

Maury pulled his headphone down over his left ear, listened intently, spoke, and then pushed it back up so he could talk to John.

"Told them we want to come back but call off that Apache first. Telling them that might buy us some time."

John looked to the glint of rotors from the Apache; it was still on course toward them. It was hard to judge distance, but he appeared to be at least several miles off.

"If he's got an air-to-air, we're screwed!" Danny shouted.

Maury looked back at John, raising a quizzical eyebrow, passing the decision on to him.

Air-to-air? He mulled that over for a few seconds. The Apache was doing ground support. Besides, air-to-air was not usual armament for a helicopter unless one was expecting to tangle with enemy air assets. Fredericks didn't have anything like that; otherwise, the L-3 would have been toast.

"Just keep going straight east for now," John replied.

"And pray both engines keep turning," Danny added.

"Can we outrun him?" John asked.

"So far so good," was all Danny said before focusing back on scanning the instrument panel.

John fell silent, letting them do their job, looking back over his shoulder to see that Forrest had his helmet off, had passed it over to Kevin to examine, the two of them talking away as if this were just another typical day.

"We got any kind of warning if something is coming up our tail?" John shouted.

Danny pointed at the blank computer screen. "It's all in there," he replied, "but I'll be damned if I know how to run it. Besides, what the hell can we do if they have an air-to-air? We're toast."

"Thanks for the reassurance," John replied, and he backward crawled to his seat, trying to avoid the mess that Lee Robinson had splashed onto the floor and to which he had added in the last few minutes.

John strapped himself back in and settled down, trying to block out the smell. He knew there was an old saying with pilots that no matter how good an engine you have, when flying at night or over water with no place for an emergency landing your engine always starts to sound rough. It had been years since he'd last been up in a helicopter, and he tried to compare what he was hearing now versus back then. Something did sound "rough." And looking forward, he could see that Danny was focused on the instrument panel and saying something to Maury, who just kept nodding in reply.

Maury was all but flying nap of the earth, at least as far as his skills allowed. John figured they were at least ten, maybe fifteen miles out from Roanoke, and if anything was going to come up their tail, they would be scattered wreckage by now. He was about to say something when Maury banked sharply, turning southwest, Danny craning to look back over his shoulder and shouting that if the Apache was still following he could no longer see him.

Maury began to gently nose up, trading off a bit of speed for some altitude. They had gone over the flight plan before taking off, figuring from the weather pattern that higher up the prevailing winds would be west to northwest. Gone were the days of clicking on a computer for flight service info, at least for the one helicopter of the State of Carolina. So it had been decided that for the return flight they would stay at a thousand feet or lower to avoid a strong headwind. When in a small plane, John always felt safer the higher up they climbed. If the engine quit, the plane just turned into a glider, and the higher up one was, the farther they could glide to an open field or nearby airport for a safe landing.

In a helicopter, he always felt the exact opposite, having witnessed during a training maneuver in Germany a helicopter having a full engine failure while more than half a mile up. According to the book, the chopper should have easily autorotated down to a landing one could at least crawl away from. Halfway down, the rotor seized up completely, and it dropped like a rock, killing the crew and the six troopers on board.

"Know where we are?" Lee said, looking over at John.

"Heading home."

"Thank God," Lee gasped. At least this time he managed to use a baggie and seal it up. Groaning, he just leaned over while Forrest and Kevin looked at him with at least some pity, even as they traded a joking comment.

John settled in, suddenly realizing that his left hand was absolutely numb from the cold. He unzipped his jacket and slid it in under his armpit and closed his eyes, trying not to listen too closely to the engine, for there was something definitely wrong. Maury shouted he was throttling back to put less strain on it, dropping their airspeed down to a hundred miles an hour. John mentally clicked off the miles; with each passing minute in the air they were subtracting an hour of laboriously walking through the winter snow to get home.

Was this trip really necessary, he wondered, or just a folly on his part? He had harbored a fantasy that perhaps, just perhaps, he would hear Bob Scales's familiar voice on the radio, inviting him to come in, land, and talk things over. Tucked into his vest pocket, he had even brought along a photograph taken of Jennifer and Elizabeth the year before the Day.

What did happen over these last few minutes, he was prepared for as well, confident of the decision not to land but still disconcerted that they had been fired upon.

He closed his eyes, suddenly exhausted, the adrenaline rush over with, now just trying to look calm as they clicked off the passing minutes for what should, he hoped, be the hour-and-a-half flight back home.

At least the message pod had been dropped, and he saw someone running over to pick it up. He had thought it out carefully the night before, writing the message on his old Underwood typewriter:

```
TO: General Robert E. Scales
FROM: Colonel John Hastings Matherson
RE: Contact
Several days ago, a man claiming to have served
with you, initials Q. R., arrived in the outskirts
of my community. He had been badly beaten by
marauders on his journey and died from the results
of injury and exposure before I could personally
```

speak to him. His message, whatever it was, never reached me. I do not have, as well, any means of verification to his claim of having served or to be currently serving with you. My flight to Roanoke is an attempt to establish contact with you. If you are reading this message rather than speaking to me personally, the reasons for my decision not to land should be apparent to you. Sir, I pray that you are indeed still alive and contact between us can be established. I will maintain round-the-clock monitoring of aviation frequency 122.9 for the next seven days, fifteen minutes after the top of any hour, day or night, if you should wish to speak with me. Please attempt to reach me first by radio rather than flying to my location. You are most likely aware of the confrontation that happened in Asheville this spring, and I regret to say any air intrusion without prior notification will be considered to be hostile and reacted to accordingly. I regret such a response, but prudence after the aggression endured by my community is necessary.

As verification of who I am, you will recognize the two photographs enclosed. Also, sir, I regret to inform you that our beloved J. died shortly after the start of the war.

Respectfully,
Colonel John Matherson
State of Carolina

He had written it out half a dozen times. If Bob was not alive, he had not given away any crucial details. He had also implied that his community now possessed air-defense capability if the message should fall into hostile hands. For that matter, he was not even sure now if Bob was indeed still a comrade on the same side or if that the tragic events of the last few years now placed them potentially on opposing sides. He had made no mention of Quentin's ramblings about an EMP, whatever that might now mean. The proof of who he was Bob would know. One photo was from a visit Bob and his wife had made to Black Mountain, a poignant trip after he passed the word that Mary was in her final weeks. It was a photograph of all of them together, Mary, still clinging to life and smiling for the photo, six-year-old Jennifer and ten-year-old Elizabeth to either side of her, John and Bob standing behind them, trying to smile as well. The second was a photo of just the two of them in the field during Desert Storm, leaning against a Humvee, begrimed, grinning, for the cease-fire—at least for the next few years—had just been announced, their brief taste of America's first open war in the Middle East at an end.

Thinking about it now caused a rush of memories. Were they still friends, or were they now enemies? Bob had been his mentor, taking a liking to John, who, fresh out of ROTC, had been assigned to Bob's staff. As Bob went from colonel to general, John had followed the more intellectual route of a military career, going on to graduate work in military history, their paths crossing again at Carlisle, where John had the pleasure of teaching for a year after Desert Storm.

If enemies, it made him think of the life of Robert E. Lee, who was somewhat of a namesake for his friend. Lee had served as superintendent at West Point in the early 1850s. Ten years later, more than one of his young cadets from West Point faced him across the other side in the fields of Antietam and Gettysburg, the burning woods of the Wilderness, and the nightmare slaughter in front of Cold Harbor. After such blood-drenched fights, Lee would read in captured newspapers accounts of yet another of those young cadets' deaths and knew deep within that the cause he fought for with such tenacity had resulted in those deaths.

Is Bob my enemy or my friend? John now wondered. *If my enemy, would he kill me, or at least try to warn me at first, and was that the reason Quentin had been sent? Or, for that matter, is this all some sort of cruel existentialist joke?*

A vibration running through the chopper snapped him out of his musing.

"What was that?"

He could see a look of concern now in Forrest's eyes and those of Malady as well.

"Might be one of the turbines is starting to break up," Forrest said calmly.

"I think I dozed off. Where are we?"

"We passed Statesville on our left about five minutes ago," Forrest said. "My God, it's all gone, John. Burned out, looted, looks like a wasteland. Those rumors that the Posse and other gangs like it just tore it apart are true. Sick bastards."

Another vibration, this one more pronounced.

"We're shutting one engine down!" Danny shouted, looking back at John.

"We gonna crash?" Lee asked.

"It can fly on one," Forrest replied. "Not fast, but at least keep us going."

John wondered if Maury even knew the proper procedure for shutdown while in flight or whether this was a learn-on-the-job situation. For that matter, how would the helicopter's flight characteristics change, and could Maury handle it?

Seconds later, he began to find out when it felt like, the chopper falling out beneath them and Maury then pitching the nose forward. At least he had a thousand feet of altitude to figure it out, but at their speed, that meant a matter of seconds. He could hear the difference in engine and rotor pitch and then the additional strain on the one remaining engine as Maury pushed it to the max, finally leveling out just a few hundred feet above Interstate 40.

Going against safety procedures, John unclipped from his harness and crawled forward. He didn't say a word to Maury, who was completely focused on keeping them aloft, Danny talking to him on the intercom, offering either some advice or just encouragement.

John could see the airspeed indicator. They were down to seventy—he was not sure if it was miles per hour or knots.

"I think I smell something burning!" Forrest shouted, and John picked up the scent as well. What the hell was it?

"That's Hickory up ahead!" Danny shouted. "Still Indian country in places. We're trying for the Morganton airport, which is ten miles farther on."

"If it holds together," Forrest replied.

"The airport in Morganton is ours. Can we make it?"

"My thoughts!" Danny shouted. "Hangar's still intact. Old Bob Gillespie still lives there, used to work on choppers."

Passing the outskirts of Hickory, flying low, they passed within easy landing distance of that far larger airport, but it was still an area not really secured. And as if in answer, there was a sharp rattling beneath them.

"Some bastard down there just hit us!" Forrest announced. "Thank God this isn't a Huey with no armor; I might have caught one in the ass!"

John crawled back to his seat and strapped back in, Danny shouting they were just minutes out if things held together.

Crossing over narrow Lake Rhodhiss, John could clearly see the Morganton airport straight ahead—one long runway up on a slight bluff. Maury aimed straight for the middle of it, approaching the runway at a right angle, not bothering to swing out the few extra miles for a standard runway approach.

He began to ease off the throttle, pulling in the collective, the nose flaring up, view forward changing to nothing but sky for John.

He looked over at Lee, trying to offer a reassuring smile. His old friend and neighbor, a man with six generations of family history in their valley, a man he would want more than anyone else by his side in a fight, was definitely having a hard time with his first flight. In spite of the cold, sweat was beading down his face and his eyes were closed, his lips moving in silent prayer.

"Almost there!" John shouted, putting a reassuring hand on his friend's shoulder. Lee simply nodded and then leaned forward to retch again.

"Brace yourselves!" Danny shouted.

Forrest leaned over to unlatch the side door and slide it open. The cold blast of air swirling in a refreshing shock washed out the stench of vomit and whatever it was that was burning.

The landscape outside was tilted at a crazy angle. With a lurch, the helicopter banked sharply to port, and John was now looking nearly straight down at a runway fifty feet below. Maury straightened the wounded bird out, throttled back more, the ground coming up fast. There was a final blast from the rotor, slowing their rate of descent, and with nose high, he slammed down hard on the runway while still going forward. They bounced and came down again for another bounce, and then he cut power back so that with the third bounce the wheels stayed on the ground. They were still rolling forward at a fair clip, Maury or Danny working the brakes, and they finally rolled to a stop.

"Out! Everyone out!" Maury shouted.

John was definitely not going to hesitate with that order. He reached over to help Lee, who was fumbling with his safety harness, the buckles slick with frozen vomit, so that John could not help but gag as he helped his friend to his feet and pushed him out the door. Command instinct told John that he should be the last one out. Forrest and Kevin, still acting if the day were routine, were already unbuckled and out the door, while up forward, Maury and Danny fumbled at switches to shut the Black Hawk down.

Maury looked back at John and motioned for him to get out. John needed no further urging, reaching over to pat Maury on the shoulder before exiting. Overhead, the rotor was still slowly spinning but winding down.

As he stepped out, he was greeted by the smell of burned metal. Old training reminded him not to breathe deeply. Burning aluminum and titanium were toxic.

"Son of a bitch!" Forrest cried, pointing at the portside turbine mounting. "Either damn lucky bastards or damn good shots."

The housing was scored with half a dozen deep dents standing out clearly, the paint having been blown off. Black smoke was trailing out from the exhaust pipe, the northwesterly breeze whipping it around them.

John covered his mouth to go up and look closer with Forrest by his side.

"None of the rounds penetrated?" he asked. "So what happened?"

"Supposed to be proof even against 20mm rounds as long as they're not armor piercing, but still, it dings the metal and bends it in; sometimes fragments of bent metal pop off inside the engine housing and get whipped into the turbine. We most likely cracked a turbine blade. If we had shut down immediately, it wouldn't have been so bad. Now I'm not sure how much damage it did."

The rotor came to a stop, Danny exiting the aircraft, coming aft to join them, fire extinguisher in hand, reaching up high to hose down the intake and then exhaust ports.

John stepped away from the Black Hawk, knees feeling rubbery. Lee was just lying in the snow, breathing deeply, looking up at the sky. John went up to his side and knelt down.

"John, we've been friends for Lord knows how many years," Lee gasped, "but I'll be damned if I ever go flying with you again. For that matter, I'll be damned if I ever go flying again, period."

Kevin Malady, who had knelt down on the other side of Lee, chuckled. "Hey, that was a piece of cake."

"Kiss my butt," Lee gasped before rolling on to his side and retching again.

Maury finally climbed out of the cockpit, took off his helmet, and tossed it back inside, and then, to John's surprise, he got sick to his stomach as well.

John stood to one side, waiting for his friend to regain his composure, while aft, Forrest had climbed back inside to fetch another fire extinguisher to hand out to Danny, who continued to douse the engine. The smoke was subsiding, the aircraft's metal ringing with metallic pings as it cooled down.

"Here comes Bob Gillespie," Danny announced, and he pointed to a four-wheel all-terrain vehicle turning out from the taxiway and onto the runway. Its driver, an elderly man, capless and baldheaded, was slowing down to a near stop a hundred feet out with shotgun at the ready.

"Who the hell are you crazy bastards?" he shouted.

Danny held his arms up, cursing back and identifying himself. The driver relaxed, set his shotgun down, and drove up, dismounting, reaching to the rear seat to pull out a heavy fire extinguisher, and dragging it up behind the chopper.

"Danny McMullen, just what in hell are you doing out here?"

"We just went for a little ride." Turning, he introduced the rest of the group. John had heard about Gillespie, who until the Day owned the airport and spent his life fixing nearly anything that could fly. When contact was reestablished with Morganton back in the spring, Danny had tried to recruit Gillespie into moving to Black Mountain to help with the L-3 and Black Hawk. Gillespie had managed to survive by going hermit and lying low when the Posse had been rampaging through the area. With no family, his wife having passed away years earlier, the airport had become his family.

The old man merely nodded a reply to the introductions because he was all eyes for the Black Hawk, and without a word, he slowly walked around it, taking a few minutes to look at the bullet-pocked turbine housing, poking his head into the cockpit, and clucking before finally going back to Danny.

"So which one of you screwed up six million dollars' worth of aircraft?"

They all looked one to the other, and John started to step forward.

"I've seen more than one crash in my career, and by God, ten minutes ago, I figured I was about to see a bunch of fools die. That was, without a doubt, one of the most God-awful landings I have ever witnessed. Whoever was flying this, do us a favor and stay on the ground. You bent a wheel strut, you idiot."

As he spoke, he pointed to the portside strut—which was indeed cantered out at an angle—and John now noticed the chopper was actually listing.

"How about the engine?" Danny asked.

"Don't know until I strip it down. Most likely some cracked turbine blades, for starters. Let me guess—you kept them spinning after you got hit until things started to burn out."

Everyone looked over Maury, who was suddenly red-faced.

"Damn it, like I told you six months ago, it's been twenty years since I flew one of these things. At least we're still alive."

It was Forrest who broke the tension, reaching into his jacket pocket to pull out a pack of Dunhills. Popping one out, he then held it up, offering it to the others.

"Oh my God!" Gillespie cried, reaching out for one.

"Can this guy maybe fix it?" John whispered, leaning over to Danny.

"Don't know until we strip the engine down."

"I think Forrest has something to trade for the work," John replied.

Danny nodded, and to John's surprise, he went over to Forrest's side and motioned for a cigarette. A minute later, all of them except for Lee and himself were smoking, Maury now shaking from adrenaline and fatigue, nervously inhaling and coughing as he exhaled but then continuing to smoke.

Forrest looked over at John, again that seductive offer. He was standing downwind of his friends and of course breathing in the delicious scent.

And then there was the memory of the photograph of Jennifer with her dying mother and the promise he made.

While putting together the drop package, he had come upon the idea of including the photographs as proof of the validity of who he was if it was actually handed intact to Bob. Fishing around in the basement of what had once been Jen's house, he found the photo albums. Going through them had caused deep stabs of pain, and Makala had found him thus, crying softly as he looked at the photos of Mary holding Elizabeth as a newborn, and then Jennifer. And as well, old photos going back to Mary's childhood, the day they announced their engagement, the day they got married.

She had not said a word about finding him thus, accepting without question his comment that he was looking for a couple of photographs to enclose in the message capsule as proof of who he was if the situation was too dangerous for them to land.

Looking out across the snow-covered landscape, still smelling the burning cigarettes, his friends unwinding and laughing as men do after a close shave with disaster, he wondered where all of this was leading—and what his reception from Makala would be when they finally got into downtown Morganton, made the long-distance phone call to Black Mountain, and found a way to get the last forty miles back to home.

I hope this was all worth it. His thoughts were more like a prayer. *Bob, for God's sake, I hope you are still alive, that whatever Quentin was raving about was just the memories of a dying man.*

He so wanted to believe it—that not only was Bob alive but that he was on the side of Bluemont, the mere thought of him being on their side a reassurance that in spite of the tragedy of the spring, it was a government he could still work with.

CHAPTER SIX

"It's seven days now without a word from Roanoke or anywhere else." John sighed, looking over at Maury Hurt, who, along with several of the ham radio operators in their community, had been monitoring 122.9 around the clock.

The response was silence.

"Could it be a signal couldn't carry that far?" John asked.

"It used to be an open channel for uncontrolled air space," one of the "hams" replied. "With a handheld unit, I sometimes picked up traffic sixty miles away. The antenna I've got set up now picks up some distant chatter—not sure from where, I suspect down toward Charleston—so we should have heard something."

"And we're certain it was monitored 24-7, at fifteen minutes into each hour? No holes, no one asleep?"

The small group looked at each other, shaking their heads.

"John, we set up a regular rotation, at least two monitoring at any given time. Zero, zilch, nothing."

"Okay, thanks for coming over," John sadly replied. The four left his home, Makala seeing them off and then coming back to sit next to John, who was gazing absently at the fire blazing inside the woodstove.

"Feel it was all for naught?" she asked.

He winced slightly as she took his left hand to examine it. He had lost a glove while leaning out of the chopper, and by the time he had finally arrived back home, his hand was completely numb with a touch of frostbite that was healing but still troublesome, along with the wrenched shoulder from getting slammed against the outside of the chopper.

Makala had hovered over him ever since their return, muttering in stern nurse manner about busted ribs and other assorted injuries from the past with this new one now added in. The trip had drained him, again reminding him that he was no longer a young lieutenant or captain in the field; those days were more than half a lifetime ago. Once home, Makala held him in a fierce embrace, stifling back tears, whispering that when their return was long overdue, everyone had begun to fear the worst—that they had crashed, been shot down, or foolishly landed into a trap and taken prisoner.

He was beyond grateful for her response, given the anger she was feeling when he left and the way she snuggled up close to him after feeding him some hot soup and then packing him off to bed for twelve blessed hours of sleep.

A day later, another storm had rolled in, dropping an additional ten inches. Before the Day, such a storm, though significant for the South, was just part of life. Lifelong residents of the area were now saying it was beginning to look like the worst winter in decades, and given how precarious living now was, a long, snowy winter could indeed turn into a starving and freezing time. In the last three weeks, John calculated that he and Makala had gone through six to eight weeks' worth of firewood. With a baby due in just about two months, it was becoming another source of worry. He dreaded the hours of work splitting and stacking an extra cord of firewood.

The other source of worry was the apparent loss, at least for some time to come, of their Black Hawk. Bob Gillespie was stripping down the damaged engine; one of the turbine blades had indeed fractured. The wreckage of the three helicopters destroyed in the battle around Asheville Mall back in the spring had been dragged into the old Sears building to get it out of the weather and still rested there. John had agreed to allocate yet more precious gas reserves for Danny and Maury to go to Asheville to see if replacement parts could be salvaged from the wrecks and then transported all the way down to Morganton.

This apparently failed venture to try to get a message to Bob Scales had cost the community several hundred gallons of precious fuel already, along with the possible permanent loss of their captured Black Hawk.

He had long ago learned to compartmentalize the multitude of issues and anxieties that had become part of his daily life, and he had to do so now, forcing a smile as Makala gently massaged his still-tender hand and then checked his shoulder, which was still sore as well. The room was quiet, warm. John sighed and leaned up to kiss her on the lips as she stood beside him.

"You know, this could kind of lead to something," he whispered, and she hugged him. Several seconds later, he received a solid kick from their baby.

"And that little devil is a mood killer if ever there was one, John Matherson." She laughed. "Maybe come spring, we can get back to some fun."

He sighed, content to just hold her, both of them chuckling as the baby continued to squirm and kick.

He finally looked down at his old-style wristwatch, hugged Makala tightly, and then reluctantly stood up. "I really should go up to the college. Ernie and the Hawkinses want to show me what they're up to."

She helped to bundle him up, went into the kitchen, and came back with a quart mason jar of canned peaches, stuffing the bottle into his pocket. "That poor girl nursing twins needs these more than I do right now. Send her my love, and tell her once it's safe to walk I'll come up to check on her."

She watched as he went out the door, calling for him to stay in the middle of the road in case he fell. Maury had brought word to them this morning that one of the Wilson boys had been found dead the day before. Out hunting, he apparently slipped on some ice, fell, compound fractured his leg, and lay there helpless until he bled out and froze. In the few years prior to the Day, when cell phones had become a part of everyone's daily lives, such an accident was all but unheard of. If in trouble while out in the woods, one simply called and cried out for help. Falling where no one could see or hear you replaced the worry last summer about the plague of copperheads and rattlesnakes that had erupted in the area, at least a dozen getting bitten and, with no antidote, two children dying.

Warmly wrapped up, wearing a scarf, which he had always disdained before but was now grateful that Makala had wrapped one of hers around his neck, he trudged down to Montreat Road by the abandoned tennis courts and headed north for what used to be a short hike up to the campus. In a different time, he would have soaked in yet another beautiful morning after a snowstorm. No wind had followed the storm down here in the narrow valley, the trees canopying the road bent under the heavy weight of the wet snow forming a tunnellike vista ahead of him. A couple of heavy branches had snapped off, which he had to climb over, a barrier that road crews once took care of within minutes. To his right, Flat Creek was still roiling downstream through the park where he used to take his children to play. A couple of students were down there, enjoying the morning, laughing, the girl chasing the young man, tackling him, the two, not suspecting someone might be watching, rolling together, laughing, and then kissing passionately. He smiled as he surreptitiously watched for a moment, again aware of the desire he had felt for Makala just moments ago, and then seeing where their frolic might lead, he figured it best to quietly move along.

Even in the midst of death, there was still life, and young life. He recalled a favorite science fiction series, *Battlestar Galactica,* when after the near annihilation of the human race, survivors aboard a few remaining ships fled their home worlds. A fierce debate ensued with one character demanding that they make a final fight while the newly appointed president declared they should flee and that if there was a priority now, it was to have children, lots of children.

In the midst of death, life was again trying to reassert itself. The historian in him knew such was true; after every brutal annihilating war, the primal instinct was to repopulate, to replace with a new generation all those who had been lost. It made him think of Jennifer. She'd be fourteen and a half now, no longer his little girl, on the cusp of becoming a young woman. The baby would be Makala's first child, but for him? In a symbolic way, was the baby about to be born a replacement for the one he had lost?

He glanced back at the couple in the snow, definitely behaving like a young couple in love, ignoring the coldness of the snow for a moment, this next glance telling him it was definitely time to move along.

A wisp of a sad, understanding smile creased his features as he pushed on, leaving the secluded park behind, reaching the road bridge over Flat Creek, walking up the steep slope past what was now the community's source of electricity. To his right was Anderson Auditorium, converted into the town factory for turning out turbines, generators, and wire, the fundamental building blocks of late nineteenth- and early twentieth-century technology.

He felt he should drop in to at least say hello, but he realized those working away inside the factory might see it as some sort of inspection tour and be thrown off their routine, and he therefore pressed on.

The road steepened for fifty yards or so, memories flooding in of one icy day when classes were dismissed early and he wound up driving down it sideways, laughing students helping to push him out of the ditch where he had finally come to a stop. It was distressing to realize now that this short walk, up a slope, trudging through nearly two feet of snow, left him so winded that he had to stop for a moment to catch his breath.

As he rested, he turned to look around at his valley. After a snowstorm, all sound was all so muffled. When still living near Ridgecrest, he delighted in the fact that the distant rumble on Interstate 40 ceased for a day or so during and after a storm. From childhood, there were memories of the sound of the few cars still on the road, tires wrapped in chains for traction, rattling by, and, blessing of blessings, days off from school. Now, except for the distant sound of hammering from Anderson Auditorium, all was silent. Whoever had penned "Silent Night" knew and understood it, as did Robert Frost when he wrote about stopping in the woods on a snowy evening.

It used to be his favorite time of year. It no longer was with all the worries about survival to spring for his family and community. The worry was compounded by the unanswered questions. Was Bob Scales still alive? Had Bob indeed sent one man on a desperate journey to reach him, and if so, why? And overarching all were Quentin's dying words about EMPs. The obsessive question haunting him. Were they ramblings of a delirious man slipping into death or a dire warning?

The thoughts of that terminated his moment of peaceful contemplation, and with breath somewhat back to normal, he turned to climb the last few hundred yards to the library.

Rounding the corner of the road by the chapel and the library, he was amused to see some of the students out sledding. Beyond their work schedule and rotation periods as community guards with the militia companies, the fact that they still had energy to enjoy such a beautiful winter day was, to him, a testament to the resilience of youth.

Going through the darkened entryway to the library, he was greeted by the musty scent of tens of thousands of books that for the last couple of years had been exposed to no temperature control and runaway moisture. The Hawkinses' living quarters in the back corner were blocked off with several layers of plastic sheets, and once through the swinging doors to the rear office, he was greeted with cheery warmth. Becka looked up at him, smiled, and put a finger to her lips. He looked over to the cribs where the twins were tucked in, fast asleep.

She smiled and offered him a chair by the woodstove that they had installed, which was giving off a cheery warmth. "Just got the little ones down at the same time for once," she announced, and without asking, she scooped a ladle of soup from a kettle on the fire, dipped it into a bowl, and offered it to John, who politely took it. Old Southern customs of greeting a guest with food still held, even now. The soup was watery thin; there was a hint of some kind of meat in it, wild onions, and he wasn't really sure what else.

They chatted for a few minutes about the babies, who were thriving, John remembering to pull from his jacket the canned peaches, which she clutched with gratitude. Finished with the soup, he asked about "the guys," and laughing, she pointed to the staircase to the basement.

"Those computers and all the other stuff have nearly turned me into a widow. Do me a favor and order Ernie to get the heck out of here at day's end and for Paul to remember he has a wife."

"Will do," John replied with a smile, and he headed for the basement, which had been renamed "the Wizard's Workshop." A joke that few caught was that long ago it was the name for Tom Edison's lab in Menlo Park, where he developed the incandescent lightbulb and helped trigger the electrical revolution of the nineteenth century that they were struggling to restore.

As John opened the basement door, he was surprised by the profligate use of electricity. The room was now brightly lit with fluorescent lights. He had always hated that type of illumination, but it used less juice than a standard incandescent bulb. A woodstove had been rigged into the basement, so it was no longer a damp, bone-chilling room, and, indeed a wonder, a dehumidifier was humming away. The stench of mold had at least abated somewhat as a result.

Six-foot stacks of magazines still cluttered most of the room, but a work area had been cleared in the far quarter, additional workbenches dragged over from classrooms and offices around the campus. Piled up around the benches were several dozen old computers—half a dozen more Apple IIes, early PCs, Commodore 64s, old Gateways, Dells, and half a dozen other models. Ernie, with Paul by his side, was hunched over a green computer board, and as John came up behind them, Ernie grunted out a curse and tossed the board to one side.

"Cooked, damn it. I would have liked to have had that one."

"How's it going?" John asked the two, obviously so intent on their work they had not heard him approach.

"Good and bad," Ernie grumbled without bothering to look back at John as he picked up another board from a pile on the table and started to examine it.

"We've got half a dozen machines cobbled together," Paul offered in a far cheerier voice.

He pointed to the restored computers off to one side, and John went over to examine them. Three were Apples, one of them an early Mac with its ridiculously small blue screen monitor, beside them a couple of 1980s PCs and a Commodore 64. The 64 was turned on, the old television it was hooked to flickering, a popular fantasy adventure game of the '80s running, little stick figures being chased by a stick-figure dragon.

While in college, John remembered, he had splurged on buying an Atari 2600 game machine, he and his friends consuming endless beers while driving two tanks around an obstacle field and shooting at each other. It had triggered the first fight with Mary, who became fed up that he was spending more time on "that damn game" than with her.

He hated to disturb the two at what was obviously an obsessive task, but he felt he had to. Paul had been absent from the factory ever since the discovery of a functional computer. It was at least keeping Ernie busy and out of his hair, but still, Ernie's skills could perhaps be better devoted to working with the ham radio operators or helping as well with the production of generators and alternators to provide power to their ever-expanding State of Carolina.

Ernie and Paul were both hunched over a computer board, wearing magnifying glasses, absorbed with testing the board, quietly arguing whether it
was fried or just one chip was bad.

"Mind if I interrupt?" John finally asked.

"In a minute," Ernie replied without looking up, overriding Paul's objec-
tions as he pried a chip off the board, fished a replacement out of a plastic
tray, and snapped it in.

"There!" Ernie announced, pointing to a volt meter that surged to life
once the chip was replaced. "It's good to go. We can use it!"

John sighed. "I hate to do this, but can I ask what we can use that board
for?"

The two looked up at him as if he was a peasant rudely interrupting
a royal banquet.

"If we can just get some computers back online, it's a huge step," Ernie
announced, still wearing his magnifying glasses, which gave him something
of a crazed look when you were staring straight at him.

"For what purposes that we can use right now?" John asked, regretting
that his query did sound somewhat blunt.

"All right, John, we'd better settle this priority right now," Ernie replied
sharply.

"I'm just asking where this can lead us, that's all," John said defensively.
"You two are a couple of our most valuable resources. I just want to make
sure we're spending those resources wisely."

"You suggesting I go out on woodcutting detail instead?" Ernie snapped.

"No, damn it."

Paul stepped between the two and put his hands up in a soothing
gesture. "John's right, Ernie. We're spending a lot of time on these old machines; there has to be a profit in it, and he has a right to know what we're
thinking about regarding all of this."

"All right, then," Ernie retorted. "God knows how many times when I
was with IBM or contracted to NASA I'd be working on something and
some damn project manager would come along, question its worth, and
shelve it. IBM could have been years ahead of Apple and the whole PC revolution if people like me had been listened to."

"Let me take this," Paul said softly, sensing that Ernie was heating up.

"Fine," Ernie snapped, "but if our supreme leader is here to tell us to shut this down, I'll just hole up at home and keep at it myself. My family and I survived through the first year without the interference of others, and, John, you were damn glad to have us blocking the left flank on the day we fought the Posse."

"Why don't you three arguing fools come upstairs for some tea and talk it out up here?"

They looked back to where Becka stood at the base of the stairs, holding a teapot up as a peace offering.

John nodded a bit sheepishly and followed her back up to the sunlit warmth of the old library office. The twins were still asleep, so after gratefully accepting the herbal mint drink, John followed Paul out into the main area of the library. It was cold, but one corner of the vast room was sunlit and offered the comfort of overstuffed leather chairs. The three settled down.

"I know the machines we are working on look like toys," Paul began. "Compared to what we had just before the war, they *are* toys, but in their day, they were cutting-edge technology and used as such. Funny that we never thought about it before. The vast majority of computers being tossed aside were not broken; it was just that advances were coming so rapidly. It's not like old cars that got sold and resold until they finally just died. Most computers getting junked simply just had a hard drive cook off or motherboard going bad, but the rest of the unit was still good. They were just junked with no resale in mind because after three to four years, they were antiques. Moore's law at work."

"Refresh my memory, please," John asked.

Ernie sighed as if asked a dumb question by someone who should know better.

Paul said, "Moore's law, named after one of the founders of Intel back in the 1960s, postulated that computing power as defined by the number of transistors per square inch will double in a very rapid progression. It meant that computing power, speed of calculations, storage, all of it will increase at a geometric progression, while at the same time cost per unit such as a hard drive for example will plummet. That Apple IIe we first brought online had around 64K, not megabytes or gigabytes, but 64 *kilobytes'* worth of chips in it for around three thousand dollars of 1980s money. Eight years later, it was obsolete and thus wound up in the basement down here, and I bet in Black Mountain alone we could find a couple of hundred of them not plugged in on the day things hit the fan and therefore perhaps still viable. Imagine if we had two hundred of your old clinker Edsels. Unlike computers, they were run and resold until finally just junked. Not so with computers, and that is what has Ernie and me fired up. Your average five-hundred–dollar computer just before the war wiped out nearly everything that was hooked up online was equal to the military's top Cray of a couple of decades earlier."

"Therefore?" John pressed.

"That's the whole interesting point that we all seemed to overlook," Paul continued. "I remember the year the college purchased new laptops for every faculty and staff member. Great idea, but three years later, they were obsolete; five years later, they were in our junk pile or just tossed into a closet and forgotten. I remember seeing a whole Dumpster load of them, recalling when they cost a couple of hundred thousand dollars on delivery and five years later we couldn't give them away, so we just tossed them out instead. There was no secondary market for five-, let alone eight- or ten-year-old computers. Files once stored on five-inch floppy disks or even reel-to-reel were transferred to three-and-a-half-inch disks, and then to just memory sticks, downloaded into the hard drive of your new machine and the old machines tossed. Those files are still alive, John. But we've got to dig up the hardware to read them again and then build off that."

"Build what? I'm worried about having enough food and firewood to see us through the winter. Everyone is screaming for more electricity now that we've got something up and running again. Hey, I'd love to have a computer in my office, even an old green-screen machine hooked to a printer. I'm sick of my old Underwood typewriter with the dang *F* and *J* keys sticking half the time. But the time to get even one computer up and running, especially now?"

He pointed to the blowing snowdrifts outside the window, and a thought flashed of the young couple down in the park. He wondered if the cold had finally driven them back inside.

"It's stuff we can use now. Databases, for one," Paul replied. "We were lucky to find hard copies of all the IEEE journals from the nineteenth century so we could figure out how to start rebuilding, using the same designs Westinghouse, Tesla, and Edison did. It'd be nice to have all those millions of words in a searchable database. Even the library cataloging went online years ago, so we are no longer even sure what we have in the book stacks around us."

"And that would help us . . . ?" John let the question trail off.

"Okay, I agree," Paul continued. "A computer working here, one in Asheville, another in Morganton . . . big deal other than the convenience of using writing machines we once took for granted. To talk with others? We already have some telephones up and running. Cell phones and Wi-Fi? Forget it for years to come, so yeah, I can see your point on that score. I agree; our more immediate concerns are firewood and food."

"I'm not saying stop working on this," John interjected. "It's just that as of the moment, I'm not seeing the short-term benefits. We replicate computer technology of the 1980s, maybe the '90s, and then what?"

"We eavesdrop," Ernie said with a smile, acting at least somewhat non-confrontational for a change, "like I said the other day when Paul showed you the first machine up and running. Come on, John, I'm talking about Bluemont. You're ex-military. When you were in the Middle East, how did the White House and Pentagon micromanage every move you guys made?"

"Commodore 64s and Apple IIes?" John replied with a cynical smile.

"Not much better, actually, if you go back a few years. When Linda and I were writing software for *Apollo*, its guidance systems were 40K computers—40K! Think of it. We went to the moon on 40-kilobyte computers."

Ernie sighed and looked out the window at the snow-covered lawn in front of the library. "America did that in the '60s, and it seems crazy today. The first shuttle flights had little more than a meg on board. All that data going back and forth on something your cell phone, at least before the system fried off, trumped a thousand times over. Again, Moore's law."

"So with what you are doing downstairs, you think you can hack into Bluemont's communications. How?"

"First of all, the data goes up and down. Sat comm. Even low-earth orbit satellites are super hardened against EMPs generated by the sun, coronal mass ejections. For military use hardened against EMP hits as well. But a lot of that stuff goes all the way up to geosynch orbit. How did you get your television before the crap hit the fan?"

John started to smile. "An eighteen-inch dish."

"Exactly."

"But it's encrypted, isn't it?"

"It all comes down to zeroes and ones in the end, John. When Linda and I left IBM, we set up our own business, writing software and providing some of the precision hardware for large-array tracking dishes—mostly civilian business contracts, but a few overseas governments as well. Recall a scandal a few years back of a high government official with an unsecured server in their home that was hacked by some guys in Poland, Romania, somewhere overseas?"

John had some recollection of it. So much of what happened before the Day, which had once seemed all so important, was now becoming hazy memories.

"John, you remember this college was starting on a cybersecurity major before the war started."

He nodded with memory of that. President Hunt had even asked him, as an historian and ex-military, to think about creating a course on the history of technology. The idea had intrigued him, and he had even done some preliminary research into the fascinating history of World War II, the tales about Enigma, Ultra, the tapping into Japanese and German radio traffic, the work of the legendary Turing and the team at Bletchley Park, England.

Is that where these two were leading?

"Take me to the conclusion," John said, looking out across the windswept yard in front of the campus library. Lowering clouds were sweeping in from the northwest, a light sprinkling of snow flurries swirling down. If another storm was coming in, he wanted to get home, split some more wood, and huddle in close to the woodstove with Makala before it hit.

"Remember those huge satellite dishes folks used to have in front of their homes twenty years ago?" Ernie asked, pressing in.

John chuckled. It was a bit of a stereotype of ramshackle trailers, with a dish half as big as the trailer planted in the front yard for television.

"They nearly all disappeared once the big mainstream servers came in with an eighteen-inch dish you could tack to your living room window."

John nodded, remembering installing one himself when he and Mary moved here with two young girls. A hundred-plus channels to choose from, and he had visions of all the educational programs that could be offered, rather than what most stations had degenerated into with the advent of the nauseating reality-show craze.

"If I could get my hands on some of those big old dishes, which hopefully were off-line and disconnected on the Day, and cobble together parts that were not cooked off, I think in a few weeks I could be tapping into communications traffic."

"Of . . . ?"

"Bluemont, for starters," Ernie replied enthusiastically. "Raw reportage from BBC uplinking and downlinking out of Canada, even the Chinese. They still must be using comm sat systems. You just point, listen, download, and evaluate."

"*Just?* You make it sound easy, Ernie. So you got gigs of data flying around, and chances are the stuff we want to know about is highly encrypted. They're no fools."

"No chain is stronger than its weakest link. No data is foolproof. Turing built a system from scratch and was able to break down the German codes, looking for patterns of usage coming from those German Enigma machines that supposedly could be programmed to create billions of variables and thus thought to be uncrackable. Come on, historian, how did we figure out the Japanese were going to hit us at Midway in June 1942?"

John smiled at such an easy underhand pitch. "You know as well as I do if you asked the question. Paul, do you know?"

John looked over at his electrical wizard who had once been a student and was surprised to see the quizzical look and shake of a head.

"I remember you being in my World War II class, Paul."

"Sorry, sir, I was diverted a lot that year," he replied, smiling. John remembered how Paul and Becka had shared the same class and spent most of it staring at each other.

"All right, then. We were picking up radio chatter about a 'Target X,' indicating the Japanese were preparing for a massive naval strike. One of the cryptanalyst guys at Pearl Harbor came up with the idea of Midway Island sending out a report that their desalinization plant to provide fresh water on the island was off-line and they were desperate, the message to be sent via a code we knew the Japanese had already cracked.

"The message was sent, and only hours later, radio traffic from Japan was monitored that extra desalinization equipment would have to be shipped to Target X once taken. Bingo—we knew where their next offensive would hit; we had our carriers waiting to receive them and wiped out their carriers in a surprise counterstrike. It is a textbook example of code breaking changing the course of a war."

"How many kids from this school's old cybersecurity program are still here?" Ernie asked.

"I'm not sure." John sighed. Too many of his students were now long gone, killed in the fighting or dead from disease and malnourishment. Those left were serving in the community's defense force, working in the ever-expanding electrical parts factory down in Anderson Hall, or assigned to other equally crucial tasks.

"If I could pull in four or five—even just two or three—and put them to work to help me," Ernie pressed, with Paul nodding in eager agreement, "John, I just might be able to get something useful out of our tinkering in the basement. Just imagine if you had known Fredericks's orders before that piece of trash even came to Asheville." Ernie pressed in with his argument, "Hell, for all we know, five hundred troops with more choppers could be on their way here right now, and we are clueless until they arrive."

"Or suppose what that poor guy Reynolds said is true," Paul interjected, "that something is up regarding another EMP. Who is thinking about it? Why? When? Do you want the answers, or do we sit back passively and wait?"

John looked back and forth at the two and then back out the window at what was obviously another storm coming on.

He sighed and finally nodded. "Okay, you got it."

The two broke into grins, the elderly Ernie and young Hawkins high-fiving each other.

"Quietly, and I mean *quietly,* run a query today. If any of our old students were in our cybersecurity program pull them off whatever they are working on now. I then want this building secured. Tell Kevin Malady and Grace

Freeman I want a guard on here henceforth. Nothing overt—just that we learned with our encounter with Fredericks that he did have spies inside our community. If we're going for something like this, I don't want it broadcasted all over town."

"John, we'd be a lot more secure if we moved this entire operation over to my place," Ernie replied.

"Why so?"

"Simple. It is out of the way of prying eyes. Easier to maintain security. Plus, my diagnostic tools are there. I can run things 24-7 at my place. Come on; it's the logical choice."

John hesitated as he thought it over and then just simply nodded. "Your place then, Ernie. I'm not going to mention this to our council. We keep it under wraps for a while. The kids stay at your place."

He hesitated and then smiled.

"You house them and you feed them as well; that will justify their being pulled off of regular work details."

To his surprise Ernie did not object to that additional requirement.

"You two got that?"

There were eager nods.

He sighed, wrapped his scarf tightly around his neck, put on his old for age cap that looked like a relic from the Civil War, stood up, and started for the door.

Once he was outside, the cold was a bracing shock, the snow coming down hard so that he pulled his hat brim low to protect his eyes. He shuffled down the path out to the middle of the road, trying to let all the concerns of his life slip away at least for a few minutes. The weather was triggering so many memories. As he walked against the renewed snowfall, he found himself recalling a time when, as a boy, a storm like this would send him out hiking up to the South Mountain Reservation a few miles away from where he lived to find a favorite secluded spot in a pine grove. Knowing the reservation patrol officers were nowhere about on such a day, he'd build a fire and enjoy the snowfall, youthful imagination taking hold, that he was a sentry for General Washington, posted along that low ridgeline to keep an eye on the British over in Manhattan.

But now? He simply longed to be back at his home for the rest of the day, sitting by the woodstove with Makala—unfortunately without any scotch to sip or cigarette to enjoy, but at least there was her company awaiting.

He glanced over at the park along Flat Creek as he stepped out onto Montreat Road and chuckled softly. He couldn't see the amorous young couple, but there was a plume of wood smoke swirling up from within a grove of trees and he smiled with the assumption that the two were nestled in there, enjoying the storm and solitude while being together.

He shuffled on in silence, turning up the steep hill to his house above the old tennis courts, glad to see smoke rising from the chimney. Stamping the snow off his boots, he stepped inside and was surprised to see Maury Hurt in the sunroom, Makala by his side.

"John, where in the hell have you been?" Maury asked excitedly.

"What's wrong?"

"It's Bob Scales," Maury announced with a grin. "We just got a message. He wants to meet."

CHAPTER SEVEN

John slowly read the message again, out loud, looking around at the nearly dozen men and women crammed into what had once been the office of the president of the college.

> *I lament the sad news of the loss of our beloved J. I recall a day in May, when I last talked to her, the same date in May that holds different connotations now. My friend, please return so that we can meet and discuss so many things of importance to both of us.*

He put the transcript down and looked around the room.

"And that is it?" Reverend Black asked. "Just that?"

"I think it is fake," Ernie stated, arms folded across his chest.

"I don't," John replied.

"Why?" Ernie's query was picked up by several others in the overcrowded room.

"*J* is obviously my Jennifer. The day in May—he knew that was Jennifer's birthday. We were on the phone talking when the EMP hit, thus his reference to 'connotations' that others held regarding that day of days. It is something only Bob and I knew, a code to tell me it was really him."

"But tapped out in Morse code, for heaven's sake, with a preface to first switch to a different frequency to receive the message, that in Morse code as well?" Billy Tyndall snapped. "It's like some bad movie. Apparently, it had been going out for several days, until one of our ham listeners even realized it wasn't just interference and remembered enough to start copying it down. Why not voice? What is this, 1941 or something? How many people even know Morse code today?"

"Maybe that's the point," Maury said in response. "Who knows how many people saw the dropped message before it got into Bob's hands?"

"If this Bob is even alive, is he someone we can trust?" Forrest growled.

John sighed and looked at the old Underwood typewriter resting on his desk, absently tapping the *F* key to see if his tinkering with it had solved the problem. The damned thing still continued to jam.

"Let's add in this latest news from the BBC," John now added. "All correspondents within the territory of the United States to be deported because of an alleged breach of national security. BBC? England, perhaps our only ally left in this crazy world? Something is up; we all know that. But what?"

"And you think your friend, if still alive, holds the answer?"

"Anyone have a better suggestion?" John asked. "If so, put it out there."

He looked around the room. Most just sat with heads lowered; Maury was shaking his head.

"I've got to take the chance and meet him."

"Back up there? How?" Maury snapped. "Gillespie thinks he can replace the coolant line, which was damaged as well, in a week or so, but the turbine blade is proving to be a real problem. But then what? Fly in, after being shot at last time, and expect the red carpet treatment? John, you and the rest of this council can order me to go, and I'll tell you to kiss off for your own good."

Maury looked over at Forrest for support.

"I only go into a hot LZ once, John, no repeat trips. I'm with Maury on this."

"And the fuel," Danny McMullen added. "We burned through a lot of Jet A just going up there and back. I thought the intent was we keep that fuel in reserve in case we ever needed the Black Hawk for defense here. Even if they are ready to kiss our butts when landing, will they refuel us?

John, they'll seize that chopper as stolen government property, and if we're ever let go, it will be one hell of a long walk back home."

John looked over at Makala, who insisted upon attending this meeting, and saw her nod of approval. The room fell silent again, the only sound that of hammering and sawing from the adjoining chapel, where half a dozen students were at work, still laboring to restore it to what it had once been before being partially destroyed during the fighting back in the spring.

John took it all in and realized if he put it to a vote, no one would support his going. This was one of those times he wished he had not relinquished the power he once held as virtual dictator of this community during the first year after the attack. He returned his gaze to Makala, who sat in stoic silence, but her glance in reply said everything. Like most women in their final months of pregnancy, she held the trump card with her husband if he in any way cared for his wife.

"All right," he finally said with a sigh. "Alternatives?"

"This guy, if he is real, is trying to reach out to you," Reverend Black said, forcing a smile to try to ease the moment. "If real, he tried to reach out to you with that tragic messenger. Now this cryptic reply in Morse code.

"Those two methods"—Black paused for a moment—"tell me that there is some important reason behind this entire affair, and he wants to keep his cards close, perhaps even from those around him. Acknowledge receipt of the message, counter with some alternative."

"If it is so all damn important, tell him to come here," Forrest snapped.

"Why not?" Black intervened. "Forrest is onto something. Tell him to come here."

The answer was so simple and obvious. As he contemplated it, John found himself wondering why he had not thought of that first. Perhaps a touch of the old hierarchy of command still held sway within him. When a general summoned a colonel to a meeting, it was "Yes, sir, where and what time do we meet, sir?" and that was it.

John smiled and nodded. "Okay, I'll go for that. How and where?"

"Asheville?" Frank Nelson, now the mayor of that town, suggested.

John shook his head. "Too public. A helicopter coming in there just might spook folks who survived the fighting back in the spring to take a potshot at it."

"The Asheville airport, then," Frank pressed.

"We disabled the runway," Black interjected, "and it means an overflight of all our territory around here. Chance for a good recon if he is not on the up-and-up."

"9A9," Danny said quietly.

"What?" John replied, not sure what he meant.

"Old FAA designations for airports. All airports in public use were given a three-letter code. CLT for Charlotte, AVL for Asheville. Shiflet is an old grass strip airport in Marion, which is our territory. You come in over the mountains to the north, and there it is. No overflight of our territory."

"Then why not Morganton?" Maury asked.

"Our disabled chopper is there," Danny replied. "Even though it's in a hangar, if he or the people with him poke around and see that and then they try to take it back, it would become a confrontation. Even if they don't try to take it back, they'll know our bird is down. Also, if they are planning some sort of nasty surprise, bringing in a lot of troops aboard an old C-130, we're not offering them a big paved strip. Stripped down, they can land at Shiflet. But take off with all that snow on the ground?" He chuckled. "They can land, but then try to take off? If we see a C-130 coming in that can carry up to a hundred troops, we just bogey off and leave them stuck in the snow.

"Shiflet would be ideal, John. Couple of dozen hangars, most of them ramshackle affairs like out of the 1930s. We put some heavily armed people in there as backup if they try to pull any stunts with a couple of choppers—hell, we might even pick up an extra bird or two if they try any crap. Plus, 9A9, you transmit that on Morse code, some geek listening in might not even recognize it and figure it is code for something else. I say 9A9 Shiflet."

John looked around the room and finally saw nods of agreement. "All right, then. Send out a response on the new frequency they shifted to. Ernie, can you and Danny figure it out? Something like 9A9, a date, and then Zulu time and see what the response is."

"And if they reply no deal, we go to meet them?"

"Politely tell them to go to hell," Makala replied sharply.

*   *   *

On the walk back from the meeting, John held Makala tightly by his side to ensure she did not slip and fall.

"You aren't trusting this, are you?" he asked.

She laughed softly. "I never understood just how much a pregnancy can mess up one's thinking. I want my husband by my side when the baby comes. I want him by my side as our baby goes through all those moments that then follow—the first smile, the first belly laugh, the first crawl, the first step, then the little hellion running amok around the house, and then one day—"

She paused and began to choke up. "Damn it, I was never this way before, John. Yeah, someday, if this world ever turns sane again, that we watch our child graduate from college, your college, and still are together when they one day come through the doorway carrying their child, our child, the same way you look at Elizabeth and her toddler. I want that, and anything that might snatch it away fills me with dread."

She struggled to hold back her tears. "You heard Elizabeth after the father of her child was killed," Makala continued, and now the tears were flowing, "bringing a child into the world with the baby's father dead, the way she would cry herself to sleep at night. The times she would look at her boy and we could sense she could see the boy's father being there, but he was not and never will be. Don't get me wrong; her husband, Seth, is an incredible, decent young man, the spitting image of his father, Lee. The fear she carries now is that something will happen to Seth the same as it did to Ben. I carry that same fear. At least the idea of this mythical friend of yours coming here alleviates some concern, but even then, what if it's a trap? Let's just say that rather than your friend coming in to meet you, it's half a dozen of those attack helicopters—or, for that matter, some plane loitering at thirty thousand feet, and they pinpoint your being at this remote airport and drop one of those fuel-air bombs I hear people talking about or even one of those neutron bombs as payback for what you did to Fredericks."

"If they really wanted me dead, they would have taken this place off the map months ago. That's why I have to believe that Bob Scales is real, most likely in command of the forces up in Roanoke, and is trying to reach out to me, perhaps to prevent further bloodshed."

"It still makes me anxious."

He did not reply that it filled him with the same concerns and fears. If there was no reason for anxiety, if Scales was indeed alive, the overture to meet would have been overt, out in the open. Not like this.

Whatever the reason, he did know one thing for certain: He had to find out the truth and find out now.

CHAPTER EIGHT

The Black Hawk, which had crested over Linville Gorge just a few minutes earlier, came sweeping in low over frozen Lake James, crossed over the
railroad bridge that spanned the Catawba River where it emptied into
the lake, and came sweeping down the length of the snow-covered runway
at well over a hundred miles an hour.

John shaded his eyes against the glare of the early morning sun, watching as it raced in, scanning it carefully with a pair of field glasses, feeling
a touch of nostalgic pride at the sight of the chopper painted in faded desert
camo, taking him back to the desert of Iraq so long ago when, filled with
awe, he watched scores of them sweeping out ahead of his armored battalion.

He spared a quick glance to Forrest, who was watching intently, silently,
wondering what this torn-up veteran of Afghanistan was feeling at the sight
and sound of a machine that meant that friends were overhead, ready to
protect, ready to attack anything in their way.

The chopper thundered past, the Doppler roar dropping in pitch as it
passed, and then it pitched up in a steep turning climb.

The pilot was hotdogging a bit, but then again, if he was coming into a
potentially hostile site, it was standard to do at least one high-speed pass and
if they drew any fire to get the hell out fast.

He had more than fifty with him, concealed in several hangars and scattered in the wood line across the runway. If this was a setup for a trap, it was about to turn into one hell of a fight. Danny, who stood beside him, clutched a flare gun firmly in his gloved hand, ready to fire off the signal if anything looked even remotely hostile.

The day was cold, crystal clear, perfect for keeping a sharp watch aloft. Several of his people, concealed under white blankets, were doing just that, sweeping the sky overhead for any telltale glint or whisper of a contrail indicating that someone was hovering up at twenty thousand feet, just waiting to unleash a Hellfire or gravity-dropped munitions.

The chopper, leveling off from its high-speed pass, circled around, the sound shifting as the pilot throttled back, pitching the nose up slightly to bleed off speed as he started to make a landing approach.

"So far, so good," John whispered as if to himself.

He looked around at his friends Danny, Maury, Forrest, and Lee, who stood to either side, all watching intently and waiting for the slightest suspicious act.

A hell of a world we have become, John thought. *There was a time when we never would have doubted the sight of a helicopter with that star on its side. But now?*

The chopper continued to settle, kicking up a near whiteout of swirling snow, the pilot edging it toward where John had ordered that Forrest's 4×6 should be parked as an indicator of their presence.

"If this goes bad," Forrest complained, "you own me a new vehicle and the gas that took it here."

John said nothing, the chopper all but invisible as snow swirled about, a glimpse of it then touching down, turbine engines throttling back, and as the snow began to settle, he saw the side door swing open.

Even from this distance, he could see that it was indeed him. It was Bob.

John stepped out of the concealment of the hangar, ignoring the protests of his friends, Lee cursing and then stepping out behind him and protectively moving in by his side. The rotors continued to wind down, and he started to lift a hand to cover his face from the stinging blast but thought better; he wanted Bob to see that it was indeed him and not some sort of setup.

Bob leaped down from the doorway, nearly fell, and came up slowly, and John could see that his friend had indeed aged, remembering long ago how in so many training exercises, inspection tours, and their brief hours of combat together in Iraq, Bob would always be the first one out with a leaping bound and confident stride, radiating self-assurance and leadership. The snow from the three storms that had rolled in within as many weeks was nearly two feet deep at the level, even down in the piedmont region of Marion. The chopper's rotors had blown most of the ground cover back as Bob moved slowly toward him. Perhaps, John realized, it was to make sure he did not slip and fall, and it be misinterpreted by his crew and what John could now see was a security team inside the chopper, that he had been shot.

Bob pulled back the hood of his parka, John doing the same, and with this mutual gesture, the two old friends could now see each other's grinning features. Bob had indeed aged, his thick short-cut thatch of gray having gone completely white, features ruddy, heavy bushy brows squinting nearly shut from the morning glare and blowing snow.

They stopped half a dozen feet apart, and old instincts kicked in, John coming to attention and raising his right hand in a near-reverent salute.

"General, sir."

Bob, coming to attention as well, silently returned the salute, the two gazing at each other, and then Bob made the final steps forward and threw his arms around John.

"My God, John! It really is you! Thank God you made it after all."

"Sir, I thought you were . . ." John was overcome by emotion, and he fell silent.

"I wish," Bob began. "I wish I could have seen Jennifer again, just one more time."

Those words nearly broke John completely. Bob had stood as godfather for both of his girls. Childless himself, he had formed a special bond, especially with Jennifer, who used to call him "Uncle Bob." A most memorable moment, at a formal review that was just wrapping up, Jennifer had shaken free of her mother's hand and raced up to Bob, who was standing in the middle of the platform where he was at rigid attention, reviewing the troops marching by. She threw her arms around his legs and loudly asked what Beanie Baby he had brought for her that day. And in spite of all the formality of the moment, Bob had motioned to the ever-present aide that hovered by a general's side. The young captain with grave features had reached into Bob's attaché case to produce a stuffed golden retriever puppy for "my girl."

And with that, the memory flooded to completion. The aide that day was Quentin Reynolds.

There was a squeal of delight as she clutched the latest addition to her collection, Bob picking her up and showing her how to salute the last company of troops marching by as he held her. There was not a soldier in the ranks of that company able to conceal a grin as they marched by. It was the exact kind of gesture that rather than creating smirking laughter later endeared him even more to his troops and their families who had witnessed the moment.

It defined the man that John was now hugging with open warmth.

John finally broke the embrace and stepped back, but Bob reached up, for John towered over him by a half foot or more, and put his hands on John's shoulders.

"Son, it is so good to know that at least you survived."

"And you too, sir."

There was a moment of awkward silence, and the two reverted back a bit to remembrance of command, that at such a moment so many were watching them for the slightest signal or gesture, friendly or hostile.

John looked back at the chopper. There were at least half dozen heavily armed men in the crew compartment, while Bob's eyes darted past John to take in the old airport, obviously evaluating.

"Yes, sir, I've got a lot of people concealed around here," John said softly, "so let's defuse them. Okay?"

Bob nodded as John turned away from him for a moment and raised his arms high, waving them over his head to indicate that all was well.

"We've got a woodstove ready to light in the airport clubhouse and packed along some MREs. Let's get your team in and get mine out of the woods," John announced. "This damn cold makes me long for the desert again."

Bob motioned for his security team to get out, gesturing as well for them to sling their weapons, while John stepped away from the chopper so those in the wood line could clearly see him, waving his arms and shouting for them to stand down.

The six-man detail in the chopper got out, weapons slung over their shoulders but still obviously wary as they spread out into a loose circle around

Bob, watching as Forrest stepped out of the hangar, M4 held casually in his one hand, followed by Maury, Danny, and Lee, who had yet to shoulder their weapons.

"Your friends?" Bob asked.

"Yes, sir."

"The one-armed character with the eye patch?"

"Airborne. Sergeant in Afghanistan, Silver Star and obviously a Purple Heart."

Even though he was moving slowly, Bob was still in his usual form as he walked up to Forrest and without going through the formality of a salute just extended his hand.

"Trooper, I'm honored to meet you."

The gesture forced Forrest to sling his weapon, catching him off guard, and John breathed a sigh of relief when Forrest actually forced a bit of a smile and extended his hand.

"First time a damn general ever offered to shake my hand, sir," Forrest announced. "Maybe you're okay like John said."

"I hope I am. If we get time, I want to hear your view on some things."

Bob's comment had a casual air to it, the type of line many in high command used as a friendly gesture but still a brush-off, but from Bob it was indeed genuine. When in command of John's battalion, Bob was the type of commander who would swoop in on a unit before dawn, ignore any officers who might be fumbling around, head straight to where breakfast was being dished out, get a cup of coffee, and then start peppering the cooks and dishwashers as to how they saw the unit. Dishing out his own meal, he'd then sit with a table of enlisted men and ask questions.

At the end of more than one such inspection swoop, an officer might very well be on his way out to reposting in some godforsaken place. Chances were that regardless of their friendship, Forrest might be asked a few pointed questions as to how he felt about John's leadership.

It was a technique John had learned as well. If you want the straight dope, go to those at the bottom of the food chain of administrations, not the middle or the top.

The two old friends turned to look back at each other.

"Any place where we can sit and talk one-on-one?" Bob asked.

"It will be crowded in the airport clubhouse. Let our people get out of the cold, grab something to eat, and mingle."

John did not add that Forrest, along with Grace and several others, had been thoroughly briefed that if the two sides did get together, they were to break out a jar or two of moonshine and pump for any information they could glean. He realized that chances were at least one of Bob's security team was his intelligence officer who would be doing the same. Forrest should be able to sniff that out quickly enough.

"The hangar we were waiting in is out of the wind and catching the morning sun; let's you and I settle in there," John offered, pointing the way.

John fell in by Bob's side, subtly gesturing for his friends to leave them be and take care of their guests. He looked back to the chopper; the rotors were slowly turning over in idle.

"Your crew can shut down if they want; there's no threat here, Bob."

Bob just smiled but did not reply to the offer, and John did not press him.

Getting out of the snow, they stomped into the hangar. Its long-gone owner had turned it into an aviator's man cave, posters of World War I and II aircraft papering the walls, along with a couple of classic pinups of nose art from that era. There were a couple of overstuffed lounge chairs next to a long-cold space heater, the chairs smelling unpleasantly of mouse or some other rodent. John dragged the two chairs into the morning sunlight while Bob examined the posters and, brushing the dust off the windshield, looked into the cockpit of a long-grounded Aeronca Champ, its tires cracked and deflated after years of sitting idle.

"I actually learned to fly in one of these." Bob sighed. "Sweet plane, post-war version of that L-3 I heard you have up and running."

John looked over at his friend. Of course he would know what John had.

There were so many questions, but Bob opened first. "John, what happened to Jennifer?"

The question took John aback, and with it returned all the pain of those tragic days. He looked away from Bob, gaze unfocused. "She died, Bob. The way so many died. In her case, diabetes." He fell silent, not wanting to say more; it was not the conversation he wanted for now.

Bob reached over and in a fatherly gesture patted John on the knee. "Sorry I brought it up. Last time we talked, it was her birthday. Remember?"

"Of course I remember." John could not keep the bitter edge out of his voice. "Her last birthday thanks to whoever, whatever triggered all this madness."

He looked back at his friend. It was, of course, not Bob's fault.

"And you, Bob? How is Linda?"

"I'll never know." Bob sighed. "She was visiting friends in Florida when it hit." A pause. "You most likely know what Florida turned into. I some- how knew she was dead within a few weeks. You know how that is with someone you love. You just wake up in the middle of the night, you know they are there in the room with you . . . and they are dead and have come to say good-bye. I just pray it was gentle and swift."

"Jennifer's wasn't," John said, and he instantly regretted it, seeing the hurt in Bob's eyes. "I'm sorry I said that, Bob."

Bob did not reply, the two old friends sitting in silence for a moment until John stirred from his seat. Remembering the thermos of coffee left by Forrest, he picked it up from the floor and motioned to it. Bob nodding agreement as John poured out the hot brew into two battered cups, hand- ing one to his friend.

"The real stuff?" Bob asked.

John nodded and could see the look of surprise.

Bob reached into his parka jacket, produced a flask, motioned to John's cup. John could pick up the welcome scent of scotch and looked quizzically at Bob, who just smiled while he poured several ounces into his own cup before raising it in a toast.

"I thank God you are still alive, John. Here's to those we lost."

"To those that we lost," John whispered.

The two sipped their drinks, and it helped to relax the tension.

"Bob, a personal question?"

"Sure."

"How the hell did you survive? You were in the Pentagon the day it hap- pened. What happened up there?"

Bob looked down at his drink before taking a long gulp. "Some of us got lucky. Most tried for their homes to get their families out. Washington went into total chaos within hours. Those that had set out to try to reach their families, some with forty miles or more of a hike ahead of them? Never heard from again. Me? Linda was in Florida—no reason to try for home. Some of us struck out for Fort Meade and hunkered down there until we tried for Fort Belvoir, the rumor being that local assets were trying to regroup there. From there, well, for a while, I was out on a carrier. The navy with assets overseas fared better than the army on that count."

"What really happened, Bob?"

"We got hit, and we lost."

"That simple? 'We got hit, and we lost'?" There was a sharp edge to John's response.

"About all I can say."

"All you can say, or all that you know?"

Again a moment of silence.

"John, you were on the phone with me when it hit. You know I and all those around me were as off guard as you and a minute later literally in the dark, same as you and the rest of the country. Pearl Harbor in spades."

"And if I remember my history, a couple of lectures from long ago at the War College, the warning signs for Pearl were clear enough to read."

"After the fact," Bob interjected. "After the fact, the patterns fell into place. But before?"

"Some read it correctly."

"Don't tell me you are buying into some conspiracy shit?" Bob snapped. "You've too sharp an intellect for that."

"With everything we had? Surely . . ."

Bob did not reply.

John fell silent and looked at his friend closely. Bob had answered a little too sharply and quickly. Was there something he was holding back? Even before the Day, Bob held many a secret that generals held while those under him were kept in the dark and knew better than to try to ask. He filed the suspicion away. Bob would only share what he felt he could share at this moment and nothing more.

Bob had aged ten, fifteen years since he had last seen him little more than three years ago. Though there was still something of his once sharp, penetrating gaze of confidence, there also seemed to be an infinite weariness behind the eyes.

His shoulders were rounded over slightly as if carrying some unspeakable burden. Gone was the ramrod-straight posture, that certain look and feel of command. There was a slight tremor to his hands as he held the warm mug. Was it just exhaustion of the moment or something far deeper?

"And out there?" John finally asked, shifting the topic away from the personal for the moment.

"Where?"

"The world. Everything, anything. We no longer trust Voice of America out of Bluemont. We try to glean what we can from the BBC, even China and their News to America program. What's the straight dope?"

Bob sighed, set his coffee mug down, unscrewed the cap to the flask of scotch, and offered it to John, who took another ounce while Bob emptied the rest back into his cup.

It surprised him. Bob always had a taste for good twelve- and fifteen-year-old scotch, but only after hours and off duty.

"John, the world has gone three-quarters of the way to hell and is tottering on the edge of the final abyss."

John sipped his coffee and waited.

"From the shores of the eastern Mediterranean to the Indian Ocean. Oil is no longer the export. Maybe when things finally cool down enough, they can sell glass where once had been a score of cities."

"Who?"

"Israel against the rest. Their ballistic missile shield held protecting Tel Aviv and Jerusalem, but the rest. Their government is now underground in bunkers somewhere out in the Negev desert. It was a full exchange. Then Indian and Pakistan cut loose on each other. Not much left on either side."

"Russia, China, Europe?" John asked.

"Holding off. Mutually assured destruction at play there. Russia was brushed by the EMP hit that went off course. Saint Petersburg abandoned. Moscow, word is some semblance of order there, the government holed up somewhere out in Siberia with their fingers on the trigger. John, the moment America was taken out of the paradigm of the balance of power, a vacuum was created. While survivors here were trying to just find the next meal, the rest of the world tottered to the edge and at least for the moment have held back from the final descent into the apocalypse."

"It was the apocalypse here." John reached over to the thermos to pour out some more coffee for the two of them.

The sun was climbing, radiating at least some warmth into the hangar, the icicles hanging along the eaves dripping puddles of water near their feet.

"John, we hang by the slenderest of threads. We still have a lot of nukes; the navy's boomers are still out there, each one packing a couple of hundred warheads. The surviving carriers and their escorts pack more."

"Surviving?"

"Guess we wouldn't admit it. When all hell broke loose in the Persian Gulf the week after the EMP strike and we launched on Iran in retaliation, they took out two of our carriers with nearly all hands. In the wake of that, with the emergency back home, the assets we had over there, we pulled out."

He nodded to the Black Hawk fifty yards away, rotors stilled but turbines still humming if things here went sour and Bob decided to pull out quick.

"John, most of what we have here now in the States we pulled out from the Middle East and Europe. After North Korea was taken off the map, equipment from the Pacific was pulled back stateside as well. We try to keep China in check by letting them know if they try anything with nukes, a boomer parked out in the Pacific will hit them with over two hundred nukes—starting with an EMP, of course. Sword of Damocles over their heads if they push us too hard."

"But Bluemont is ceding half our country to them, Bob. I don't get it."

"Let's just focus on the here and now," Bob replied, obviously diverting the direction the conversation was taking.

That triggered another suspicion for John, but he knew better than to press the issue—and besides, Bob was right. It was the here and now that he had to focus on.

"Blunt question, Bob, for the 'here and now.'"

"Go for it."

"You got other assets nearby just in case this meeting went bad?"

Bob nodded. "Couple of Apaches and an extraction team set down on the far side of Linville Gorge. Sorry, but that's the way it is."

"Hell of a position for two old friends, isn't it?"

"Yeah."

"So why are you here?"

"To talk as we are right now."

"Why?"

"John, you most likely know the political and military situation for our country. BBC has been rather close to the mark, and I assume you've been monitoring that."

"We have."

"I eventually was assigned out west, commander center in Cheyenne Mountain for a stint. We all knew it was a no-win with China. Sure, humanitarian aid was the guise; they wanted it to look like another Marshall Plan, with 'hearts and minds' thrown in. Can't blame the folks out in California and on the rest of the West Coast. Infrastructure down, Los Angeles, San Francisco, Seattle, even Vancouver turning into snake pits of chaos. Someone trying to keep their family alive, feel that our government has utterly failed to protect, and container ships flying red flags start coming in. Rations, water purification plants, medical supplies."

He paused. "Things like insulin, John. What would you have done?"

That barb, if it was intended as such, stung deeply, and he did not reply.

"Their first troops even wore UN-blue helmets. Three-quarters of the population out there already dead? People forget LA was built on what was near desert. Without the Colorado River being pumped in from hundreds of miles away, along with a dozen other reservoirs off-line, people were killing each other for a lousy bottle of water after just three to four days. Someone hands your kids water and a meal—"

"So they are there to stay, is that it?"

"Unless we want to go to nuclear war, yes."

"These reports that we are abandoning the line along the Continental Divide, military assets pulled back to east of the Mississippi?"

"It's being defined as neutral air space to defuse any chance of a confrontation. That and Mexico, with backing from half a dozen Central American countries pressing up over the Rio Grande. What do we do?"

"It was once our country, Bob."

"Argue that with Mexico, who now claims we ripped them off in a long-ago and forgotten war."

"And they ripped it off from those who were there before them."

"History, John. It has always been thus. Take the veneer of civilization off, a major power receives a visceral blow and totters. Nature abhors a vacuum. Amazing—the years of political correctness pumped out in our colleges became an education of national guilt. Some out there along the West Coast actually say we deserved what we got for our past sins and welcomed a chance to try out socialism. Just feed us, and we'll get along with whoever is in charge."

"Anyone fighting back?"

"Yeah, Texas, of course. Voice of America isn't reporting it, but some group in Texas declares they're the new government, cite what they claim was the original treaty of annexation from the 1840s, and they are justified in withdrawing from the Union. They got representatives with them from half a dozen other states saying the same. It is ripe for a blowup. Logical, therefore, that our regular military pull out completely to avoid the prospect of this going really bad and what is left of our country getting sucked into the conflict."

"Meaning nuke?"

"The Chinese are just as afraid of that as we are. They know if we popped three or four EMPs over their mainland, they would be in the same boat we are. But if we do that, they blanket what's left of our country with ground bursts. We do the same back. Who wins other than death?"

"Thus we concede west of the Mississippi, and Bluemont focuses on bringing everything east back under their control. Are those the orders you're following, sir?"

Again, Bob did not directly reply. "Full-scale war with China now?" he finally said. "Then who gets to grab what's left of the radioactive pie? Mongolia?"

John actually chuckled and shook his head.

"Some years back, I was over there for a conference," Bob continued. "Great people, beautiful country. Remember camping with the head of their military up in a northern province for a weekend of fishing." He smiled wistfully and took another sip of coffee. "Anyhow, we were finally talking shop. That guy said they assumed someday it was all going to hit the fan. Russia against us, China against Russia, or just the whole world goes crazy. He then said, and I swear the guy was serious, that when the dust settled and radioactivity cooled off, they would mount up and ride again. Maybe that's who wins if this unravels any further. John, we are balanced on a razor's edge. A couple of third-rate powers triggered all of this; I swear that pudgy nutcase in North Korea did it just to see if they could do it. Iran joins in on the plot for whatever it was they used to believe about their hidden imam returning. We allowed them to get their nukes and missiles to hand off to terrorists like ISIS. Damn all who allowed that to happen. Any idiot could see eventually they'd go for us.

"Anyhow," he said, sighing wearily and staring into his coffee cup, "I saw the report that where the well is that their imam was supposed to come out of is now a crater a thousand feet deep. Same is true for the cities controlled by the terrorists and all of North Korea. Some vengeance.

"That's all moot now as far as you and I are concerned. It happened, and we lost. The job now is to pick up the pieces of what is left and try to re-assemble some sort of united front. A United States out of what is left and project outwardly that, though our backs are to the wall, we're standing again as a united country. If not, we completely cease to exist."

There was a long moment of silence, the two friends sipping their scotch-laced coffee, a cold breeze sweeping into the open hangar so that they zipped their parkas back up, while outside the helicopter turbines contin-ued to turn over with a low steady hum.

John wished he had not accepted the scotch. Never have a drink, even with a once trusted friend, until whatever issue was between them was settled.

"You're here to either pull me in or take us out, is that it, Bob?"

His friend looked over at him and slowly nodded.

"What exactly is your job now?"

"Military governor of this entire region. Everything east of the Appala-chians from Charlottesville down to the wreckage of what was once Florida. Navy is working the coast; I'm to deal with everything inland."

"I assume you know what happened between us and that idiot Freder-icks that was sent down here back in the spring."

"Yeah. Don't look at me, John; I had nothing to do with that screwup and the idiotic idea of the Army of National Recovery. Those of us left from the regular military were appalled with that idea. You can't pull a bunch of kids out of surviving communities where they are needed most right now, throw a weapon in their hands, given them twelve weeks of basic, and send them into hellholes like Chicago, Pittsburgh, or what had once been D.C. or New York City. It was the same kind of stupid thinking about how to fight Vietnam, and remember, I'm old enough to have been in on the tail end of that one. Draftees who barely knew how to wipe their own butts out in the jungle without getting jungle rot or snake bit didn't stand a chance. Same with the ANR. After that battalion got taken prisoner in Chicago and every last one tortured to death by the gangs running that place, the whole concept was quietly dropped.

"That's why what is left of our regular military was pulled back from the face-off with the Chinese and Mexico out west and redeployed here. We got to get things back into a single, unified whole—at least east of the Mississippi. That's my job now."

"Did you send a courier to me by the name of Quentin Reynolds?" John asked.

"He was a good man." Bob sighed. "Said he grew up in the area, knew his way around. After we took Roanoke, I wanted to get word to you outside regular channels." He paused, obviously carefully choosing his words. "Let's just say that Major Quentin took it upon himself to try to reach you with that and some other things."

"What other things, sir?" John asked.

"Let's stick to Quentin for now. He left with several others in a Humvee. Did he get through?"

"He's dead, Bob. Don't know about those who came with him. Some of my people found him along Interstate 26, on foot, badly beaten. It is still no-man's-land up in parts of these mountains, and he met the wrong folks. Only thing one of my men got out of him before he died was that you sent him and wanted to talk."

Bob sighed and then stared straight at him. "Obviously, he had some contact to you; otherwise, you wouldn't have tried to reach me. What exactly did he say?"

The way Bob spoke the last few words, John could sense his friend was tense. "I never spoke to him directly, sir. He reached an outlying community run by my friend Forrest, the one-armed Afghan vet. They fetched me back to meet him, but Quentin died before I could talk to him."

Again silence from Bob.

"Why him?" John asked. "A trek from Roanoke to here by land, that is damn near suicide, especially at this time of year. Why not just send a message in the clear? You got the air assets."

John nodded out to the Black Hawk that, in a profligate display, was still burning precious Jet A fuel.

"I couldn't, John."

"Why?"

Bob stood up, downing the last of his coffee and setting the cup on a cluttered workbench next to the dust-covered Aeronca Champ.

"Because I have orders to kill you. Kill you and either rein this so-called State of Carolina into line or wipe it out."

Bob turned his back on John as he spoke, and John wondered if his old friend and mentor did so because he could not look him in the eye as he spoke.

"John, I would like you to come back to Roanoke with me to talk this thing out further. I promise you no harm will come to you or your community while you are away. I'm asking you to trust me on this."

"Is that an order, sir, or a request from a friend?"

"I'd prefer the latter." He paused for a moment. "John, I'm doing this as a dark op. No one further up the line knows I'm here talking to you privately. I'm doing this as a favor to a trusted friend. Please come back with me for your own good and that of your community."

"And if I say no?"

Bob sighed and turned back to face John.

John shifted his focus to the pilots in the chopper. One appeared to be talking, attention focused toward Bob. Had there been some sort of signal? Was something being called in if he refused Bob's "request"?

"John, I hate to say it, but I think you can assume I can bring hell down on this place in less than five minutes. I assume that the men who were with you when I landed are some of your closest friends and advisors."

"They are."

"If this goes bad, they will be caught up in it as well."

"I know that."

"Therefore?"

John looked into his eyes and could still see his old friend, a commander he respected and would have given his life to protect. Was he really capable of doing this?

"Why, Bob?"

"Orders."

That left him stunned, and he lowered his head. "I recall an ethics class you personally taught at the War College," John said softly, voice tinged with sadness. "A code that stated that an officer must refuse an immoral order, even if it meant his career or even his life. Bob, I know you too well to accept that you are—and God forgive me for saying it—only following orders."

Bob bristled at the reply and did not speak.

"I sense this order is one that you yourself have inner questions about, sir."

"What the hell do you think?" Bob replied sharply. "An order to either arrest or kill a man I saw as a son, his children substitutes for grandchildren I would never have? Just what the hell do you think?"

"You know I won't go with you."

"I kind of assumed that."

"So I guess this is at an end," John said, coming to his feet. "It's your call, Bob, and I'm leaving it to you. You asked me what Quentin had said. And as I just told you, by the time I reached his side, he was dead. But he did spill something beyond the fact that you were alive." John paused. "At least what he rambled about to my friend Forrest and the nurse trying to save him. Like I said, the poor man was damn near dead when he was found and out of his head."

"And he said what?"

"Something about another EMP."

Bob stiffened and broke eye contact.

"Bob?"

"John, I'll ask you one more time. Come back with me to Roanoke. We can talk further then. Bluemont wants you dead. If I've got you stashed away in a safe place, believe me, it's for your own good."

"Sir, I'm not going back with you, and if all was reversed, you'd say the same."

"Yeah, I assumed it would be thus."

"So, what's next?" John asked. "You're free to go. I won't stop you, and you knew that before you even stepped foot off that chopper. You get your people back in, lift off, I tell my people to scatter, and in five minutes, you and I are personally at war. Is that it?"

Bob did not reply.

"Kind of like what we read happened at West Point a long time ago, when the superintendent was ordered to hold on charges of treason any cadet or faculty that would not renew the oath of allegiance to the Union. Instead, he told the secretary of war to go to hell and let his old friends and students—now enemies preparing to serve the Confederacy—leave without a fight. Is that it?"

Bob nodded. "I've served my country over forty-five years. If not for this current mess, I was about to retire out, settle down with Linda; she was already picking out a place down on Marco Island, and you know how it is. Old soldier writes a book or two, kills the boredom by fishing, and quietly grumbles how the country continues to go to hell but there is nothing he can do about it. And now, instead, I'm here, freezing my ass off."

"Then why did you really come, Bob? Really? Your comment a few minutes back tells me that if I don't go, you are most likely expected to lift off, and five minutes later, this place is toast. Is that what Bluemont expects?"

Bob did not reply.

"So why not do it?"

"In reply, John, I assume there are at least a few heavy weapons stashed in this hangar and you got extra personnel in a hangar next door to this one. You could hold me hostage and back out. Chances are if I'm taken prisoner, in spite of my orders to hit you even if I am being held, my people would hold back on a strike, allowing you to escape."

John sighed, shook his head, and gestured for the general to sit back down by his side. "You know I wouldn't do that to you, and unless this damn war has twisted you inside out, I know you won't order a strike on me, at least not like this."

"Oh, damn all this shit to hell," Bob whispered, and with a weary groan, he returned to sit at John's side. "It's cold out here, so damn cold."

"Yeah, I know." John emptied the last of the thermos, most into Bob's cup, the last few drops into his.

"What did they used to call it? A Mexican standoff or something like that, though I guess that became politically incorrect to say years ago."

"Something like that. 'Mutually assured destruction' kind of fits better at the moment. Both of us die or both of us walk away."

"Stupid, all of it."

"You need not tell me, sir. So who ordered me dead?"

"Bluemont."

"Again Bluemont. Can you give me a straight answer?"

"Maybe."

"Just who the hell are they? They claim to be the legitimate government of the United States. Claim line of succession as defined in the Constitution. But who are they really?"

"They are the government, John. At least that's something."

"How did they survive?"

"By coincidence, on the day things went down, there was a simulation attack training exercise, with some people evacuated up to the FEMA fall-back position, which was the Bluemont facility. You know the president went down while aboard Air Force One. Damn fools in charge had never hardened it to the current level of a high-yield EMP. Congress wasn't in session, so nearly all those people were scattered around the country. There-fore, the survivors lucky enough to be at Bluemont were it."

"You ever meet them or been there?"

Bob looked down at his coffee, swirling it around in his cup before drink-ing down the now-tepid brew. "No. I was bounced around after the Day, out west, briefly in Cheyenne Mountain—like I said, out on one of our surviving carriers that for a while served as a joint command center. Then took over assets coming back from the Middle East and the Far East that began to deploy out of what was left of Norfolk with orders cut several months ago to, as I already told you, reestablish control in the southeast. No, I've never been there. At least on the inside."

"Mind if I ask a few questions, sir?"

"Maybe."

"Why keep meeting me a secret? Do your friends in Bluemont know you did this?"

"Did what?"

"Came down here like this, based on a somewhat cryptic transmission back and forth? Why didn't you tell them?"

"John, to be honest, at the moment, I'm really not sure."

"Come on, sir," John replied sharply. "Do you trust Bluemont?"

"What?"

"Just that. You claim you have never met anyone up there face-to-face. Do you trust them?"

"I trust the Constitution of the United States, which I am sworn to uphold. We have to have something to hang on to. There's nothing else out there now, John. Bluemont is at least something."

"I took the same oath, sir, to defend the Constitution of the United States against all enemies, foreign and domestic." He emphasized the last word, *domestic.*

Bob stared at him and finally nodded. " I'm not in the loop on a lot of what is going on. Just rumors—you know how it is—and my focus is the mission to bring this entire region back under control. Your community, what you folks are calling the State of Carolina, is part of that mission."

"But you've been hearing rumors."

Bob nodded in reply.

"Quentin rambling about an EMP—is that a rumor or fact, and from whom?"

"John, my entire life I've served. I served under some brilliant men in the White House, and yes, some that I thought at best were naïve when it came to the harsh realities of the world and what warfare truly is. And yeah, I served under more than a few I thought were an outright danger to the survival of my country, at least my country as I saw it. But always, in the end, I saluted.

"I recall Lincoln once declaring that across four years, no president could do ultimate fatal harm to the Republic, and at the end of those four years, the people could vote him out and replace him with someone they thought more capable. Even when I passionately disagreed with a president, I took solace in that and forced myself to salute even when I felt the person I was saluting was unworthy of that. At such moments, I saluted the office and not the person."

"EMP, General Scales," John pressed in, unable to contain the question any further. "Fact or rumor? If fact, by whom and when?"

"I can't give you a straight answer."

"Because you aren't sure yourself, or if you are sure, you can't say?"

"Damn it, John, don't press me on this!" Bob shouted back, an action so rare in the past when they served together that it startled John.

He stared straight into his old commander's eyes. "I believe you at least suspect something is up. That perhaps I'm even tied into it, directly or indirectly."

Bob returned his gaze without blinking.

"I suspect you are disobeying them right now," John whispered as if someone might overhear their conversation. "You said you had orders to detain or kill me. But here you are when it would have been just as easy to lure me into this meeting, confirm I was here, and then take this whole place out."

Bob stood back up. "I'm freezing. Let's at least go outside and stamp around a little bit and stretch."

John followed him out of the hangar. The glare reflecting off the snow was so intense that John wanted to put on his old scratched sunglasses but decided against it. Sunglasses were often the cheap trick of concealing a man's eyes—or worse, the way some cops used to wear them to intimidate.

The air was sharp, crisp puffs of wind kicking up crystals of snow that glimmered and danced in the morning sunlight. If not for the presence of the Black Hawk, the landscape would have been one of peace. It was an unnatural sound now after more than two years of near-total silence with the death of nearly all man-made machines. There were times he missed those sounds, the hum of traffic on the interstate, the near-constant whispering of jets passing high overhead, all the multitude of sounds of an advanced technological world.

Now it was usually silence except for the whispering of wind in the trees, the delightful sound of summer thunderstorms coming down off the mountains, and what had always been his favorite, the winter sound of wind cracking the ice out of trees, the hissing and tinkling of snow swirling down, and the scent of wood fires carried on the breeze. As they walked along the row of hangars, he could catch a glimpse back to the airport's cinderblock clubhouse. Smoke was wafting up from the chimney, a bit of a crowd gathered outside, weapons shouldered, his people pumping Bob's for information, and Bob's troops undoubtedly doing the same.

His orders had been that if such a situation developed to be friendly but reveal nothing about their numbers under arms, praise the food situation as well supplied—though the reality was that it would be tough going by spring—and convey confidence that all was well. The precious supply of moonshine that Forrest had brought along was to be applied liberally to any of Bob's people who were willing to try a swig, but except for Danny and Forrest, who seemed to have a prodigious capacity for holding their liquor, the others were to refrain.

He assumed nearly the same orders had been given by Bob to his personnel.

"Things seem okay over there," John announced, nodding back toward the clubhouse.

"I understand you have created a highly capable fighting force."

"Old tradition of militia. Remember a favorite movie of ours, *Drums Along the Mohawk*. We had to defend ourselves or go under."

"John, there are a lot of places like yours, actually. Not around the cities—they all became death traps. The enclaves of those who had tried to prepare beforehand, some survived a year or more, and then the barbarians just finally overran them. You most likely know that every major city of a quarter million or more east of the Mississippi is gone—a twisted, burned-out, perverted wasteland. They just were not sustainable without modern technology. That and all social order broke down within a matter of days.

"But once you got farther out, some of the smaller cities like Asheville somehow hung on. Those in the south had a better chance during the first winter, but even in the north, remote rural areas banded together. A fair part of West Virginia rallied around an eccentric old congressman a hundred miles west of here in Tennessee; there's an area nearly as big as what your community claims to be the State of Carolina. They're reviving the old name of the State of Franklin. More than a few, especially in mountain areas where folks rebuilt long-abandoned hydro dams, even have power again. So you are not just the only pocket of survival."

"So why does Bluemont want us suppressed?"

"I saw my mission as assimilating back in."

"Ever hear of the Borg? Jennifer was fond of the old reruns of that show. And, Bob, it looked like you had one hell of a fight going around Roanoke when I was up there a few weeks ago. Obviously, whoever was there was not happy about being assimilated."

"It hasn't been easy. I heard about that Posse group you took care of. There's a lot like that still out there. Most have pulled back into what is left of the cities, gleaning whatever can still be looted and raiding out into nearby countryside. That's why nearly every major urban center is dead ground. As for Roanoke, that was what we were fighting to put down. A number of decent folks were hidden in there and glad to see our return, but there were holdouts who we had to finish off. Did you know a group of maybe a thousand or more are still dug in at Winston-Salem? Chances are they've been eyeballing you for some time."

That did catch John by surprise. Of course they would be fools not to assume that Charlotte, Winston-Salem, and major urban area were hotbeds of groups like the Posse, who had taken to settling in to one spot and systematically stripping out anything that could provide another meal until absolutely nothing was left and then striking out again. It was a good bit of intelligence. With the small city of Hickory coming into the State of Carolina, he'd have to look at beefing up their security.

"Thanks for that info."

"It is the upside of why I took on this assignment. The ANR was a total failure. I saw my mission as reaching out to communities like yours. In more than a few, I had to separate the wheat from the chaff, and it got tough. But most survivors want to be pulled back into the fold. Bring stability and law and order back. That is the upside of my job, tough as it is. Network them together. I heard you've got electricity strung up. Sooner or later, after you get some electricity flowing again, you might start digging around in closets, basements, and realize that computers that had been tossed aside and not online the day we were hit just might still be functional."

That caught John off guard. Had someone leaked that info, and if so, how had it reached Bob so quickly? Surely it had to be a guess or an observation of what had happened somewhere else. But as he looked at Bob, he was all but certain that it was a warning that someone within his own community was at the least talking too openly, or perhaps far worse, was a spy for Bluemont, maybe slipped in by Fredericks.

"Interesting guess, Bob."

"Just an observation, that's all."

"Sir, we've drifted from the question I asked earlier."

"And that is . . . ?"

"Do you trust Bluemont? Are they truly the legitimate government of the United States as defined by the Constitution?"

There was no reply.

"Do you?"

Bob remained silent, finally breaking the moment by shading his eyes to look at the snow-covered mountains to the north. "Beautiful spot you have here. Linda wanted us to retire to Florida and after following me from pillar to post for near on forty years—how could I say no to her? But this is where I wanted to come. I even remember visiting this airport once. Thought about after retiring, getting my pilot's license again, buying a plane like the one in the hangar we were just in. A nice club here to join."

"Sir, dare I press that you are dodging me?" John said softly.

"Yes, John, I am." The old general sighed and slapped his hands together several times to get the circulation going. "I'd better head back."

"So that's it?"

"Kind of."

"It's good to know you're alive, sir."

"And you too. I have a strong sense of faith, John. Your reason for coming here so many years ago was motivated by a tragedy, the illness and impending death of your wife and a place to raise your girls after she was gone. But as I look at it now, I feel you were led here by God for a higher purpose."

"You helped to lead me here, sir."

"Be that as it may. I'd like to think there is a purpose to all of this and a purpose for the position I know you must take."

"If it means we will wind up as enemies, it is one I can barely grasp after everything you, I, and our country have been through."

"You've given me food for thought. The trip was worth it." Bob reached out, taking off his glove to grasp John's hand. "As used to be said back during the Civil War, if a day comes when you and I must face each other across a field of conflict, each of us doing what we believe our duty compels us to do, know that I will do what I must do as my sense of duty and honor compels me to act." He sighed, his voice going thick. "And it will be the worst day of my life."

"For me as well, sir."

The handshake turned into an embrace. Looking over Bob's shoulder, John could see that the gathering outside the clubhouse stood silent, looking their way. John finally let go of the embrace, stepped back, came to attention, and saluted. Bob stiffened and returned the salute.

"God be with you, John."

"And with you, sir."

Bob started to turn away, hesitated, and then turned to face John again. "A word of warning: watch your back. Please watch your back every single minute until we meet again."

John stood silent, parka hood back, hand up to shield his face from the stinging blast kicked up by the rotors as the Black Hawk lifted off. Fortunately, he could explain the tears clouding his vision as a reaction to the bitter cold.

"I think we'd better get the hell out of here!" Danny shouted as the chopper lifted heavenward. "I managed to get one of those guys a bit toasted; some of what he had to say doesn't sound good. They've got four Apaches just on the other side of Linville. They can rip the shit out of us in five minutes."

John nodded. "Order everyone to disperse, no vehicles. Just scatter out for an hour and see what happens. If we don't get hit by then, we rendezvous and head back to Black Mountain. But it won't happen now, today; I'm certain of that."

"Why?"

"I trust him."

"A general working for Bluemont?"

"No, because I trust him as a friend. He came here to warn us."

"Of what?"

"That a war is coming."

CHAPTER NINE

This is the BBC News. It is 3:00 Greenwich War Time.

As stated in prior broadcasts, all our correspondents have been ordered to leave their posts within the territories still controlled by the United States immediately. We can report that our correspondent who was briefly stationed in Bluemont was, this day, placed under arrest and is in detainment with the charge that he had disseminated false information harmful to the goal of completing the reunification of the United States east of the Mississippi River. We have no information at this time as to his safety or whereabouts.

It has been reported by other sources that the government's efforts to regain control of territory along an east-west axis, Norfolk to Richmond and Roanoke, Virginia, has been completed with minimal loss to either side and that former local governments in the latter two areas have greeted the return of central authority. This same source that we are now relying upon added that the next step shall be establishment of a new zone of unification and security along an axis from Charleston, South Carolina, west to Atlanta and shall include urban areas amongst which are Raleigh, Charlotte, and Asheville, North Carolina. It is claimed that significant progress has already been made in those areas, though there are reports of significant resistance as well. It shall be recalled that in the spring, the central government faced a major setback in the Asheville area with the report that an entire battalion of ANR troops had been annihilated with no prisoners taken, though contacts in that region deny the reports of the refusal to take prisoners.

On other fronts, China has again issued a stern warning to Bluemont that it must regain secured control of any and all weapons of mass destruction or that China, in order to defend the security of the regions it has extended humanitarian aid to, will be forced to take, and I quote, "rapid and stern action."

It was the first time John had actually been to Ernie's house, located out on the edge of town above Ridgecrest. John could see that the well-concealed so-called Franklin Clan had built their mountain retreat with an eye toward security, though before the Day, to an untrained eye as it came into view, it would just appear to be yet another upscale mountain home built for its remarkable view of the Mount Mitchell range.

John was getting extremely weary of bouncing around in old open-air all-terrain vehicles, but today the journey was in Maury's World War II–era jeep. It was open air, but given the history of the vehicle, it was a pleasure to experience a ride without racing to some confrontation—or, as happened in the spring, dodging the choppers that Fredericks used against the town. Nevertheless, it would eat up a couple of more gallons of their ever-diminishing gas supply. Just the day before, he had learned that the fuel within one of their remaining storage tanks had gone bad in the extremely cold weather for lack of the proper preservative. It meant that come spring planting, the few remaining functional tractors would have to burn some sort of recycled oil. He did have hopes that a team of old hobbyists living in Morganton were making progress in actually getting a couple of steam-powered machines up and running.

They turned onto Ernie's steep driveway, Maury shifting into low four-gear drive, and ascended the short road with ease even though it was snow-covered. Ernie's house was solidly built, most of it poured concrete, and John noted what looked like small bunkers flanking the driveway, covered by snow for now but that regardless provided clear fields of fire. The bunkers were assets that had saved Ernie's home when the Posse had attempted to flank the town's defenses two years ago and found themselves confronting a well-fortified position.

They pulled up to the front of the house, Ernie opening a garage door and beckoning for them to pull in and get out of the lightly falling snow.

As they climbed out of the jeep, John looked around with envy. Ernie had a full workshop in the basement garage, and not just the workshop of a casual handyman. There was arc-welding equipment, tool-and-die-making equipment, and a hoist for pulling an engine block out of a vehicle, and lining one wall were boxes of unopened rations.

Ernie noticed John looking around and smiled. "Were you a Boy Scout?" he asked.

"Yes, made Eagle."

"Well, Boy Scout, remember, 'Be prepared.' My family and I took it seriously. If everyone had, we wouldn't be in this damn mess now."

Ernie led the way upstairs to a spacious two-story-high living room, a cheery fire roaring in the fireplace, radiating warmth. Ernie's wife, Linda, was in the kitchen in the vast open room, looking up, smiling, and coming around the counter—carrying two cups of coffee, no less.

John sighed. "Why is it everyone seems to have a stockpile of coffee stashed away except me?"

"Again, Boy Scouts: 'Be prepared.'"

John tried not to bristle. Ernie could be so darn annoying at times rubbing in these types of things, but on the other hand, whether the final incident with Fredericks had been a setup by Ernie or not, he had dropped the guy, and now he just might be on the verge of unlocking some deadly serious questions as a follow-up performance.

The rest of Ernie's extended family came out from the far side of the house to meet them—his sons, grandchildren, and daughter and her reclusive author husband, the daughter offering to help John and Maury shuck off their parkas, scarves, and gloves.

Ernie produced a bottle of fine brandy from under the kitchen sink and offered to put something extra into their coffee, and though tempted, John declined. This was not a social visit; the business was dead serious, and he wanted a clear mind to evaluate why Ernie had so urgently requested his visiting the "Franklin Enclave," as everyone now called it, a visit that few had been permitted to experience.

"Let's head upstairs," Linda announced without further ado and social small talk with the rest of the family. Linda had rarely attended community meetings, and John thought her to be somewhat standoffish, until Makala, after meeting her, told John she suspected Linda had Asperger's. Unlike most, John knew what it meant, and for him it carried no negative stereotypes. An "Aspie," John knew, might not be up to par on most social skills, especially the ability to wander a crowd, meet and greet, and engage in small talk hour after hour. They tended to be mono-focused at times to the point of absolute obsession. It might be something society might think inane—the history of pinball machines and how to repair them or nineteenth-century railroads and the hauling capability of every engine ever made back then. In fact, if he could find people with that knowledge, he would have embraced them and put them to work to actually make such a machine to use on the abandoned Norfolk and Southern rails.

For Linda, it was software design, and in a long-ago world she had been one of the first programmers for the guidance systems for *Saturn V* rockets. She was a lone woman in a sea of techno-geek males of the early 1960s, writing guidance software for computers that had yet to even be made, so intense was the space race back then to get it done within President Kennedy's timeline. He had learned that Linda's task was to write the software for the third stage of the *Saturn V* rocket, several years before it was even built and flown, for what was called TLI—trans-lunar injection. It was software that at a very precise moment would fire off the third-stage rocket to propel the *Apollo* spacecraft out of earth orbit and send it soaring toward the moon at nearly twenty-five thousand miles per hour.

The challenge: she was aiming at an imaginary place in space where the moon would be three days later in its orbit around the earth so that the *Apollo* spacecraft would skim past the edge of the moon at a precise angle just sixty miles above the lunar surface. It was compared to aiming a pistol shot at a piece of paper set edgewise at fifty yards. Miss by even a fraction and the command module would crash into the lunar surface; too far out and lunar gravity would not sufficiently grab the spacecraft and it would just go winging off into deep space with no hope of return.

She did all of that before she was twenty-three.

Reaching the second-floor landing, John paused for a moment to soak in the view of Mount Mitchell, hidden briefly by a snow shower and then standing out again, cloaked in deep snow. The heat from the fireplace radiated up from the living room below, and John took off his sweater and enjoyed the warm, comfortable feel.

"Good morning, sir."

Several of John's old students were sitting at a long table where half a dozen computer screens were set up, several of them old Apple II screens, the others a mix from a first-generation Macintosh with its terrible blue nine-inch cube screen and two PCs, one in full, vivid color. As always, John felt a touch of embarrassment with his inability to remember names, though he recognized the young faces who at one time had sat in his one hundred– and two hundred–level history classes but could usually be found across the hall from his classroom in the room set up as a lab for the college's cyber-security program.

Linda motioned to a couple of chairs set up behind the three and then pulled up a chair herself in front of the color monitor. "Ernie just finished another calibration this morning on a geosynch sat comm device we think is of interest."

"Froze my ass off up on the roof in this damn weather," Ernie growled. "Samantha, that's your job from now on."

He tapped the shoulder of one of the girls sitting in front of an Apple screen. The young woman's hair was unruly, pulled back in a ponytail, and definitely needed a good washing. John remembered her as someone who had been quietly defined as 4-F for service with the college's militia due to asthma and a propensity for catching any bug floating around and had been down with pneumonia more than once. If not for the town's production of antibiotics, the last bout would have killed her. She had finally been tasked with helping to weave the wire for the generators being produced down in Anderson Hall and was doing a rather poor job even with that, but now she apparently had found her niche.

"Ernie, you keep this girl out of the cold," Linda said protectively. "She's needed more right here."

"So I freeze at my age, and she sits here snug and warm."

"Just shut up and leave her be."

Even as the two started to argue, Samantha pointed at the screen where an endless stream of numbers and letters without any semblance of order or reason were cascading down at a near-blinding rate at times. "There it is again, same pattern." Samantha hit a button on the keypad, which froze the image with an old-fashioned screen capture.

Ernie leaned over her shoulder to look.

"What is it?" John asked, curiosity filling him.

"Encrypting," Ernie announced, continuing to stare at the screen.

"Bluemont?"

"No way of knowing yet. If we were sitting on top of a hill looking down at the Bluemont facility, that would be easy enough. Aim a little eaves-dropping antenna at one of theirs and start listening in. Most people just assumed everything on computers just flashed around on fiber optics or microwaves, but a lot was going up and down as well, especially government stuff, and of course it was encrypted. You have the right software on your computer, and what looks like gibberish in raw form becomes standard text.

"Do you remember Kindles? You buy a book, and thirty seconds later it's in your computer, but what was sent was not the actual real text and photos; it was all encrypted to keep hackers from snatching it and then torrenting it out on their own."

"Torrenting?"

"The bane of every author, for starters. Easy, actually. Some bum just scans the text of a book into his computer and then just put it out there as a PDF file. They make a buck or two, the author gets ripped off. Go downstairs and ask my daughter's husband about it, and he'll start raving like a crazy man about getting robbed of hundreds of thousands of dollars from torrenting."

Ernie continued to stare at the screen while talking. "All those Internet sources for books, music—like Kindle, Nook, iTunes—were dependent on encrypting, and they were damn good at it and were updating their codes almost daily. So that is what we've got to get around."

John looked at the other screens. The color one that Linda was sitting in front of was actually showing a wavering video image filled with static.

"And that?"

Linda smiled. "Raw feed from the BBC. Off-the-air stuff. A reporter somewhere up in Canada cursing about getting kicked out of the country. Stuff like that is going out all the time."

"Can we talk to him?" John asked hopefully.

Linda shook her head. "We don't have any kind of uplink here, just listening."

"Should we get our ham operator guys to try to establish contact with them?"

"Already doing that," Ernie replied.

"Remember one of them talked with us several days after we snatched that Black Hawk," Maury interjected. "Then nothing. We can only run the radio in the chopper for so long before we have to fire it up to recharge."

John looked around at the equipment scattered on the table—boxes of additional equipment, computer boards, old empty mini-frame stacks, heavy-duty backup batteries that used to be standard external equipment for most home computers so that if the power blinked off the battery kept the system running. John spared a glance into the open door of a bedroom across the hall and saw where there were yet more boxes piled up, some of them stamped *Montreat College.*

A couple of more students whom he had vague recollection of once being in his classes were in that room, leaning over a ubiquitous green computer board, probing at it with a voltmeter.

John caught Ernie's eye and motioned for him to follow, not sure where to go until Ernie gestured toward a back room, a spacious affair, and within were yet more boxes, stripped-down computers, television monitors, some flat screens, others old-style heavy fourteen- and sixteen inch monitors. There was barely room for a desk and a couple of chairs, with Ernie gesturing for John to sit down in one, while from under the desk he pulled out a bottle of brandy, opened it, and without asking poured a couple of ounces into two rather dingy-looking glasses.

John did not argue the point this time and was glad for the warmth of the drink coursing through him seconds later. Ernie also pulled out a cigar and looked to John quizzically at least for this offer. John reluctantly refused, and Ernie shrugged, bit off the end of his smoke, produced an old-fashioned friction match, and lit it up, the blue smoke curling around John.

"Something bothering you?" Ernie asked.

John wasn't sure how to start as he sipped his drink. "For starters, I finally relented and said it was okay to recruit a couple of kids for this scheme of yours. Then I find out you all but hijacked the equipment from the college library basement and hauled it all over here without a by-your-leave. I now see five or more kids working here. Where did you get them from?"

"Paul Hawkins recommended them."

John nodded slowly. "And what jobs did you take them from?"

"Here and there," Ernie said with a bit of a grin.

"I would have liked to have known."

"John, you know you are sounding a bit like a bureaucrat with that. Were we supposed to ask permission?"

"Ernie, you know how many mouths we have to feed between now and when food starts to get produced come late spring. Every hand counts."

"And we've got hundreds working on making generators, retrofitting vehicles to burn alternate fuel, even some on your obsession with steam-powered tractors or some sort of mini locomotive."

"We try to find a job everyone can do, but unless under attack, our first priority is food and more food."

"And those tech nerds out there, how much food or whatever can they make versus what they are doing now?"

John nodded, finishing his drink and putting his hand over his glass in refusal while Ernie poured several ounces more for himself.

"Dare I quote someone we both disdain?" Ernie pressed. "'From each according to his ability.' You know the rest."

"I'm not saying that, Ernie."

"Well, in defense of what I am doing here, I'm saying it. Those kids are bloody geniuses when hunched over those old screens and damn near useless when it comes to canning beans, trapping rabbits, or toting a gun through the woods without accidentally shooting themselves or someone else. I'm maximizing their effectiveness, and their effectiveness might actually mean figuring what in hell is really going on out in the rest of the world and how it might hit us. Hell, you're the historian; you tell me what role kids like that played in previous wars."

John took that in and finally nodded. "You telling me you got a Bletchley Park out there in the next room?"

"Could be. Maybe one of them is the next Turing who will figure out how to crack the German Enigma code by building a machine to mimic how it works. Maybe not that dramatic, but if you are here on some kind of inspection tour and are about to order them back to whatever they were doing, I'm kicking you out of my house. The Franklin Clan will close up the gates and survive on our own again."

"And those kids stay here!"

John looked up to see Linda standing in the doorway, most likely having listened to the entire conversation.

"You feeding them as I requested?" John asked.

"That's right," Linda replied with a smile.

"You have that kind of surplus?"

"Be prepared, as my husband said."

John looked down at the freshly opened bottle of brandy stashed beneath Ernie's desk, the cigar resting in the ashtray, and wondered how, after two and a half years, this family still seemed to have enough to keep going without ever asking for additional help. But as he had resolved back in the first days when the responsibility fell upon him to try to organize his community to survive and defend itself, when it came to those who had prepared before the Day, his policy of "don't ask, don't tell" had to stand. He was not a commissar out to redistribute what was left or, as most likely happened in far too many places, point a finger at the 1 percent who'd had the foresight to be ready and shout for the other 99 percent to kill and loot them, just so all could fill their stomachs for a few extra days and then go back to starving.

"We'll feed and house them," Linda announced, pressing in on John's musings. "That poor skinny rail Samantha was half-starved to death; most of her peers pitied her but saw her as not good for much of anything other than consuming a ration a day. Here she is back where she belongs, and the others view her as some sort of guru and definitely a leader they turn to for advice. John, in the vicious triage of the world you have to deal with— and God save you, I know what a hell it must be—that girl most likely would have died before spring and except for a few close friends been mourned by few."

Linda's words were a slap of reproach, and they stung. He lowered his head. "Point made, Linda. She stays."

So many like her had indeed died, so ill-suited to be hunters—at times hunters of other men—or gatherers and sowers. Samantha was the luxury of an advanced technological age that so many like her had actually created. A world that all others once lived off of, even though they did not understand the hows or whys, but would curse if their sixty-inch flat screen hooked to a satellite dish went on the blink during a Super Bowl, or news of what some star had done that day to further titillate a society even as it headed to the brink of disaster and then fell.

The "nerds in the basement," which too many once mocked—even while dependent upon them for their jobs, their entertainment, and indeed their very lives when it came to the infrastructure—had been held in mocking disdain by far too many. Little did anyone realize their importance until the moment everyone was brought to their knees in sharp flashes of nuclear light far above the atmosphere.

"All right, it stays as it is. Now tell me your goals," John said.

Ernie, seeing that John's hand was no longer covering his glass, poured him a few more ounces, and for once John did not resist. Linda and Ernie were running the show for the moment, and he realized it was time to just listen and perhaps relax a bit.

"Something is about to happen," Linda announced. "Ernie and I worked in our fields for about fifty years. Good years with NASA, IBM, and then our own business with the satellite antennas. We were good because we learned to have a gut feel for things at times and stay a jump ahead of the game."

"What she is trying to say—" Ernie started to interject.

"Damn it, Ernie, I know what I am about to say," she snapped, and John could not help but smile. Ernie might intimidate most folks in town, but in this house, he could see it was an open fight at times, and at times Linda won. "We knew *Apollo* would work, but the shuttle was an insane design. Putting a manned crew atop solid rocket boosters that could not be turned off once lit, the way a liquid engine could be shut down, was asking for disaster. We and others warned and were ignored. We along with others tried to point out the fatal flaw of the insulation coating in the liquid fuel tank as well. It might just be spray-on foam, but if a piece the size of a kitchen counter snapped off and struck a wing during liftoff, it could prove fatal.

The math was simple; regardless of mass, it was about velocity at impact that counted. Again we were ignored, and then we watched in horror as *Columbia* broke up on reentry because of that exact reason."

She was digressing from the discussion of the moment, but he let her continue, knowing she was reaching toward a significant point and expressing frustrations that still haunted her.

"IBM was going to miss the boat with the PC market. We tried to tell the management idiots in business suits that. Their reply? No one really wanted a computer in their house but would rely on them to provide big mainframe systems, run of course by IBM people in white jackets. Of course that meant all of America would pay to be able to dial in and pay yet another fee via old AT&T to hook in to our machines. I remember them pitching that in one of their *World of Tomorrow* programs at a world's fair. So here we are in the world of tomorrow," she said with a sigh.

She gestured back to the room where the students were working. "They just might crack something, and it might mean the difference between our surviving or not. Your friend the general was giving you a warning. He is going to come down on us. He wants it to be without bloodshed, but regardless, he has his orders already. But what are the orders? Not just against us but long term. He didn't say anything about what that poor dying fellow . . . what was his name?"

"Quentin."

"What that poor man said about an EMP. And your friend didn't reply. Why?"

"I think he isn't sure himself," John replied, hoping that was the real reason, and not because he was already aware of some plan and going along with it.

"Then let's find out."

John downed the rest of the drink Ernie had poured for him, and it did go to his head. It was a welcome relief. He realized Linda was right. Something was coming, and unlike the threat of the Posse, or even Fredericks who showed his hand, before he fully struck, this time he just was not sure what the hell was about to happen next.

"And something else is worrying me, John."

"What is it?"

"You. The general was giving you a personal warning as well. I pray for you every day, and that prayer now includes that you take heed of his warning."

John smiled but said nothing.

"Be careful, John, very careful."

"Of course," he said, trying not to sound dismissive. "And okay. You win. Put them to it, and while you do, you feed and house them. Is that all right with you two?"

Linda smiled. "You see, Ernie? I knew he'd see it our way."

"Five extra mouths to feed." Ernie sighed. "Sure we can't draw some rations for them, John?"

"Five, I only saw three in that room."

"There's two more up on the roof installing another ten-foot-wide satellite dish we salvaged yesterday from a trailer down near Old Fort."

As John had already conceded who fed and housed the students, there was no sense in arguing about two more and he let it go.

"Those things will be damn visible on your roof," John ventured.

"Don't worry, we already thought of that," Linda replied. "They're screened with some camouflage made from bedsheets to blend in with the snow covering our roof."

John shook his head. If anything, he was feeling a twinge of guilt over the kids like Samantha. Until the realization that there were at least some computers capable of being restored, put back online, and then turned to a useful, perhaps crucial purpose, kids like her had languished, no longer fitting in. And without doubt, more than a few of them had died in this harsh new world. If they again had purpose—perhaps a crucial purpose—then he felt at this moment their society had at least taken yet another small step out of the darkness.

"I think you Franklins have more than enough rations to go around for five extra mouths, at least until the next harvest starts to come in."

Ernie barely cracked a smile. "Be prepared, John. If all of us had thought that way, we wouldn't be counting every bean or ear of corn and calculating if we should throw them to a pig or eat them ourselves. Yeah, we can feed them."

"Point taken," was all John could say.

"Fine, then. Now, I've got a stew ready to ladle out. You and Maury stay. Agreed?"

John felt no guilt with accepting. Too often, someone else would offer a meal of watery soup or a stew with some fragments of squirrel or raccoon mixed in with wild onions and greens, and he always politely refused such paltry fare, not because he wasn't hungry but because it was one extra meal that whomever he was visiting could better use with their raggedy-clad children.

The entire extended family, Franklins and their newly adopted charges, gathered around their dining room table, Ernie standing to offer grace while all joined hands. The room was actually warm in spite of the cold wintry blast swirling outside their south-facing windows, the fireplace glowing hot with heavy crackling logs stacked in. John felt a wave of nostalgia with the gathering. He often lost track now of exactly what day of the week it was. In warm weather, going to church on Sunday had become a looked-forward-to weekly event in the college's chapel, which was still under repair from the battle back in the spring.

But with the harsh weather of the last month and Makala's advanced state of pregnancy, the walk from their home up to Gaither Hall had been set aside. It wasn't just the gathering around a family table for a filling meal that hit hard; it was the way everyone held hands with heads lowered, offering a prayer of thanksgiving that filled him with emotion.

Perhaps Linda and Ernie were putting on a bit of show for their guest and new lodgers, but then again, he knew they were above that. It was a continuation of old Southern traditions, of family and friends gathered together for a Sunday afternoon of sharing and thanksgiving.

And that realization hit him now as well. When was Thanksgiving? Was it next week, or was it already past? Had they lost touch with that after but two and a half years?

As Ernie ladled out each bowl in turn and passed it on, John found he could not help but watch it hungrily. The meat did not strike him as fresh—it most likely came from a freeze-dried can of emergency rations—but it was still meat, mixed in with what appeared to be real potatoes and a sprinkling of greens. What truly set his mouth to watering was not just the stew but the scent of freshly baked bread as well. Part of the modern kitchen fixtures had been pulled out long ago, with an old-fashioned kitchen woodstove set in as a replacement, with Linda leaving the table for a moment to pull a large loaf of bread out of the oven and setting it down in front of Ernie to be cut into thick slices and then passed around as well.

Stew and bread set before him, he looked down at the feast and found it hard not to fill up with emotion, wishing that Makala was here as well. He felt guilty that such a meal was before him.

"John Matherson, don't let that get cold!"

He looked up and saw Linda gazing at him not sternly but with a glint of affection, as if reading his thoughts. "There's more than enough to go around, and I'll have a bowl and a slice of fresh-baked bread for you to take home to your good wife."

He could not find the voice to reply and simply nodded, not used to such maternal gestures, especially now that Jen was gone.

He ate in silence and barely listened to the family chatter, teasing of a brother to their daughter implying she might be expecting, the grandchildren announcing that they planned to go sledding down the driveway, Ernie admonishing that there was still the wood splitting and hauling detail to see to.

As for the students now living with them, Linda, without any overt show, just quietly walked behind them with a steaming ladle and put a bit of extra stew in each of their bowls. No one else at the table complained about this second helping, and John felt a flood of emotion as Samantha looked up at Linda, whispered a thank-you, and then struggled and failed to hold back tears of gratitude for a meal unlike any she had most likely seen in years. Linda leaned over to hug her, and the girl began to cry openly.

No one spoke, and then, to help cover the girl's embarrassment with her emotional display, one of the grandchildren insisted she go sledding with them after the meal was done.

It was the most John could recall having eaten in weeks—or was it months? Perhaps the meal the evening after the battle that had taken out Fredericks when he and those who had fought that day were each handed to eat at one sitting, at John's insistence, an entire MRE from the stockpile they had captured. Nearly four thousand calories of food all in one sitting.

As he looked around at those gathered with him, a favorite hymn came to mind that Aaron Copland had titled "Simple Gifts." As if there were some sort of mental prompting, with the meal done, the daughter got up, went over to the piano in the living room, thumbed through a layer of sheet music, picked out a piece by Debussy that John recognized, and began to play.

There was a moment of silence from the others as they listened appreciatively. It flashed John to the day he was in Gaither Chapel with Makala and a student was singing the haunting song "Try to Remember," a song that so symbolized to John the world they now lived in. The daughter just simply playing a song took John to the thought of a world that must have existed even before his own time, when a family would gather for Sunday dinner, and then afterward someone would play the piano and perhaps others might even sing.

We've lost so much, he realized, *but then again, maybe we are learning again about the simple gifts of still being alive.* The gifts of a warm, filling meal, family and friends together, and rather than the cluttering noise of some ridiculous game turned up too loudly on a television afterward, it was instead a family entertaining themselves while the cold wind of winter swept down from out of the mountains and across icicle-coated orchards and snow-drifted fields beyond.

He realized, that at this moment, whatever was about to come . . . it was good to be alive.

CHAPTER TEN

"John, wake up. Wake up! We're under attack!"

It was the dream, the jumble of dreams that always ended with him bolt upright in bed, sweat soaked, shivering. Out on the desert, the Bradley up ahead burning, racing forward to find the medics already pulling out the charred bodies, two of them still alive, faces burned black, red mouths open, screaming, and he stood helpless, could do nothing other than stare in shock . . . Doc Kellor pulling back a blanket revealing Ben, the father of his grandson, features contorted in the agony of death . . . then Jennifer . . .

"John, wake up!"

He was sitting up, shaking, the room freezing cold, Makala's arms around him, kissing him awake. He opened his eyes. This time, there was no soothing, kissing his forehead, wiping the sweat from his face, whispering it was okay; it was just "the dream" again.

"You've got to wake up now. Reverend Black's on the phone. We're being attacked!"

He nodded, standing up, bare feet hitting the freezing-cold floor, shocking him, Makala helping him to put on a heavy bathrobe, steadying him as consciousness returned.

"Who's calling?"

"Reverend Black. John, there are helicopters circling." She started to lead him to the sunroom where the phone was.

"Who? Where?"

She picked up the receiver of the phone, an old-fashioned black rotary unit, and handed it to him.

"Matherson here."

"John, it's Black. I'm at the campus office. We've got three Apaches overhead. Can't you hear them?"

That finally startled him awake, and he realized the room was reverberating with a low, steady rumble. He walked to the sunroom window, which was half-covered with frost, looked out, and caught the glint of flashing rotors sweeping by overhead.

"Any shooting?"

"Not yet."

John continued to look out the window. The choppers were staying high, circling out along the crest line of Lookout Mountain. He watched them for a moment, catching glimpses. "Any come in low over the campus?"

"Not yet." He could hear the nervousness in Black's voice.

"Get on the phone to downtown Black Mountain, Asheville, any connections we have. Tell them not to shoot unless fired upon first and report anything they're seeing. I'll be right up."

He hung up. Makala was already scrambling to fetch clothing and boots, helping John to get dressed.

"What is it?" she asked.

"Not sure, but if it's a surprise attack with intent to kill, they'd already be hitting us."

Pulling on his boots, he heard a vehicle outside, and opening the door, he saw that it was Maury in his jeep. John ran out to him, looking up, the distinct thump of a helicopter rising in pitch as the chopper raced by overhead, still keeping altitude.

"What the hell is going on?" Maury shouted as John climbed in, brushing snow off the passenger seat before sitting down.

"They're military, desert camo pattern. They must be with General Scales. Get me to the office."

Maury spun the jeep around through the deep snow and set off downhill to Montreat Road, the vehicle skidding as he hit the base of the road and went sideways onto the main street through the village without slowing. Maury edged off the road to get around a tree that had fallen in the last storm and had yet to be cleared and then turned to race up to Gaither Hall. As they skidded to a stop, John looked up again and saw that there were several Black Hawks as well, slowly circling at more than a thousand feet above the narrow valley.

Black was at the office door, motioning for John to come in. Out on the snow-covered front lawn, a dozen or more students were looking up, all of them with weapons. One of them was Grace.

"Do not point your weapons at them! Everyone get the hell inside!" John shouted.

"Someone on the ham radio, asking for you."

John went to the radio, the tinny-sounding speaker crackling.

"Matherson, this is Bob Scales; please respond."

John picked up the old-fashioned handheld mike and clicked it several times before replying.

"Matherson here. Bob, are you overhead?"

A momentary pause.

"Affirmative, John. Assumed you were in that jeep."

"Yes, sir."

"Nice vehicle. I'd like to see it up close."

John hesitated for a moment. "You're welcome to land, but flag off those Apaches and send them home."

"Can't do it, John. Please listen carefully. I'm asking for your immediate surrender."

"You've got to be kidding."

"John, I've got assets over you that can take down your campus and all those kids in five minutes. We're already landing in Asheville. You might have disabled the Asheville airport, but I have two C-130s touching down on the interstate next to it. I've also got a support column on the ground coming up from Greenville, and they have some Bradleys. It's your call. I'll give you five minutes to think it over."

John put the mike down and looked at Reverend Black and Maury.

They were silent, staring at him.

The phone began to ring. Black picked it up, listened for a moment, simply said, "We already know," and looked at John, still holding the receiver.

"That was Dunn in downtown Asheville. He said several Black Hawks have touched down near the county office complex. They'll be in his office in another few minutes."

"Any fighting?"

Black relayed the question, sighed, and looked back to John. "One of the security team there is shot, bad. Fired on them as they landed."

John looked back out the window, helicopters still circling, and in spite of his orders, students were coming out of buildings, some already in winter camo, weapons up.

"John, what are you going to do?" Black whispered, still holding the phone.

He looked at his troops, his kids. Against the Posse, even against Fredericks, it was one thing, and those two fights had cost dearly. This time?

It would be a bloodbath, and for what?

"We don't stand a chance against them." John sighed. "I know Bob Scales. This is the A team, not those pathetic ANR kids they threw at us last spring."

"John, I need your answer now." It was Bob again on the radio. "I just got a report a couple of your people and mine were shot in Asheville. Stop it before it turns into a full-scale fight."

He wanted to shout back that it was Bob who was starting it with this surprise assault coming in at dawn.

"John, they've got us," Maury said softly, and John finally nodded.

"Reverend. Tell Dunn to stand down, disarm, and surrender. Get on the phone to all locations, tell them not to fire, to stand down, and await word from me later. Repeat, do not resist. You got it."

Reverend Black sighed. "John, you're making the right move."

"Yeah, I know," he replied bitterly. "Maury, get outside, tell those darn kids to get back inside. Find Kevin Malady, tell him everyone is to return to their rooms, stack weapons, and show no resistance. Got that?"

Maury could only nod and went back out the door as John picked up the mike and clicked it.

"Okay, Bob. We surrender on your word that my people are to be treated with respect, no reprisals or arrests. It's got to be the code we once lived by, sir."

"Agreed."

"Wait fifteen minutes so I make sure the word is out. There's a baseball field above the campus; you can set down there."

"Fifteen minutes, then. Bring your jeep up to meet me, John. Make sure your people do not fire. If they do, you know what I have to do in reply."

"Understood."

He could hear Bob click off.

I should have expected this, he thought bitterly. *But then again, what could I do differently?* After two and a half years of successfully managing the defense of his community, to be caught like this was galling.

Frustrated, he threw the mike down and walked outside.

The rotor of the Black Hawk came to a stop, John at last able to lower his hands from his face as the swirling snow settled down. Three Black Hawks had landed, troops piling out of the first two, weapons raised, forming a defensive perimeter, while overhead the three Apaches continued to circle. Their nose guns were turned away, outward, and not in toward the campus—a smart gesture on Bob's part—but their presence was menacing nevertheless, the sounds, the sights, and smells taking John back to the desert of Iraq so long ago.

John stood by the jeep, Maury at his side. The world felt cold, empty. Could he trust Bob? Or was this all a ruse? He'd grown used to winning, to always somehow pulling the chestnuts out of the fire. And now after two and a half years, the game was up. Whatever it was that Bluemont wanted, they now had it. How brilliantly it was done, to send in a man John once served under, had trusted, respected, and considered to be his friend.

It was all up to Bluemont now. He had defied them because of Fredericks, the type of man who across his years of military service he had learned to hold in contempt. The quintessential bureaucrat, the type where in the face of all logical argument, at times with the lives of men in the balance, would smile that disdainful smile, implying that an Ivy League degree in public administration trumped reality in the field.

Was that what Bob was serving? If so, regardless of the promises made minutes ago, John could see what would follow. Local community control was finished, the high talk back in the spring of a reaffirmation of the Constitution, of their expanding out across the Carolinas, bringing at least some semblance of a technological infrastructure back online to themselves and their neighbors . . . gone.

There would be no fight now. Perhaps the first gesture to smooth things over would be a bribe of reassurance, some truckloads of MREs brought up from the coast, perhaps even already packed along with the column invading up from Greenville, South Carolina. Then? A new administrator? Another Fredericks? And with him new rulings? The logic that a local militia was no longer needed for self-defense now that the regulars were here, but the young men and women of his community would be needed elsewhere and an order given?

He could see it all so clearly, even as he felt a surge of emotion as the side door of the third Black Hawk slid open and Bob Scales alighted, behind him a detail of eight well-armed men, some in desert camo, others in winter uniforms, who joined the defensive perimeter.

John did not make the gesture of going forward to meet Bob, waiting as he struggled alone through the knee-deep snow, moving slowly.

Bob stopped half a dozen feet away from John and gazed into his eyes, saying nothing.

"Sir, if you are expecting me to salute this time, I'm sorry, I can't."

A flicker of a smile creased his old friend's features. "At least present your sword as a token of surrender, and I'll return it graciously," Bob replied.

John kept his features fixed. Memories flooded in of his year with Bob at the War College, participating in the traditional staff rides to Gettysburg, the hours spent together analyzing the battle while walking the fields with the rising young officers who were their students and getting a lesson not only about the battle itself but also the traditions of the military in which they served. That they would fight ferociously for the cause they believed was right and to which they had sworn their sacred honor, but could as well show compassion and share the last drop of a canteen with a foe who had tried to kill them but minutes before.

"Okay, forget the sword. But can we at least get out of the cold?" Bob suggested.

"Can I request that you call off those Apaches overhead? They're making my people extremely nervous. Last time we had Apaches here, they shot up our chapel and hospital and killed dozens."

Bob nodded. "You can assure me that where they set down no action will be taken?"

"If they land back at the airport where we met, there is no one there, close enough to cover you if needed, far enough away to ease things here a bit."

"Your word of honor on that, John?"

"Yes"—he hesitated for a few seconds—"on my word of honor . . . sir."

"By the way, I already have a team there," Bob announced.

"Why there?"

"Seemed like a good staging area, and besides, they're looking for a lost Black Hawk. Figured it might be stashed in one of the hangars. All right, I'll order them back to that airport."

Bob turned and shouted an order. One of the troopers deployed on the security perimeter around the choppers nodded and went to the pilot's window of the Black Hawk Bob had come in on. Seconds later, the three Apaches turned sharply to the southeast and began to climb out of the valley.

"Satisfied?" Bob asked.

"It helps."

"Now can we get in out of the cold?"

John nodded and pointed to the jeep. Bob climbed into the passenger seat. The trooper who had passed his order to the pilot shouted a protest and started to come forward, weapon not pointed toward them directly but raised to the ready.

"It's all right, Captain!" Bob shouted. "Wait here."

"But, sir!"

"I'm with friends. Order the men to keep perimeter and wait. I'll be back in one hour."

The captain nodded reluctantly, saluted, and turned away.

"He gets a little too nervous about me at times," Bob said.

"I hope he doesn't get nervous while we're gone. Not a threat, sir, but there are well over a hundred heavily armed people down there." He nodded back toward the campus.

"I trust you. Just make sure they stay away from where the choppers are waiting."

John did not reply.

"You do know that if I am not back in an hour, things can quickly grow ugly."

"Are you doubting my word"—he paused—"General?"

Bob looked back at John, who was climbing into the narrow backseat, smiling but glance firm. "I trust you. We both have to trust each other now."

Again John did not reply. "Take us to Gaither, Maury," John said to Maury, who switched the jeep's engine on and put it in gear.

"Your name Maury?" Bob asked.

"Yes, sir."

"Nice jeep. Original?"

"1942 Wills."

During the short drive back to Gaither, Bob chatted with Maury about the jeep, its history, and how he always preferred them to Humvees.

As they passed the library on one side and the girls' dorm on the other side of the road, John could see anxious faces peering out of windows, nearly all still in winter camo, weapons slung on their shoulders. Malady stood in the doorway of the dorm, ready to go. John told Maury to stop.

"Kevin, keep everyone inside, weapons grounded. And for heaven's sake, no one is to go near where the choppers landed. You got that? Once you feel things are secure with our people, report to me down in Gaither."

"Yes, sir." Kevin made the gesture of saluting even as John told Maury to head on to Gaither Hall.

They turned into the rear parking lot of Gaither, slid to a stop, and dismounted. Bob offered his hand to Maury, who reluctantly took it, and thanked him for the ride and brief history lesson about jeeps.

John climbed out of the back of the jeep and led the way inside. The corridor was packed with anxious students and staff, all of them suited up, all of them armed.

John stopped, looking over his shoulder at Bob, who came in behind him, pulling back the hood of his parka. The old general did not hesitate or show fear. He actually smiled, coming up to John's side.

It was a tense moment.

John took a step forward and held up his hand in a calming gesture. "This is General Scales. He is an old friend from long before the Day. General, these are some of my troops."

Bob actually stiffened and offered a salute, which some then returned, though many continued to just stand in silence, their hostile gazes obvious.

"Colonel Matherson, my compliments, you have a good-looking command here."

Good-looking? John tried to not show any reaction. In an earlier age, a world long ago, those standing in the hallway would have been described as a ragtag-looking bunch at best, winter camo made out of bedsheets, most of the young men unshaven, all of them thin, wiry after two and a half years of privation and two deadly campaigns behind them. A few had offered salutes in return, but the rest were wary, eyes cold and obviously expecting that before the day was out it would turn into a fight to the death . . . and though scared were ready to face it.

"All of you," John said in a calm voice. "We are in stand-down. I want you to keep your weapons slung and follow proper procedure to ensure chambers are empty. We don't need an accident. Remember what I told you about how things went out of control at Lexington Green. We don't want that here because one hothead takes matters into their own hands. Do we understand each other?"

"Sir, are we surrendering without a fight?" one of them cried.

"We are not at war here. The general is here to talk things over."

"With Apaches as an opening move?" another student shouted angrily.

"All of you listen to me. This is not Fredericks. I know this man. He could have come in here with gunships tearing us apart before we even knew what was hitting us. He's here to talk. So I want all of you to relax, get back to whatever your assigned duties are, ground your weapons, and for now leave them in Fellowship Hall if you are going outside. No one is to go near the ball field. The troops up there have firm orders to protect those helicopters, and that means shoot first and ask questions later. Your venturing up there could be seen as a hostile approach, and then . . . Lexington Green again. You all got that?"

There were nods, a few soft "Yes, sir" replies, all of them saluting John while avoiding eye contact with Bob, an obvious gesture to indicate who was still in charge as far as they were concerned, and the group started to disperse.

John opened the door to what had been the president's office, motioned for Bob to step in, and then closed the door behind him.

"You handled that well, John, thank you."

"What else was I to do? Order them to shoot you and then storm the field and get slaughtered?"

Bob looked around the room, offering a smile as he took his parka off. "Lord, I do recall this room. Remember I visited this campus years ago." He paused for a moment. "Mary was buried out of this chapel. Our friend Dan Hunt was president. I sat in here with him after the service for Mary. I remember he was in tears for you that day."

John offered a chair at the long meeting table and turned away for a moment so emotions wouldn't show as Bob conjured up the memory of that day. It was Bob who had recommended John for the job at this college, having served with Dan Hunt, the two of them classmates from West Point.

"I don't see him here," Bob said softly.

"He didn't make it—died during the starving time after everything went to hell."

He looked back at Bob, who was gazing at Dan's favorite painting, George Washington kneeling in the snow in prayer at Valley Forge.

"The list goes on and on," Bob said softly, "all those who didn't make it."

"I wondered about you across these years, sir," John replied, "but now you are here."

"You take inspiration from that painting?" Bob asked. "Is that why you kept it?"

John studied it for a moment. "Only recently started to use this office, just for state council meetings. I felt it was kind of a shrine to a good leader. But yeah, on a day like this, it's worth studying."

Bob did not respond to John's obvious touch of cynicism. "How Washington kept his strength through that winter at Valley Forge is beyond me at times. If he had lost his way, the American Revolution would have truly been lost."

"That's worth thinking about now."

Bob turned his gaze from the painting to John, and there seemed to be a flash of warning. "Let's get to business, John," he announced, and he sat down at the far end of the table.

"Formal surrender, is that it, sir? It's Appomattox, you're Grant, and I'm Lee?"

"I prefer not to think of it that way. Call it rejoining the Union we both swore an oath to."

"You mean Bluemont?"

Bob hesitated. "You seem damn hostile to them."

"I have every reason to be hostile. This community lost over a hundred dead to that tin-pot dictator they sent down here back in the spring. Before we leave, I want you to take a look at our chapel; we're still repairing it. Those troops out in the hallway, they have every reason to mistrust. They all buried friends, several of them spouses, by the time it was done. How else should we react?"

"Were they students of yours, John?"

"You mean now, or before the Day?"

"You know what I mean."

John smiled sadly. "Yes. That girl who spoke up asking if we were surrendering."

"You mean the one who would not salute me but definitely saluted you?"

"That one, yes. She was a Bible studies major. Loved history, good kid from a good family that came up here every month to visit, and all of them would sit in on one of my evening classes. Her family lived in Florida."

With the mention of Florida, he saw the sudden look in Bob's eyes.

"Sorry I mentioned that place, sir."

Bob sighed. "Like I said, I know my Linda is gone. I just pray it was peaceful."

"Same for that girl. She got married in our chapel across the hall a year ago. Had a baby three months ago. No husband now—he was killed in the attack where Fredericks was holed up at the end."

"I understand the tough edge to her now," Bob replied.

"We all have tough edges now, sir. No father for her baby, nightmares as to what happened to the rest of her family. This school is all she knows now." He hesitated. "She feels she has nothing to lose if she dies fighting to defend it."

"There is no need anymore to fight, John."

"Really, sir?" He could not control the sarcasm in his voice, but Bob did not react.

"Damn, I'm cold and thirsty."

"It's a dry campus, Bob. At least we try to keep it that way."

"Coffee, then?" Bob asked hopefully.

"None of that either. All those K-Cups of coffee belong to my friend Forrest—you remember him, the sergeant who left an arm in Afghanistan—but I can roust up some herbal tea."

"Please, if you don't mind."

John nodded, left the office, and leaned over the dutch door that led down to the old business office, which had been converted into the formal administrative office of the town. He shouted down the stairs, Reverend Black opening the door down below, and John passed along the request.

He returned to the president's office, where Bob had returned to staring at the painting of George Washington.

"Do you think he really prayed like that in the snow of that winter?" Bob asked.

"He was a man of faith, and if ever this country needed faith, it was that winter. So yes, I believe it is real."

"So do I," Bob said softly.

The two were silent for a moment, both gazing at the painting.

The historian in John knew that the weather during that first winter at Valley Forge was nowhere near as severe as the one at Morristown, New Jersey, a couple of years later when the army was encamped at Jockey Hollow. Several units—unpaid, unshod, desperate, and hungry—had finally mutinied. Washington had taken the hard choice of executing several of the ringleaders and in a tense standoff was ready to order troops still loyal to the cause to fire, if need be, on the regiments in mutiny. The revolution had indeed hung by the slenderest of threads on that desperate day. Only Washington's strength of character and leadership had prevented a complete breakdown of the army and the collapse of his years of effort with all disintegrating into chaos and most likely dictatorship or capitulation.

There was a tap on the door, his friend Reverend Black bringing in two steaming mugs of herbal tea. John thanked him, and there was a moment of hesitation.

John made the formal introductions, Bob coming to his feet to shake Black's hand.

"Everything all right? Everyone standing down?" John asked.

"It's not good over Asheville. Half a dozen dead and wounded. I spoke on the phone with some officer who said he had just placed our person Dunn there under arrest."

John looked over at Bob.

"I'll straighten that out once I'm done here, John."

"So, are we all under arrest?" John asked coldly.

"I didn't want any bloodshed," Bob replied. "I promise to straighten it out."

"Tell that to the families of the dead," Black snapped back.

Bob nodded, keeping his composure. "If you're still on the phone with them, tell the officer there—it's most likely Major Minecci—that I am safe and secure here, will be up there in two hours, and expect a full report. If fired on, he is not to return fire unless the situation is life threatening. Can you help me with that, Reverend?"

Black looked over at John, who gave a nod of reassurance, and he left.

"You could have given us warning," John said. "It would have prevented what happened in Asheville."

"Maybe, maybe not. The way I read things when we last met, I knew I could trust you. But my people who mingled with yours while we were talking? It wasn't good. Reports back were that your people would fight if we just tried to walk in."

"Can you blame them after what the last attempt to bring us into the fold of Bluemont turned into?"

"I balanced all and finally felt this was the right approach. It's tragic that anyone had to die. God knows after what happened in Roanoke, Richmond, and Lynchburg, I know the cost. The only way I felt could work was to show overwhelming force in the first move and count on you being moral and sane in response. It could have been far worse, and you know it."

"So my next question, Bob. Why this?"

"I already told you that before. I've been tasked with establishing a re-unified state east of the Appalachians from central Virginia down to the old border of Florida."

"Why not Florida as well while you're at it?" Again, he could see the flash of pain in Bob's eyes at the mere mention of that place.

"We've written off Florida. I remember some years ago—I think I read it in *American Heritage* or some magazine like that—until DDT and air-conditioning came along, except for the coastal regions, the state was relatively empty. Well, it most certainly turned into that after the Day with tens of millions living there, a high percentage of them elderly and dependent on that air-conditioning, modern sanitation, a reliable supply of medications, modern hospitals, a freezer full of steaks, cold margaritas out on the screened-in lanai every evening, and of course mosquito control. Word is the few left down there again face malaria, cholera, Nile Valley, you name it."

He paused, obviously not appreciating having to dwell on what for him was personal history as well. "Remember, Central Command for our operations in the Middle East was based in the Tampa, Saint Pete area. Within two months, they collapsed, the survivors, the lucky survivors, evacuated by our navy. From Miami to Jacksonville—on the other coast Fort Myers to Pensacola—disintegrated into a sinkhole of anarchy, looting, murder, and then disease and starvation. There are some pockets of survivors along the coast, living again by what they can harvest from the sea as long as pirates don't get them first. The navy tried to control the waters around there for a while and clean out the pirates but finally gave up. Florida, like I said, is a write-off."

It was obvious to John that he wanted to leave that subject behind.

"Florida's gone, but you were ordered to take this place, is that it?"

"I'd prefer not to use the term *take,* John. Call it *unite, reunite.* Bring you back in under a central federated government."

"But after Fredericks, suppose we don't want to join?"

"John, you have no choice. To be blunt, it is unite or die."

John chuckled at that and shook his head. "I seem to remember that was on our flags during the revolution against an overbearing authority four thousand miles away."

"You're taking it the wrong way, my friend."

"Bob, who actually are you serving? I mean, *really* serving? Bluemont, or the oath you swore to the Constitution?"

Bob fell silent, and there was a look of anger in his eyes.

"My trust for Bluemont? It's about as far as I can spit into a hurricane," John interjected.

"My God, John. So you are going to take that decision upon yourself. You don't trust them, so go to hell and leave us alone, and that's it?"

John offered no reply.

"I have my orders. I hope you can trust me to see them through and avoid a senseless conflict that you know you cannot win."

He wanted to retort with a conjuring of memories about military ethics classes, the tragic, horrific example of the German army in the 1930s, when the oath of allegiance was one day switched from defending the state to accepting without hesitation all orders from the führer.

"So what are your orders regarding here, what we have come to call the State of Carolina?"

"A bit aggrandizing, that name, isn't it? State of Carolina. Last time I checked a map, your state here controls what, five thousand square miles? What about Charlotte, Greensboro, Raleigh? For that matter, there is a garrison in Greenville-Spartanburg put there by Bluemont, and they have a corridor of control all the way down to Charleston."

"It's a start," John offered, "and if left alone will continue to expand in an orderly way. Groups like the Posse either move out or, if need be, we take them out. We were doing okay with local folks reaching out to the next community and inviting them to join in. Unite or die? Maybe it is unite and live."

"John, there are a hundred enclaves like yours that are making 'a start,' as you put it, from here clear up to Maine. But then what? We devolve into a hundred feudal-like states that eventually balkanize the way Europe did after Rome collapsed? You and your friends have done a masterful job of restoring order, civilization, and—from what I could observe even bringing some technology back online. But reunite everything? Do you have any idea what some other so-called states have devolved into? You most likely know about Chicago, Cleveland, Pittsburgh, New York, even D.C."

"I've heard some stories."

"You haven't *seen* it; I have. D.C. is of course gone, a write-off, same as Florida. There are some whack jobs running what they call a kingdom not a hundred and fifty miles from here that are told to worship their leader as the son of God, and if you don't go along, you are crucified."

"So why not go after them first?" John offered.

"Weak argument, John. Bait-and-switch logic. It is precisely places like here, where things are being restored, that old values still hold, that we need in our fold before I can take out places like that."

"So we are back in the fold, is that it?"

Bob nodded, finally sipping his tea and grimacing slightly. "Damn, this is awful stuff, John."

"Sorry, but that is what we live on."

"Don't take it as a bribe, but once we get this settled, I've got a convoy coming in with two hundred thousand MREs. Remember each of them has a packet of coffee. Do you still smoke?"

John shook his head.

"Why, I remember you as being really addicted."

"I promised Jennifer before she died."

Bob lowered his head. "Sorry." John could tell the emotions were genuine. "We can talk later about all that we lost."

"And your specific orders."

Bob looked back up at him and sighed, obviously not happy about what he had to say next. "I'm ordered to place you under arrest and transport you in an expedient manner to Bluemont to stand trial for murder, the execution of prisoners, and treason."

"Oh, really?" John said, and he could not help but offer a sarcastic grin. "Can I have time to say good-bye to my wife?"

"Wife?"

"Guess you wouldn't have known, or would you? I assume Fredericks, before we killed him, was sending up reports."

"Actually, I didn't know. Who is she?"

John offered a brief explanation to his old and perhaps now former friend as to how he and Makala had met on the Day and all that had transpired afterward.

"I had hoped to see my child born," John concluded, "but guess you need to haul me out of here ASAP."

Bob shook his head. "I'm not going to do that."

"Bob, you have orders to follow."

Bob's gaze turned icy cold. "Don't push it, John. I'm putting my neck out as is. The original orders were to take this place by force."

"So why didn't you?"

"Again, don't push it. Just that I knew there was a better way. And part of that better way is to leave you in peace."

"So I can be a puppet figurehead?"

"Damn, you are hostile," Bob replied.

"I have every reason to be hostile," John snapped back. "We were doing just fine until two hours ago."

"There is a far bigger world out there than this 'State of Carolina,' as you call it."

"I know that."

"No, you don't. Not really."

"Enlighten me, then, sir."

Bob began to stand up. "I understand your feelings, but if this is how it's going to be, let's just cut the crap. I'm not going to put you under arrest and transport you to Bluemont. Nor anyone else here." He paused. "I just implore you to keep things stable with no resistance. You do that for me, and I can skirt around that other order for a while."

"Aren't you breaking orders?"

"Come on, you know there is always leeway for a commander in the field if he knows how to play it."

"And something called the Fifth and Sixth Amendments of the Bill of Rights. Does Bluemont even have the right to accuse me of treason, prosecute me for a capital crime? And the Sixth Amendment is about being tried in my state or district where the alleged crime took place by a jury of my peers. Something about our revolution and protest against those being arrested without warning and transported away. It was so important an issue back then that we wrote it into the Constitution. I could cite a few other points from that document as well."

"Damn it, of course you know I am aware of that."

"And Bluemont isn't? I find that troubling, Bob."

"Again, don't press me, John."

"I'm not pressing you, sir. Perhaps it is you who are pressing yourself."

"Damn it, listen to me! Just listen for a minute."

John nodded and sat back, breaking eye contact and deliberately focusing his gaze on the portrait of Washington at Valley Forge.

"Asheville and Greenville-Spartanburg are to become the staging area to bring Atlanta back under control."

"My God, sir. Who is your head of intelligence? Atlanta is a hellhole. You'll be facing tens of thousands down there, the survivors of a dog-eat-dog existence the last two years. I know. The southern extent of what you dismissively call the State of Carolina is not a hundred miles away from there, and we still on occasion have refugees staggering in from there. Word is that Fort Benning collapsed within weeks after the Day. After that, posse-like groups moved in and looted out weapons from there. Your force might be facing some nasty ground-to-air stuff. Bob, taking back Atlanta . . ." He sighed. "It will make Sherman's job look easy in comparison."

"I already know that. Look, John, we've got to get our act together east of the Mississippi, and Atlanta is part of that job. This world is still totter-ing on the edge of a full-scale nuclear exchange. We are all playing a game of brinkmanship now that we have been pushed off the table as the one re-maining superpower we thought we were back in the '90s. It's as bad as—if not worse than—when you were a young lieutenant back in Germany watching the Fulda Gap against the Soviets. There's good intelligence the Chinese have moved surface-to-surface nukes onto our mainland, aimed at here. That is a seven- to ten-minute launch-to-strike time at most."

"And our boomers out in the Pacific?"

"I can't discuss that with you."

"Have we abandoned even that?" John snapped.

"Our only hope of survival is to present a unified nation and do it damn quick. Atlanta is but one part of that equation. To the rest of the world, we look like we're in tatters. That whole damn experiment with the Army of National Recovery made us look even more the fools. Bluemont has deci-ded to go to whatever extreme necessary to get the job done and finish it before spring."

Bob fell silent, John returning his gaze to his old friend. He could sense the strain he was under. Something within him felt it was time to finally ask yet again.

"You sent Quentin to try to reach out to me first, and you did so behind Bluemont's back, didn't you?"

"Kind of."

"What do you mean, 'kind of'?"

"I talked with him about it. Originally, he was to be airlifted down to you as an envoy. I was thinking of dropping him off inside your territory, do it covertly."

"But then?"

"He deserted and did it on his own."

"What?"

"You heard me correctly, and that stays here. Okay?"

John nodded.

"Why desert?"

"He picked up on some rumors. Told me the night before he lit out that he could no longer abide by those orders, and the following morning he was gone, along with three others in a Humvee."

"What rumors?"

Bob hesitated for a moment and then relented, speaking softly.

"You asked me about this at the airport the other day and I didn't feel comfortable telling you then, but now? I think it is time you realized what I am trying to contain, what all of us are facing. There's some talk. Can't say how, where, or from whom. Just talk that if need be, Bluemont will trigger an EMP."

"What the hell are you talking about?" John cried. "Against who?"

"Southern United States." Bob shook his head and then stood up. "You repeat that to anyone and I'll have you gagged and hauled out of here today, whether it turns into a fight or not. I've said too much already." There was a sharp edge of warning—or was it panic in his voice for having said more than he should have?

"You say a word anywhere, and by God, I will ship you to Bluemont, let this place rebel, and then you know the results. Do you read me, Colonel Matherson?"

During his entire career under this general, John could only recall several real dressing-downs, though he had witnessed it delivered to many another. Bottom line, it was why some stayed majors and colonels and only a select few had generals' stars pinned to their uniforms. There at times had to be this ruthless edge no matter whom it was being delivered against.

"John, I'm trying to beat the clock. I have orders to neutralize Atlanta and bring it back into the fold within the month. It's to demonstrate to, China and the rest of the world that we are firmly in control of our territory east of the Mississippi. I need Asheville along with Greenville-Spartanburg as secured staging areas for the push south. I need that now."

"Whoever gave you that order is insane. Atlanta is now the lower circle of hell, Bob. You could sink an entire army corps into that place and it will be another Fallujah."

"Don't you think I know that?" Bob replied wearily. "Asheville is part of a far bigger game. And if it doesn't work, Bluemont is willing to do whatever they deem necessary to get their point across to everyone here. It's seen as a message as well to China that we will use any means possible to pacify remaining resistance within our territory and in turn a clear warning as well to not press us any further."

Whether what he said was planned and intentional or not, he must have inwardly realized he had spilled a highly classified secret.

"All right, sir, it stays in this room. You have my oath on that. But please go on."

Bob sat down and looked at the half-empty mug of herbal tea. "You sure you got nothing else here?" he finally asked, motioning to his empty cup.

John nodded, stood up, and without another word went out into the hallway. Several of his students were still hanging about, and he asked them to fetch Kevin Malady. His campus commander of their battalion was before him less than a minute later. John whispered a request, and Kevin grinned and ran off.

It was, of course, a dry campus, but even under the strictest of rules at any such place, there were always some ready to bend those rules, and one had to be foolish not to recognize that fact. Kevin was back in less than five minutes, handing over a small hiking backpack. John took it back into the office, closed the door, and produced a quart bottle of moonshine, half-full, and just handed it to Bob, who took a long swig and passed it to John, who took a drink as well before putting the lid back on and passing it back.

"One of the traditional products of these mountains," John said, coughing a bit since it certainly was strong stuff and burned on the way down.

Bob took another long sip and nodded his thanks. "Good stuff," he gasped, and he motioned to push the jar back.

"Keep it."

"Thanks, I will. Not Dalwhinnie fifteen-year-old scotch, but one lives with what they can these days." He took another sip and sighed. "All right, John, do I have your sworn oath that what I have said will stay in this room? Not even to your wife, who I hope to soon meet?"

John finally nodded.

"Just rumor, mind you. Some chatter my own people picked up off encrypted sat comms. Speculation that to bring down Atlanta and any other pockets of resistance in the South, an EMP will be burst above the Gulf of Mexico coast to knock off-line any technology they've managed to bring back up over the last two years, and then we move in the following day. Line-of-sight effect, as you know. It would include here."

"In the name of God, why?" As John asked, he thought of just how delicate the infrastructure his community had managed to bring back online over the last year and a half was. Even a low-yield burst would destroy everything they had managed to re-create.

"Knocks whatever is left down and takes them off balance. You aren't the only one who is getting the genie back out of the bottle when it comes to electricity, getting some cars and trucks running again." Bob now fixed him with a sharp gaze. "Or the Black Hawk here and there that has gone missing and could raise hell with our side."

"Isn't this a sledgehammer to blot out a fly? What threat do we present?"

"It would be a message to the rest of the world as well even if Bluemont says someone else did it—that we are ready to do it to the entire rest of the world and will not hesitate to do so. We've been pushed back as far as we will accept and no further. It is a game far beyond you and me, but it will bring down everything you and your friends have created here."

John felt sick inside just thinking of how each small step back from the darkness had so lifted the morale of all. To suddenly have that go entirely down again would be a final deathblow. If it was delivered, whoever was left afterward might as well crawl into their graves and pull the sod over themselves and die.

He could not reply and just sat there in silence. If at this moment Bob had produced a cigarette, he would have taken it, his pledge to Jennifer gone, for indeed there would be nothing left, no hope left, no dream of rebuilding if this was indeed the level that Bluemont was willing to go to.

"It is why I had to bring you in now, John," Bob said softly, taking another sip from the mason jar. "I'm trying to forestall it, to make a stab at Atlanta first and hope for the best. If that fails, at least I can argue that this region is back in the fold, and if an EMP is detonated to do it farther out to sea or at lower altitude so you are not impacted."

"Bob, just sit back for another year or two, let those barbarians left in Atlanta literally eat each other, then you might be able to move in. But try it now? EMP first or not, you damn well had better have a lot more troops than General Sherman did; otherwise, it will be a bloody disaster."

Bob nodded sadly and then made a show of looking at his old-style wrist-watch. "It's been nearly an hour. I don't want my young officer up there to get anxious and come looking for me. It might trigger something."

"The mood my people are in, if he comes down here like gangbusters, yes, it will go bad."

"Then I'd better get back." Bob stood up, John rising as well.

"What next?" John asked.

"I'm setting up forward headquarters in Asheville. Can you assure me there won't be a fight?"

"Asheville? Not sure. Chances are there won't be resistance; the fight was already punched out of that town long ago. I think, though, your safer bet would be to laager in at the airport, far enough out of town so you don't have to deal with some nutjob sniper, but close enough that everyone will know you're there. If that convoy that's coming up from Greenville, South Carolina, gets through the Green River Gorge safely, the airport would be a good place to rendezvous."

"I'll need the airfield there," Bob replied, "so your suggestion is a good one. We have a couple of C-130s with us in Roanoke that have already touched down on the interstate, but getting the runway at Asheville back up would be preferred. And the navy can fly some things in as well once we get that runway your people chewed up repaired."

Bob looked down at the mason jar. John gestured for him to take it, and Bob slipped it into the pocket of his parka. "This is the way it is, John. You stay on, function as before, and if you follow my rules, I'll report to Bluemont the situation is under control here and you are under house arrest for now—or better yet, we can't find you—and that this area has achieved level-one stability. You've got to stay low. For heaven's sake, don't screw it up by letting Bluemont catch wind that you are out and about. If you do that, I want you to continue to function as before but behind the scenes, and for God's sake, don't go broadcasting that around, so stay off the radios."

"And in return?"

"I report this area is secure."

"And the EMP?"

"Let me cross that bridge a month from now. Maybe I can talk them down from it. You're right; I know as well as you that trying to take Atlanta now would turn into another Fallujah or even a Stalingrad. I need your help with this. Can I count on you?"

John finally nodded in reply, for after all, there was no other alternative short of seeing another war fought by his community.

"You got a landline down to the airport?" Bob asked.

"We have a line to Hendersonville."

"Is the wire near the airport?"

"It runs along the interstate."

"Get one of your people down there today, have them point it out, and I'll have my people link it in. I want that done by tonight. That will then be how we stay in touch."

John nodded. "EMP. If those bastards are going to do it, what do you do?"

"Don't ask me that yet," Bob said wearily.

"Will you give me warning?"

Bob stared at him and finally nodded. "If you see me pulling out of here with everything we can haul, pulling back to Roanoke to be out of line of sight, you'll know it's coming. That's the best I can do for you."

"And you would let them do that?"

Bob looked back at the painting of General Washington kneeling in the snow of Valley Forge. "Ask me again in a month."

"All right, then," he said, finally adding, "sir."

"Thank you, John. I'm sorry it had to be this way. Please keep your people reined in; let's make this as easy as possible. From here, I'll go straight to

Asheville to make sure things are settled down there. Once that phone line is in, I'll be in daily touch."

Zipping up his parka, Bob opened the door, John following him out. Bob paused, looked through the open door into the adjoining chapel, and stepped in. Students up on a high scaffolding, working to repair the damaged ceiling, were hammering away, disturbing the silence. Bob stopped at the back of the chapel, taking it in, John coming to his side.

"I remember this place well, from when Mary was laid to rest."

"It's the heart of this campus," John said. "Lot of days, even before the Day, this is where I'd come to pray by myself, to sort things out. A lot of hearts and memories are tied to this place."

Bob nodded and then simply knelt down, lowered his head, whispered a prayer, made the sign of the cross, and stood back up.

"Pray for me, John."

And at that moment, John again fully trusted his old commander. Coming to attention, John saluted him, Bob returning the salute and then embracing him. The chapel was now entirely silent; the students who had been working had stopped and were watching them. Though not planned at all, John knew that word of the prayer, salute, and embrace would spread from one end of the campus to the other within minutes, and for the moment, it had defused the potential of a deadly confrontation.

He walked his friend to the outside door where Maury was patiently waiting. Bob offered him a friendly smile, jokingly asking if he could drive the jeep on the way back, and his two friends drove off, Bob at the wheel, tires spinning in the snow.

As he drove off, John made a mental note to immediately call Ernie and tell him to check the camouflage for the antenna array on the roof of his house. No sense in Bob getting wind that they were already working on their own to try to listen in to Bluemont. And with what Bob had just told him, now there was true urgency to that task.

John returned to the chapel alone, sat in the rear pew, lowered his head, and, like Washington at Valley Forge, began to pray while outside snow again began to fall.

CHAPTER ELEVEN

Makala was fast asleep out on the sunporch while John dozed in his office, unable to sleep the night after the conversation with Bob and all that had transpired in the previous twenty-four hours, when the phone on his desk rang, startling him awake.

He picked it up before it rang a second time.

"Sir, are you safe?"

It was Kevin Malady.

"Sure, why?"

"Something is up."

John looked at the old windup clock on his desk; it was nearly two in the morning.

"What?"

"Get your wife, get out of that house now, into the woods, and lie low."

"What's going on?" John snapped.

"Get out now. We heard a chopper come in, sound muffled, a special-ops type machine. One of my people on watch with night vision just saw eight people get off at the ball field, and they're heading your way. I'm getting a team together; they'll be down there in five minutes. Sir, get out of your house now!"

John put the receiver down, raced into the sunroom, and grabbed Makala by the shoulders, shaking her awake.

"John, what is it?"

He put his hand over her mouth. "We gotta move now," he whispered, and even as he did so, he thought he saw a glimpse of movement out on the moonlit road. "Now!" he snapped, dragging her out of the bed.

A laser dot suddenly flashed on to the wall just as she stood up, and he shoved her down to the floor. One of the windowpanes shattered, three bullets impacting the wall behind where she had been standing but a few seconds before.

"Down, stay down!"

He pulled her to the doorway into the hallway, pushing the door shut behind them.

Outside? Whoever it was would expect that. Upstairs was the only alternative. Upstairs and hope for enough time for Malady to bring help.

"The stairs quick," he hissed.

As she started up, he diverted to his office, crouching low, grabbed the Glock off his desk, and turned to follow her.

The explosion of a flashbang in the sunroom blew the door he had just closed open, knocking him off his feet. Stunned, he managed to regain his footing, following her up the stairs to the second floor.

Which way to go? He had thought out so many different scenarios across the last two years, but never this one, to be caught by surprise in their own home in the middle of the night. Jen's old bedroom? No, too obvious; whoever it was would hit there first. Even as he hesitated, another flashbang blew downstairs.

The attic. It was a dead end, but it might buy a few more minutes of time.

He shoved Makala to the attic steps, following up behind her, moving backward, pistol raised, ready to shoot if closely followed. A third flashbang and then the sound of more glass breaking, several short bursts of gunfire.

Behind him, Makala fumbled with the attic door, finally shoving it open. He came up behind her and tried to close the creaking door as quietly as possible.

Makala started to speak, and he put his hand over her mouth. The house-length attic was dimly illuminated by moonlight streaming in through one window. He inwardly thanked God that Jen had been a pack rat, the attic filled with old trunks, racks of clothes from fifty years ago, long-forgotten family heirlooms. He scanned it, seeing where several old steamer trunks were set against a far wall and motioning for Makala to get behind them. She hesitated, and he shoved her into the dark, musty corner and pushed her down to the floor.

She was beginning to sob, and again he had his hand over her mouth and pressed his lips to her ear.

"Are you hurt?"

"What is happening?"

"Just stay quiet. Help's coming."

He could see her pale, frightened features in the moonlight. She was protectively clutching her stomach.

"Baby okay?" he whispered

"I think so."

"Matherson!" The voice echoed up from down below. "Only you we want. Come out, hands up, and your wife is okay. It's just you we want to go with us."

He looked at her, the offer just a fleeting temptation of a few seconds. They had fired without any warning. Whoever it was undoubtedly had night-vision gear and could have seen she would have been hit. This was not for a capture; this was a raid to kill both of them.

And if this was from Bob Scales, and he survived, he would find a way to ensure his former friend roasted in hell.

"Thirty seconds, Matherson. Just come down with your hands up."

He knew better than to reply. From down below, he could hear that someone was creeping up the stairs to the second floor. Even before the thirty seconds were up, another flashbang went off, just beneath them, the concussion startling him and Makala, who was unable to suppress a gasp of fear.

He put his hand on her shoulder. She was shaking like a leaf. Seconds later, a long burst of gunfire swept the master bedroom below.

Silence for a moment, and then footsteps creaking along the old wooden floor corridor below.

Three more flashbangs popped off, detonating in the guest rooms and bathroom, dust from the low ceiling of the attic swirling down from the concussions. More gunfire as they swept each room.

"Matherson, you're cornered. Save your wife and just come down; we know you're up there."

Makala reached out to clutch his side, an affirmation that he was not to surrender.

"It's going to hit hard. Be ready; keep your mouth open," he whispered.

He heard the door up to the attic creak open, and something arced up into the attic. He crouched down behind the steamer trunk, opening his mouth wide to lessen the impact of the explosion on his eardrums. It detonated with a blinding flash, the shock wave hitting so hard that Makala gasped.

He knew he had but an instant to be ready and was back up, Glock firmly held in both hands, resting on the top of the steamer trunk. Gunfire snapped up from the stairwell. And then the first assailant appeared.

John knew the target would be small, face only, helmet and body armor covering the rest. The man rose halfway up, laser sight flashing along the opposite wall, and then turned toward where John waited thirty feet away.

The laser light sparkled in John's eyes, nearly blinding him, and he squeezed off shot after shot. One of the 9mm rounds must have hit squarely; the killing shot he anticipated in return was a long burst going up over his head and then stitching across the ceiling as the man he hit tumbled back down the stairs.

He could hear muffled cursing, and then a fusillade of fire erupted, smashing up through the floor of the attic, and started to stitch toward them.

"Curl up on top of the trunk!" John yelled, pushing Makala up as he remained crouched, weapon trained on the stairwell.

How many shots did I fire? he wondered. *How many left?*

And then he heard it: an explosion of gunfire outside his home. Shouts, curses, more shots, several grenades going off.

He waited for whatever came next. A grenade came up from out of the stairwell. He pulled Makala back down from the trunk and held her tightly. This time, it was fragmentation showering the room with a deadly spray that, if not for the packed trunks, would have surely killed them.

There was more gunfire from outside, several long, sustained bursts, and he waited, the seconds dragging into minutes. Makala was by his side, curled up, sobbing. He did not dare to look over at her for even a second, all attention focused on the staircase. To add to it all, he could smell something burning, and smoke was beginning to curl up from the stairwell.

"John! John and Makala!"

The voice was high-pitched, frantic.

"It's Grace Freeman! For God's sake, please answer. Please!"

Long-ago training. They take one of yours, put a gun to their head, and get them to cry out. He didn't budge.

"The house is burning. My God, sir, where are you?"

He could hear someone running in the corridor downstairs, continuing to shout his name.

There was a pause, and then the stairs up to the attic began to creak. He was still holding the Glock, a weapon where the safety was built into the trigger. Just apply a few extra pounds of pressure, and it would go off again.

A head appeared, hard to distinguish due to the ever-increasing smoke.

"John and Makala?"

"Grace, don't move," John hissed, still not sure if she was being pushed forward by an attacker, but he had to take the risk of replying.

She looked his way.

"Are you safe?" he whispered.

"Damn it, sir, this house is burning. We gotta move." She cried. "We got the place secured. Come on! Come on!"

John reached down, pulling Makala to her feet, Grace coming around to Makala's side to help.

It was no time for questions as they headed for the stairs. John paused for a second, looking around. He saw an old shirt dangling from a clothes rack, tore it off, and covered Makala's face, shouting for her to take a deep breath and then hold it.

With Grace leading the way, they fumbled down the stairs. John guided Makala around the body sprawled out by the attic door. A round had caught his would-be assassin just below the nose, and he thought to actually pause to see if the man was still alive. Smoke was pouring out of the master bedroom. Makala was clutching his hand tightly and dragging him along, guided by Grace. With a cold sense that even if the man was alive he would be dead anyhow in a few minutes from that wound, he left the body behind.

Coughing, gasping for air, Grace led them down the steps to the ground floor. The sunroom was engulfed in flames. Grace staggered from the blast of heat, and John, coming behind the two, shoved them forward and out the back door.

"I got them out!" Grace cried, and then she leaned over, retching and gasping for air.

John could hear shouts, and through watery eyes he saw Malady come up, weapon raised. He shoved John to the ground, another of his students shielding Makala with her body and more gently easing her down to the ground.

"Situation?" John gasped, looking up at Kevin.

"At least four got away!" Kevin shouted.

"One dead up on the second floor," Grace gasped.

"At least three, then."

Someone had peeled off a parka and was putting it over Makala, crouching down to help shield her. John started to come to his feet, but Kevin snapped for him to stay down; whoever was after him was still out there.

He looked back at the house. An upstairs window burst, flames licking out. All of it was going up. Whoever they were, they must have dropped thermite grenades to set it afire like that. Jen's house was going . . . all of it going.

And then the thought hit. Someone was draping a parka over him. He pulled it off, held it to cover his face, and ran back into the burning house, tearing free from someone who was trying to hold him back.

"John!" It was Kevin coming up behind him, trying to pull him back.

"No!" John tore himself free and staggered into the sunroom. Nearly blinded by the smoke, he fumbled about on the windowsill, found what he was looking for, and crouching low, parka held up against the heat, he staggered back out. Once outside, he collapsed into Kevin's arms.

He clutched Rabs tight to his chest. He would never let Rabs burn like that.

Sitting in President Hunt's office, he gratefully took another sip of moonshine and looked over at Makala, who was resting on the sofa, two of the girls she had trained as nurses hovering over her. One of the girls looked back at John and smiled reassuringly.

"She's okay, and so is the baby."

He could barely see her smoke-smudged face looking toward him in the blacked-out room, curtains drawn.

She started to cough and then managed to clear her throat. "Moonshine is the last thing you should be drinking now, John Matherson," she whispered, her voice husky.

"I know."

"And damn it, if not for the baby, I'd join you," came her reply.

A burst of gunfire echoed in the distance, and he could tell the difference of who was firing. Sustained bursts versus three-shot replies. Whoever they had cornered next to the cafeteria was firing back like a professional, conserving ammunition.

John stood up and went to the window to at least slip the curtain open to see what was happening, but Kevin reached out and blocked him.

"Their goal, sir, was to kill both of you. You're staying here until this is over."

"Those are"—he hesitated for a moment—"my kids out there doing my job."

"They're your troops doing the job you trained them for"—Kevin paused to add emphasis to his next word—"sir."

There was a sudden explosion of gunfire—long, sustained bursts—and regardless of Kevin's orders, he was not going to cower here, not after what they had done, and he carefully parted the curtain a few inches to look.

He could see the tracers snapping into the side of the cafeteria and what had once been a peaceful outdoor patio. Several dozen students had the area surrounded and were unleashing a fury of fire. One of their targets got up, trying to pull up someone else. John had ordered that if possible take them alive, but the rage unleashed by the assassination attempt could not be contained. In spite of body armor and helmet, their target's legs and face were nevertheless exposed, and he was finally dropped. The other one, obviously wounded, tried to get up, and another explosion of fire took him down.

More shots continued to pour in until finally the cries went up to cease fire.

John started for the door, but Kevin blocked his way and made it clear by the way he stood in front of John that if need be, he'd physically take him down, something that Kevin was more than capable of doing.

"Let someone report in," Kevin snapped.

"For once, John," Makala whispered, "listen to someone else. He's right."

John simply nodded and then went over to his wife's side, sat down on the floor by her side, and took her hand. "Are you really okay?"

"Just some smoke, John, that's all."

"The baby?" he asked nervously.

She tried to laugh but started to cough again. "Scared the shit out of the little bugger; he's been squirming like a kickboxer ever since it started." She paused. "Our baby is okay."

She leaned over and wrapped her arms around his neck. "Why would your friend do this to us?" she asked. "You said he was honorable."

"I don't know," John whispered. "I just don't know."

"Matherson." It was a whisper from the corridor, followed by a knock. He recognized Reverend Black's voice and started for the door, but Kevin stepped in front of him and opened it, shielding John.

It was indeed Reverend Black, and Kevin let him in.

Black went past John, knelt down by Makala's side, and, taking her hand, whispered a brief prayer of thanks and then looked back at John.

"I got him on the phone, John. Pick up the line here."

John nodded. "Did you tell him what happened?"

"I just did as you said—told him it was an emergency and to hold on the line."

"John, don't talk to him," Makala said. "It will tell him you're alive, and they'll come back."

His rage was nearly out of control. Hit him, that was part of it all, but to include his pregnant wife? For that matter, Elizabeth, her baby, and husband could have been in the house as well. The attack was not to just capture him; it was to kill him and anyone with him. He looked at the two girls tending to Makala and then at Kevin.

"As soon as you think it's safe to move her, take her somewhere secure, and don't tell me where it is until this is over with."

She started to protest, but a sharp glance from him stilled her voice.

"It is about you and the baby now, not me," John said sharply, and she did not reply.

He walked back to the desk and picked up the phone. "General Scales, are you on the line?"

"Yeah, John, what the hell is going on?"

"Perhaps you should tell me exactly what the hell is going on, you son of a bitch."

"John?"

"Come after me, fine. That's part of this game you're playing, and I'll accept that. But my pregnant wife?"

"John, in the name of God, what is going on up there?"

"You tell me," John said again, uttering each word slowly and with unrestrained anger.

There was a long pause.

"John, whatever it is, tell me exactly what is going on."

"Why don't you come up here yourself and explain it"—he paused—"sir?"

Another long pause.

"John, just tell me, will you?"

"Fine then, play innocent. I trusted you, and less than an hour ago, eight of your storm troopers hit my house. If my people had not spotted them first and reacted, they would have killed my wife and the baby within her, and then me. That's what happened up here."

"God in heaven," Bob whispered.

"Yeah, God in heaven, Bob."

"Where are you, John?"

"Do you honestly think I'd tell you? Just know that wherever Makala is now, she is safely stashed away."

There was another tap at the door, the person out in the corridor identifying herself as Grace. Yet again, it was Kevin who answered. He cracked the door open and, recognizing her, let her in.

"Don't hang up, General Scales. I'll be back."

He put the phone down and looked at Grace. Her once beautiful hair was badly scorched, the right side of her face blistered. She tried to talk and began to cough.

"Young lady." It was Makala. "You get that burn treated right now."

"In a moment," Grace replied, and then she looked back at John. "Seven accounted for, sir. We think one slipped through and is heading up toward Lookout Mountain. We've got a full platoon tracking him. He's wounded and trailing blood."

"Our side?" John asked, suddenly nervous. "How bad?"

She hesitated and then looked over at Kevin, who nodded.

"Five dead, twelve wounded at last count."

"Who?"

She began to rattle off names, and John sagged with a sudden weariness. One was the girl he had seen running with her lover in the snow just days ago, another Jim Southerland, a beloved art teacher who had decided to live on campus and wasn't even part of the militia but apparently had turned out with the others.

"Let the last bastard go," John said, shaking his head. "These people were well trained. I don't want anyone else hurt in this affair. You got that, Grace?"

"Yes, sir."

But as she turned, John saw the exchange of glances with Kevin. They were out for vengeance and knew as well that as long as one of the hit squad was still alive, their beloved leader and his wife were not safe—at least for the moment.

Grace closed the door, and John picked the phone back up. "Bob, you still there?"

"John, I've ordered a chopper to start running up. I'll be there in fifteen minutes."

"General, you come up on a chopper, and I promise you, my people will shoot it down. They're in a killing mood. Five of my students and friends died rescuing my wife and me."

The enormity of their sacrifice hit him. It was amazing it was not five, even ten times that number given whom they went against.

"I got at least another dozen wounded. You fly up here, and you and your crew will be added to the list. Now, if you want to bomb the place, just go ahead, but this entire campus will be evacuated before you get here."

"John, please listen to me. I don't know what the hell you are talking about. Are you hearing me?"

"Yes, I'm listening."

"Whoever it was, it was not me or anyone in my command."

John sat down. Bob's words were what he wanted to believe.

"Can we do this, John?"

"What, damn it?"

"I'll come up alone, in a Humvee with just a driver—at dawn, so there is no confusion in the dark. Your people can stop and search me at the security gate you have out on the interstate."

"Until you prove yourself different, Bob, it's on your head. Okay, come on up.

"Stop at the security gate, but if my people see one additional vehicle or hear anything overhead, all bets are off."

"All right. I'll be at the gate come dawn."

"And what's to prevent you from having a few F-18s up at thirty thousand feet?"

"I have no reply other than my word." He paused. "And memory of your Jennifer to guide me now."

With that, John looked down at flame-scorched Rabs, whom he had placed on the desk.

"Dawn, then."

General Bob Scales stood with arms extended straight out as two of the security guards at the Exit 59 barrier roughly patted him down and then none too gently pushed him forward.

Contrary to Kevin's, Reverend Black's, and his own wife's appeal, he had decided to meet Bob at the gate. If anything was to go down, he'd rather it be here than down on the campus. He had forsaken Maury's far too easily identifiable jeep and instead had Black drive him to the meeting in his old Volvo. Lee had shown up and insisted he go along as well. Kevin had already gone ahead with several carloads of the militia and a pickup truck with a "package" in the back for Bob.

The guards pointed to where John waited, standing under the roof of a makeshift shelter that had been erected to protect the interstate security team. Bob approached slowly, keeping his hands out and clearly visible.

There were no salutes, no friendly exchanges other than a warning from Kevin that if he made the wrong move, it would be the last gesture he would ever make.

"How is Makala?" Bob finally asked. "Are she and your baby okay?"

"They're fine," was all John could say, and then he looked past Bob to Kevin. "Go ahead and show him what we brought along."

Kevin put his hand on Bob's shoulder and guided him to the back of the pickup truck and pulled off the tarp covering the rear of the vehicle. Bob stared for a moment and then looked back to John.

"Upon all that I hold sacred, John, I swear to you they are not mine. I've never seen them before."

"We stripped them of their gear," Kevin said coldly. "High-quality stuff, regular army. The one Colonel Matherson shot in the face was roasted to a crisp when his house burned. His grave is the rubble that's still smoldering. We're still hunting the last one, but he won't last long; he's trailing blood. You want them back, sir?"

Bob looked over sharply at Kevin and shook his head. "Bury the bastards wherever you want. They're not mine, and that's final."

"Kevin, take them to where we dumped the bodies of the dead Posse. That's all they deserve."

As he spoke, he watched Bob closely. Both he and Bob had been taught a code of honor when it came to their own dead. Not even a body was ever to be left behind, no matter what the cost of retrieving it.

Bob did not flinch or show the slightest emotion at John's cold words of scorn.

"John, if there is nothing else, do I have your permission to leave?"

John could only nod.

Bob turned and started to walk back to his Humvee.

"General Scales?"

Bob turned and looked back.

"If not you, then who?"

Bob stopped and then slowly walked up to John, stopping almost within touching distance. Kevin was on one side of him, Lee on the other, and both were tense, ready to spring.

"Look me in the eyes, John."

John did as requested.

"Upon the memory of Jennifer's grave and wherever my Linda now rests, I swear to you I did not do this."

"Then who?"

"I gave you a warning. There are more than a few who want you dead, John Matherson. I hate to think it is who I now suspect, but maybe it is."

John took that in but did not reply.

"And if so, and if they tried for you in your home, they know more about you than even I do. It means you have someone in your community who has given information out." He paused as if suddenly realizing something. "And it means they know that you and I have talked."

He stood silent as if evaluating that thought.

"God be with you, John," Bob whispered, "and maybe I should ask that He be with me as well in the days ahead."

John did not reply as Bob turned again and walked back to his Humvee, which backed up, turned, and then sped off.

"I don't believe him," Lee finally said, and Kevin nodded.

John kept his thoughts to himself and then finally looked at Kevin. "Dump their bodies like I said," John finally said. "And, Kevin, keep a twenty-four-hour watch on Makala, and I am not to know where she is."

"Already taken care of, sir."

"Lee, mind if I bunk with you?"

His friend smiled and nodded.

CHAPTER TWELVE

"Ernie, I need something, and I need it now," John announced while still standing out in the snow in Ernie's driveway.

For once, Ernie was out the door to greet him and actually grabbed John by the hand. "You okay? We heard about what happened last night. Makala, is she okay?"

"Yes, just fine. We're fine."

"Those sons of bitches."

Lee had thrown a fit when, at midday, John had roused from his exhausted sleep and announced he was going to visit Ernie.

That had triggered an explosion of anxiety, with Kevin appearing with a pickup truck–load of their troops, fully armed, several of them wearing the captured gear taken from the dead raiders.

The last attacker had been found dead, shortly after dawn, having apparently bled out from his wounds, and after being stripped, he had been dumped with the others.

At least for the moment, it meant to John that he was safe and would not let what happened stop him from his routine, and that included using Maury's jeep when it was snowing, so he ordered Kevin and the others to relax and get some sleep. An order reluctantly obeyed.

"Mind if we come in?" John asked, nodding over to Maury, who was standing beside his jeep and throwing blankets over the seats to keep the snow that was falling from covering them.

"Why don't you have a top for that damn thing?" Ernie asked, shouting to Maury.

"Couldn't find one that was authentic to the period."

"Oh, great, historical accuracy before comfort."

Maury did not reply. John knew it was painful enough for his friend to redo the paint job back early in the spring to cover over the white star on the front hood and paint the rest in a speckled camouflage pattern, which of course Maury had to match up with the Normandy 1944 look, so it was less easy to spot them from the air.

Maury just glared at Ernie and did not reply.

"All right, you two, come on inside." He motioned to the door into the garage. Slamming it behind the two, Ernie turned, arms folded defensively.

"Are you going to shut me down?" he asked sharply.

"Hell no."

"Well, I heard you are taking orders from our new potentate down at the Asheville airport and assumed you were sent here to pull the plug after he failed at his attempt at killing you."

"Damn it, Ernie, did anyone ever discuss diplomatic conversation skills with you?"

"Nope. And if anyone ever does, I'll tell them to go to hell."

John couldn't help but smile. "Yeah, okay. Everyone knows. I surrendered without a fight. You got an alternative short of a bloodbath for our side? As to damn near getting killed, just leave that be for now."

"How many troops does he have with him?"

"He's got at least half a dozen Black Hawks, maybe as many Apaches, a couple of C-130s, and from what our lookouts in Hendersonville told us, at least half a dozen Bradleys and a dozen truckloads of supplies and additional troops up from Greenville. And you suggest we fight that?"

"Go up into the hills and wait him out. He'd be facing half a thousand or more very pissed-off, well-armed folks."

"Ernie, you have been a burr under my hide from day one, but this tops it. I'm supposed to go back to those kids at the college and tell them to suit up and head out into the woods in this weather?" He snapped out the last words and pointed back outside where a lightly falling snow was being whipped along by twenty-mile-per-hour winds. "Half of them would freeze to death within a couple of days out there with no fires to keep warm. Light a fire, you got an Apache with infrared seeking on top of you."

"He's right, Ernie."

The two turned to see Linda slowly coming down the basement stairs. "So stop needling him. You know as well as I do there was no chance to fight back, so let it be."

"I was just suggesting an alternative, Linda."

"Fine. You suit up, take a rifle, go sit out on the ridge for a few hours, and then come back and tell us if we should fight or not."

"I'm seventy-five; those kids trained to fight are in their twenties."

She ignored him and walked up to John and Maury, holding out two mugs of coffee.

"We don't have much of that stuff left," Ernie muttered.

"They need it more than we do warm inside here," she snapped and then turned her attention to John. "Really, are you and Makala all right?"

"Just fine, Linda. It was bad, though, for those at the college. Five dead, a dozen wounded, and I doubt if a couple of those will make it."

He tried to say those words without becoming emotional again. They had died saving his family and him. All of this was becoming too much to bear. He knew if he broke in front of Linda, she would go all to pieces as well. He shook it off and just offered a weary smile of resignation.

"My only other question, John: Do they know about our operation here?"

John shook his head. "So far, I don't think so; that's why I called and said to double-check the camouflage on your satellite dishes."

"You can't see them from the road or from up above. I had the kids make some netting out of bedsheets to blend in with the snow. I think we're safe."

"Good. That's the way I want to keep it."

He could see that Ernie was still glowering and felt it necessary to smooth the waters. "Ernie, I'll admit now, it was a smart move to shift your operation down here. The last thing I want is another war. You saw what a couple of Apaches under Fredericks did to us in the spring. Their only tactical mistake was basing out of the mall. If they had been based at the airport with proper security, Fredericks would have won. We don't have Stinger ground-to-air missiles, and any Hollywood hokum about taking one of those birds out with an old-fashioned RPG is absurd. General Scales held the trump card, made sure we saw it in his opening move and won."

"He played it well," Maury interjected. "There was nothing we could do in response, at least for now."

"But—" Ernie started, and Linda cut him off.

"But what? A hundred, two hundred kids dead?"

"They're not kids, Linda."

"We've got grandchildren that will be in the militia units in another year, Ernie. To me, they're kids."

John caught her eye and nodded.

Strange, when his second lieutenant's bars were pinned on him, he was twenty-one and felt he was indeed a man. His father had been flying combat missions at twenty-three, his grandfather at twenty-one. Of course he felt like a man then. But now, when there was an entire generational difference between him and those who were actually the ones who would carry the fight, it was all so different.

He recalled the old photo books of soldiers from World War II. The haunting image of a shell-shocked Marine covered in filth and blood, staring at the cameraman with vacant eyes. One had to look deep into that photograph to conjure out the realization that the frightfully aged Marine most likely was, in fact, not more than eighteen or nineteen years old.

Those whom he called kids, when looking up at the Apaches circling over the campus, were again ready to fight, but in their eyes they had as well that same haunting gaze. They were veterans of two major battles, and they knew the price and the loss even when they won. They were ready to fight even though with the pragmatic realism that only a veteran could gain, they knew without doubt the fight would most likely be futile.

Memory of his walk up to the campus of several weeks back came to him, the young amorous couple playing in the park. That should be their world, holding with it some hope of a future, not another fight to the death. And now one of them was indeed dead. The thought of that stabbed deep, but he had to push it aside for now.

Damn all that created this world for them, he thought bitterly as he nodded, still looking at Linda.

"You're right, Linda; they're still kids, or at least should be kids. I'm not going to spend their lives in some final gesture of defiance."

And even as he spoke, the nightmare of what Bob said might happen—that Bluemont might unleash another EMP—hung over him. After what had happened just hours ago, he was no longer sure of Bob, though as emotions settled, he did want to believe him. Perhaps now the answer to it all was to find out, on their own, what the truth really was regarding Bluemont—and what was happening in this house might be the key.

He suddenly realized that he had been standing in quiet contemplation for several minutes while Ernie and Linda had launched into what he realized was something of a standard method of communication between the two. Ironic as he focused attention back on them. They obviously loved each other dearly, and yet they sure had a strange way of expressing it.

"All right, you two, let's chill it." It was Maury who finally interrupted the argument.

The two looked at him, and Linda smiled. "Thank you, Maury. Point taken. At least by me."

Ernie said nothing and finally turned back to John. "Let's answer the first question, then. If you are not shutting us down, why are you here?"

"I just want an update and to pass along a few suggestions. I want your team to lie low, but keep the kids working here on task 24-7."

"So you are not this General Scales's lackey?" Ernie quipped.

"You know, Ernie, someday when all of this is over, you and I are going to have a real serious discussion."

"Just remember, Matherson, I saved your life. Fredericks was ready to shoot you in the back."

"Yeah, right."

Ernie smiled. "Well, some are whispering I just simply saved you from the dilemma of what to do with that son of a bitch by just shooting him and getting it over with. Either way, I did you a favor."

John finally relented and nodded.

"This basement is freezing," Linda announced. "Let's go up to the Skunk Works."

"The what?" John asked.

"That's what we're calling it now. The kids like the name, especially after

I told them about a little side contract work we once did at the real Skunk Works Lockheed had."

John smiled at that. Lockheed had been a prime contractor for highly specialized spy planes back during the Cold War, their secret R&D lab dubbed the "Skunk Works." It fit for what they were doing now.

Linda led the way up to the main floor of their home, again cheerily warm thanks to the fireplace and the wood-fueled kitchen stove. She led them up to the second floor, moving a bit slowly, bracing her knee as she climbed the stairs, muttering that she wished she'd had the replacement knee surgery done before everything had hit the fan.

As they reached the top of the stairs, John looked up and grinned at the hand-drawn sign hanging in front of them: "Linda and Ernie's Skunk Works." Whoever had drawn it was indeed creative. Linda and Ernie caricatured as cartoon skunks, arguing with each other, with an array of $#*#%& erupting from the skunk image of Ernie's mouth, even as they were holding hands.

The entire room was now cluttered with electronic equipment, most of it retro from the '80s and '90s but some of it looking fairly recent. The work crew had grown from the five he had seen last time to nine, hunched over screens, empty plates and cups strewn on the tables and floor. That alone made John wonder how many precious rations Linda had been lavishing on them. The mere sight of a half-eaten sandwich, packed with what look liked hamburger meat, by Samantha's work area triggered hunger in John. A half-eaten sandwich remaining unconsumed was something he had not seen in a very long time in this starving world.

All were at work, two arguing in the far corner, each pointing to their respective screens, one of them a fairly new nineteen-inch flat screen.

"How and where did you get all of this?" John whispered to Ernie, those at work not yet noticing his presence.

"Here and there," Ernie whispered.

"I need to know. If word gets out we are salvaging equipment from people's basements and attics, it might leak out."

Bob's comment about a spy in their midst had been troubling him ever since he'd woken up.

"Let's just call it Dumpster diving from abandoned buildings in Old

Fort. I figured on hunting down there; it's only five miles away if you take the abandoned road for which I have a key to the gate. I took my sons along, and we prowled around a bit. Hell, the old police station and town hall are down there. Anything that looked to be online down there I assumed was fried, but in a back-room closet, there was a whole stack of tossed-off equipment. Someone told me they had just had a major refit of their entire computer system just a few weeks before everything happened, had stashed the older stuff, most likely to be quietly taken home after being formally written off as junked. It was still there, so I took it, and no one the wiser. Who the hell wants computers anyhow in Old Fort? Smarter than prowling around Montreat where curious eyes might see us and gossip about it."

It was important to keep this man happy, John realized, and he made the effort to pat him on the back.

Samantha at last turned in her chair, saw John and Maury standing watching them, and smiled.

Whatever Linda was feeding them, the girl looked the healthiest John could ever recall. She must have put on five pounds or more since he had last seen her. She nudged those working to either side of her, and for a moment, all work ceased.

"Don't let me interrupt," John said with a smile. "I just dropped by to see how things were going."

"Is it true that we've been occupied by military from Bluemont?" Samantha asked. "We heard the choppers coming over and shut down while they were overhead. We also monitored a BBC report, claiming they had reports of heavy fighting in Asheville and that you were under arrest and standing trial for the murder of ANR prisoners after they surrendered."

Those bastards, John thought. Of course they would spin it that way.

"None of it true, Samantha, at least my being arrested. I'm still here, aren't I? Yes, the military has occupied the area. Yes, several of our people and a couple of theirs were killed in Asheville and a dozen others on both sides wounded. But no one over here. There is no more fighting on either side. The general in command is an old friend of mine. We have a peaceful understanding for now. So don't worry about it, and just stick to what you're doing."

He could see their doubtful gazes.

"Please trust me. There is no fighting at the moment. What I am asking of all of you is to keep at what you are doing. I'm counting on you for that."

Several started to talk at once, but Linda held up her hands like a schoolteacher bringing her class back to order. "Stay on those screens. We'll have a team meeting over dinner to evaluate the day's data. Now get to it." Her voice was gentle but firm, and all followed her orders.

Linda beckoned to the back office. As they left the work area, John leaned over to Linda. "Do they know what happened this morning?"

"Ernie and I decided not to tell them, though one said they thought they heard a helicopter passing overhead. Until we know who the casualties are at the college, we figured it best not to get them upset and not focused on their work."

John nodded his thanks as they followed Ernie, with Maury by his side, into the back office.

There was no comment from Linda as Ernie fetched out the bottle of brandy, a jug-handle quart and a half, broke the seal, and without comment poured three glasses, keeping one and handing the other two over, with Linda abstaining.

"Here's to a blessing to the health of your family and you," Ernie offered.

"And to those who gave the last full measure this morning," John whispered before taking a sip.

Ernie put his glass down and smiled. "John, I think we are onto something."

"What?"

"We're not having much luck at all with breaking the encrypting. Bits and pieces at best, which is mostly guesswork. We've figured out a header to messages that indicate place of origin is Bluemont. A couple of names and titles. Their encrypting is sophisticated, as to be expected. What shows as the letter A might mean the letter M the first time it pops up. If that were the case, any fool can just sit down with a chart and a frequency table of how many times a particular letter is used. For example, A is used a hell of a lot more than X or Z in anything we write. Kind of like playing that old television game show but without lovely Vanna pointing out the letters as the players guess.

"But of course it's not that simple. A might mean M the first time we see it, but the next time it might mean *L* or *W,* and so on and so on. It is the same problem Turing faced when building a machine to mimic the German encrypting machines back during World War II. The trick was to try to see patterns. One of the Germans' big mistakes was daily submarine check-in reports with longitude and latitude, three groupings of two numbers each for degrees, minutes, and seconds. At the same time, naval intelligence reports in they're tracking a sub at, say, twenty degrees west and fifty-five degrees north, and they think it is U-Boat 111. Add in that French intelligence had reported U-Boat 111 putting to sea and a drunk sailor had told his girlfriend who is with the resistance where they were bound for patrol. Put those three different data points together, look at what we are getting via the Enigma machine—most likely from that sub—and it puts another piece into that puzzle to breaking the code."

Maury, the World War II history buff, interjected, "But they had hundreds working at Bletchley Park on breaking Enigma. They already had parts of the machine snatched by the Poles out of a German embassy just as the war started, machines later captured from subs, and like you said, data to correlate from other sources. Even then, it took several years to even start to get it right, though eventually we were transcribing the orders their high command was issuing almost as fast as they were being decoded by their own people."

"We don't have hundreds of people, and we don't have years," John replied softly.

"We do have our computers up and running," Ernie interjected.

"But how fast can we get results that we can use?"

"It depends on what you are looking for," Linda replied with a smile.

"How so? I fear this is a needle-in-a-huge-haystack problem."

"I recall stories from before the war of highly placed government officials, damn idiots, using their personal e-mail servers for classified data and transmitting in the open rather than on government-secured lines."

"And?"

"During the war," Maury interjected again, "I mean the Second World War, it was found that some bored sailor on a U-boat was playing chess via Enigma with a friend back at naval headquarters. 'Queen pawn to queen pawn four' type stuff."

The two looked at him.

"Well, it was stupid, but when the pattern was realized, people at Bletchley Park were decoding it and then transferring that knowledge to important stuff, even while they were laughing about how the guy back at headquarters was a lousy player and placing bets as to who would win."

"My point is," Linda replied, taking over again with the conversation, "you look for someone using the system in a declassified or inappropriate way. In one case, a couple of hackers in Europe were able to get inside the system of a very high-level official before the Day and cracked into thousands—tens of thousands—of files because that high-level government type was using their personal server. Letters going to friends asking about a kid's birthday mixed in with very deep stuff about military operations."

"How does that help us?" John asked, feeling that he was swimming in seas beyond his understanding.

"We've got an idiot like that," Linda said with a grin.

"I don't think it is that important, Linda," Ernie announced.

"Well, I think it is, and John should hear it."

"Go on."

"Within all the reams of encrypted data, something has been popping up. We're almost certain it is from Bluemont."

"We suspect it is from Bluemont," Ernie said.

"All right, suspected, then. What is it?"

"Personal notes. Short ones," Linda interjected.

"So?"

"John, this is high-level stuff, and we think we are getting into the stream."

"What kind of personal notes?" John asked, feeling numb from exhaustion and the impact of the brandy, now desperately trying to fathom where Linda was going and why it was important.

"It reads like husband to wife. I-miss-you type things."

"And?"

"A comment that in a few weeks the sender is scheduled for two days off and will visit."

"That's it?"

"It could mean anything," Ernie snapped. "Maybe it's to a girlfriend. Hell, maybe boyfriend to boyfriend. I don't put much on it."

"You would say something like that, Ernie. I don't care who it is to or how you see their relationship. It just caught me as strange, popping up unencrypted."

"Linda, you're losing me here. So far, I'm leaning with Ernie."

He hesitated, going over in his mind his promise to Bob Scales versus what was already out in the community as to what Quentin had said while dying.

"When we started this endeavor, there were questions about what that dying messenger said. Something about an EMP. Are we picking up and deciphering anything that looks like messages about an EMP?"

Ernie perked up with that. "Why, John?"

"It was a reason I decided to green-light this project."

"Did you get something out of General Scales?" Ernie pressed, staring up at John.

"I'm dealing with what we know from Quentin," John replied, trying to sound calm but knowing he was never the best of liars or one able to cover up facts that were troubling him.

"I see," was all Ernie said in reply while offering to top off John's drink, which John firmly refused but then wondered if his gesture not to drink was a clue to Ernie that he wished to remain absolutely sober during this conversation.

"No, nothing clear yet. Thought we had a code word for it yesterday, but that fell flat on its face. Remember, good encrypting can mean billions of permutations changing all the time. The machines we've got are way behind the ability to tackle that with the speed we wished we had. The machines out in the next room are not even doing gigs of calculations a second, when we actually need terabyte capability. So no, nothing yet."

"Then just please keep at it."

"You dodged my question, John," Ernie replied.

"Maybe I did," was all he could say in reply. "But I want to shift this back to Linda. Why are you interested in these personal messages?"

"They just strike me as odd. We have no idea exactly what Bluemont is, other than it was listed before the war as a center for FEMA in the event of a national emergency. Their updated version of the Cold War bunkers is out of some movie like *Dr. Strangelove* from back in the '50s and '60s.

"Ernie and I knew about them. Gossip when we worked at IBM, people sent off for a couple of months to set up computers and when asked about what they were doing, they'd smile and act all hush-hush. You know how it is—you were military once—and how some of those with a secret just walked around all so self-important."

John nodded. Such types always drove him crazy. Just because they had a security clearance for some particular project, they would strut around with an oh-so-superior air, like a child taunting, "I know a secret you don't know."

He often wondered how any secret actually could survive at all when placed into the hands of so many people with such ego issues.

"What are you leading to?"

Ernie started to speak, but Linda overran him. "I think tracing out these short notes might bear some fruit. If nothing else, there might be something classified spilled in one of them. It's happened before, I bet."

"Code words during World War II." Again it was Maury. "Manhattan, Big Boy and Little Boy, Omaha and Overlord. You put them into a letter that had to go through censors and the FBI was at your door. The double edge there. The mere fact that you used those words innocently could bring a whole lot of hurt down on you, but that it did bring down a whole world of hurt meant you had stumbled onto something. There's the story about some innocent guy who wrote crossword puzzles and by chance had the code names for three of the five invasion beaches for D-day in a puzzle. He winds up in an FBI office getting grilled. Of course, no one reported it, but suppose it had been in a radio broadcast then, or an e-mail today, and suddenly that person is grilled and others find out. That's a tip-off."

"And fat chance we'd have such luck today," Ernie replied. "Anything going up to the sat and back down to wherever from Bluemont is a closed loop. If somebody screws up, who are we to even know they screwed up? Assigning a code word to an EMP, they sure aren't going to use *flashbulb* or *big boom*. It'll be subtle—*Starfish* or *Rose*—and we'll never notice it."

"I'd veto *Starfish*," John said softly. "Might make you think about looking up at the stars, and beyond that, it was used by us, *Starfish Prime,* for a test launch of an EMP back in 1962."

"I knew that," Ernie replied with a smile. "I remember that test—just testing to see if you remembered."

John wondered if he was for real or just pulling his leg, but it did not matter.

"Okay, let's cut to the chase," Linda said. "Whoever this lonely guy or girl is in Bluemont, the single letter *R* has turned up in every one of the unencrypted correspondences between the two separated lovers. 'To R,' and 'Re: R.'"

"So?" John asked.

"I want to put half our assets on looking for anything related to *R* in any message headers and addresses."

"You're crazy," Ernie retorted.

"Yes, I was; I married you," Linda snapped back.

John held his hands up in a calming gesture, looking one to the other. *Who do I side with?* he wondered. Ernie was the one who had pulled off creating what was now the Skunk Works—did so under his nose—and his foresight had been proven because if still located in the college library basement, chances were Bob Scales would be onto it. But on the other side, Linda was proving that she had a deep intuitive sense about some things.

He recalled years ago, while at the War College, interviewing a retired four-star general, who as a young colonel was first wave ashore at Omaha Beach. The dignified elderly man spoke about Napoleon's famous interview question for a candidate for promotion to general: "Are you lucky?" The old man had laughed in a soft, self-deprecating voice and said that luck was about intuition and listening to an inner voice of warning. He recalled a night when his battalion dug in to an orchard for the night and he awoke a few hours before dawn with an overwhelming dread that something was about to go wrong. He ordered his battalion to decamp immediately and pull back a quarter mile. Shortly before dawn, the Germans laid down a killing barrage on that orchard they had vacated but a half hour earlier and sent in a dozen panzers to finish the job. His battalion's reply was to annihilate the panzers.

It wasn't luck, he said, it was some inner warning that had awakened him. That the orchard must surely stand out on a map to the Germans—a likely and comfortable place for a battalion of motorized artillery to laager for the night—and with that realization bringing him awake, he moved out. He never doubted his intuition again or tried to rationalize it away. He acted. Often he was wrong, but the times he was right made the difference between him sitting in John's office to be interviewed and being buried in France.

He realized his meeting with Bob at the snow-covered airport should have set off every alarm bell, for surely Bob was feeling out the situation prior to striking. He should have prepared better and had failed to do so. If he had acted, would he have fought Bob? He realized that was futile; his reaction would have been the same, but nevertheless, he should have listened to his inner warnings far more closely.

He looked over at Linda, his decision made. "I'm with you. Put half your kids on it. Focus in on any communication that looks personal and has some sort of reference to *R*. I think you are onto something."

"Oh, hell, I knew you'd agree with her," Ernie growled.

"That's because he's smart," Linda said with a smile. "Now I saw the way you were looking at a half-eaten sandwich, John. I still have some burger meat left over. Let me cook one up for you two visitors and enough left over to take home to your wives and kids."

CHAPTER THIRTEEN

At last the weather had broken, with a stretch of over a week in the upper forties, so that there were actual bare patches of pavement visible on the roads again.

He had heard no more from Bob other than a terse daily phone exchange with each telling the other that there was nothing new to report. No further reference, especially over an open phone line, about the assassination attempt or what might be unfolding regarding Bob's plans regarding his stated position that he would go in on Atlanta within days.

Work on the mill dam and generator to provide power to Old Fort and even on to Marion was completed, and with a ceremony to be held in downtown Old Fort at the train station, John felt it would be good for Makala to end her week of being in hiding. He found that he had to take something of a fatalistic view regarding the threat. If they, whoever they were, intended to try again, it would come, and nothing he could do would prevent it. He could either cower in hiding with his wife or live life.

The baby was due in little more than a month. Protective like any expectant father, he had first vetoed the idea of her riding down the mountain in the old Edsel. Then one of the citizens of Swannanoa had shown up toting an old-fashioned set of tire chains that would fit the car. It was something folks in the South had rarely seen, but as a boy growing up in the North, he well remembered the struggle of fitting them to the tires of his father's car before a major storm, and he always associated the sound of them with when he was six, a blizzard on Christmas Eve, believing they were Santa's sleigh bells. Driving to Old Fort and back would consume two gallons of gas, but the council insisted they go for the ceremony as a demonstration of the bond between the mountain communities and those down in the piedmont below.

He felt a little more justified when Paul and Becka, along with the twins, were crammed into the backseat, for after all, they were the architects of the entire electrical system that was gradually spreading out. He had debated with Paul the wisdom of risking his family out in the open by traveling with a man who most likely had a price on his head, but Paul had insisted they go along.

The drive down the old interstate was more than a little white knuckled. Several had attempted the run after the last storm, but it was the Bradley that had gone up and down several days earlier that had packed down a pathway that was now melted clear in places. Unlike in areas in north where the effects of several heavy snows coming nearly weekly could linger on the ground for months, this far south, a stretch of days up in the forties in December with clear skies could trigger a lot of melt off even in the mountains of North Carolina.

Still, he took the downhill run at little more than ten miles an hour, carefully staying in the middle lane. Other than the journey back from Morganton after the adventure in the Black Hawk, this was only his second foray down the long interstate climb through the mountains since the Day.

Evidence of the wreckage left from the Posse attack littered the road. For the folks of Black Mountain, the road had a certain taboo quality to it. At the top of the pass was where the town had established its barricade against the tens of thousands of refugees seeking entrance in the weeks following the Day. The barrier was still there but for the moment no longer manned with a passageway cut through it on the eastbound side.

Right at the crest of the mountain, at the truck safety stop where heavy vehicles used to pull off to examine a large map and safety information before beginning their descent, was the place where John had personally supervised the executions of Posse prisoners, including their ringleader. Several frayed ropes still swung in the breeze from the stoplight overhang. He knew the bodies that had once dangled there as a warning had long ago rotted off, what was left consumed by buzzards and coyotes, but as he drove past, he could still imagine them there as they kicked out the last minutes of their lives. The cliff just beyond had become the dumping ground for hundreds of Posse dead, and even after two years, some claimed a stench still wafted up on damp mornings. Seven bodies had been added to that pile, but he made no mention of that fact to those traveling with him.

Abandoned vehicles still littered both sides of the road on the way down. Most had been picked over in the months after the fight but with little enthusiasm or careful checking, for some still contained skeletal remains. It was a foreboding place, and all in the vehicle were silent as John negotiated his way around the wrecks until finally halfway down the mountain the wastage of war was pretty well left behind. The driving became a bit easier as well, for it was not uncommon that while a foot of snow was coming down atop the mountains, down in the piedmont it would be rain. Long stretches of the road, especially where the highway weaved about facing to the south and east, the pavement was melted nearly clean and just covered in slush.

Nevertheless, he made a mental note that once the ceremony was completed and he had performed some ritualistic handshaking and small talk, he would turn back and head for the home that he and Makala now occupied across the street from the campus. There was the feeling in the air that another front was starting to come through, and the prospect of driving the Edsel back up the mountain with the slush turning to ice and snow again falling was of concern.

They finally reached the exit where the remains of a burned-out McDonald's marked the turnoff. For that matter, all the buildings lining this part of the highway were scorched ruins. The Posse's taking of Old Fort had been an act of utmost wanton brutality, nearly all caught by surprise in the town before they could flee the onslaught, and most had been murdered. As he turned onto the main street, the same dreary sight greeted him, everything burned out and looted, charred ruins covered in a coating of snow and ice.

It was deeply depressing, the first time he had actually come here since before the Day. By the railroad tracks crossing through the center of town, there was an abandoned flatbed eighteen-wheeler. Obscene graffiti spray-painted on the cab indicated it had been a Posse truck, and an equally graffiti-covered Cadillac made John wonder if this was the vehicle of the Posse leader he had hung.

No one had expended the energy to move these and half a dozen other vehicles off the road, giving most of the downtown area a tragic postwar visage. It wasn't until they crossed over the railroad tracks that John saw that the old train station by some twist of fate had been spared, along with several shops and the town office on old Highway 70 as it headed east.

Several dozen were gathered outside the station for the ceremony. The same with nearly all the citizens of his world, they were slender, wiry looking, wrapped in oversized stained and soiled jackets and parkas. He recognized Gene Bradley, the nominal head of the community, an old, retired postman for the town, who wore the gray uniform jacket of his profession as if it was a badge of office.

John let the Edsel drift into the parking area behind the train station where half a dozen all-terrain vehicles, a battered old VW bus, and even a horse-drawn wagon had parked. A heavy truck retrofitted to burn on waste oil was actually out on the railroad tracks. The old telephone and telegraph poles once used by the railroad had been the convenient way to string wire from the power dam up in Mill Creek Valley five miles away. Quite a few old-fashioned glass insulators had been found on the poles along the way, even long stretches of sagging copper wire that had not fallen prey to scavengers and boys armed with pellet guns who always felt the insulators made excellent targets long before the Day.

The truck had several spools of wire on the back, and sitting around it was the work crew who had accomplished the feat of running the wire into town over the last few weeks in spite of the weather. Paul got out to check with them, proudly shaking hands all around while John worked the crowd of citizens with Makala by his side, of course all the women asking how she was doing and when she was due.

"I think we're ready to start," old man Bradley announced, and he opened the door to the train station, letting the crowd in. The interior triggered a wave of nostalgia for John. When his girls were little, they had spent many an afternoon "train chasing," following a heavy coal or freight train down from Black Mountain by taking Mill Creek road. They'd stop to watch it circle around the local attraction of what folks called "the Geyser" but was actually just an oversized fountain set in a small park and then race ahead to downtown Old Fort, get ice cream in a shop across the street, and then sit in front of this station to watch the train come thundering through before heading home.

They were warm memories, and he suddenly felt Makala's hand slip into his as if she were sensing his thoughts.

There was the usual round of "speechifying" that good days were finally coming back with the arrival of electricity and offering thanks for all the help they had received from the citizens of Black Mountain and Montreat College in bringing a modern world back to them. There was even a joke, but it was half-serious as well, that the next step was to again see trains, powered by steam, pulling into the station.

It dragged on a bit long, and John waited patiently. This was an important day for these few of the town who had somehow managed to survive. John was asked to say "a few appropriate words," and he did keep it to just a few, looking past the happy group to low scudding clouds that were starting to come in from the northwest, possibly the harbinger of another storm.

It was finally time to light things up. All eyes turned to Paul and Becka, each of them holding one of the twins, who were taking in their first journey to the outside world with wide-eyed wonder, both parents keeping back a bit protectively, for Becka was indeed paranoid about the prospect of the twins catching a cold or something worse from those gathered around.

A bit of a friendly argument ensued as to who would actually go up to the old-fashioned switch, which look liked it belonged in a Frankenstein movie, and snap it down. Finally, one of the children of the village was pushed forward, picked up by her mother, and did the honors. A string of lightbulbs and other strings of the ubiquitous Christmas lights brought in from somebody's attic flashed to light. Again, there was that same look of wonder on all the upturned faces, cheers, and some even started to cry. Someone turned on a CD player, and Lee Greenwood's "God Bless the U.S.A." hit John hard as it always did. Nearly everyone joined in at the chorus, and nearly all were in tears by the end.

Next was the usual country song, more than a few beginning to dance, while outside there was a shout that the food was on. John walked out of the now-stuffy room, Makala by his side, to where several women had lugged over kettles of what smelled like venison stew. He could never admit, even now after the starving times, that venison stew made him queasy. While he was a student at Duke long ago, one of his roommates had come back from a weekend hunt toting a four-point buck, hung it up in the backyard, and butchered it himself. Being students on a tight budget, the group had pretty well lived on venison for a couple of weeks. They had teased John as a wimpy Jersey boy for not enthusiastically joining in for their meals of venison steak and ground venison stew, always washed down with plenty of beer. He had of course partaken, but there was something about the smell that had bothered him ever since, even when hunger gnawed away and a student at the college had come in with an increasingly rare kill.

He politely took a bowl of the stew and struggled with it, Makala smiling at his discomfort and his white-lie responses to the elderly ladies about just how good it was to have fresh venison stew, though he wondered just how fresh the meat truly was.

There was a side to John that only those close to him really knew how to read; at heart, he was an introvert. If given the preference for an ideal day, it would be to just spend it with family, maybe a friend or two dropping over, and then plenty of time in the evening to curl up with a good book about history. During his years as an officer, when in direct command of a platoon and then a company, he'd had to force himself to be out there, to be patient and listen, to learn how to work with others rather than just be the type to issue orders and expect others to instantly obey, even when he knew he was right.

He had walked backward into his entire role as leader of his community, never wishing it. It was why friends like Lee Robinson, Maury, and others said that he was actually highly efficient, because at heart he did not want a role that others would have greedily grabbed on to and never want to relinquish.

He had to play the role now, enduring more than one handshake that turned into an embrace of gratitude from someone who had not bathed since winter set in.

Paul and Becka had already placed the twins in the back of the Edsel, Becka claiming they were tired and that it was nap time. It finally served as an excuse for John to disenthrall from the enthusiastic crowd. He did not want them to think he was rude or standoffish—he definitely was not—but now he doubted the wisdom of agreeing to get Makala out of the house for a while in her eighth month of pregnancy with a potentially icy drive back up the mountain.

Paul and Becka were already in the backseat, huddled over their precious cargo as John helped Makala into the old Edsel after passing the word to Bradley to give a call up to the town hall at the campus to let them know they were leaving. It was a safety gesture that if they did not get back within the hour, it meant they were stuck, and it was also a holdover from not all that long ago whenever venturing out of Black Mountain, because there were still the occasional marauders lurking along the roads, ever ready to jump on a lone traveler in a highly prized functional car.

He did not add that if they were still singled out as a target there was little that could be done, and now that worry was hitting him hard. Going out on his own in a different car was one thing. Doing it this way in light of what happened was a show of courage that he had to do, but he was putting those whom he loved at risk and now just wanted to get back home.

He absolutely refused Kevin and Lee's demand that he travel with a well-armed escort. Long before the Day, he had come to disdain the near-absurd lengths that security teams went to around even the most minor of officials after 9/11, and he refused to bow to that level.

Strange world, he thought as he reached the interstate and swung onto the opposite side of the road since on the way down it appeared to be clearer. Strange as well that though he had an extremely pregnant wife in the front seat and parents in the back with twins nestled between them, all four adults were armed, Paul and Becka each carrying sawed-off shotguns and Makala, like him, armed with a .45 Glock.

A couple of times up the long climbing slope, the Edsel fishtailed a bit. John was glad that they had left while the sun was still high in the sky for this time of year; the temperature was beginning to drop, and a breeze was picking up, with a thickening spread of clouds drifting in from the west. At such moments, the four did what people nearly always do: speculated about the approaching weather.

"John, look up to your right!" Paul suddenly cried, breaking the relaxed and friendly conversation.

John leaned forward at the wheel and saw a Black Hawk crossing up high over the ridgeline to their right, swinging about in an arcing turn, and then diving back down and disappearing from view up toward the top of the crest.

John hit the gas as much as he dared, the Edsel fishtailing even more until the chained tires dug into the slush and propelled them forward, blue exhaust swirling out behind them.

"Are they after us?" Makala asked nervously.

"Doubt it," he said, trying to reassure her.

"If they wanted to arrest you, John, this would be the convenient place to do it, away from the town." She didn't add that killing them would be all so easy now.

If that was indeed the intent, he thought, then he truly was a fool for leaving the security of the campus and partially trusting Bob's words.

Coming around the last bend in the road, he saw that the Black Hawk was going into a hover at the top of the pass at the long-abandoned truck stop, the place of a major battle and executions.

"Back it around!" Paul shouted. "Head back down to Old Fort."

John wearily shook his head. "Whatever is about to happen, they have us." He sighed. "Keep your weapons down and out of sight."

John slowed the Edsel and stopped fifty yards out, turning the Edsel sideways by the exit ramp of the truck stop.

"If it goes bad," he said, looking over at Makala, "take the wheel and try to make a run for it."

Her arms were around him, hugging him fiercely.

He forced a reassuring smile. "The baby comes first, lover. Don't worry— if they wanted us dead, it already would have happened."

He carefully got out of the Edsel, made a show of holding up his Glock by the grip and then placing it back into the vehicle, and walked toward the Black Hawk with hands out to his sides and clearly showing he was unarmed. The chopper's rotors slowed to a stop as he approached, the side door sliding open, and Bob Scales got out, doing the same as John, arms extended out, showing he was unarmed.

The two approached each other cautiously. Behind Bob, John could see that there was a door gunner at the ready, weapon not pointed directly at him but ready to be swung around.

"Hell of a way to meet, General!" John shouted over the whine of the Black Hawk's turbines, which had not been shut down.

"Yeah, hell of a world, John," Bob replied as he slowed and came to a relaxed attitude of attention.

John did the same and finally raised his right hand in a salute, which Bob returned.

"We have to talk," Bob announced.

"I was hoping that was all. Just as long as you leave my family and friends out of it."

Bob looked past John to the wreckage scattered about the truck stop, the horizontal pole where frayed ropes swung slowly back and forth in the increasing breeze from what appeared to be an approaching storm.

"So this is where you held the Posse off?"

"Yes."

"Exceptional choice of ground. I heard how they nearly succeeded in flanking you from over there to the north." As he spoke, he pointed to the deep ravine of Mill Creek.

"Something like that."

"I just took a look over there and saw something interesting, John."

He did not reply.

"You should tell whoever is over there that the white camouflage netting was fine right after the snow fell, but those antennas kind of stick out clearly now."

Again John did not reply.

"It was spotted yesterday, John. Actually, I don't mind, but I am curious as to who you are eavesdropping on over there."

"Why don't you go ask yourself?"

"I was thinking just that, but didn't want some sort of misunderstanding if I or some of my people just showed up unannounced."

"Is that the reason you flew all the way over here?" John asked.

"One of several," he replied, and John sensed the tension in Bob's voice.

He said no more and continued to look around, gazing again at the ropes, the only evidence left of the mass hangings that had taken place here at John's orders.

"You did what you had to do here," Bob finally said, "but knowing you, dealing out justice summarily must have been tough."

John looked up at the ropes, remembering the insane gibberish the leader of the Posse was screaming in his final seconds before being hoisted aloft to slowly die of strangulation. The hysterical pleas of the others with him as one by one they were hoisted aloft or taken to the edge of the ravine and shot in the back of the head until he finally relented and let the last few survivors of that murderous gang go to spread word of what would happen to any who dared to approach again.

"They were cannibals. There was nothing else I could have done."

Bob looked over at him.

"When you've seen too much, sir, strange how all higher emotions can just drain away. I'm haunted by other things now, but not this."

"I know."

John looked up again at the ropes, and he suddenly felt a strange sense of detachment—no fear, no desire to try to flee. He looked back at the Edsel, where Makala had slipped over to get behind the wheel.

"Whatever it is, you're leaving her out of this, aren't you?"

"Of course, John."

"You've orders to take me to Bluemont that you can no longer dodge around, is that it?"

Bob did not reply.

"Bob, I prefer a bullet. I remember a class with you once about George Washington, how he had to handle the Major André case, even though every judge of his court-martial appealed for mercy, or at least a bullet rather than the rope."

"I remember that," Bob said softly.

There was a moment of silence, and Bob looked at the Edsel. "You know, John, I think that is one of the ugliest cars ever made."

It broke the tension for a moment as John smiled and explained how it had belonged to Mary's mother, the old oversized machine impervious to the effects of an EMP.

"And that is your wife down there?"

"Yes, sir."

"May I say hello? I'd like to meet her."

"Of course. But if I am being arrested, I'd prefer no word. We have a baby due in a few weeks; I don't want anything to upset her."

"Of course."

"All of them are armed," John said softly as Bob started down to meet them, "and more than a bit nervous as well."

"I understand."

Bob approached the driver's side of the car. Makala opened the door and started to get out, Bob smiling and telling her to stay inside where it was warm. She rolled down the window.

"Ma'am, I wished we had met under better circumstances," Bob said gracefully.

"So do I." Her voice was anything but friendly.

"John said you two are expecting." He continued to smile and leaned in slightly. "And excuse me, ma'am, but you look like it will be any day now."

"Yes, any day now, and I expect my husband to be by my side."

"Of course. I understand."

One of the twins in the back of the car began to fuss, and Bob turned his attention to the backseat.

"Now there's a lovely package."

John offered quick introductions, Paul and Becka looking up at Bob warily and not offering any reply other than curt hellos.

"I wish I had more time to meet all of you properly and someplace warm where we could sit and get acquainted. I can guess you want to get those two little ones safely home. You can pull around the chopper and go on your way."

"With my husband?" Makala asked sharply.

"We need to chat for a while, ma'am."

"But he'll be home directly afterward?"

"All will work out just fine," Bob said smoothly.

"I see," was all she said back, her gaze now fixed on John.

John offered a smile of reassurance. "I'll be along shortly, sweetheart. Why don't you get the Hawkinses and their babies settled in and stay with them until I get home? Okay?"

Makala had the uncanny ability to know when he was holding something back or lying, and he knew she sensed it now.

"John?" She started to crack the door open.

He stepped forward, leaned into the car, and kissed her. "Baby comes first," John whispered even as he kissed her again. "Get home safe, sweetheart. I love you both. Please do that now."

She began to sob, arms reaching out to hug him, to somehow pull him into the car, but he broke free of her embrace, pushing the door closed as she tried to open it again.

"Now, Makala, please. Do it for me. Get the Hawkinses safely home."

Unable to hide her sobs, she shifted the car into gear, rear wheels spinning as she hit the gas, swung the old vehicle out onto the road, and floored it, tires spinning in the slush and then gaining traction. She swung around the tail rotor of the Black Hawk and disappeared from view, John's gaze on them until out of sight.

"A beautiful woman, John. Lots of guts. Can see why you fell in love with her."

"Thank you for playing your part, Bob. But she knows."

"Yeah, I could see that. What loving wife wouldn't see through it?"

There was a moment of silence between the two.

Bob put a reassuring hand on John's shoulders. Now that they were gone and he no longer had to playact, emotion was hitting him. "I hope you two have a daughter on the way. I always feared that Jennifer wouldn't make it through the times after the attack. I remember how aggressive her diabetes was. Is it any help to you now that I prayed for her every day, even tried to figure out how to get through to you with some insulin? But it was impossible. You know that."

"It wouldn't have made any difference. A few extra shots, six months' worth, her fate was sealed along with so many other kids like her on that day. We both know that."

"Nevertheless, it haunted me. Same as my Linda and so many others."

John could hear the emotion in his voice, and then there was silence between them as they walked back up the slope to the helicopter and climbed aboard, the gunner offering each of them a hand as they stepped up and strapped in.

"So this is it?" John asked as the rotors began to turn.

"Not quite yet. I'm sorry, but we've got to take down your eavesdropping as well. One of your ham operators screwed up, put it out on the air that you and your people were listening in and suspected that Bluemont was plotting some sort of attack. Sorry, John; I got direct orders to take it off-line."

John wearily shook his head. It was the age-old bane of any secured operation. All it took was one loudmouth and all cover was blown.

"Only one of two ways I could see of doing that. We hover over the building, half a dozen of my troopers rappel down on to the roof, and chances are a lot of people—yours and mine—get shot, or you just walk in with me and we peacefully take it off-line. It's your call."

"We walk in," John replied. "One question, though. How did you know where to find us?"

"There are spies, and then there are other spies, John. I think you were bloody insane for driving down to Old Fort after what happened last week. But in my case, it made it easy to pick you up without any fuss and take care of your listening post at the same time."

"Just great." John sighed.

"Maybe you should count yourself lucky."

The walk from the Ridgecrest conference center up to the Franklins' steep driveway was just a short distance but damned tiring as they slogged up through the slushy snow. A couple of times John came to a stop so Bob could catch his breath, and there was even a bit of tension-breaking joking about how both of them were getting too old for this type of hike. As they rounded the last turn in the driveway, John came to a sudden stop as four figures rose up from concealment—Ernie's sons, daughter, and her husband, all of them pointing weapons at them.

John held his hands up, whispering for Bob to do the same as John identified himself. Weapons were lowered but still casually held in their general direction as they ascended the last fifty yards to the garage entrance, where Ernie awaited them, arms folded in his usual defiant gesture.

"I suspect this is not a friendly visit," Ernie announced without offering any kind of welcome. "We saw the chopper circling earlier and heard it land at Ridgecrest. One hovered above us for a few minutes last evening as well."

John tried to make formal introductions, but Ernie cut him off. "So, we've been found out, and your friend decided to come here personally to have a look-see before shutting us down. Is that it?"

"Let's not go off half-cocked, Ernie," John replied.

"Half-cocked? Let's look at this from a different light, John. So this your legendary friend Bob Scales?"

John nodded.

"And our new military dictator. At least he looks a damn sight more official than that damn Fredericks that I put a bullet into."

"Oh, for God's sake, Ernie, can we just mellow out for a moment?"

"So you're the one that shot Fredericks?" Bob interjected.

"Yeah. You got an issue with that? The bastard was about to shoot my foolish friend here in the back, so I gave it to him first."

"From what I heard of everything that happened here"—he paused—"can't say I blame you. And if you saved John's life in the process, I thank you."

"Just great, I feel exonerated," Ernie replied. "So now that I've confessed, am I on the arrest list too?"

"No."

"But my friend here is?"

Bob was silent.

"Tell you what. A quid pro quo. You let him go, we let you go. You hold him, we hold you. You execute him, we execute you. How's that sound?"

"Damn it, Ernie, stop being an ass," John snapped. "One volley from an Apache will take this place apart—you, your entire family, all the kids you got upstairs. I won't be part of that."

"Thank you, John," Bob said softly, still forcing a disarming smile. "Mr. Franklin, I respect your loyalty to our friend John. I feel the same way about him. But to try to hold me—actually, I'm okay with it, but some of my people would not be—they'd try a rescue and evac the moment they heard I was being held, and a lot of innocent people on both sides would get hurt. We don't want that. I know John doesn't want it either."

John nodded.

"Well, maybe I'm willing to take the risk."

"Ernie, go upstairs and ask Linda what she thinks."

"Oh, for God's sake, John, don't pull that card on me."

"Smart decision, husband," Linda announced from the landing of the stairs that led up to the first floor. "Now will you invite our guests in?"

John looked up at her, smiled, and could see the look of worry clouding her features.

Ernie relented, motioned for them to go up, while behind them, his sons, daughter, and son-in-law were taking off their camouflage smocks and stacking arms.

As they reached the first floor, Bob breathed in deeply, smiled, complimented Linda on whatever was simmering atop the woodstove in the kitchen, and then went over to the fireplace in the living room, extending his hands to warm them. John joined him, and looking up to the second-floor balcony, he could see nearly a dozen anxious faces peering over the railing and looking down at them. He motioned for them to disappear, but they did not comply.

Linda came over, helping John and Bob to take off their parkas while the daughter approached the two with steaming mugs of broth, which both gladly took.

It was all so surreal for John, as if he and an old comrade from his army days were paying a friendly visit. But he could not help but notice the sea of cold, decidedly unfriendly gazes from Ernie's family who were gathered in the kitchen and leaning over the balcony railing.

Bob could not help but notice as well, and after taking several long sips of the warming broth and thanking their daughter, he turned to face the assembly, "Can I ask that all of you join me down here by the fire?"

There was an initial reluctance, no one moving.

"Please. It's okay. Let's gather round," John said, and the tense spell was broken for a moment.

The students came down from the second floor, family members coming out from the back rooms of the first floor, filing into the spacious living room. As almost twenty of them gathered in, John could see just how much the Franklin Clan had been putting out to support their Skunk Works. Even though the house was large, it had become decidedly crowded. Rations that had been long ago planned for eight or ten to survive for a couple of years were now being doled out at what must be a prodigious rate. He figured

Ernie must have been using either gas or propane to at least power the well to keep a cistern filled. How much more was that taking now?

With two surviving sons—a third had been killed in the fight with the Posse—a daughter who now appeared to be pregnant and her husband, four grandchildren, and nine students, the strain of supporting all of it must certainly be telling. He could see Linda was the matriarch of the entire arrangement and could sense her near-infinite weariness with all that she had to see to as she continued beyond that to be something of a project manager as well. But it was all now coming to an end, the future indeed uncertain and most likely dark.

Bob put the mug of broth down, looked around at the gathering, and offered a somewhat military "Let's all just stand at ease and relax" opening statement.

But no one did relax; the tension was palatable.

"I'm sorry, truly sorry, to tell you that whatever it is all of you are engaged in, I have received orders to shut it down."

"From who? Why, damn it?" a chorus of protest rose up.

Bob extended his hands in a calming gesture, but it did no good, anger rising by the second.

"Damn it, everyone shut the hell up!" John snapped out sharply, and the room did fall silent in response to his outburst.

"Listen up. What General Scales is saying here is the way it's got to be. I don't like it any more than you do. I came here with him with an understanding. No harm was to come to him, and realize he's made one hell of a personal gesture of his showing his character by doing this personally rather than sending some underling to do it. He put his life on the line to deliver this message."

No one said anything, but John could still sense the righteous anger.

"Look, it is the way it is, and I don't like it any more than you. Either we shut it down and start disassembling it now, today, or I know for a fact that come tomorrow, his people will be back and do it for us."

"Let them try it!" Samantha cried, voice near to breaking. "We haven't busted our asses for weeks without sleep just to have it come to this."

"I know how you feel. Remember I was the one who first said go ahead with it when Ernie and Paul Hawkins figured out we could get computers back up and running and use them for what you've been doing. Please listen to me. We don't agree, you try to put up a fight, and thirty seconds of an Apache helicopter hovering over this place will end it anyhow. There is no arguing with that. Most of you saw what an Apache can do when we faced off against Fredericks back in the spring."

"So we surrender to another Fredericks, is that it?" Samantha pressed. "Go ahead and try, damn it. We can haul this stuff out of here before you hit and hide it in the woods, and then try to find it all."

Bob edged past John and looked straight at Samantha. "I admire your courage, young lady. Yes, you can do that. If I were you, that would be my first reaction. But please think. If forced to act rather than resolving this peacefully, this house is gone. If forced to, your power station—which you need to run things here—is gone. Then what? You are dead, and a lot of young men and women about your age are gone as well. Please, I do not want that, but the orders are firm. This operation shuts down today. I'm asking your help to ensure it happens without anyone getting hurt. If I didn't care about that, I just would have sent an attack helicopter in and not put myself here in front of you."

John looked over at his old commander and actually did feel a surge of emotion. His words, his caring, hit hard. Fredericks, and so many others like him, would have hit first, and those killed on both sides not a concern.

There was a long moment of silence broken only by whispers back and forth between those assembled.

"He's right," Linda finally interjected, breaking the tension. "All right, General, we shut it down, but before we do so, I want you to look at a few things and answer a few questions. Can you agree to do that first?"

"Of course, ma'am."

"It's Linda."

"All right." Bob hesitated, some emotion showing. "My wife was named Linda as well."

Linda looked back at the gathering around them. "Why don't you kids relax for a while? You all look pasty faced as zombies. Get some coats on, go out, and enjoy the air and a bit of sunshine before that next storm rolls in. Now get going."

She shooed them out of the living room like a protective hen, the group breaking up, but it was obvious that none of them were pleased.

"How about we go upstairs to talk?" she offered. "Ernie, time for some cigars and brandy."

"Share a cigar with him?" Ernie growled, nodding toward Bob. "And Matherson doesn't smoke."

"I'll sit next to you and inhale deeply," John said, trying to smile and break the tension.

Once into his office, Ernie opened the cigar humidor, and there were only two left within.

"These are my last two Cubans, and don't ask how I got them before the Day," he announced sadly as he held one up and sniffed it. "My homegrown stuff tastes like shit, but at least it is something after you two are gone."

Bob actually smiled and nodded a thanks as Ernie clipped off the ends, offered one to Bob, struck a match, and held it for Bob as he puffed his cigar to life. Ernie hoarded the precious friction match, managing to light his own cigar as well before tossing the match down to the tile floor.

"Classified info," Bob said, smiling after first inhaling the cigar, taking it deep in without coughing. "A year back, the navy seized a shipment of these, and I was able to trade a bottle of real scotch with an admiral friend of mine for a box. First one I've had in half a year or more. Thank you."

"So that easy to get contraband stuff out there?" Ernie queried sharply.

"Not as easy as you might think," Bob replied without breaking his smile, showing to John that he could still keep that poker-face grin even when someone was needling him.

Linda came in bearing a bottle of wine, and Ernie groaned. "That's one of the last of the Malbecs." He sighed as Linda handed it to him to uncork.

"Might as well send our friend John off with a proper wine," she said.

"Who said I'm going anywhere?"

She looked at him, and her composure let down for a moment.

"You're arresting him and taking him away, aren't you, General?"

Neither Bob nor John replied as Ernie, taking that in, uncorked the bottle and poured out four drinks into slightly dingy glasses and held his up.

"America," was all he said in a very formal salute.

"America," the other three whispered, and at that moment, John picked up a subtle nuance when Bob drained off a good portion of his glass and put it down without further comment. Old tradition was to toast the commander in chief as well in any such setting when glasses were raised. He looked over at Bob, who did not return his glance.

"Shall we pull the wires now?" Linda asked without preamble. "Smash the motherboards and hard drives in front of you?"

Bob shook his head and then took another sip of the wine. "That won't be necessary at the moment, but yes, I'm afraid it will come to that. If you can promise me there'll be no confrontation, a couple of my people will come over tomorrow to take the computers away. I just ask that you disable them in some way now."

"How about we fire off a mini EMP for you?" Ernie snapped, and Bob looked over at him sharply. Ernie smiled at his joke, which was definitely flat. "But then again, I suspect Bluemont has the same plans soon enough."

"Why do you say that?" Bob said, and again John could see the poker-face smile.

"What you saw out in our Skunk Works isn't there to play some damn games or set up a new Facebook or those damn Twitters. Yesterday, we noticed a real increase in traffic. We managed to capture and decrypt a few lines here and there after a lot of sleepless nights. Does Wallops Island, Virginia, sound familiar, General?"

"Nice beaches. Camped there years ago."

"It was also a NASA and NOAA facility for lofting short-range rockets, not usually orbital, but they could launch from there for small payloads— say, what used to be known as a suitcase nuke. We've got something about a 'package' being moved there. Wallops Island, package, mix in my paranoia and I read it as something really dark."

"I'm not privy to such information," Bob replied calmly, and then he masked his reaction by taking another sip of wine.

Ernie smiled but did not press further, a reaction that John thought strange coming from this man. He saw Ernie glance over at Linda and read that there was something else up their sleeves, something beyond speculation regarding a "package" at Wallops Island, a place John was finding hard to place on a map.

"General, we've been picking up something else," Linda interjected.

"Go on."

"You know as well as I do that all systems, no matter how secure, are porous, only as secure as their weakest link, meaning personnel link. Recall some high-level types before the Day who would sit at home late at night, using their personal servers to send out chatty e-mails and then mixed with notes to friends, family, something official and classified?"

"I do," Bob said, his features clouding with obvious disgust at such stupidity.

"Easy enough to crack if they break security protocols. Do that and a door might be wide open for someone to snoop into. Well, we've got such a person at Bluemont."

"Go on." After taking another drink of wine, Bob put the glass down on the table next to Ernie, who did not hesitate to pour in several more precious ounces while Bob took another puff on his cigar, and John gladly inhaled next to him. The entire Internet and computer security game was something he would readily admit was beyond him, so it was always fascinating to listen in on something like this.

"General Scales, what is 'Site R'?"

John could see Bob stiffen at Linda's query.

"Could you repeat that one, Linda?"

"Site R, and your response tells me that means something to you."

There was a long moment of silence from Bob. Cigars had always been an excellent means of giving a man a moment to gather his thoughts as he appeared to examine the glowing tip, knock off a bit of ash, and take another meditative puff, which is exactly what Bob did, and it spoke volumes to John, who remained silent.

"Linda, I am not sure what you are driving at, and as far as this Site R is concerned, I have no comment."

"Then it's classified?" Linda snapped, her voice like that of a prosecuting attorney closing in for the kill.

She stood up, went over to a filing cabinet alongside Ernie's desk, pulled it open, drew out a file folder, and tossed it on Ernie's desk next to where Bob was sitting.

"My Site R file, General. Sorry, but our regular printer was fried off on the Day. We did scrounge up an old dot matrix printer from the college library and a couple of boxes of paper but no extra printer cartridges. My handwritten notes—excuse them, some people say I have a miserable left-handed scrawl—but take a look, General."

Bob picked up the file folder, opened it, and held it up close to try to read the faded printouts and all but illegible handwriting. He finally gave up and put the folder back on the table. "What are these?"

She smiled, the smile of the legendary Cheshire cat, luring by its cryptic words its prey coming in closer for the kill. "We started to monitor this person over a week ago. He was breaking standard encrypting. Our profile, a bureaucrat at Bluemont. E-mails bouncing all the way up to their satellite system and back down to an address at a place called Site R. Personal stuff; hope it is his wife rather than a girlfriend, because if it is a girlfriend and he's married, the bastard should be hanged. Some of it the usual sticky stuff, some of it, well, all this proper Southern girl can say is, it got very randy at times between the two, though that girl Samantha who was tracking it day and night got more than a few laughs."

Linda smiled at that, and even Ernie chuckled.

"He sure is horny."

"Ernie!" Linda snapped.

"Well, he is. And in this starving world, you gotta be damn young or very well fed to have enough surplus energy to think the way those two are. It used to be called sexting, I think."

"You don't have to tell me," Linda shot back, and Ernie visibly wilted.

"Hey, let's call that TMI," John snapped, though he was now curious to look at the files as well, even though from Bob's expression it was obvious Linda had hit a major nerve at the mention of Site R.

"Please continue," Bob said softly as he picked up the file folder and began to thumb through it again.

"Site R, as I was saying. We wondered where it was. For all we knew, it could be some island in the Indian Ocean, England, Antarctica, and the e-mails just pathetic longings. But then it cracked open wider. Our horny Romeo appears to be making his plaintive cries of undying love and long-ing right under Juliet's balcony."

"How do you know that?" Bob asked.

"He said he had a seat on the weekly shuttle chopper. Once things settled down when the package was delivered, he would be able to visit her again. Something about a five-day personal leave, a quick flight, and plenty of time then with his lover. She replied that she is getting sick of being stuck in Site R and asked why can't she just get a posting to Bluemont and then they could be together all the time. He then dodged off on his reply and, get this, said that no one is supposed to know that he, and I quote, 'got you out to safety at Site R.'"

Bob looked at her wide-eyed, obviously taken completely off guard, and she indeed did smile openly now. Whatever her game, John realized, she had just sprung it on an obviously unsuspecting general.

He opened the file folder again, held up the pages closely, and started to scan through them one by one. Cursing softly, he reached into his breast pocket to produce a pair of reading glasses, put them on, and for long minutes scanned through the files.

All were silent. Ernie puffed on his cigar, and after draining the precious glass of Malbec, without offering to those around him, he pulled out the nearly empty bottle of brandy, poured a stiff drink, and swiftly downed it, earning a sharp glance from Linda.

Bob finally put the file back down with a sigh. "Damn all to hell," he whispered, and he held his empty glass up for Ernie to reluctantly refill with what was left in the brandy bottle and took it all down in a couple of quick gulps. "Can I keep this file?" he asked.

Linda shook her head. "If it's as important as I think it now is, the answer is no."

"And if I just take it?"

"You don't leave here if you try."

He nodded, looking over at John. "You reason with her. I want this file. I need this file."

There was an urgency to Bob's appeal that spoke volumes to John, who wordlessly gave an appealing look to Linda. She was silent for a moment, considering her answer.

"I assume John is under arrest and going with you, General Scales."

Bob, who was leaning over toward Ernie, who was relighting his cigar, looked back at Linda. "Yes, he is, but don't tell your family and the students here that. We don't need a scene."

"John?" She looked at him sharply. He realized all he had to do was announce he had no intentions of going and all in this house would resist his leaving and if need be hold Scales as hostage.

"Give the file to me, Linda," John said. "You can trust me with it. Bob, can I take responsibility for the file?"

Scales nodded in ready agreement. John reached over to pick it up without waiting for her reply and then turned his gaze back to her.

"All right, John." Her voice was choked with emotion.

"Thank you, ma'am," Bob said, and setting his glass down, he swiftly stood up.

Linda stood up and went up to John and hugged him. "When do I see you again, John Matherson?"

"Don't worry; just keep everyone here safe."

She started to stifle back tears.

Bob reached out to put a reassuring hand on her shoulder. "Ma'am, you just might have changed the paradigm. I hope you can trust me."

She looked back at him sharply. "I don't."

"I can understand that."

"Anything you wish to smash on your way out?" she asked sarcastically.

He did not reply, leaving their office, slowly walking out into the large room dubbed the Skunk Works and then turning to look back at the three who were following him.

"Keep this up and running. Focus on this—how did you put it, Ernie? This 'horny Romeo'? Focus in on him with everything you have."

Linda and Ernie looked at him with obvious surprise.

"As far as your team knows, they are being shut down. Find whoever is your loudmouthed ham operator—for that matter, all your ham operators—and I want them off the air now, immediately. I want a full shutdown on any kind of uplink traffic. Silent listening only. Nothing even on the phone line. I'll have a courier down here tomorrow to pick up anything new, but it will be made to look like he is occupying this place and shutting it down. Do you read me?" Those last four words were spoken sharply in a clear command voice that carried the type of threat a general knew how to conjure up when need be.

Ernie and Linda stood silent, just nodding in reply, until Linda broke the silence. "And John's fate?"

"He is still under arrest and will face charges in Bluemont," Bob said sharply, loudly enough that the eavesdroppers gathered in the living room below could obviously hear.

Shouts of protest rose up as family and former students gathered at the base of the stairwell as the four came back down.

Bob made a show of shouldering his way through, ignoring the curses and threats hurled at him, John following in his wake, shrugging off more than one plaintive attempt at a hug and appeals for him to stay.

Though the climb up to the home had been a laborious one, Bob descended the driveway at a near run, John following in his wake.

Whatever it was that had so hit the general, it was obviously big, and not another word was said as he approached the waiting helicopter, its turbines kicking over as he approached. John hesitated to climb in. He could not help but sense that doing so was sealing his fate for whatever was ahead.

Bob climbed into the chopper, the rotors overhead beginning to turn, and looked back at John.

"Matherson, you can turn and run and I won't follow. That or get your ass in here now and face what is coming next. It's your call."

Wondering if he would ever see Makala and his newborn child, he hesitated for several seconds and then climbed in after Bob, and the Black Hawk lifted off.

CHAPTER FOURTEEN

He didn't feel free or that he was actually under close arrest. After landing at the Asheville airport, Bob had disappeared into the cavernous hangar that had once housed National Guard aircraft at the north end of the airport while John was led to what had been the headquarters for a couple of private aviation firms. Bunks had been set up in the foyer and corridors to house troops, some of them fast asleep. Those relaxing off duty and still awake gazed at him with curiosity but said nothing as a sergeant major led John to what had been a private office, desk pushed to one side, a standard collapsible bunk with sleeping bag set up in its place. The sergeant told him to wait for a moment and returned with a sleeping bag and an MRE-supplied cup of instant coffee, which John took a sip of and set down; it was laced with whiskey, and for the time being, he definitely wanted to keep his head clear.

"Anything you need, sir, I'm bunked next door; just come and get me."

"Mind if I wander about a bit, Sergeant . . ." His voice trailed off, the middle-aged man's name tag concealed under his parka.

"It's Sergeant Major Charles Bentley, sir. Just call me Charles or Sarge. Okay?"

"Fine, Sergeant. About wandering around?"

"Sorry, sir, but you are under arrest until I hear differently. I'm responsible for your well-being. Play along and we keep it as it is now. You try to walk off, sir, and sorry to say it, I will have to put you under restraint. Those are the general's orders."

"I won't be a cause for concern, Sergeant," John said as he turned to look out through the half-open venetian blinds. A couple of dozen private planes were still out there—Bonanzas, Mooneys, the usual Cherokee 140s and 180s, Cessna 172s that must have belonged to the flight school, and even some high-end turbo props and a couple of corporate jets. All of them abandoned. Long ago, he had sent a crew down here to drain off their avgas and Jet A, but even before his people had arrived, looters had already been at the planes, taking all the gas and most likely just for the hell of it smashing them up. The planes, once worth millions, had all been pushed to one side to make room for the eight Black Hawks, six Apaches, and a C-130, and as he watched, a second C-130 was taxiing in from landing.

"Is that everything you have, Sergeant?" John asked.

"You know I can't answer that, sir."

"John is okay with me."

"Sir, orders from the general are to consider you as a colonel reactivated to service. So it remains *sir* or *Colonel*."

"All right, Sergeant. Mind if I ask a few questions?"

"Those I can answer, fine by me, sir."

"Been with General Scales long?"

"I'm his top enlisted aide. After Major Quentin left, I've been his sole adjutant."

"Can you tell me anything about Major Quentin?"

The sergeant politely shook his head in reply.

"He left us with a hell of a mystery, Sergeant. This talk about an EMP. You know anything about that?"

"Sir, you know as well as I do what I can and cannot answer."

John smiled, pulled out one of the chairs stacked up in the corner of the room, and sat down, taking off his parka, stretching his legs out to relax, and making a show of just sipping the whiskey-laced coffee but not gulping it down. "Sergeant, how about sitting down for a few minutes? I'd appreciate the company."

"Sir, you are bunked in the same room as the general. When he comes back, perhaps it would be better to direct your questions at him."

The man was good. Firm without being disrespectful, and he would stick to his orders—perhaps one of them to get John a bit tipsy and pump him, or even to see if he could be made tipsy.

With that thought, John made a show of going over to the window, cracking it open, and pouring out the laced coffee. He looked back at the sergeant, who actually grinned a bit.

"Waste of a good drink, sir."

"I prefer to keep my head on straight. Here and then wherever it is you are eventually taking me."

"If there's nothing else, sir, I'll be next door down." The sergeant turned to leave.

"Charlie?"

The sergeant looked back.

"At least tell me about yourself. Were you in the Pentagon on the day the shit hit the fan?"

"No, sir. I was actually part of the ceremonial team at Fort Meade for duty at Arlington. Final assignment before mustering out after twenty-five years."

The sergeant's trim but muscular build, ramrod-straight posture, and demeanor was a giveaway to John. The ceremonial guard was one of the most exacting assignments in the military. It was not just the very public task of standing guard at the Tomb of the Unknown Soldier but also for all military funerals and beyond that any ceremonial event requiring military presence in D.C. itself. Behind the scenes, it was also a highly efficient combat force, one of the top ready reaction forces inside the beltway.

"How did you meet General Scales?"

"He and some others from the Pentagon came in the evening of the first day." He seemed reticent to continue.

"And then?"

"Well, the general and I sort of fell in together, and he asked me to stick with him."

"Mind if you tell me more about what happened in D.C. that first day, Sergeant?"

"No, sir. There was a lot of confusion. The whole city was down, communications down. By the middle of the first night, the city was burning." Again there was a drawn-out silence; he was obviously reluctant to say more.

"Nothing classified—just curious," John prompted him.

"After a couple of days, it was obvious to some we were doing nothing effective where we were. Some said we should try to link up with Andrews Air Force Base, but that was on the other side of the city, and we hadn't seen any air traffic, at least not going out from there."

That struck John as curious. "Did you see air traffic?" he asked.

"Yes, sir. A number of choppers, looked like special-ops-type equipment, most likely proofed against EMPs. They were moving about."

"So something was at least flying?"

"Yes, sir. But nothing toward us. All our comm gear was down, and we were obviously written off."

"What were these choppers doing? Where were they going?"

"Don't know, sir," he replied a bit too hastily.

John knew the sergeant would not speculate anything with him and dropped that line of questioning. "So you then went to Andrews?"

"No, sir. A group did set out that way." The sergeant smiled. "A lot of those wandering in from the Pentagon were men like General Scales. Well, I should say around the same rank. There was a lot of arguing back and forth, which I stayed clear of."

"Smart move, Sergeant. If two generals got into a row, I always made myself scarce."

"The general said we should strike out for Fort Belvoir and link up with whatever was there. Most of us went along with him."

"Most?"

"Well, sir, it did get a bit ugly. Not often you see a two star telling a couple of three stars to go to hell. The general, he had a hell of a lot more ground experience, not a paper pusher—we could see that and went with him."

"Good analysis and smart move."

"I understand you served under him, sir?"

At last, a question back, and John openly went over the times they served together, even how when he had decided to retire because of Mary's cancer, it was Bob who had helped him find a position at Montreat College, which was Mary's hometown.

The sergeant took it in, most likely not much that was new there if his job was to pump John as a "good cop" interrogator.

"Sergeant, you have family?"

And now the man did stiffen up. "Yes, sir."

"And?"

"I'd rather not talk about it."

"I understand. The general told me about what most likely happened to his wife."

There was a momentary pause again.

"They lived on the other side of the Potomac. My wife, two daughters, a son. My boy was a plebe up at West Point. My daughters still in high school. I didn't want them in some crap hole of a school in Washington. Unless you were able to pay forty grand apiece to send your kids to one of the schools where all the elites were sending theirs, you were stuck. I had in-laws up near College Park, good schools at least up there, so that's where we bought a small, very overpriced house to ensure the kids were safe and at a good school."

Again a moment of silence.

"I wanted to try to get to them; the general talked me out of it. I guess he was right. One man alone, trying to get through all that chaos. It was something I would think about at times before the Day. You know, trying to plan what to do if everything ever hit the fan. But you know how it was, sir. It was always figuring ten, maybe twenty megatons on Washington, an equal dose on Baltimore—one minute we're here, the next we're together with a lot of other poor souls waiting to talk to God. You know what I mean."

John could see that the mere recollection was painful. All the worst nightmares possible most likely kept him up night after night. No quick, near-instant deaths. A woman with two teenage daughters. What chance did they have? And the sergeant knew it.

John decided to tell him a bit about Jennifer, a choice to perhaps share a bit of the misery to help bond. The sergeant listened sympathetically.

"At least you were with her at the end, sir."

"Yes, I'm grateful for that. Also the most painful moment of my life, but yes, at least grateful that I know what happened, unlike you and General Scales. Does he ever talk about it?"

Again a moment of silence.

"Some nights I can hear him praying about her; that's all I'll say."

"I understand."

It was obvious the sergeant was not going to offer more. He did try, a bit woodenly, to ask about what assets John had, even as to where the Black Hawk was stashed, to which John just smiled politely and replied that he'd prefer not to answer. The sergeant finally relented and stood up to leave.

"Sergeant." As he spoke up, John held his coffee cup back up. "Can I hit you up for another cup—this time straight, no cream, no whiskey, no Xanax. Okay?"

The sergeant smiled. "Sure thing." He returned a moment later with a steaming cup and a plastic MRE pouch filled with hot stew. John took both gratefully.

"Again, sir. No wandering about or talking with other personnel. If I have your word of honor, I'll leave the door unlocked. There's a bathroom down the hall; we managed to get water running for the toilets, but no hot water yet. I'll loan you a razor, soap, and a heat packet from an MRE for shaving if you want."

"I'd appreciate that, Sergeant. I really would."

Several minutes later, he was in the bathroom, looking into a mirror, as always shocked by his appearance. It seemed he had aged ten years in the past two. His hair, cut short, had gone nearly entirely gray; the rough stubble of a beard actually was looking white, his features gaunt, eyes a bit sunken, complexion sallow. It was the look of his world, again reminding him of photographs of long ago, the aged and chiseled features of boys in their early twenties after a couple of years with the Army of the Potomac, having survived Antietam and Gettysburg and all wars since.

The sergeant came in, offering over a disposable razor that looked fresh, a small, still-wrapped packet of soap, a small toothbrush with a travel-size tube of prewar paste, and a plastic MRE bag, its chemical charge having been activated and the pint of water within hot to the touch. John thanked him with genuine gratitude. For the first time in more than two years, he was no longer struggling with an old-fashioned straight razor. He splashed some of the scalding-hot water onto his face, opened up the soap pack, rubbed it on to the stubble, dipped the razor into the hot water, and began to shave. When he turned on the faucet, a trickle of rusty-colored cold water dripped out. Several nicks and a lot of scratching later, he looked back up at his red-faced image in the mirror.

Well, if they are going to shoot me, he thought, *at least I'll look halfway decent.* The bag of water was still hot, and on impulse, even though the room was freezing cold, he stripped off his heavy flannel shirt and sweat-encrusted undershirt, leaned over the sink, poured several ounces of the water on his head, and scrubbed a bit with the small bar of soap, his short hair so oily he barely worked up a lather. Alternating between the freezing-cold water and what was left of the warm water in the bag, he rinsed most of the soap out. How he longed for a full shower, but the building was without heat, and at least he now felt semicivilized as he pulled the graying T-shirt back on and heavy flannel shirt over it. He finished up by brushing his teeth with real toothpaste, a heavenly feeling after two years of charcoal mixed with mint leaves.

Coming out of the room, he found the sergeant loitering in the hall, and thanking him, John handed the razor back, the sergeant motioning for him to keep the small bar of soap, toothpaste, and brush. He realized the sergeant had shown a subtle act of trust. Even though it was a modern disposable razor, a desperate man could still cut his wrists with it, an act unthinkable to a man like John, and the sergeant knew that.

"You almost look like an officer again," the sergeant said, offering a smile. "Don't let your stew chill down; the coffee has nothing in it. Chances are when the general finishes up with whatever it is that bit him in the butt, he'll want to talk to you."

"So you wanted me to look good and well fed before the execution, is that it, Sergeant?" John said it as a joke but saw that it had misfired.

"The general follows the rules, sir, same as me, and I believe you as well. In his eyes, you are a standing officer in the American army. There will be no summary execution, sir; you will have a proper court-martial. Yes, we executed some in Richmond and Roanoke, and that was for the same kinds of crimes you faced with that Posse group. So, sir"—and his voice now took on a harsh warning edge—"do not insult General Scales in my presence, sir, by implying he would act in any way contrary to the Articles of War."

John admired this type of loyalty and extended his hand in an offer of apology, which the sergeant, going formal, did not at first return.

"Sergeant major, I hold the general in the same respect as you do. I know I am under arrest by orders from Bluemont, not by the general's."

"I suggest you get some rest, sir," the sergeant said. He drew back and offered a salute, which John formally returned.

"Thank you for your help." He paused, continuing to hold the man's gaze. "And my sympathies regarding your family, regarding all our families, including that of General Scales."

There seemed to be a flash of easing down on the sergeant's part. He nodded and turned away while John went back to his assigned quarters.

The stew was barely lukewarm. He downed it hungrily, gulped the black coffee, unrolled the sleeping bag the sergeant had provided, and, in spite of what he figured was his condemned status, he was asleep within minutes.

"All right, Colonel Matherson, out of that sack and on your feet."

Momentarily confused, John sat up. How long he had been asleep he wasn't sure. It was dark outside, Scales standing over him holding a Coleman lantern that was hissing loudly, turned up to full illumination.

John sat up, rubbing his chin, surprised with the realization that he was freshly shaved and his mouth did not feel sticky and taste rancid.

Scales set the lantern down on the table pushed to the corner of the room, pulled a chair behind it, and placed another across from him, motioning for John to sit down. "I trust Sergeant Bentley saw to your needs and treated you well."

"A good man. You know how to pick them, sir."

"Fine. He told me you behaved okay—no tricks—and kept to the code, not revealing anything. Sorry about lacing that coffee with whiskey. In part, it was to get you to just relax, but yeah, we both know it's an old trick."

"Figured that one, of course, though it was tempting. So, when does the court-martial start, or are you really transporting me up to Bluemont for trial?"

Bob sighed, leaned back in his chair, and rubbed his eyes. "You got a good eight hours of sleep, John, I've been at it nonstop since midnight, and it's just past six here."

John waited for him to continue.

"We've orders to pull back to Roanoke and before we leave to take down everything you have here."

Even as he spoke, John glanced out the window and saw that several floodlights powered by a loud generator had been set up around the perimeter where the Black Hawks and Apaches were parked, crews busily at work.

"And that is it?" John said coldly. "Why?"

"Those were my orders, and don't you dare to try to throw the line at me about 'only following orders.'"

He knew better than to do so and raise that infamous moral argument.

"The attack we were supposed to be staging for to move on Atlanta has been put on hold. We don't have the assets to do it."

"Bob, if what I see parked outside is everything you've got, there is no way in hell you're ever going to secure Atlanta."

"What I was trying to tell them all along. I actually did pass up what you suggested—of course you can understand I did not peg your name to it—that we need to sit back through the rest of the winter at least, let them tough it out a while longer, and perhaps be more tractable come spring. They weren't happy up in Bluemont with that. They tried to push it. I said it was impossible. and they just got back to me to pull back to Roanoke but to take down whatever you've built here first."

"It means they're going to do it. They're going to pop an EMP. That's the real reason they want you to give up what you've just gained."

Bob looked over at him and said nothing.

"Anything else?" John asked.

Again silence.

"I assume I go with you."

"Something like that."

"It's what I figured."

Bob went up and looked out the window as a Black Hawk's engine started to turn over, was revved up for a minute, and then shut down. A light snow was falling, and once out of the sleeping bag, John could feel that the temperature in the room had dropped by quite a few degrees.

"Among everything else, John, the fact that you are still alive and managed to dodge that hit squad has made life even more complex."

"So it was Bluemont?"

Bob simply nodded.

"You suspected they would pull it; that was what you were warning me about."

"You twisted a lot of tails up there the way you took out Fredericks and then several days later talked with the BBC about it. They had to brand you as an out-of-control terrorist." He sighed. "And yes, I had orders to summarily execute you as a renegade. I didn't dare to try to contact you directly with a warning. There is someone in your ranks that was infiltrated in— most likely by Fredericks, who I guess gave a GPS of your house and your routine. I was able to bullshit my way around that you had slipped by me and that trying to take you out would trigger a full-scale riot. So they decided to act on their own with, as used to be said, 'extreme prejudice.'"

John took all that in, and there was an inward relief at last. He believed him, at least for now.

"And a huge subtext as well, John. They hit you, everyone will believe I did it, and it will trigger a regular civil war. It was a stab at me as well." Again he sighed and looked down at the floor. "One of the final acts that is triggering what happens next."

Bob stood, went back to his bunk, opened a briefcase, and pulled out what John recognized as an aviation map. Bob spread it out on the desk, anchored one corner with the Coleman lantern, and just stared at it for a moment. "So in your service, you never heard of Site R?"

"It's some place out in Nevada, isn't it?" John asked, but then he paused as Bob placed an old-style aviation slide rule on the map. The circular part was mounted in the middle of a rectangular sheet of metal, a foot long and four inches wide, one side hashed off with lines like a ruler, which John recalled could be used to measure distances on an aviation map.

Bob was not trying to hide anything as John came around the table to look over Bob's shoulder. John could see lines already penciled in, originating in Asheville and then tracing north by northeast. He leaned closer. To an untrained eye, the map was a nearly insane jumble of circles, numbers, and symbols for airports, some surrounded with air-controlled demarcation zones, the surface color shaded to indicate ground altitudes, inverted V-like symbols of such obstacles as antennas.

He focused his attention on the penciled lines that crossed into an area bound by Washington, D.C., on one side and extending westward for a considerable distance, all of it colored over in light gray.

Bob saw where John was focusing his attention.

"All that gray area was heavily restricted to air traffic, even more so after 9/11. It is just under 350 air miles from here."

John followed the line that Bob now traced out on the map and then looked up at him in surprise.

"My birds down there have an operational radius of just under 350 miles. I'm having my people mount some extra fuel tanks to extend that. It is eating up nearly every gallon I have left. We're lifting off in a couple of hours." He looked over again at John. "You're going with me."

"To hand over to Bluemont?"

Bob glared at him. "I'm leaving some of my personnel behind for this. It will be a handpicked team that goes with me. I don't think I need to tell you when it comes to really trusting everyone who is with me in this command, I know who I can count on, who might hesitate, and some just might jump the other way. My Major Minecci is one of them, so he stays behind. I can carry ninety with me in the Black Hawks."

He continued to stare at John. "I want you to pick half a dozen of yours to go with us."

"In heaven's name, why? So they can be executed too?"

"I want them as witnesses," Bob replied sharply, obviously insulted by John's accusatory response. "I want civilian witnesses who are about to learn the truth. I want you to pick six people that you trust."

"And that means trusting you, General."

"Yes, it does. Again, I leave the decision to you." Bob turned away and looked out the window. "You can walk out of here now, and no one will stop you. I publicly arrested you to protect you, because I had orders to either give you a speedy trial and execution or take you to Bluemont for the same. I am not going to do that. I had reason to believe another unit might be sent to visit you—or, for that matter, just drop a fuel-air bomb on that beautiful valley of Montreat to finish it—and let me take the blame. Arresting you as I did bought a little extra time, but Bluemont is expecting me to deliver you alive or dead before the day is out. Knowing that, you are free to go if that is your decision, but get your people evacuated now, today."

"Or what, sir?"

"This morning, my ass is on the line as well. I'll explain it later, but things with Bluemont have never been a love match from the start, of late have gone very sour, and you, Colonel Matherson, you and your friends have finally pushed me over the edge."

"Which means?"

"Your call, John. If you don't trust me with this, and suspect I am playing some game to deliver not just you but six of your friends to Bluemont as icing on the cake, then get the hell out of here now. If you trust me I want six of your best with me within two hours. I want them as additional witnesses as to what is going to happen next. When all is said and done this day, many might not believe me, but they just might believe you and your friends."

John again looked at the map. He was not sure exactly what it was that Bob was plotting, but it was not what he expected just twelve hours ago when arrested.

"Okay, sir," was all he could say in reply. Across a lifetime he had learned that far too often when someone said "just trust me," it was a prequel to getting a knife in the back. Bob was asking him now to not just put his own life on the line, but those of some of his closest friends and comrades as well.

But there was a cold logic to it all at this moment. If they were about to be betrayed, Bob's prediction that Bluemont would take his community off the map with an air attack was undoubtedly true and his friends would die anyhow.

He again looked at the lines Bob had drawn on the map, what it implied, and he finally made the decision. If Bob's intent was to betray them, they were all dead anyhow. If not, he would have to trust his old commander's offer.

"Okay, sir, I'll give them a call, but chances are they'll refuse."

"I won't blame them if they do, but I sure would appreciate their presence this day. I can have a Bradley up there in an hour to pick them up and bring them back. I hope they sign on."

John looked at the map one more time, still not sure where this was all leading. Some pieces were beginning to fall into place, memories surfacing from his time at the War College and a stint in the Pentagon.

"I'll make the call."

CHAPTER FIFTEEN

John climbed into the troop compartment of the Black Hawk and looked across to the opposite row of benches. Maury, Grace, Forrest Burnett, Reverend Black, and Kevin Malady seemed relatively at ease, but Lee was already cursing under his breath while Maury helped him to adjust his safety straps. They had all been roused out by his call to the town office. By chance, Forrest had come in from over the mountain when hearing that John had been arrested, demanding to lead a rescue operation before he was hauled away. The fact that all of them had actually trusted his voice, over a phone, to board a Bradley sent up from the airport and that it was not a trap to round up those who had served with him spoke volumes.

The door was about to be slid shut when, to John's surprise, Bob Scales climbed in, followed by Sergeant Major Bentley and a young staff sergeant toting several different radios. Behind them, extra boxes of small-caliber ammunition were loaded in, finally followed by a medic dragging aboard a couple of boxes of medical supplies.

The pilot looked back over his shoulder. "Sir, we are overweight!" he shouted.

"Just get us the hell up, burn off some gas, and we'll be fine!" Bob shouted back. "I've seen worse!"

"Your orders, sir," the pilot snapped back.

Bob looked around at John's friends and smiled. "So I suppose you're all wondering why I asked for this meeting at eight in the morning with the snow coming down."

"You're damn straight," Forrest muttered, and he finally added on, "sir."

"Time later—now just enjoy the ride, I always get a kick out of liftoff."

The eight Black Hawks and six Apaches started to taxi out from the parking area in front of the National Guard hangar, ground crews watching them, bundled up against the blasts of the rotors and the moderate snow coming in from the west.

Rather than do a straight vertical takeoff, they actually taxied down to the end of the runway, the lead Apache turning to face the wind and with wheels still on the ground built up forward speed before finally nosing up. John looked forward through the windshield of the Black Hawk to watch the show.

Forrest was leaning up out of his seat to watch as well and started to chuckle. "Remember that damn movie, the one with the bugler blowing charge? We actually used to do that in the 'Stan if a bunch of us were lifting off and going in harm's way. Got your blood up."

"Shut the hell up," Lee muttered, already clutching his vomit bag. "If I'd known this involved another flight, John, I'd have told you to screw off."

Three Apaches lifted off first and then circled high to protect the rest of the formation. The Black Hawks were next. John's pilot shouted a warning to hang on. He rolled forward at full throttle, shifted the collective, and nosed up high, Lee moaning as they lifted into the swirling snow. Gaining just a few hundred feet, they leveled off and turned to a nearly due north heading.

"It's going to be nap of the earth most of the way!" Scales shouted. "Might get bumpy at times with this weather. We're going to follow Interstate 26 over the mountains, angle east once through the pass until we pick up Interstate 81, and then straight on from there. Low and fast. Should take about two and a half hours. We've got a hot thermos of coffee for those who want it; otherwise, just settle back, try to get some sleep, and enjoy the ride."

His words were met by a heavy retching from Lee, and there were a few gags from the others until the slipstream shrieking past the helicopter whipped the stench away.

There had been a barrage of questions from John's friends as they wearily alighted from the Bradley at eight in the morning and were handed Kevlar vests, helmets, M4s, and combat packs. The situation was not helped when Lee saw that they were being shepherded to a Black Hawk, its engines already running.

Maury started to shout questions at John about what was going on and where they were headed as the chopper leveled off. John pleaded real ignorance as to what was transpiring, and all looked to Bob, who remained mum. The group settled into sullen silence as they raced north, interrupted only by Lee's pathetic heaves. The medic finally plastered an antinausea patch behind his ear and give him a couple of pills to swallow, and just as they were clearing the top of the I-26 pass at the Tennessee border, Lee finally settled down thanks to the medication and drifted off to sleep.

John sat lost in silent contemplation. He was putting one hell of a lot of trust in Bob at this moment, trusting not just for himself but for the lives of his closest friends on the line as well. The penciled lines on the map, whatever they meant, could have been just an elaborate ruse to lull him into belief and ultimately to lure in his best combat leaders and closest friends, one of them the only man in their whole community who could, in a clumsy way, actually fly a Black Hawk. For Bob to personally deliver them to his leaders in Bluemont, the murderers of their precious Fredericks, would be quite the coup.

He looked over at Bob, who, like any old hand with likely thousands of hours in Black Hawks, had settled into his bucket seat, stretched out his feet, lowered his head, and simply dozed off. There was precious little to see out of the frost- and snow-covered side windows. Up front, the view was just a blur of snow and glimpses of a deadly still interstate highway as the chopper banked to a northeasterly heading with Interstate 81 on their left. John caught a glimpse of what looked like an abandoned airport, its snow-covered runway running parallel to the interstate. John had a flash of memory; it might have been Mountain Empire Airport. He recalled it as a friendly place when several years back he was up with a friend in an Ercoupe, and they landed to get gas and some Coke and crackers. One of the mechanics noted that a cowling flap had cracked loose on the antique plane. It looked to John that the bent-back metal from the cowling would mean they would

be stuck for hours. The mechanic simply bolted it back in place and literally charged them just a dollar and a half for the bolt.

He hoped that whoever had helped them had survived and that he was
perhaps peering out with envy at the eight Black Hawks and six Apaches
racing by, just barely above the pavement.

Time stretched out, John nodding off as well after the tension of the last
few days. As he was stirring awake, he saw Grace and Kevin sharing a joke
and laughing, leaning in close against each other. The way they looked at
each other, he wondered if something was developing between the two. If
so, good; they'd make a fine match.

John dozed off again, to be awakened by Bob talking to the pilot and
then looking back to John.

"We just lost one of our Apaches. Turbine overheating. They're landing
on the highway, see if they figure it out, but we're pushing on."

"Where are we?" John asked.

"Near Winchester, Virginia. It really is nap of the earth now, so you'd
all better hang on for this last part."

Winchester?

If so, John knew that Bluemont was just fifteen or so miles to the east,
dug into the slope of the Blue Ridge Mountains, which too many mistak-
enly called the Shenandoahs. If they continued on the current heading, it
really did mean Bob was not heading there after all.

"How far to wherever it is we are going?" John asked.

"Fifteen minutes by air at most, but if Robert E. Lee was leading us as
infantry," he said, smiling, "it'd be about two days' forced march."

It took a minute to decipher that, and John smiled. His last remaining
doubts had just been set aside.

The helicopter flared fifteen minutes later as Bob predicted, nose high,
coming in to land, snow swirling up around it, nearly blinding the view.
John looked out eagerly. He recognized the terrain as if it were darn
near his own hometown. The chopper, nose into the wind, thumped down
a bit hard, bounced, and then finally settled. Bob, unstrapped from his
safety harness, was already up. He hunched over, went to the side door, slid
it open, and then leaped out. *Typical Bob,* John thought. First one in with
boots on the ground. John eagerly followed him. Bob shaded his eyes

against the rotor blasts as one helicopter after another settled down along the road, doors sliding open, troops leaping out with weapons raised.

John looked over at Bob. "Why land here?" he shouted.

Bob grinned at him. "Because I miss the place."

John could only shake his head in wonder.

Bob called over one of his captains and shouted some orders. The captain nodded and turned to issue a command, and nearly all the troops dismounted, spreading out to form a defensive perimeter—except for one squad, two of the men toting sniper rifles, another what looked to be a ground-to-air missile, and two others backpacking heavy loads that John could not identify.

"Care to come along?" Bob shouted to John.

"You're damn straight I'm coming along. Mind if my friends join in?"

Bob looked back at the Black Hawk they had been on, John's people tentatively climbing out, all of them with looks of confusion, Lee obviously unhappy until he looked around, eyes going wide before he ran a dozen yards forward to look up at a road sign.

"My God!" Lee cried. "Taneytown Road and Wheatfield Road! You have got to be kidding me!"

"No joke," Bob replied. "Care to follow me?"

"You're damn straight, sir!" Lee shouted, and it was he who eagerly broke the trail with his towering bulk, heading up the Wheatfield Road, plowing through the snow, which at places was drifted nearly two feet deep, clearing the way. Behind him, the two snipers—both men nearly as big as Lee—followed, kicking snow aside, obviously laboring to clear a path for General Scales, who, though obviously enthusiastic and eager to go, nevertheless was a man well into his sixties, and after five minutes of uphill ascent, it was apparent the hike was beginning to take its toll.

They reached the intersection with Sykes Avenue, where Lee had paused, looking back almost like an eager child ready to push on whether the adults were following or not. Bob nodded and pointed south, a steep ascent even on days when the road and hiking path beside it were cleared of snow. John paused at the intersection, waiting for General Scales to come up, the man bending double for a moment to catch his breath. While waiting for him to continue, John took in the view, limited for a moment as a snow squall swirled around them and then opening back up again. It truly did take his breath away, and he felt a surge of emotion.

"Let's go," Bob announced between hard gasps for air.

"Maybe wait a few minutes, sir, catch your breath," John offered.

"Go to hell, Matherson. I can still hack it," the general replied. "General Warren and a lot of others did it on the run with full gear. Then there was that artillery battery manhandling their guns up this slope as well."

"And they were in their teens and twenties," John replied cautiously.

Bob smiled at him and then without another word pushed forward. John noticed that the two snipers had held back a bit and were obviously working hard to tramp down the snow to form a path, as was Sergeant Major Bentley, who came along, invited or not—he had to be by his general's side. None spoke to the general or dared to offer a hand, but it was obvious they were keeping a sharp eye on him as they climbed the last few hundred yards up the steep slope.

John, walking by his side, found even he was breathing hard, a memory flooding back of when he was a boy and had actually run up this hill in his eagerness to reach the crest.

And indeed there was the crest just ahead, crowned by an iconic statue.

Bob was breathing so hard it started to worry John as they came nearly to the crest and turned off on to a walking path that wove its way through the heavy boulders.

Lee was already up atop one of the boulders, shading his eyes against the wind, looking west. "Down there, straight down there, one of my great-great-grandfathers came in with Hood's division." Then he swung his arm to the northwest. "Another one of my great-great-granddads was in the thick of it up there by the Seminary on the first day."

Lee's voice thickened. "My God, on the third day, he went in with Pettigrew and lost his arm. Oh my God." He turned away and tears flowed. "Why did you bring us here?" Lee asked of Bob, who smiled.

John was brimming with the same question, having recognized where they were within seconds of touching down. They had landed behind Little Round Top on the battlefield of Gettysburg.

Bob motioned for all to gather round, unable to speak for a moment, still breathing hard, coughing and spitting. "It sucks to get old, gentlemen. My first time here, I was twelve and ran my parents into the ground."

John was smiling and nodding as his mentor spoke.

"Colonel Matherson and I must have hiked—or should I admit driven it—a dozen or more times together for staff rides while we were at the War College up in Carlisle, which is only thirty or so miles off that way." He pointed to the north.

"I'm not getting it, sir," Kevin Malady said. "I've always wanted to visit this place, but why now?"

Bob turned and pointed out toward the west. "Site R is over there," he announced. "That is why we are here, gentlemen."

"Site R?" Lee asked, but it all came to John in a stunning rush of realization.

When Linda had first mentioned it, that they were monitoring some personal traffic back and forth from a Site R, it had not registered with John since he had assumed it was some government site out west. It wasn't until he saw the lines drawn on Bob's map that it finally had clicked. It explained why Bob had put a full clampdown on everyone in his command as to their destination and why he had made some obvious choices to leave certain personnel behind, while letting it appear he was personally delivering John to Bluemont and asking some of John's team to come along as well. To throw off anyone within his own command who might squeal to Bluemont after he lifted off, the game of luring in some of John's top people to be handed over as well hopefully worked.

Bluemont was far behind them now, and Gettysburg sixty miles farther on—as Bob adroitly put it, a few days' march away for Robert E. Lee. Site R was not much more than six miles away from where they now stood and clearly visible from Gettysburg's Little Round Top.

"Site R was built back in the early 1950s," Bob began, and John smiled. It was almost like the start of one of his lectures delivered at the War College.

"It was built as the fallback position for the Pentagon and civilian government in case of nuclear war. At the time it was built, the thinking was that the commies"— he paused with an ironic smile—"excuse me, I mean our good friends the Russians, if they launched an attack, it would come in with bombers, and we'd have six to eight hours' advance warning. So the military decided they needed a bunker, a damn big bunker to house upward of twenty-five thousand personnel. It had to be far enough away from D.C. not to be caught in the blast radius of a twenty-megaton warhead and the resulting fallout, but close enough that it could be reached by ground within two hours, by air within twenty minutes.

"Thus Site R. That's why a modern four-lane highway was built from D.C. to Frederick, Maryland, back in the 1950s. Convenient as well that, with Eisenhower as president, it was damn near in his backyard with his farm just down there on the other side of Seminary Ridge. Whenever things were looking hairy, Ike could always just go to his farm for a while without triggering a panic and be just a few minutes away from the biggest shelter in the country. Same with Camp David less than five minutes' air time away from here."

As he spoke, almost like a tour guide, he pointed to the west, but for the moment the snow squalls obscured the view.

"All the times I was visiting here, I never knew about it," Lee offered.

"Well, it was kind of a secret that wasn't a secret. Impossible to hide something like that, not like some of the sites out west. It's just we never talked about it, even with officers getting trained up at Carlisle just thirty miles from here.

"Anyhow, work crews that had been drilling all the tunnels for the Pennsylvania Turnpike, coal miners from the fields north of here, a couple of thousand of them were brought in and hollowed out an entire mountain. I've been in it. You go down half a mile deep, a regular three-lane highway, and come out into subterranean caverns that just seem to go on forever. They put up hundreds of recycled World War II barracks, officers' quarters, rather nice private trailers for high-rank civilians, mess halls, a giant cistern fed by artesian wells, storage areas, years' worth of survival food, and a meeting room that looks like it came straight out of that movie *Dr. Strangelove*. It's something like a time capsule down there actually. I was part of an emergency evacuation drill back when the Cold War was still on but winding down. Of course we all thought it absurd. It wouldn't be bombers hitting us anymore. It would be sub-launched ballistic missiles from off the coast, launch to impact on D.C., little more than five minutes."

He laughed sadly, shaking his head.

"During that surprise drill, just herding us onto the buses took an hour before we were even out of the parking lot. Your typical snafu. Kind of sad and creepy actually how we laughed about it on the drive up here. At least it was an overnight away from the Pentagon."

"When was it still operational?" Maury asked.

"I think that exercise we were in proved how futile it all was. If the shit hit the fan without warning, we were all toast, so why sweat it? Got moth-balled back when everyone was told the Cold War was over. Rumor is it was reactivated and the vice president was parked in there for a while immedi-ately after 9/11. But since then?"

He sighed and shrugged. "I know this. On the Day, there was no men-tion of it whatsoever to anyone in my wing of the Pentagon."

He turned to look back to the west and walked over to where the two soldiers who had been lugging heavy backpacks had already shucked off their loads and were pulling them open.

"But in a few minutes, we'll find out the real truth of it all."

Bob leaned over, pointed to the west, both of the men nodding, and as John watched, they began to unfold and open up a couple of portable dishes and several other antennas. They then pulled out of their packs a couple of high-grade military laptops and turned them on while the other trooper, squatting down, secured the dishes, aimed them west, and began to slowly adjust them while listening to directions from his companion with the com-puters hooked into the antenna arrays. Bob walked away and came back to the rest of the group.

"I thought about Site R off and on after the Day, even asked about it. All I ever got back from the government in Bluemont was blank stares and what I sensed were bullshit answers. The so-called reconstituted government at Bluemont was hunkered down in the FEMA fallback position and was told that was it. I just let it go since it was obviously a 'don't ask and we won't tell' type of issue. But there were whispered rumors. And then yesterday, your friend Linda Franklin handed me some data." He looked off to the west. "And if confirmed, my friends, the shit is about to hit the fan big-time."

He walked over to where his eavesdropping team members were still at work. One of them looked up at the general.

"A few more minutes, sir."

Bob, obviously agitated, turned back to John and his friends. "Bluemont was a more recently constructed site, actually the headquarters not for the military in the event of a catastrophic attack but for a civilian agency, FEMA. Not as big a facility by a long shot—could house four or five hundred at most—but a lot more up to date. Half the distance as well to D.C. for evacuation. Rumor was it was the parking place for whenever there was a ceremonial gathering in D.C.; a member of the cabinet, a representative from each House, and some administrators were sent there just in case something really bad happened. So Bluemont seemed the logical place for those that were able to be extracted out after the attack to set up the government and start over.

"Also"—he paused for a moment and then shrugged as if the topic were no longer a secret—"there were rumors that some personnel were already up in Bluemont on the day we were attacked, taking part in some sort of drill. Those allegedly lucky ones thus became the core of the reconstituted government. At least that is how I saw it all until Linda tossed those papers in my lap last night with e-mails leaking back and forth between Bluemont and Site R."

His features reddened slightly. "Some juicy tidbits, for this old guy, if not for how deadly it all is, I could almost laugh with how pathetic that guy in Bluemont sounded—what did they call it?—*sexting* or something like that to a woman in Site R?"

He shook his head. "So now we are here," Bob said, looking back to the west. "The snow's clearing for a moment. Go ahead and take a look. It's just to the left of that ski slope. That's Site R, just over there; you can see the antenna array atop the mountain."

John squinted and looked to where Bob was pointing, and sure enough, he could see the antennas jutting up from atop a ridgeline as a snow squall drifted clear for a moment.

"Wouldn't those antennas have fried off on the Day?" Maury asked.

"Yes, but for a place like that, they have backups and more backups stored inside. Remember it was built to come through a nuclear war. If that place is somehow operational, they got the replacements up. So that is why I decided we should park here—eavesdrop in the best way possible, with our gear literally aimed straight at them from only six miles away. I knew this to be as good a spot as any to do so and figured we'd soak up a little history as well while my tech boys listen in. Feel free to wander around, but don't go out into the open. I doubt anyone picked us up flying in twenty feet off the road for the last fifty miles, but one can never be positive, especially when coming up on a place like this. So now we sit back, wait for my team to get up and running, and see if this is a wild-goose chase or not."

"And if it is a wild-goose chase?" Kevin Malady asked, looking over at Bob suspiciously.

Bob sighed. "Let's just hope this is the final straw," he said coldly, his tension obvious to all.

"Let's take a look around," John announced, working to ease that tension down.

If this was indeed a wild-goose chase, what would his friend do next? For that matter, John now wondered, what would he do with whatever it was he was about to find?

John felt it best to step back for a few minutes. He motioned for his friends to follow and set off along the crest of the hill. He cautioned all to remain inside the wood line, while pointing out the statue of General Gouverneur Warren, hero of the Battle of Gettysburg, his bronze figure forever gazing toward where the Confederate attack had come in.

Near Warren's iconic statue, the gaudy and imposing two-story-high mini-castle dedicated as a monument to a New York regiment towered above them, which John suggested they not climb up. He noticed that Bob was following along.

Bob's features were drawn, pale in spite of the icy blasts of wind whipping about the hilltop. *What is he contemplating next?* John wondered.

"Wish we had time to really visit this place," Bob said. "Maybe when better times come again, we will do so."

In the silence of a winter morning, the landscape clad in snow, visibility at times dropping as another squall came in like powder smoke obscuring this field of action, John felt a strong profound connection with this land and its history. With all that had happened, would history eventually forget this place, its location returning to primordial forest such as what greeted the first settlers a hundred years before the battle? It was a sobering thought that a day might come when their descendants a score, maybe even a hundred generations hence might walk this ground, look at the broken fragments of long-gone monuments, and ask, "What happened here?"

Already, the first signs of neglect were showing. The once heavily trodden pathways were beginning to be reclaimed by the forest. Looters and vandals had already defaced many of the monuments, stealing the bronze plaques emblazoned with the names of the gallant for their metal. Even a couple of the artillery barrels had been stolen from their cast-iron gun carriages.

The path led down the slope to a simple granite monument tucked into the southwest slope of the hill. John, with his friend Bob by his side, approached it reverently. It was the monument for the Twentieth Maine, which had held the extreme left flank of the Union army on that grim, terrible day against odds as high as six to one. Even Lee Robinson, whose ancestors had assaulted this hill, stood in reverent silence as John spoke a few words about what this place meant to him, how the commander of that regiment, Joshua Lawrence Chamberlain, when returning years later to this now-quiet glen declared that where great deeds are accomplished, greatness lingers and that this was indeed the vision place of souls.

All stood silent, Bob then offering that they pray together for the repose of the souls of all who fell here, both North and South, which they did, Lee openly in tears.

As the group turned to start back up the slope, General Scales interrupted their departure.

"It might be legend, it might be true," he began, struggling to keep control over his voice. "Some claim that when the few hundred men of Maine who were sent to hold this position started to dig in, piling up rocks to form a low wall to huddle against and hearing a tidal wave of thousands screaming the rebel yell heading their way, Colonel Chamberlain stepped forward to address his men. Back then, officers actually did that kind of thing.

"Legend is that he cried out, 'Men of Maine,' and then went on to proclaim that perhaps only once in a century were so few men gifted to hold such responsibility, that whether their Republic lived or died now rested in their hands and their hands alone and let each man embrace that duty, if need be with his life.

"Maybe that is us this day," Bob said. "The Republic might rest in our hands before this day is out."

With that, he turned and started back up to the crest, shoulders braced back, walking with a purposeful stride. John followed in his wake, sensing that his friend had reached a profound decision.

As they reached the crest of the hill, Sergeant Major Bentley, who had stayed behind, came racing down to meet the group.

"My God, General, you got to see this!"

Bob moved ahead swiftly, and this time Bentley did not hesitate to put his arm around his respected commander and help him up the slope.

John fell in behind them as they reached the crest. The two snipers were hunkered down behind the boulders, and the antenna arrays had been covered with gauzy white camouflage netting, one of the snipers forcefully suggesting that the rest of the group stay low.

"We monitored a Black Hawk taking off from there not ten minutes ago," Bentley announced. "It was a tense moment, feared it might be coming over this way to check us out. But it turned southeast, and from the chatter we picked up, it was bound for Bluemont."

"Okay, and . . . ?" Bob asked.

"My God, sir, that place is bursting with chatter, uplinking to a sat, take a look!"

Bob went over to where his two surveillance people were hunched over their laptops, capturing data. One of the surveillance team looked up at Bob, but he wasn't grinning, and there was a chilling, icy look of rage in his eyes and clarity in his tone of voice.

"Sir, those bastards—" He paused for a moment. "Those people over there, the flow is near constant. The stuff going up, not much and highly encrypted, but we can break some of it down. It is the other traffic, though. Personal notes to people back at Bluemont. Personal! One of them complaining that they're sick of the frigging rations!"

The young man looked down at the ground and slammed his fist next to the laptop he was monitoring. "They're complaining about the food they're stuffing themselves with while I found out my father was killed trying to protect our family dog from being taken for food, and my mother was . . ." His voice trailed off into tears of rage.

Bob squatted down by his side, rubbing the back of the young man's neck, but as he did so he looked at the data scrolling down on the screen, eavesdropping on transmissions from Site R but six miles away. He remained thus for long minutes, at one point picking up the laptop and asking the other technician how to freeze the screen so he could reread something. As he did, his features reddened, and he put the laptop down and stood up.

"Okay, we've got enough here," he snapped sharply. "I want you two to stay here and keep monitoring. Capture everything you can."

He then looked back at the two who were the security detail and ordered them to stay as well, along with one to follow him back to the choppers and pull out some survival gear and rations and then come back.

He now looked at John and the others. "Let's go," he snarled.

"To where?"

Bob pointed across the fields of Gettysburg to the ridgeline beyond. "We're going to take that damn hill."

CHAPTER SIXTEEN

A thunder echoed in the valley behind Little Round Top as the five Apaches and eight Black Hawks started to rev up. General Scales had gathered his men around once back down from the hilltop and briefed all on what was to be done. Standing with his friends, it struck John just how concisely the man had thought out a tactical plan within a matter of minutes. He outlined the reasons for his decision first and offered that if any did not want to participate, they were free to stay behind. Upon hearing what the general had to say, every man and woman volunteered, all filled with a deep anger. Next he laid out the tactical plan for the assault to the pilots and troops and, having caught his breath after the grueling hike in the snow, did so with a calm radiance and voice of authority.

As he broke word to his command of exactly what they were facing and that they were going straight in, John could see the entire demeanor of the eighty troops, the pilots, and copilots shift within seconds to determination and bitter rage. Many of them cursed foully as they gathered round their choppers and geared up for a flight into what might turn into a hot zone, zipping up Kevlar jackets and loading up with extra ammunition from the boxes hauled in on the helicopter John had ridden in. The medics were tearing open the box of supplies carried on John's chopper, each of them shouldering several fully loaded emergency bags, checking to make sure they had medic armbands on both arms. Forrest quietly whispered to John that in Afghanistan the medics took those off since the bastards they were fighting would single out medics for special treatment.

Once loaded up, Bob circled to each team, bowed his head, and led them in a short prayer before helping them to load in. Bob chose to go in with the lead copter, telling the pilot for the one John was on to hang back and be the last one to come in once the LZ was cleared.

"This is why I wanted you and your friends with us!" Bob shouted. "If we find what I suspect is over there, I want civilian witnesses. You might not know it, John, but your reputation extends beyond just Black Mountain, Montreat, and Asheville. So if things get hot, you are to stay back and stay alive. You got that?"

Bob led this last group in a short prayer with heads bowed, and he shook hands. He told Forrest and Malady—who was a marine vet—to make sure everyone's gear was squared away and then stomped off to the lead chopper.

"Let's double-check each other's equipment and get ready for some shit!" Forrest shouted enthusiastically, and John could see that in a perverse way, PTSD was forgotten for the moment; he was back in his old element and enjoying it.

As each climbed into the chopper, Forrest and Malady checked their Kevlar jackets and helmet straps, Forrest giving John an admonishing look as he zipped up John's jacket and then helped him up while Kevin double-checked that each was properly strapped into their safety harness.

"It could be hot; we might get hit. If we do and have to ditch in, follow what I do!" Kevin shouted.

Their pilot looked back over his shoulder, holding up one hand in a thumbs-up gesture, which all returned.

"Bugler, sound charge!" Forrest shouted as they lifted off, this time rising nearly vertically, the Black Hawks spacing out into line astern with Bob in the lead Black Hawk, while two Apaches fanned out on to either flank, the other three moving ahead of the column.

John looked over at Lee, who was sitting next to him, his gaze fixed forward, and for once he did not look nauseous.

They swung a bit to the north, following the Wheatfield Road rather than cresting up over Little Round Top. Lee, wide-eyed, rattled over the place-names—Wheatfield, the Peach Orchard, Trostle Farm—his voice filled with emotion. John recalled years ago at the town's Civil War round-table meeting when Lee had nervously presented a talk on his family's role in the war, how two of his ancestors fought in this battle, one losing an arm. There were tears in his eyes as he leaned up to take in the view.

"If only we had half a dozen of these at that battle, good God, how it would have changed things."

"Suppose we had them instead," John quipped back with a smile.

The choppers swept low over the snow-covered battlefield, hugging the earth, climbing up the gentle slope of Seminary Ridge, pitching up slightly to just barely clear the trees. Ahead, Sachs Covered Bridge could be seen, beyond that the open fields of the Eisenhower Farm, and then directly ahead . . . Site R, the ridgetop bristling with antennas.

Lee took a deep breath and looked across at Forrest, who was sitting silently, eyes half-closed.

"How bad is it going to be?" Lee shouted.

"Don't know. Maybe just some garrison types who will pee themselves and run as we come in. Or special-ops types with orders to shoot to kill anyone who comes close and tear us apart as we come in. You'll know in about three minutes."

"Now I know how my granddaddies felt." Lee sighed, his features set and grim. He started to whisper, and John caught bits of the Ninety-First Psalm, what many called the soldier's psalm, "Thou shall not be afraid for the terror by night; nor the arrow that flieth by day. Nor the pestilence that walketh in darkness, nor the destruction that wasteth by noonday . . . "

"Minute out!" the pilot shouted. "Doesn't look hot; we circle while the others touch down first."

John strained up to try to catch a glimpse. The mountain filled the windscreen before them, the pilot pitching up slightly to clear space beneath him for the Apaches that were already skimming along the face of the ridgeline. There was a paved runway at the base of the ridgeline, John noting that it had been cleared of snow. Between the airfield and the ridge, there were a half a dozen helo pads, cleared and marked as well. A Black Hawk rested on one of the pads.

So far, no shots were fired. The Apaches zoomed back and forth along the face of the mountain as the chopper with Bob in it skimmed in low, flared up, and touched down on one of the pads. Bob was the first one out before it had even settled down, followed by troopers with weapons raised.

Another came in, and then a third while a couple of hundred feet up, the Black Hawk that John was in turned in sharp sixty-degree banks, circling about. Lee, absolutely wired up, for once did not complain while Forrest, chuckling softly, hung on to his safety harness with one hand, M4 strapped across his chest.

"Shit, we've got incoming!" the pilot shouted, and he snapped the Black Hawk over into an opposite turn. For a few seconds, it looked to John as if he was about to go straight into the mountain before pulling around.

John caught a glimpse down and saw that a firefight was opening up, tracers arcing back and forth between where the Black Hawks were landing and bunkers set to either side of what appeared to be a massive steel door at least thirty feet wide and twenty feet high. What appeared to be orange tennis balls snapped past the Black Hawk's windshield, the pilot cursing and going into sharp spiraling evasive turns.

"I'm putting us down before we get hit up here!" the pilot shouted, and he nosed nearly straight down. The helicopter pads were now all occupied by the Black Hawks, John's pilot opting for an access road, plowed as well, that circled round the pads. He flared up sharply, the medic that was flying with them reaching up to slide a side door open. Even before touching down, he was shouting for them to get out, stay low, and hit the ground.

Forrest was the first up and in spite of his old war injuries was out the door. He ran half a dozen feet and flung himself to the ground, M4 up and ready to engage.

John had not done anything like this in more than twenty years, but training did kick in, as it did for Malady and even Maury, who leaped out and sprawled into the snow alongside Forrest. John looked back and saw Lee standing in the open doorway, Grace behind him.

"Lee, Grace, get out!" John shouted, and at that instant, a burst of shots laced down the side of the helicopter, shattering its forward windshield, hitting the pilot, and then stitching across Lee. He collapsed back into the Black Hawk, the long burst raking down the length of the helicopter, tearing

across the turbine housings, and from there into the tail rotor, which disintegrated into deadly shards arcing out in every direction.

Smoke billowed out between the still-rotating rotor blades. John got to
his feet and ran back even as the medic was grabbing hold of Lee, pulling
him feet first out of the crippled bird. There was blood covering Grace's face,
but she was up, helping to push Lee out, John grabbing hold of his friend's
legs and pulling him to safety.

His friend was wide-eyed and gasping. It looked as if his vest had taken
a shot, and for a few seconds, John thought he had just been stunned by the
blow, turning to Grace and shouting at her if she was wounded.

"I don't think I'm hit!" she cried. He then looked back at Lee, who at
that instant started to cough up blood.

The medic frantically tore the Kevlar jacket open, cursing. There was
an entry wound that had punched through his jacket just above his heart.
The medic rolled Lee up onto his side, slipped his hand down the back,
and came up with a bloody hand.

"Damn it!" the medic cried, and he looked at Grace, who had been standing behind Lee in the helicopter, her face splattered with blood.

"You hit?"

"No, not sure . . . no."

"Then put pressure on Lee's wound!" the medic shouted, pushing down
hard with his own hands first and then grabbing Grace's hand and guiding
her to take over. He looked back to the front of the chopper. The pilot was
staggering out, arm drenched with blood, copilot running around the front
of the Black Hawk to help him get clear. The medic returned his focus
to Lee.

John knelt beside Lee, not sure what to do other than hold his old friend's
hand. The medic was cutting through Lee's parka and shirt underneath,
stabbing the exposed arm with a syrette of morphine, and seconds later the
look of panic in Lee's eyes cleared a bit while the medic worked frantically
to set up a bag of plasma.

"What's his name?" the medic cried, looking over at John.

"Lee Robinson."

The medic leaned down close to Lee's face. "Lee, you are going to make
it, but you've got to stay with me. I've got to keep you breathing, I'm going

to work a breathing and suction tube down you; don't panic. You got that? Stay with me. I'm going to get you through this!"

Lee looked around wide-eyed, gaze resting on John. "Gettysburg. Good place to die, my friend."

"You're not dying, Lee!" John cried.

Lee coughed up more blood. "Thought we'd share being grandfathers together. Tell them I love them."

He started to convulse. The medic gave up on the breathing tube for a moment, pulling Grace's bloody hands aside and actually slipping a couple of fingers into the entry wound.

"Jesus God," the medic whispered softly, and then he leaned back, reached into the tote bag dangling from his shoulder, pulled it open, and drew out an emergency surgical pack.

"I've got to try to go in," the medic announced, "stop the bleeding there."

He unrolled the pack beside Lee and then drew out another morphine syrette and stuck it into Lee's arm.

John looked at him, questioning this decision.

"I've got to all but knock him out," the medic snapped before John could even ask.

All this time, gunfire was snapping around them, several shots stitching up the snow within feet of where the medic was working. He looked back over his shoulder. "Damn you, you sons of bitches, can't you see I'm a damn medic?" he cried.

Lee was still frothing up blood. His lungs were clogging with aspirated blood, the medic whispering for Grace to cover her friend's eyes and keep reassuring him.

She began to sob as she leaned over him and started to whisper calming words that he would make it.

Another convulsion tore through Lee's body, blood spraying up out of his mouth in a torrent, and then he just started to relax.

The medic leaned back and said nothing, lowering his head.

Lee looked up at John and actually appeared to smile. "Gettysburg. Bury me here, John." And then he was gone.

John could only kneel beside his friend of so many years, holding his hand, finger resting on his pulse, feeling the last faint beat, and he was gone. All he could do was kneel over, embrace his friend . . . and cry.

"Matherson!"

He looked up. It was Sergeant Major Bentley gesturing for him to come forward.

John ignored him for the moment, looking back to the medic.

"It was .50 caliber most likely. Kevlar won't stop that. Felt like his aorta was nicked, pulmonary arteries shot up as well." He stared at Lee for a moment and then turned to look at the pilot, who was crouched down next to him, blood pouring down his arm.

"Let's take care of that," the medic said, and he turned away as if Lee had never existed.

"Damn it, Matherson, on me!" Again it was Bentley. John forced himself to stand up and then paused, leaned back over, and closed his friend's eyes. Grace was kneeling by the body, crying.

"Grace, stay here with the medic. You can help him."

"I'm going with you," she snapped sharply.

"Damn it, I'm not losing you too, Grace. Now stay here with the medic. He needs you more than I do."

"Stay here, Grace; I need you," the medic ordered even as he tore away the sleeve of the wounded pilot to reveal arterial blood pulsing out.

"Matherson, damn it, the general wants you. Move it!"

John looked back to where Bentley was standing out in the open, arms on hips, as if oblivious to the firefight that was going on.

John spared one last glance for his fallen friend, stifled back his emotions, and crouching low started toward Bentley.

Maury, Forrest, and Malady, who had been deployed forward, got up to join him.

"Lee?" Maury asked.

"Gone," was all he could choke out.

A loud tearing sound, almost like that of a bedsheet being ripped in half, echoed against the face of the ridge. One of the Apaches, angled down, was at a hover fifty feet up, pouring in a stream of 30mm shells across the face of the huge steel doors, then turning its fire into a bunker on one flank for several seconds, pivoting, delivering the same deadly blow to the second bunker on the other side of the door. Its tracer rounds made its efforts look like a garden hose of liquid fire pouring down from an angry heaven. A second Apache was swinging back and forth, sweeping the ground above the door with the same river of death. There was a secondary explosion from what must have been a concealed bunker positioned partway up the steep slope.

John came up to Bentley, who without comment turned, set off at a slow jog, and led them to where General Scales was down on one knee, snapping out commands into a handheld radio.

"That's it, you've torn the shit out of them!" he cried. "We take one more shot. Don't wait for me. Cut loose again!"

The two Apaches broke away from their attacks, turned, and with rotors thumping loudly pivoted and climbed up.

Bob stood, went over to a Black Hawk, and held up his hand, and the pilot offered him a microphone linked to a loudspeaker strapped to the helicopter.

"That's it!" Bob shouted. "We didn't want a fight. You opened fire first. You saw what you got. Lay down your arms, come out hands over your heads, and I promise safe surrender. You've got thirty seconds, or some Hellfires will come in next."

The bunker to the left flank of the steel door let go with a secondary explosion, ammunition within lighting off like a long string of firecrackers, men around Bob ducking. He remained standing.

"Fifteen seconds or you'll really get a taste of hell."

Three men came staggering out of the second bunker, hands up, one of them obviously burned, smoke swirling up from his scorched uniform.

"Medic forward!" Bob shouted. "Surrender; we'll take care of the wounded. This is General Bob Scales, Eastern Command. I am giving you a direct order that will save your lives. Now give it up."

One of Bob's medics raced forward and actually knocked the man in the smoldering uniform down, rolling him back and forth in the snow and shouting for one of the other surrendering men to help him. The sight of this finally broke the standoff at last.

More men and women began to emerge from concealment, many of them wounded.

"That's it! Keep coming forward!" Bob shouted. "All medics up front and center. Treatment center on me. Move it!"

The Apaches continued to circle overhead like birds of prey eager to strike. Looking up, Bob picked the transmission mike up, clicked it, and passed the order for them to climb a bit higher, hover, and hold fire unless directly ordered to attack.

He let the mike drop, grimly surveying those coming in, and then looked over at John. "Thank God you're okay," he said. "I looked back when your bird was hit; I thought it was you in the doorway."

"It was my friend Lee," John replied, still struggling with emotion.

Bob looked at him questioningly.

"He's dead."

Muttering a curse, Bob turned away. "Damn them, damn them. There was no need for this. I had to come in sharp and fast, not just go up to the gate, knock politely, and ask to please come in. But it didn't have to be this way. Damn fools should have seen we had the firepower edge."

Several dozen surrendering were now coming forward, the majority injured in some way. A captain, dragging a wounded leg, approached Bob and stopped half a dozen feet away, and just glared at him. "Who the hell are you?" the captain snapped.

"First off, I am your superior officer, and you will salute before addressing me," Bob snapped.

The captain glared at him and those around him, attention focusing on John and his people for a moment, who, other than their flak jackets and helmets, were decidedly unmilitary.

"And this rabble?"

Sergeant Bentley stepped forward and got within inches of the captain's face. "You will address the general as *sir,* you son of a bitch, and salute a superior officer. Now close your damn yap and answer when spoken to."

The captain began to reply, and Bentley leaned in almost nose-to-nose, exactly like a professional DI intimidating a jerk of a recruit who, if behind the barracks and out of sight, would get his butt kicked.

The captain relented, stepping backward a few paces and to one side, turned his focus toward the general, and finally offered a salute.

"Captain Dean Hanson, United States Air Force."

Bob barely returned the salute. "Your unit?"

"223rd Security Battalion."

"Oh, Christ, air force security," one of the men behind Bob growled. "No wonder."

Bob did not look back at whoever spoke out with disdain. "Why did you fire on us, Captain?" Bob snapped.

"Sir, our standing orders are anyone enters this compound, we shoot first and ask questions later."

Bob looked around at the carnage. Lee was not the only casualty on their side. Several men near Bob were down. Dead and wounded were being carried in where one of the medics was shouting that he was setting up a clearing area, literally next to the command Black Hawk. The ship John was in was beginning to burn, and no one was bothering to try to suppress it.

"Now listen to my orders," Bob snapped at the captain. "That steel door over there, open it now."

The captain stiffened and shook his head. "My name is Captain Dean Hanson, United States Air Force, serial number—"

Bob stepped closer. "Cut the bullshit, Captain. Open the damn door."

"Sir, what you are ordering is in direct contradiction to my orders."

"From where?"

"Sir, I do not have to answer that question."

"Bluemont?" Bob shouted and John saw a flicker in the captain's eyes, and he knew Bob saw it as well.

Bob shoved past the captain and strode the hundred yards to the door, ducking down for a moment as more munitions from one of the bunkers ignited like a Fourth of July display. A dozen of Bob's troopers and John and his friends fell in behind him. As they approached the vast steel door, they could see it looked almost like a safe, its face pockmarked from the strafing runs by the Apaches that still circled overhead.

"Captain, open that door!" Bob said, looking back at Hanson, whom Bentley was shoving along behind them.

"I can't."

'What do you mean you can't?"

"The control mechanism was inside the bunker you just destroyed." There was an edge of triumphant sarcasm to his voice.

John looked at the captain with unconcealed hatred. In a world of starvation, those like Hanson stood out. He was full fleshed, actually overweight, face round and florid, obviously spending more time sitting in a comfortable office, three good meals a day, and not out scrounging for enough calories to struggle through one more day.

"Bullshit," Bob snapped. "There's always a backup. Something like this, no idiot built it with only one way to open the door. You've got a backup."

"My name is Captain Dean Hanson—"

The captain's words were cut short by a scream of panic as he ducked down, falling to his knees, Sergeant Bentley, with an old-style 1911 .45 semi-auto standing over him, having discharged the weapon only inches from his head.

"Next one will be to the head in thirty seconds if you don't answer the general," Bentley said.

The captain looked up at Bentley, obviously terrified, and then looked to Bob.

And then there was actually a bit of a smile. "Screw you. I know you. You'd never execute one of your own," he snapped, but his voice was quavering.

Bob glared at him, all around them silent. John took it all in and knew the captain was right. Bob was trying to bluff him, and the captain knew it. Though they had come all this way, that steel barrier blocked them from the answer they sought.

There was only one way out, John realized. He stepped forward and went up to Bentley.

"Give me that pistol!" he snapped.

Bentley looked back to his general, who gave a subtle nod of agreement.

John took the pistol, stepped in front of Hanson, and leveled the weapon straight at his forehead. "Now listen very carefully, you son of a bitch," John said, his voice icy cold. "My name is John Matherson. For a year, I was military commander of my community down in the mountains of North Carolina. Do you hear me, Dean?"

There was no response.

"I am not part of General Scales's command. I'm here as a witness to whatever is behind that door. Less than a week after the shit hit the fan and everything went down, I put a bullet into the head of a thieving drug addict in a public execution. Do you hear me?"

Again no response, but he could see the man was looking up at him wide-eyed.

"I've personally executed dozens more since then without hesitation. Ten minutes ago, one of your bastards killed one of my closest friends; the blood on me is his blood. Do you read me?"

There was a faint nod.

"I've extended your life by two minutes. Maybe the general would not order you shot, but by heaven, I have no such compunctions. I'm giving you thirty seconds to do as the general ordered. If you do not, I will blow your frigging head off and not hesitate. At this moment, I might blow it off any-how as payback for my friend even after you answer, but your odds are better if you answer. After I shoot you, I'll single out another and another of the prisoners until someone finally gives the general the answer he wants. Now, Captain Hanson, do you read me?"

He paused and looked around at those gathered and then back at Hanson. "Fifteen seconds!" John snapped.

"John?"

He looked up. It was Scales, who was shaking his head.

"Stay out of it, damn it!" John shouted. "We've been through hell for two and a half years, and I want the answers now. Lee didn't die just for us to stand around like a bunch of assholes in front of a door this bastard can open."

He looked back at Dean. "Ten seconds . . . eight seconds!"

Several of the prisoners, obviously terrified, shouted for the captain to re-lent, one crying out that he knew the answer and would give it.

John could see that the man had lost control, his trousers soaking through.

"Six seconds." He pressed the cold muzzle of the gun to the captain's forehead.

"All right! All right!" Dean screamed. "I'll talk."

John nodded and stepped back, suddenly feeling completely drained.

"Get him to open the door now," John commanded. "If he doesn't open that door in three minutes, bring him back here and I'll kill him."

John walked back to Sergeant Bentley, easing the hammer of the .45 down to the safe position. He held the weapon by the muzzle, which was warm, and offered it back to the sergeant, who took it.

Bentley stared him straight in the eyes. "By God, sir, would you have done it?"

"After all we've been through?" John said, not answering the question. "And, Sergeant, don't ever ask me that question again."

A couple of troopers of Scales's command dragged Dean up to the door. He fumbled to open the collar of his uniform and drew out several keys on a chain around his neck, muttering that the electronic controls had been shot out. He handed one to a guard accompanying him, explaining that they both had to insert the keys in locks ten feet apart and turn them simultaneously. They did so, and with a metallic hiss, the vast doorway cracked open.

Bob stepped forward. "Hold it there!" he shouted, going up to Hanson's side. "You got a security detail in there?" he snapped.

A moment of hesitation.

"You play us wrong now and I hand you back to my friend Matherson. Do you have a security detail inside?"

"Yes, sir."

"Then you are in first, and order them to stand down. I got a sniper aiming straight at your back. You play us false and you will be the first to die, and I turn those outside over to Matherson and his men. You read me? If the killing is to stop now it is up to you, Captain. I want any security to come out, weapons held overhead, or by God I'll have an Apache outside this door pouring 30mm and then a Hellfire down inside."

"It's over!" Hanson cried.

"Then make sure it is."

Hanson, shaking and barely able to walk, approached the front of the blast door, which had slid open just a few feet, hands held high over his head.

"This is Captain Hanson. We are surrendering this facility to forces of Eastern Command. Safety your weapons and come out with them held over your heads."

John could hear voices from within arguing back and forth for several long, drawn-out minutes. Dean started to step into the cavernous darkness but froze in place when Scales barked out an order for him to not take another step in, shouting loudly that he was General Scales, in charge of Eastern Command, and was taking control of this facility and those who surrendered would be treated honorably.

Dean, voice breaking, began to sob, crying out that it was over and for the detail within to come out as ordered.

Finally, they began to emerge, and within minutes, half a hundred were out the door, dropping weapons as they emerged to be hustled off by a detail set up by Sergeant Bentley.

Finally, there was no one left except Hanson partway into the half-opened doors.

Bob finally came up to his side. "How do we open these things wide?"

Dean nodded to a control panel inside the doorway. Bob told him to go ahead. Dean entered a code, and the doors slid the rest of the way open.

John watched this in angry silence. The doors must have weighed several dozen tons or more and were at least three feet thick. Fifty yards into the tunnel, there was another set of doors, not as substantial but still significant, and for a second time, the same ritual was played out of cracking them open, Dean taking a few steps in, shouting for the security detail behind them to come out with weapons secured and surrender.

It was a tense few minutes with several of them refusing until Bob, with his excellent command voice, talked them down, that the entire firefight had been a tragic misunderstanding and as he was commander of all troops east of the Appalachians, those within were under his command, to obey immediately or face court-martial. They finally surrendered.

"Another security detail beyond here?" Bob asked as he nodded down the wide, cavernous corridor carved out of solid rock, three lanes wide, illuminated every hundred feet or so by a dimly glowing fluorescent light set into the ceiling.

"Just those off duty and everyone else."

"Everyone else?" John asked.

Dean looked at him but said no more.

"Get this bastard out of here," Bob snapped, looking back at Sergeant

Bentley. "All prisoners secured outside. All wounded regardless of side treated ASAP. I think ten of our men can handle this rabble now that they've sur-rendered. I want the rest on me. I want you with me as well, Sergeant, so get it squared away and then catch up."

Bob watched as Dean, staggering from shock, was led back into the brilliant midday light of the entrance.

"Would you have done it?" Bob asked, looking at John.

John just gazed at him, still feeling cold, nearly broken inside, wonder-ing now what shock would confront him next.

Bob put a reassuring hand on his shoulder. "We've all been through too much," he said, gesturing down the long tunnel. "Let's see what's down there and if this trip was worth the price."

CHAPTER SEVENTEEN

It was a very long trip down, a hike of well over half a mile. John and those with him and Scales fell silent except for occasional whispers and Bob explaining this entire facility was carved out of solid rock and was not a natural cave.

The road began to level out from its five-degree pitch, the air within warmer so that parkas were unzipped. Bob cautioned those with him to keep their Kevlar jackets buttoned up tight and weapons held up in a nonthreatening manner and to only return fire if fired upon first.

A babble of voices began to echo—shouts, cries, yells of confusion and fear. Bob ordered the main group to stop, and he sent several scouts ahead, again reminding them of orders not to shoot.

Long minutes passed. Bob squatted down on the hard tarmac, reaching into a pocket and pulling out some hard candies from an open MRE pack and passing them around.

As they waited, Bentley came up. There was a wordless exchange of glances, and it was an indicator to John that this officer and top NCO truly worked as a team, respected each other, and could work on instinct of mutual trust without a word being said.

Bentley unclipped a flashlight from his vest, snapped it on, and continued down the tunnel until finally he was only a pinpoint of light. Several more minutes passed and then all jumped with a start; a single shot, followed a second later by two more, echoed like a cannon in the cavernous hall, the flashlight snapping off.

"Son of a bitch," Scales snapped. "Up, get ready to move, weapons on safety, but be ready to engage if fired on."

The troopers with them began to move out, edging along either side of the tunnel. Bob gestured for John and those with him to hold back for a moment, passing a quiet order to the one medic who had come in with them to get against the wall and be ready to set up an aid station.

"I don't want a bloodbath," Scales announced. "If we find what I think we're about to find, I don't want a bloodbath."

They started forward, crouching low. A flashlight came back on down at the end of the corridor, blinked twice, and then several seconds later blinked five more times. Bob, unclipping his flashlight, repeated the signal back, and came fully erect.

The flashlight at the end of the corridor grew brighter, moving up and down, obviously held by someone walking toward them, shifting the high-intensity beam up toward the ceiling so as not to blind them. The troopers advancing ahead of John and those around him stopped in place. There were some whispered exchanges, and then Bentley came into view, illuminated by the dim overhead fluorescent lights, left hand holding his .45. In the pale light, John could see blood soaking his arm. He had his right hand firmly gripped to the collar of a civilian dressed in what was the nearly ubiquitous uniform of government officials of chinos and a blue dress shirt. The man was short next to Bentley, nearly bald, features heavy, looking back and forth nervously at the troopers who were poised to either side of the tunnel.

Scales stood in place, not coming forward, John falling in by his side.

A few more steps and Bentley showed just enough restraint not to send the man he was hanging on to sprawling to the pavement, but he did shove him forward so he nearly lost his balance.

His dignity obviously insulted, the pudgy-featured man drew himself up, tucked his shirt back in—which had been disheveled by Bentley's rough handling—looked down at his left sleeve, which was splattered with blood, and shot an angry glance at Bentley, who remained by his side.

The medic was already up by Bentley's side.

"It can wait," Bentley snapped. The medic looked over at the civilian.

"That's my blood on him," the sergeant said sharply.

"Just who the hell are you?" the civilian cried, voice a bit quivery, but Scales ignored him.

"Sergeant Major Bentley, are you hit?"

"I'll be all right, sir; it can wait."

Scales glanced to the medic.

"Don't see anything arterial, sir; I guess it can wait a few minutes."

"Fine, then."

The civilian cleared his throat to try to interrupt, but Scales continued to ignore him.

"Report, Sergeant—what was that shooting about?"

"This man here had a bodyguard who decided to take issue with my presence. He fired first."

There was a pause.

"So I killed him."

He said so as if it were just a typical day's work, and Scales nodded.

"A lot of others around—you'll see in a minute. I had to aim for the center of his body. Didn't want any stray shots to get someone else."

"He murdered my man—"

Again Scales cut him off. "Let the medic tend to your wound, Sergeant, and thank God you are safe." At last, he turned back to the civilian. "You are damn lucky my sergeant was able to walk back; otherwise, it would have gone very badly for you and a lot of others. Do you read me?"

That caught the man off guard.

"Now you can talk. Who are you, and what is your position?" As he spoke, he took a step forward, hands balled up and resting on his hips. John had seen this more than once when his friend wished to convey a very strong "don't mess with me" attitude.

The civilian nervously cleared his throat. "I'm Richard Pelligrino, head administrator of this facility."

"And this facility is . . . ?"

"Site R."

"I already know that," Bob snapped. "What is it now?"

Pelligrino hesitated, looking around at all those who were gazing at him. "Who the hell are you to come barging in here like this, slaughtering my security team?"

"You are answering the questions, not I, and you'd better answer me now, Mr. Pelligrino. I've got over two hundred troopers outside who are very pissed off. I've got a full battalion airlifting here within the hour. I have the assets. Maybe you know who I am, my command, and what I can bring to bear. Do you realize that, Mr. Pelligrino?"

Pelligrino's gaze drifted to Scales's name tag. He hesitated and then looked back up at him. "Why are you here? This position is not part of your command."

"It is part of my command now and you are answering the questions. Therefore, my question. Who are you, and why are you here?" His voice rose as he snapped out the last few words.

"Like I said—" he began.

"'Like I said, *sir,*'" Sergeant Bentley interjected sharply, still standing by Pelligrino's side while a medic was cutting open his sleeve to examine his wound.

Pelligrino cast a sidelong glance at the sergeant, who was still holding on to his .45 with his good hand and then back to Scales. "Like I said"— he paused for a few seconds—"sir. I am the head administrator for Site R."

"And Site R is . . . ?"

Pelligrino hesitated, which provoked Sergeant Bentley to pivot slightly. The .45 was still down at his side, but the threat was apparent.

"Answer General Scales completely," Bentley directed, articulating each word slowly and clearly. "We already know this is Site R. What is this place for now, today, Mr. Pelligrino? And no more game playing."

"It is a designated civilian emergency relocation center," Pelligrino finally replied, his voice barely above a whisper as if conveying a great secret.

"*Sir,*" Bentley again interjected.

"Sir," Pelligrino whispered, head slightly lowered.

"Then let's take a look at this emergency relocation center, shall we?"

"You can't!" Pelligrino cried. "This facility has the highest level of security requirements, which I doubt you are qualified for. I am ordering you to turn around, leave now, and we can just call what happened a tragic mistake that I won't report."

Bob looked at him with absolute contempt. "My security clearances existed long before you most likely crawled out of your frat house at some Ivy League hole. I've put up with shits like you for over forty years, but not this day. If you want to debate it further, look around you. These men with me have as much security clearance as I do after the hell they've been through for the last two and a half years and every right to see what is down at the end of that road."

Pelligrino started to bluster, and Bob, contempt obvious, stepped past him. "Someone drag this bastard along," he snapped.

John, who had remained silent throughout the exchange, could not help but smile as Pelligrino was shoved to one side, a trooper grabbing hold of him by his collar and pushing him along. He had endured far too many like him during his brief stint at the Pentagon, some of them in uniform, who were just ticket-punching their way up the career ladder and to hell with what was actually right or how many got hurt or even died as a result of their actions.

The tunnel began to widen out. The troopers keeping pace with Bob along either side advanced with weapons raised but not positioned to fire, but could do so swiftly if need be. If there was danger around the corner, Bob did not seem to show the slightest concern, walking down the middle of the paved road that leveled out and then went into a curving turn to the left at the bottom. Half a dozen troopers ahead of him reached the corner where the road turned left and came to a stop, raising weapons and shouting at someone unseen to drop their weapon and keep their hands visible.

Bob motioned for the trooper pushing Pelligrino along to bring him forward.

"Now listen carefully, Mr. Pelligrino. Do you have more armed personnel around that bend?"

He hesitated, and again Sergeant Bentley was menacingly by his side.

He could only nod.

"Then you go forward and tell them to lay their weapons down and come out with their hands up, that the fight is over and no one gets hurt. But if one of my troopers gets shot, Sergeant Bentley or my friend John Matherson here will gladly put one into you. The fight is over, Pelligrino; let's make sure no one else gets hurt."

The thoroughly frightened administrator was shoved forward. He cautiously advanced the last few dozen yards, turned in the middle of the road illuminated by several floodlights, and squeaked out a command for those waiting on the far side to give up.

What sounded like an argument started until Pelligrino shrieked out that they were outnumbered and everyone would die if they didn't surrender immediately.

Seconds later, the first men and women of what John hoped was a final line of defense emerged, hands over their heads. Bob's troopers, weapons pointed high but still aimed in their direction, shouted out for them to move up the road on the double.

Several dozen emerged, and as they were moved up the road, John could see the looks of fear.

It was the medic who was trying to follow Bentley and work on him who helped defuse the tension, walking in among them, offering reassurances, announcing that if any were hurt they should fall out and she would take care of them; otherwise, they should just keep moving up the road toward the exit. To John's amazement, one of them was actually smoking a cigarette, the scent of it wafting around him as they passed him.

A cigarette? Here? Just what kind of place is this really?

"Any more?" Bob shouted. A trooper at the very front of the ground turned, looked back, and replied with a hand gesture that all were cleared, but John could see there was a look of confusion from the other troopers who were standing at the bend in the road.

"Let's see if all of this was worth it," Bob said softly, starting out again.

Whatever they were about to see, John could not get out of his mind that his friend Lee was dead. Whatever they were to find, was it worth Lee's death?

And then he turned the corner of the road dug half a mile down into a mountain and came to a stop in silent amazement.

The underground cavern, if it could be called that, was illuminated nearly as bright as day and seemed to stretch off into infinity. The road, which had broadened out into four lanes as it went through the curve, emptied into a vast, open underground chamber, the road just continuing straight on until it was actually lost to view. There was a turnoff to the right, an illuminated sign overhead announcing all entering had to first report for decontamination and security clearance. Bob ignored it and up at the front with his troopers just pressed straight on, Bentley dragging Pelligrino along.

The ceiling overhead arced more than thirty feet high. The spread of the cavern from his left to right was at least several hundred yards or more.

The broad street was actually lined with barracks. World War II–era wooden barracks, row after row, each two stories high, and strangely, even topped with shingled roofs, interspersed with curved aluminum Quonset huts. At regular intervals, natural stone pillars rose from the floor to the ceiling to support the vast mountain overhead so that the interior almost looked like some strange, surreal, military cathedral.

All stood in amazement—except for Bob, who looked around, hands on his hips.

"Like I told you, John," he said softly, "I was here once, more than twenty-five years ago as part of a drill. This was designed in the 1950s to be the fallback position for the Pentagon in the event of nuclear war.

"The barracks you see laid out down this road—it's actually called Main Street—were left over from World War II. After the place was hollowed out, it was felt that the cheapest and easiest thing to do was just build these; we still had hundreds of them as surplus, prefabricated and sitting in a warehouse a couple of hours away. No weather here, no termites, they'll stand a hundred years or more.

"Off to the right, there used to be a motor pool, even used to have a couple of old Sherman tanks down here, rigged up as earthmovers if we had to dig our way out if a nuke hit close by. There even used to be old-style electric golf carts for driving around inside. I think that was Ike's idea."

A hundred yards or more down Main Street, a small crowd had gathered.

"How many are here now?" Bob asked, looking back at Pelligrino.

"Who?"

"Civilians, damn it."

Again a hesitation. "About fifteen hundred, maybe two thousand. Some leave at times, and others are brought in." A brief pause, and with Bentley glaring at him, he finally added, "Sir."

The man's features had gone to nearly purple, his knees were shaking, and with a moan, he slowly sank to the ground. The medic ran up to him, knelt down, felt for his pulse, and then looked up at the general.

"Might be his heart, sir."

"Given what I think is here," Bob said softly, "I have to ask: What heart?" He then announced, "Shoulder all weapons. These are civilians here. Unless he dies on us, drag him along."

He gazed down coldly at Pelligrino. "Which way to the command center?" he snapped, and the ailing man pointed straight down Main Street.

He set off with a purposeful stride, right up the middle of the main street, troopers—with weapons shouldered as ordered—flanking to either side. John trailed along behind him; his friends Reverend Black, Maury, Forrest, Kevin, and Grace, who had disobeyed John's orders to stay behind and had caught up with the group and was still obviously in shock over Lee's death, followed behind Bob.

They passed several of the wooden barracks, relics of what seemed another age. The paint was peeling from the wooden sides, but other than that, they seemed well tended. There were even nameplates tacked to doors.

John slowed as he passed a Quonset hut on his left. There was a single name tag tacked to the door. He recognized the name. The same as on the personal e-mails that Linda had snatched out of the ether and which had finally led them to this place. Surely it couldn't be?

As he stared at the nameplate, similar to the types of nameplates set in front of an officer's home on a military base, the door cracked open, an anxious young face looking out, a girl in her early teens at most, still gangly like a young colt.

He smiled at her, and a flicker of a smile creased her slender face as she nervously brushed back an errant wisp of reddish hair. John stopped, his friends staying with him.

"Are you here to arrest us or something?" she asked.

He shook his head and gestured toward the front porch as if requesting permission to approach. She hesitated, nodded, and opened the door wider.

He caught a glimpse of inside the barrack. Though the exterior was of World War II vintage, the interior looked something like a typical living room—a sofa, several chairs, and what appeared to be the back of an old-style television from thirty or more years ago.

"Don't worry, young lady. There was a misunderstanding, but it's been settled. You're perfectly safe."

He spared a quick glance back down Main Street. Bob had gone far ahead of him, surrounded by the troopers who had entered with him. John looked over his shoulder. His friends, however, had lingered behind, waiting for him out on the street.

Grace was still with him, and it was she who broke the tension.

"Hi. My name is Grace," she announced in a warm, friendly voice, and she simply stepped past John, advanced up a step onto the porch, and extended her hand.

The nervous smile on the young girl's face within the hut broadened slightly. She opened the door wider and took a step out, reached forward, and politely shook Grace's hand.

"You sure everything is okay?" the girl asked. "We heard gunshots."

"*We?*" John asked.

"I live here with my mother and two kid brothers. The emergency siren went off. Our teacher told us to go to the shelter, but I ran home to get Buster before going to the shelter area, because sometimes we're in there for a day or two and I can't sleep without Buster, and then I heard shooting."

"Who is Buster?" John asked.

She hesitated, a bit embarrassed.

"It's okay," Grace said softly.

The girl reached behind her and then produced a stuffed bear, obviously well worn from constant loving attention, and her features turning red with embarrassment.

The gesture, the sight of her holding the stuffed bear, struck John like an electric shock, and he lowered his voice. "It's okay, young lady. My daughter had a friend like him named Rabs." He could barely get the words out.

Among his friends, there was no one who did not know about Rabs, his daughter's beloved stuffed companion who sat on the windowsill in the sunroom and watched over her grave, and which John had gone back into his burning home to retrieve, more cherished to him than any other memory of the past.

Maury came up to John's side.

"You're about the same age as my son, who is eleven," he said. "He won't admit it, but he has a friend like yours—a panda named Pandi—that sits on his nightstand. It's okay, young lady."

"I'm twelve. My name is Laura."

"We're pleased to meet you, Laura," John interjected. "Don't be anxious; everything is okay now. Just a misunderstanding, and no one was hurt. We're just visiting here."

"That's good," Laura replied, still obviously a bit rattled. "When I heard the shooting and I wasn't in the shelter area, I went to the far corner of the room and curled up behind the sofa with Buster as we were drilled to do and waited for the all clear. But I haven't heard the all clear."

"I think it might be broken," Grace replied. "They should have sounded it by now."

"Should I go to the shelter?" she asked.

"If you would feel more comfortable," Grace said smoothly. "If you want, I'll walk you there."

"Okay."

Grace took another step up, reached out, and put a reassuring hand on the girl's shoulder and then looked down at Buster. "I have a bear almost just like him," she said warmly, and there was genuine emotion in her voice. "Mine is named Winnie. How did Buster get his name?"

Laura instantly began to choke up, tears coming to her eyes. "They kept telling me that they would go back and get our dog, Buster, and bring him here, but they never did."

She started to cry, and Grace gently embraced her.

"Come on, let me help you to where the shelter is, but you'll have to show me the way."

She nodded, sniffing back tears, clutching tight to Buster.

John struggled with his own emotions. The frightened girl was the same age as his Jennifer. At least the same age as Jennifer was when she was still alive . . . and dying.

Something she said forced the question he had to ask, sensing that if there were going to be straight answers, it would be here and now from this girl.

"How did you get here, Laura? You haven't always lived here."

"Some men came to our school and called out my name and those of a few other kids. And now I'm here."

John knelt down in front of her, looking up at Grace, shaking his head slightly for her to wait. Grace picked up on the signal, stopping in place, a protective arm around Laura, holding her tightly to reassure her.

"Can I see Buster?" John asked. Laura reluctantly held him out, and John took him.

It was nearly impossible to keep his own emotions in check. The scent of the stuffed bear, the worn fabric, a bent ear that had obviously been stitched back into place. For a moment, in his heart, Buster was Rabs.

He kissed Buster and handed him back to Laura with a whispered, "Thank you."

She snatched him back, but her eyes were on John. "Are you okay, mister?" she asked.

John could only nod.

"He misses his daughter," Maury said, voice thick with emotion as well.

"Where is she?"

"She's back home in North Carolina," Maury quickly interjected, sparing John from giving a more honest answer.

John took a deep breath and forced a smile. "So you were in school, some men came in, called out your name, and you left with them. Is that it?"

Laura nodded.

"Where did you go to school, Laura?" Maury asked.

"Sidwell Friends in Washington."

"And why did the men take you out of class?"

"It was all kind of scary. We all knew the men. They work for the Secret Service."

"Secret Service?" John asked, startled but trying to not let it show.

"Yes, sir. They're always there because the president's kids go there too. The men are very nice to us, though it's a bit scary at times since we all know they have guns on them. One of them would always sit in the back of the classroom where the president's kids were in class. Out on the play-ground, they'd even bat some balls for us, so we all knew them."

"So the Secret Service men took you out of your classes?"

"Did anyone else go with you?" Maury interjected.

"Yes, sir. About twenty or so. They said we were going on a special trip." She clutched Buster a bit tighter. "They let me bring my backpack, and I had Buster in there, so he came with me."

"And then what happened, Laura?"

"We went out to the ball field behind the school, and there were two helicopters there, and they had me get on board."

"Just you?"

"Oh, no, sir. About twenty kids or so."

"The president's kids as well?"

"No, sir. We thought it strange, but they were left behind."

"And then?"

"We flew here. It was a fun ride. The Secret Service men told us to buckle in tight, that it was going to be like a roller-coaster ride, and it sure was. My friend Becky threw up all over the place." She smiled at the memory.

"Where did you go on this ride?"

"Here. We landed outside, and they had us run in here. It was a bit scary; there were some men with guns outside. They had us get into the backs of a couple of trucks and brought us down inside here."

"Laura, when did you take this helicopter ride, and how long have you been here?"

She looked around, suddenly a bit nervous. "We were told we're not sup-posed to talk about it, sir."

"Laura." It was Grace now, bending over to face the girl at eye level. "It's okay, sweetie. You can share it with us. Mr. Matherson trusts you, and I do too."

Laura was silent for a moment, and tears began to well up. "It was a scary day. We were taken to what they call the shelter here. All day long, more kids were coming in, parents, some old people. I had to put on a large name tag that hung from my neck with my parents' names on it.

"Finally, I saw my mom with my two little brothers. She had one suit-case for all of us"—she paused, welling up—"but Buster, our dog, wasn't with her. She was crying and told me that Daddy was safe but in another place. Then they told us they had to shut off all the electricity for a day, except for emergency lights, and we all slept in the shelter area."

"What day was this?" John asked, and now his voice was insistent, growing impatient.

She just stared at him.

"Laura, sweetheart. What day did this happen?" Grace asked softly.

"The day the war started," she whispered.

"When on that day?" John pressed, trying not to sound insistent and frighten the girl. "What time of day did the helicopters take you away from your school?"

Again silence.

"When?" This time, he nearly shouted the question so that she blanched and began to cry again. Grace shot a look of admonishment at him, and she moved between the girl and John.

John felt a hand on his shoulder. He looked back, and it was Forrest, who shook his head and pulled him back.

"I'm sorry, Laura," John said softly, standing up and backing away.

"We're all sorry if we scared you, Laura," Grace pressed. "It is just we want to learn the truth, and we trust you to tell us that. Okay?"

"It was in the morning," she whispered. "I don't know. Classes started at 8:15. About an hour later, we heard the helicopters landing outside, and some of us were told to leave with the Secret Service men."

"My God," Maury whispered. "Before ten in the morning?"

John could only nod as he struggled to absorb all that what she said implied.

"What about the other children in the school who didn't go with you?" Grace asked.

"I don't know. We were told they were safe, but we never saw any of them again." There was a pause. "You're from the outside?" she asked plaintively. "My best friend, Halle, didn't go with us. Are they safe? I wanted to send an e-mail to my friends that didn't go, but I was told only official things can go out on e-mail, but someday soon I can see them again."

With that, John turned away, unable to hide his pain, his rage. It was not the girl's fault. The kid was terrified by this encounter. It was not her fault, but as he looked back at her, he could see his Jennifer standing there.

Forrest, with a firm hand on John's shoulder, led him back out into the middle of the street that went the entire length of the deep underground cavern.

"Do you know what this means?" John snarled. "Do you know what this means?"

Forrest, features emotionless, could only nod.

"They knew. At least some of the damn bastards knew. They got theirs out at ten in the morning of that day and hid them here before the shit hit the fan. They knew!"

He shouted out the last words. Several of Bob's troopers who had lingered behind to secure the entryway tunnel were standing close by, and he could see in their eyes, their features, that the truth was dawning on them as well. One of them was crying, cursing foully about his own wife and newborn son, an unrelenting stream of obscenities, a comrade holding him tightly, telling him to let it go.

John was feeling the same rage.

On the Day, it had been like any other day but for one great difference: it was Jennifer's twelfth birthday. After teaching his early afternoon class on such a beautiful warm spring day with half of his students dreamily looking out the window, he had gone down to the village and at a favorite store purchased twelve Beanie Babies for his daughter and raced home to be there before she arrived. Jen, dear now-gone Jen, his first wife's mother and such a beloved grandmother to Jennifer, had arrived as well to greet their birthday girl.

The rest of that final afternoon of peace had unfolded without incident. Jennifer and a friend had gone up into the neighbor's orchard to play with the family's two golden retrievers while he grilled up some burgers and hot dogs for dinner. Then Bob Scales, the same Bob Scales who just an hour ago had led the assault on this facility, had called from the Pentagon to wish Jennifer a happy birthday.

They had then chatted. There was no warning, no Bob sending some sort of coded message that the shit was about to hit the fan and to get ready. Just a friendly chat until suddenly it was obvious even Bob was being caught off guard. Some shouts of panic in the background from Bob's end, his suddenly saying, "Something's up. Got a problem here. I gotta . . ." and then the line went dead.

The war, the Day, had begun for John and the rest of the nation as all power just went off, the sound of traffic on the interstate drifting into silence, a few minutes later a puff of smoke rising from a distant ridgetop, to be learned later it was a commercial jet that had gone in, killing all aboard, one of a couple of thousand jets going down across America.

All of it coming to a stop . . . at just after four in the afternoon . . . hours *after* young Laura said that she had been evacuated to safety.

And yet now, at this moment, after two and a half years of struggling to survive, to reluctantly rising to being essentially an emergency dictator of his town, of having to personally execute a thieving drug addict only days after it started, to carrying his dying father-in-law out of a dying nursing home where the dead were literally decaying on the beds where they had been left to die because no one could help them . . . to all the starving, the death, the fending off lone marauders that devolved into wandering gangs of hundreds who would actually kill someone so they could feast upon them . . . and then to hold his twelve-year-old daughter as she died for want of a single vial of insulin, while down here, a select few were hidden away before it had even started and had lived comfortably since?

"Laura!"

He turned to look up Main Street. A woman who appeared to be in her late thirties or early forties, well dressed in a clean white blouse and jeans, figure healthy and definitely not starving, was running toward them.

"Mommy!"

Laura broke free from Grace's protective embrace, leaped down the steps of the Quonset porch, and ran toward the woman, who slowed, grabbed the frightened girl by the shoulders, and pushed Laura protectively behind her. She looked toward Grace, who had been following behind Laura.

"Back off and leave my child alone," the woman snapped, and then she half-turned to look at Laura. "Are you all right? Did they hurt you?"

Laura was sobbing too hard to answer.

The woman turned back to face Grace.

"She's all right. No, we didn't harm her, ma'am."

"Who the hell are you?"

"My name is Grace Freeman."

"Listen, damn you, you keep your hands off my child. You're armed; you are dangerous. You stop where you are and get the hell out of here now!"

Grace looked over at John, obviously confused. John stepped toward the woman. "Miss Freeman is with me," he announced. "She is no threat to your child."

She glared at John with an icy, dismissive gaze. "And who the hell are you?"

Her sanctimonious, superior tone was to John like sandpaper grating on an open wound, reminiscent of so many like her going back to childhood, the rich kids who lived up in Short Hills, the wealthy community that adjoined where he lived for several years in a working-class neighborhood. Their parents were the power brokers of firms in New York while his father was putting his ass on the line in the skies over Vietnam. The wives and daughters of haughty generals, unlike men like Bob Scales who truly came from the salt of the earth himself. To college professors one had to bow to in order to have any hope of getting a passing grade with their all-so-superior attitude, cramming their political views down his throat. She was of that ilk, and that attitude would not have survived a week if she had been trapped in the world up on the surface.

He took a deep breath and tried to control his own rage. "I am Colonel John Matherson, State of Carolina, and this young lady is a lieutenant under my command and will be treated with respect."

"I don't give a damn where you're from. I'm ordering you to clear out now and stay away from my children, or you will face charges, Mr. Mather."

"That is Colonel John Matherson," Forrest retorted.

"Do you even know who I am?" she shouted.

John tried to extend his hands in a calming gesture, but she overreacted, as if he were drawing a weapon.

"Security! I need security here now!" she screamed.

John looked past her. Wherever Bob had gone with most of his command, he was long lost to view. A crowd was beginning to mill about out along Main Street. All of them looked to be civilians. Well-clothed, well-fed civilians, from mothers holding infants to several elderly, one of them in a motorized wheelchair.

Some were looking their way, and as if this woman was indeed some sort of leader, they started to head in their direction to witness the confrontation.

John looked back at the nameplate on the barrack's door.

"Your husband is . . ."

"Yes!" There was a definite superior gaze as if with that question being asked she could now play her trump card and he would wilt away. "He was a senator and is now acting secretary of state."

"At Bluemont?" He said the two words slowly.

"Yes, you idiot, at Bluemont."

"If I were him and married to you," Forrest growled sotto voce, "I'd stay there."

"How dare you!" she cried.

"I dare because I have a right to dare," Forrest replied.

"And you were evacuated here hours before our country was taken down by an EMP?" John snapped, voice filled with bitterness.

"I don't have to answer that question," she replied, but there was a slight loss of confidence in her voice. She turned away from John, looking back over her shoulder. "Someone get security here now and throw these bastards out!"

"We killed most of them," Forrest replied. "If you'd care to, go up outside, take a look at their bodies. And then take a look at the entire damn world out there while you were hidden away down here."

He was about to say more, but John could see that Laura was behind her mother, terrified, clutching Buster and sobbing uncontrollably.

It took all he could do next to try to control his voice. "Ma'am, I suggest that someone take your daughter to what she said is a shelter area, but you stay here. I have a few questions I'd like to ask you."

"I want security now!" she screamed. "They're assaulting me!"

The crowd was drawing closer. John looked past her. They numbered in the hundreds while Bob had brought less than a hundred with him when they stormed this place. More than a quarter were dead, wounded, or still deployed outside in a defensive perimeter protecting their precious airlift assets or dealing with the prisoners and wounded. He realized he should have stayed with Bob, who had forged ahead to find the communications center. All who was with him at this moment were the three guards that had been detailed to hold the entry to the tunnel and those left of what could be called his command—Grace, Reverend Black, who was gazing about, obviously in shock, Kevin Malady, Maury, and Forrest.

He could sense it was unraveling.

He glared at the woman, who was obviously trying to provoke a reaction.

"Ma'am, this can go one of two ways," John announced, struggling to control his voice, his emotions still overwhelmed by all that he had learned in the last few minutes. "We're going to back up to the tunnel entrance. I ask you to tell those folks behind you to get back in the other direction and we wait to let this sort out. We don't want this to go out of control, so please help me."

"Get your filthy asses out of here now!" she screamed. "Security, they're trying to assault me!"

John saw several men pushing their way through the crowd, M4s up and aimed toward him, the crowd parting to let them pass but following in their wake, some shouting obscenities and threats.

"My people, get back!" John shouted even as he unslung the M4 over his shoulder.

"He's going to shoot me!" the woman screamed. Her scream was picked up by the approaching crowd, most of them scattering or dropping to the hard tarmac floor of Main Street.

It was happening too fast for him now to hope to control. He began to draw back. Forrest was already crouching low, weapon aimed. Grace was out front, crouched low and moving forward, and John could see that she was trying to snatch Laura and knock her down while the girl's mother remained upright, screaming.

A shot rang out, another, and then another.

Grace tumbled over onto her side, blood spraying out. Forrest, weapon leveled, opened up, aimed shot after aimed shot, dropping those who were firing on them. The crowd behind the action started screaming and running in panic. John stopped his retreat, crouching low, crawling the dozen feet to Grace, and flinging himself over her to protect her with Kevin at his side. Maury had his weapon leveled, shooting as well, while the three troopers who had been guarding the tunnel entry came running forward, weapons

at the shoulder, one of them firing several times at a man in civilian clothing who had a short-barrel automatic, catching Maury in the leg.

A well-aimed shot from Forrest dropped that man as well as he tried to
dodge behind a barrack.

The firing from down Main Street stopped; John, still prone over Grace,
looked up. The street, so crowded but a minute earlier, was empty, the smell
of cordite heavy in the air, wisps of smoke being sucked up by a noisy ventilation fan set in the ceiling over the street.

The three troopers pressed forward past where John was, and throughout
it all, amazingly, the woman who had provoked it had remained standing,
most likely so startled by the frightful onset of violence she had not yet even
grasped how to react. Grace was lying prone over Laura, who was gasping for
air and trying to crawl out from under her protection. Horrified, John saw
that Laura was bleeding, blood leaking out of a wound in her back.

John drew back from his covering of Grace with his body. Her eyes were
glazing, going out of focus. She had been hit in the head.

"Laura okay?" she whispered.

Crying, he could only nod. It would be like her to sacrifice all for a child
she barely knew.

"She's okay, sweetie," John lied.

"Good. Tell my daddy . . ."

And then she was still.

It was near to painless and all so quick, unlike so many deaths he had
witnessed, so many he had held while they were dying. All he could do was
gather her into his arms and cry while Forrest knelt by his side, weapon
protectively raised, and screamed for a medic. Kevin Malady went forward
with the three troopers, reaching the security troops they had just engaged,
all of them apparently down. One of them started to rise up, swinging his
weapon around and cursing with rage, and Kevin put three more rounds
into him.

Only now did the woman who had triggered all of this realize that her
daughter was hit as well.

The medic came running up, still crouched low, knelt down by Grace's
side, put a finger to her carotid artery, snapped on a flashlight, and shined
it into her eyes.

"I'm sorry, sir, she's gone." Without delaying even a second, the medic crawled over to Laura, felt the wound on her back, gently ran a hand underneath her, drawing it back to reveal she had an exit wound in her upper chest, and then frantically went to work. Even as she did so, she looked over at Maury.

"Where you hit?"

"Leg."

"Where? Upper?"

"No, calf; might have broken my leg, though."

She glanced at him as if evaluating his injury. "You'll have to wait!" she cried and then focused her attention back on Laura.

Laura's mother now started to react, sobbing, squatting down by her daughter, screaming, "All of you murdered her!"

John, still in shock, was still holding Grace, brushing her long, dark hair back from her battered face.

"Sir! Sir!"

He looked up. It was the medic.

"You got to get control of this. Start by getting this damn woman out of here."

The young medic's orders snapped him back. John forced himself to focus, to let go of the moment, try to think a minute, five minutes ahead as he was once trained to do, no matter how horrific the situation.

He looked forward. Kevin and the three troopers had pushed forward by fifty yards, Kevin shouting with his booming voice for everyone to stay calm, keep back, to get inside shelter and no one would be hurt. But then he looked back anxiously toward Grace, obviously wanting to go to her side.

One of the troopers was checking the four dead, kicking their weapons aside, picking up the light automatic carried by the one in civilian garb who had been killed and slinging that weapon over his shoulder.

Laura's mother, hysterical, was trying to push the medic aside, but Forrest was already reacting, roughly grabbing her by the shoulder and shoving her back, half dragging her away.

John stood up, went to Forrest's side, and pulled the woman to her feet. She was continuing to scream, an almost sure provocation for more chaos to ensue. He held on to her, pushing her toward her barrack house. The last thing needed now was for her to run off screaming that those with him had been responsible for the shooting of her child and not the other way around.

"You were the one that triggered her getting shot!" John shouted. "Now let my medic try to save her!"

Laura had left the Quonset hut door open, and John shoved the woman up the steps and inside. What he saw startled him. The quarters were spartan and yet comfortable—a bit of a strange mix of retro furniture that was obviously from the '60s and looked like it had come off the set of *The Brady Bunch,* complete with the ubiquitous olive-green color so favored back then. A twenty-five-inch console television, once considered an indicator of the height of affluence, was in the room along with the usual recliner lounge chair, mixed in with standard government-issue gray desks, straight-back chairs, and a bookshelf that was half-empty.

The woman was beginning to sob. John looked at her without pity and glanced at Forrest.

"If she starts getting loud or tries to leave, you have my permission to punch her out," John snapped.

She looked at him with open hatred but then fell silent.

M4 at the ready, John opened the door into the rear of the Quonset hut. There was a small kitchenette to his right, a sink, a two-burner range and fridge, and an unopened pack of MREs on the counter. To his left, a door half-open. Looking in, he saw there were twin bunk beds against one wall and a single standard military-issue bed against the other wall. A few toys were on the floor, a wooden-track train set, several dolls, and a model of a spaceship, obviously the children's room.

Next to the kitchenette, there was a small but nevertheless complete bathroom with a shower, wash sink, and toilet. Curious, he turned on the hot water for the sink, and after about a minute of running cold, warm, hot water finally poured out, and the toilet most definitely flushed; there was even a roll of toilet paper beside it.

All of this filled him with a mix of rage but then strangely nostalgia as well for such simple comforts of a lost age that a few had managed to preserve down here.

He now noticed for the first time that it was all climate controlled. There was no heat running. It was cool, perhaps in the midsixties, but not uncomfortable. The entire cavern was at the same temperature and humidity as well from what must be a vast climate control system and sanitation support for the entire cavern. The energy demands must be prodigious, at least by the standards of the world after the Day.

At the far end of the room, there was one more door. There was perhaps a one-in-a-thousand risk, but still, after all the tragedy of the last few hours, he was not sure what to expect, so he flipped off the safety on his weapon, leveled it, and then popped the door open.

It was the master bedroom. She was indeed high-ranking. It was no two cots pushed together; there was actually a queen-size bed that took up more than half the floor space of the room but nevertheless looked damned comfortable when compared to the freezing cold nights with Makala when they would revert to zipping two heavy down sleeping bags together in order to be close and then snuggle together on their double bed. Jen's room did have a king-size bed, but that had been her room and, in his heart, taboo to ever move into even though she had been dead for close to half a year. All of that gone in the fire just a week ago.

He glanced around the room. It was typical military construction from the '40s and '50s—particle walls, flimsy doors of half-inch plywood, standard government-issue fixtures, from toilet to light sockets . . . and all of it looked at that moment to be luxury all but undreamed of.

There was a flash memory from Orwell's *1984* when the author had written that in a world of desperate scarcity, possession of a kilo of coffee or a few grams of real chocolate could define the ruling elite from the rest of the world and be worth fighting for and many willing to die for in order to possess.

A few pictures were pinned to the wall, apparently taken out of wallets. The woman out in the living room, perhaps five or six years back in a maternity ward bed, proudly holding newborn twins with a six- or seven-year-old girl horning in at the edge of the photograph at least appearing to look happy. From what had just transpired, he wondered if she truly had been happy at that moment.

There was a photo, framed, over what he could only assume was her husband's small dresser. He recognized the face.

So this is our acting secretary of state, standing next to the person who was

*once the president of the United States and died on the Day when Air Force One,
insufficiently hardened, had gone down.*

He read the autograph from the president written across the bottom,
a person who, if he had met him while in the military, he would have been
forced to salute but nevertheless held in contempt, an autograph expressing
friendship to the couple, naming both of them, and the memory struck with
such force as he read the names of whom the president was addressing the
autograph to that he actually spoke out loud.

"So you are the idiot who was using the unsecured e-mail not to your
wife but to a girlfriend that finally brought us here?"

He did not know whether to laugh or scream in rage as he tore the
framed photograph off the wall, turned, and headed back to the living
room.

Forrest was sitting by her side, but his attitude had shifted as she at least
appeared to have calmed down.

"Done prowling around my home?" she asked, looking up at him coldly,
cheeks streaked from spoiled makeup.

"Is your name Alicia?" John snapped.

"No, Janice."

He could not help but smile, an almost cruel smile after all the tragedy
she had created. "You want to know how we found out about this place?"

She looked up at him and tried not to show a reaction. "Go on, enlighten me."

"Your idiot husband was sending out a few e-mails to this place that
we did not even have to crack. It was a correspondence with some woman
named Alicia."

He hesitated. Was this even too cruel for him? "He certainly had a thing
for her and was looking forward to—how shall I say it?—a romantic inter-
lude with her next time he was here."

Her eyes widened with shock and then growing rage. "You're a damn
liar!" she shrieked. "He said he gave her up a year ago!"

"That's how we tracked this place down, your husband sending unsecured sexting to Alicia who apparently he stashed here as well," John replied sharply. "Sure, he protected his family"—a pause—"and his mistress
as well."

She glared up at him, struggling for control. "Matherson, you are cruel beyond any words to describe."

"Madam, it was men like your husband who turned this world into a place of such cruelty," John said coldly.

She lowered her head but then looked up at a trooper standing in the doorway.

"Ma'am, your daughter is going to make it. The medic stabilized her; some folks are helping us to take her to the hospital."

She nodded, tears continuing to well. "Thank you," she whispered.

John looked out the front window. Someone, a civilian, was bringing up a stretcher. Another was holding up an IV bag while the young medic was hunched over Laura, still working on her, but the girl was obviously conscious.

But next to her, Grace lay as she fell, Reverend Black and Kevin kneeling by her side and crying.

"Get a blanket, something over Grace," John whispered. "When we leave here, she goes back with us."

"Understood, sir." A pause. "I'm sorry; she seemed like a good kid. I saw it happen. She was trying to knock the little girl down to protect her when she got hit. She gave her life trying to save someone else."

"That was Grace," John whispered.

"I'll see she's taken care of, sir."

John could only nod.

The woman looked at John. "Who was she?"

He stared straight at her. "In a way, you could say she was a daughter as well."

The woman lowered her head. "I want to go with my girl. Let me leave."

"In a few minutes. She's in the best of hands until then. The way you behave, your being around her might upset things again, maybe trigger another incident."

The woman was obviously in shock, and she just seemed to sag, the fight out of her.

"Your husband is the acting secretary of state," he asked.

She nodded.

"And he is at Bluemont?"

Again a nod.

"How did all of you get here and when?" John pressed.

She looked over at him.

"Answer my questions and in five minutes I'll see someone gets you safely to your daughter. Again, how did you get here, and when?"

"I was flown in along with my twin boys."

"When?" John tried to keep the tension out of his voice.

"On the Day."

"When?"

She seemed to recoil backward, and he realized it was again becoming difficult to contain his anger.

"When?"

"The morning of the Day," she whispered.

"The morning of?" He paused for a moment. "It was before five in the afternoon in North Carolina when we were hit and everything went down. And you are telling me you were flown in here that morning?"

She could only nod.

"How can that be? Part of me just doesn't want to get it, to believe it. Are you telling me that some in Washington knew we were going to get hit and got their families out?"

There was a long, drawn-out silence.

"You see your daughter after you answer me."

"All right. Yes. Some knew. I don't know all the details; even my husband wouldn't tell me. He just would say there are some questions never to ask, and you are now asking one." She looked back over at John. "I want to see those e-mails you claim he was sending to that Alicia bitch."

"General Scales has them."

"Of course he'd get her out too, the bastard. I knew about it even then." She sighed and looked at John out of the corners of her eyes. "I need a cigarette."

"Don't look at me; I quit."

She motioned to a side table. He started to indicate she could go herself, thought better of it, and without taking his eyes off her reached over, opened the side table, and sure enough, there was a pack of cigarettes—British imports—and a lighter. He tossed them over to her, and with hands shaking, she lit one up, and he looked at it hungrily.

"You want one?" she asked.

After two years and a half years, he finally broke, nodded, took one out of the pack, and, whispering an apology to Jennifer, he lit it, taking it in deep, the nicotine hitting hard so he felt a bit light-headed for a moment. He felt deeply ashamed about breaking his vow to Jennifer and hoped she would understand at this moment.

"I don't know who, whether it was NSA, CIA, or some other agency, picked up the warning we were going to be hit later in the day. Only a few knew. Apparently not even the president, who was flying back to Washington when it hit."

"Who are these few?" John asked, head swimming from the nicotine and all that he was now learning.

"I don't know for sure." She hesitated, leaning forward to look out the door where her daughter was being loaded onto a stretcher, the child whimpering.

"You can go with her as soon as we're done talking," John said, and she looked back at him. "Who are these few that you said knew?"

"I'm not sure. You can guess, can't you? Not the ones in power up front. Just those behind them that few ever really see. Not many I recognized, but my husband was one of them." She paused and took another deep drag on her cigarette. "He got drunk one night and said that the country was going to hell anyhow. Some whispered that a reset button was needed to put them in control. Some operatives got a warning that North Korea and Iran were about to hit us by handing nukes and launch systems to terrorists who actually did the attack. They thought it would be a standard nuclear bomb strike, most likely against Washington and New York."

She took another drag. "So to play it safe, they set up some sort of practice drill. You know, he said like it was a war game or something. Practice evacuating certain key personnel, leaders to Bluemont, while families and a select few higher-ups were sent up here and stashed away.

"Then, as you all say, the shit hit the fan for real. Not a mushroom cloud over Washington but far worse, he said. The kids and I were already here. Others were brought in secretly in the weeks afterward. We were told to wait."

She sighed after taking another long drag on her cigarette. "Wait. I've been in this shit hole for two and a half years, and now you tell me my husband's slut mistress was here all along as well?

"That's all I know about what everyone calls the Day."

"Why aren't you in Bluemont?" John asked.

"My husband said the place was too small to take care of us all. Also, after it was all over, with representatives from other countries going there, even that damn pesky BBC could be there at times. If families were seen by them . . ." She paused again and looked at him coldly, and he realized that regardless of the enormity of what she was revealing, it was the news about the mistress that was driving her to now talk.

"Family and other people of special interest," she continued, "if we were there, outsiders might start asking why. Those in Bluemont, which is half the distance from Washington as this place, could claim a lot of excuses for getting to that place, even that they were part of a training exercise. But nearly two thousand of us? Some of them with very deep pockets who in reality controlled most of the political machines, at least before everything went down?"

"Two thousand?" John asked in surprise.

"Yeah, something like that." She took another drag on her cigarette, which burned clear down to the filter. She didn't bother with the ashtray, just let it fall to the shag-carpeted floor and ground it out. She got out another cigarette and lit it, continuing to smoke.

"More would come in after everything hit. Those with the real deep pockets—you know what I mean—people who shoveled out the cash before the war to buy what they wanted in Washington and could pay even more to survive here in safety. The ones that came afterward said it was beyond hell up above."

She stopped looking at him, head lowered as if waiting for an angry response or even a physical blow.

"It is indeed hell," was all he could say, and she took another drag on the cigarette. "So all of you have been here for over two years?"

"Yeah. Hell of an existence, isn't it?" She looked around at the sparsely furnished Quonset hut. "Water rationed to one shower per person every third day, one load of laundry a week in a communal laundry area. A communal laundry area with everyone else. Can you believe that?" She actually had rage in her voice over that indignity. "Meals are usually MREs, some of them twenty years old. Television is a library of old videotapes. I've watched every episode of *Three's Company* and *Sesame Street* maybe twenty times each until I'm ready to scream. The cigarettes he brings to me he gets through some trade deals—bet he gives most of them though to that bitch of his."

John looked around at her quarters, her slightly frayed but clean clothes, the electric lights outside illuminating Main Street, the subdued rumble of the ventilators lining the street that kept the temperature in the midsixties year round.

"Yeah, one hell of an existence," John whispered.

She could not even catch his bitter irony, she was so consumed with her own self-pity and rage at this moment.

"You ever go outside?"

"During the day, no. They say we can't be seen by anyone that might be watching. On special occasions, they'll let the kids out at night to run around and play for an hour or two."

"And your husband coming here?"

"Him? Every week, they bring a big helicopter in from Bluemont for what they call 'family visit weekend.' He gets to come once every six weeks for what he claims is one night, but I have the answer now." She glared at him, features bitter. "He got that bimbo who was his administrative assistant out as well, stashed her in the highly secured area at the far end of this damn cave, and spends the other night with her."

Her early attempt at sounding upper class, arrogant, and used to power had all but disintegrated. Her tone was now that of a bitter shrew.

"I can't wait to see him again," she announced coldly as she simply let her cigarette fall to the carpet, watched as it burned a hole into the worn green shag, finally crushed it out with the heel of her shoe, and lit yet another one.

"I'll loan you my gun when you see him again if you want," John said softly, and she looked at him, and he could see a dark glimmer in her eyes.

"Who else is here?"

"I don't know. Those in charge keep us kind of separated. My neighbor Gal, her husband was a senator as well; Pamela across the street, her husband was with the CIA. There's a section in the back, some nice modern trailers back there, that's cordoned off separately. Some say that's where the big-wigs, the elite, are stashed. You can smell their cooking at time, real food, not the shit they give to us."

"I would think acting secretary of state would be a high rank."

She sniffed derisively.

"Yeah, right. He's a puppet. I mean the real high rankers."

"The president's family, maybe?"

"You mean that fool in office when it hit? They never got them out—at least that's what my husband said. But the acting president now, yeah, that family is back there somewhere."

John looked down at his cigarette, which had burned out. He let it fall to the carpet.

She looked over at him, and he could see tears. "Maybe it was as I heard someone whisper, it was to reset things, others like my husband would take over, figuring just D.C. would be hit. I don't know. I asked my husband more than once what happened and why. He gets drunk a lot now, and all he says is that it's 'better to reign in hell than serve in heaven.' He says that a lot."

He looked at her, no longer with contempt but almost a sense of pity. He looked back out the window. The stretcher with her daughter was up, being moved, medic still by the girl's side, a civilian walking along the other side of the stretcher holding the plasma bag high. Maury was sitting across the street while a trooper was cutting his pant leg back and wrapping a bandage around the wound. Maury was crying, but not for himself; he was looking down at Grace, whom someone had thankfully covered with a poncho.

"They're moving your daughter. Go with her," John whispered.

She stood up without comment and started for the door, paused, and looked back. "You want any more cigarettes, go ahead and take them. That bastard of a husband brings me a new carton every time he comes here."

"I hope your daughter is okay," John said in reply, but her back was already turned to him, and she disappeared from view, suddenly shouting melodramatically that she needed to be by her baby.

John could see that Forrest was leaning against the wall, just outside the open door. Their eyes met, and Forrest, scarred and wounded veteran of Afghanistan, came into the room and sat down by John's side.

"I heard most of it," Forrest said softly.

John could not reply.

"Scales sent a runner back; he wants you with him."

"In a minute."

Forrest reached over to the carton of cigarettes. There were still several packs inside. He opened one, lit it with his battered 101st Airborne Zippo, and looked over at John, offering him a puff, which John gladly took.

CHAPTER EIGHTEEN

Having been escorted through the vast cavern labyrinth by the runner sent back by General Scales, John passed row after row of old-style barracks and Quonset huts. Most of them were empty, windows dust covered with no sign of habitation.

There was a grim triage logic to it. Designed back in the 1950s to house twenty-five thousand for how long? A month, six months, maybe a year? Two thousand could stay down here for years, a decade if need be. Also, moving twenty-five thousand in? Surely it would have drawn notice. Bob had been in the Pentagon on that day of days and was clueless as to what was going on at the moment everything hit. The number who were in the know and slipped away earlier that day or even before that? A hundred or two at most? Their families added in?

It was the sick mathematics of living versus dying. Who is the inner elite who cared no more for their duty and moral responsibility and thought only of themselves? Triage at its most sickeningly self-centered. It was time to confront it.

As they hiked to wherever Bob had gone, John could see scores of civilians lingering, watching. Some were even tanned. My God, did they even have tanning beds down here to get a dose of vitamin D and look good in the process?

He looked at his friends Forrest, Reverend Black, and Kevin, so clearly showing the ravages of two and a half years of survival, and he knew how he must look to them. Kevin was struggling to keep it together, an affirmation of what John suspected: that he and Grace had become close. Reverend Black was whispering to him, a supportive arm around his shoulders. He was barely keeping to his task, and John was tempted to relieve him and send him back to Grace's body and see that it was tended to with loving respect, but at this moment, he needed him far more than sentiment could allow.

After nearly a half mile of walking, John could see, of all things, a Cyclone fence that went from floor to ceiling, warning signs to either side of the entryway that they were about to enter a secured area. That almost made him laugh if it hadn't been so ironic. The gate was wide open, two of Bob's troopers posted to either side. A dead body covered with a poncho lay to one side, a massive pool of congealing blood having leaked out from underneath the poncho. He paused and made eye contact with the troopers.

"One of theirs," a trooper announced, her voice clipped, grim. A field bandage was wrapped around her upper left arm.

"You all right?" he asked her.

"Yes, sir. But that son of a bitch isn't." She nodded to the body. "He nearly shot the general."

There was a gaze of intense hatred in her eyes, and it was obvious she had killed him and now showed no remorse. How could he blame her? How could he blame any of them? After all they had been through, after all they thought they had been fighting for, and now to see this?

"The general is in that bunker complex over there, sir," she announced, nodding back beyond the fence, wincing as she did so from the wound to her arm.

He looked over at the other guard, a sergeant. "Can't we get her over to a hospital?" John asked.

The sergeant nodded back down the street that John had just traversed.

"Sir, we've got less than fifty in here," the sergeant whispered. "No telling how many we've yet to secure who will fight back once they get organized for a rush on us. The general said everyone who can hold a gun stays on station until we get things straightened out."

The sergeant turned his attention away from John, shouldered his weapon, and aimed past him. "You there! Halt and keep back, or I will shoot!" the sergeant snapped.

John looked over his shoulder. A group of milling civilians was getting closer and at the sergeant's command sullenly started to draw back.

"If they were all armed, we'd be in the shit," the sergeant said softly. "Word is that there are some additional personnel in a highly secured area." He paused. "You know anything about that, sir?"

"I do," was all that John felt comfortable with saying. "Just be ready; there could be some well-trained personnel in there." He looked just beyond the gate; there was a Humvee parked inside. "See if you can get that thing to start. If not, drop it into neutral and roll it to block this gate. Stay behind it as cover just in case."

He looked over at Forrest, who was nodding in agreement. "Mind staying here?" John asked him. "Kevin, Reverend Black, maybe you two as well?"

"Okay." Forrest smiled. "Sir."

The two guards were obviously grateful for the reinforcements, and leaving them behind, John started for the bunker complex. As he approached, he eyed the building. Unlike the living quarters, it was made of poured concrete. A lone guard from Scales's unit guarded the door, offering a salute as John approached and opening the door for him.

As he went through the door, it felt as if his ears were about to pop. The room was overpressured, the air pressure higher within to keep any ambient dust or anything else, such as chemical or biological agents, from filtering in. He could see wire meshing in the heavy glass of the door. It wasn't armor against bullets; it was faraday caging of the entire building, proofing it against an EMP. Of course it was known about back in the 1960s, and he could recall some of the secured briefing rooms down in the basement of the Pentagon having the same kind of protections.

Once through the double doors, it truly was a *Dr. Strangelove* world. A vast projection screen filled the opposite wall. It was dark, but he could easily imagine a global map display, arrows crisscrossing back and forth showing the trajectory of incoming missiles. Several dozen desks were arrayed in three tiers facing the darkened screen.

They were standard military issue of a generation or more ago. Most had old standard rotary phones on them as well, a few early model desktop computers, all of it having the feel of a time capsule. There were glassed-in rooms in a semicircle set around the main room, half a dozen feet higher than the main floor. John could see one was lit up with fluorescent lights; Bob Scales and half a dozen of his troops were in that room. As he approached, Bob looked down and waved for John to come up.

There was an unpleasant scent in the air, and as he drew closer, there was yet another body, not covered, shot in the head. He had seen so many dead like this one, but in this surreal room, the corpse seemed so out of place. John hesitated for a moment, looking down at it and then up at the lone guard stationed at the door telling John that the general was waiting for him, and he went into the room.

Far-more-up-to-date computers and communication gear lined two walls of the room, some of it lit up. The far wall was covered by a dark blue curtain, in front of it a desk, flanking the desk to either side American flags. Parked at an angle were a couple of television cameras that looked to be twenty or more years old, and glassed in to one side a small control booth, apparently to operate the cameras and sound equipment.

Besides Bob and his security detail, there were several civilians in the room as well. One of them Pelligrino, ashen faced but still alive. Standing nervously behind him were two men and a lone woman.

"John, are you all right?" Bob asked.

"Sir?"

"There's blood all over your jacket."

John looked down and for the first time realized that he was indeed caked in blood. "It was Grace. The girl with my unit," John said softly.

"She going to make it?" Bob asked.

John could only shake his head.

Bob looked back at Pelligrino. "Another death I am holding you responsible for."

It looked like Pelligrino was beyond rattled and just sat in dejected, terrified silence, eyes darting back and forth like those of a hunted rabbit.

"What's going on here, sir?" John asked.

"Get these four things out of this room and have them wait in the hall,"

Bob snapped, and the guards with him shoved the civilians out without any display of civility, leaving Bob and John alone.

Bob leaned back in the old chair, put his feet up on the table, and sighed. "You want the 'sit-rep'?" Bob asked, motioning for John to pull up a chair.

John sighed and nodded, fishing into his pocket for the pack of cigarettes he had taken and pulling one out.

"I thought you quit," Bob said, raising a quizzical eyebrow.

John did not reply as he tossed the pack on the table. Bob reached over, pulled out one as well, and motioned for the lighter.

"Didn't know you smoked."

"I didn't other than the occasional cigar."

The two sat in silence for a moment, Bob coughing as he exhaled but then nodding. "I can see how you can get hooked on these damn things.

"We're in the shitter," Bob finally said. "For that matter, the whole damn world is in the shitter."

John knew that he was serving as a sounding board and the best thing to do now was to just listen.

"I came in here with eighty people. We've taken about twenty casualties." He paused, looking at John. "I'm sorry about Grace and Lee."

John could not bring himself to reply.

"All I could worm out of that administrator Pelligrino is that we are in a world of hurt. There are a couple of hundred civilians at the back end of this facility in a highly secured area who are family members of high-value types. 'Movers behind the movers,' they call them. Anyhow, the security we faced at first, standard garrison types, you could see that. But there are some definite A-team types holed up in that highly secured area, and if they try to retake us, it could go badly. I was on the phone to someone up there. She wouldn't identify herself, but I told her she keeps her people in place and there's no threat. But if they move, all bets are off, and this place turns into a free-fire zone."

"Do they know how many we really have with us?" John asked.

"I don't know. If they have access to outside cameras, they could see how many came in with us and do the math. For now, I think I've got them convinced I've got a full battalion in reserve coming in and if they start a fight, we can hold until that battalion arrives and all hell will come down on them. They're not pushing, at least for the moment, and if they don't, we don't shove."

John nodded.

"They'll buy it for a while," he finally said while Bob took another drag and coughed again but did not toss the cigarette down.

"What else?" John asked, for obviously there was more.

"I had that piece of crap Pelligrino out there get on the phone with Bluemont."

That momentarily caught John by surprise, but then again, the moment they started to hit this place the alert would have gone to Bluemont, which by land was less than sixty miles away and by helicopter a quick twenty-minute flight.

"And?"

"I'm ordered to surrender my entire command. They're sending up a battalion by land even as we speak."

"Air?"

"Assume so."

"Our choppers?"

"I've already ordered them to clear out. They get caught on the ground, we truly are screwed. They're pulling back to where we landed earlier today. We can stay in touch with the comm team I left up on Little Round Top. That way no transmissions can be locked in on. Our choppers lifted off a few minutes ago. Security teams at the gate are pulling in and securing that huge steel door. Wounded are inside the gate and being tended to."

John nodded, crushed out his cigarette, and lit another. Bob, coughing, just let his drop and did not bother to try another just yet.

"We caught them by surprise," John replied. "If they hit back, we'll be ready and can hold this place against a damn armored brigade. Are there any back doors?"

"I've got some of my people talking to the prisoners we took. Hate to say so, but I told my people to be persuasive if need be."

"What doesn't happen in front of CNN never happened," John said softly. It was a bit of advice John remembered being spread among the troops just before going into Iraq. Of course there were rules of engagement with his army. But there was also the fundamental fact that war ultimately was and is the application of brutality, and if it saved the lives of men under one's command, all bets were off, at least if CNN wasn't there.

Bob did not reply.

"So what next, sir?" John asked.

Bob pulled another cigarette out of the pack lying on the table and lit it. His feet still up on the table, he exhaled the first puff and watched in silence as the smoke swirled up. "John, at a moment like this, it might seem strange, but I'm going philosophical on you. In fact, you were one of the few I ever served with I could go philosophical with."

John said nothing, but it was indeed an ultimate compliment.

"Do you remember our oath when we were sworn into the service?"

"Yes, sir."

Bob continued to stare at the coils of smoke. "'I do solemnly swear that I will support and defend the Constitution of the United States against all enemies, foreign and domestic,' there's a bit more, and then it ends with 'I will well and faithfully discharge the duties of the office on which I am about to enter. So help me God.'"

John remained silent.

"I have just been ordered by the person claiming to be the president of the United States, headquartered in Bluemont, to surrender my command and all those serving with me." He took another drag on his cigarette, gaze unfocused. "You ever take an order from someone you thought was a total ass and the order was dead wrong?"

"Yes, sir."

"I hope not me."

John chuckled softly. "Of course not."

"For enlisted personnel, their oath includes that they are only required to obey orders that are lawful and are held morally and even legally accountable if the order is immoral or violates the military code of justice and/or the Constitution. That became important post-Vietnam, after the Mỹ Lai Massacre.

"That is not specified in the oath for an officer, but it is clearly implied because we have an option enlisted personnel do not have; we can resign our commissions in protest and are expected to do so." Another puff on the cigarette followed by a moment of silent thought.

"Are you going to resign?" John finally asked.

Bob looked over at him. "Your thoughts, John?"

"Is it about here?" John asked. "The fact that someone—in fact, quite a few—knew on the morning of the Day that we were going to get hit, took care of their own, and said the hell with the rest of us?"

"In part."

Bob was silent for a moment. He took another drag on his cigarette and sighed.

"So damn much is clear now. We knew a practice drill was going on the day we got hit and most of the personnel that took over after that day by chance had been in Bluemont. At least I and others believed it was by chance. Hell, drills like that are being pulled all the time. We just came to assume that a few more that took over made it to Bluemont in the weeks afterward."

He stood and looked out the window of the room to the open floor of what had been built in the 1950s to serve as the War Room to keep on fighting from if Washington was destroyed. "This was built to fight a nuclear war from. Once ICBMs with flight times of but minutes came online in the late 1950s and warning time went from hours down to just a few minutes, those of us working in the Pentagon knew we'd all be gone in those first few minutes and this place was all but forgotten. A relic of a different type of war from a different time. And now to find it was activated and running with families stashed here?"

He looked back at John, tears in his eyes. "Six hours' warning and I could have gotten Linda out of Florida. All of us could have done something. For that matter, we could have scrambled everything we had and perhaps even targeted the container ships in the Gulf of Mexico and off the California coast before they hit us. It's all too much to absorb, John."

"I spoke to a woman who said her husband claimed that a select few knew something was coming but assumed it would be just a nuclear strike on D.C., and I would guess maybe New York." John wearily shook his head. "*Just* D.C. and New York," John whispered again. "Just ten to fifteen million dead. My God, what kind of mentality thinks such a loss would be a small number and that would reset the political paradigm in their favor."

"There's intelligence chatter all the time." Bob sighed. "If one believes all of it, every day you go crazy. You know that. Maybe they thought that it was just a mid-level alert. I guess we'll never know for sure. Bastards who would sit back for that think of themselves first. I doubt if we'll ever get the truth from them."

"By the way," John said, breaking the tension of the moment with a sad smile, "it was her husband sending those love notes, not to his wife but to his mistress stashed away in the highly secured other end of this facility, that gave us the clue about Site R. I told her you have the letters. She is so pissed off I'm certain she'll sing like a canary for us if we need more info later."

"Typical," Bob said softly, wearily shaking his head. "So typical of so many moral scum we all had to salute at one time or another."

"But to the core question, sir?" John asked. "Is it about what they did to us all or what they are going to do to us next?"

"Go on."

"I see one side of the dilemma that you are dwelling on being what happened. But, sir, the more pressing issue is what they're going to do next and how you will reply."

"Keep talking." Now Bob lit his third cigarette.

"All of this started to unravel when you received orders—when was it, not much more than a day ago?—to pull your entire command back to Roanoke. It meant that Bluemont was preparing to pop an EMP to destabilize Atlanta, take out communities like mine that are resisting them, and I guess send a message to China as well not to push beyond the Mississippi. It comes down to the fact that they are willing to hold and execute power whatever the cost. I just heard someone quote Milton: 'Better to reign in hell than serve in heaven.' They scrambled to protect themselves when all hell cut loose and then seized the reins of power afterward. Whether that was their plot beforehand or not we most likely will never know. But since the Day? What they've done, what they are planning to do next? That, sir, is the issue of the moment to focus upon."

Bob closed his eyes. "'By the rivers of Babylon, there we sat down, yea, we wept when we remembered Zion . . . If I forget thee, O Jerusalem, let my right hand forget her cunning . . . If I do not remember thee, let my tongue cleave to the roof of my mouth . . .'"

He looked over at John. "The 137th Psalm," he whispered. "I dwell on it often when I think of all that has happened."

"And you are saying we cannot let our tongue cleave to the roof of our mouth or our right hand forget its strength."

Bob made no gesture of reply.

"Enemies, foreign and domestic—it all turns on that, sir. Not just what they did but what they are about to do to hold on to their power. To protect the Constitution, it is therefore right for you to act."

His gaze was no longer fixed on John, as if he was staring off to some distant place

"And to not forget the Jerusalem that they allowed to be destroyed," John interjected, "Whether they thought it would be—forgive me for even saying it—just a strike on Washington and New York that would reset the political paradigm and power structure or some suspected it would be a full-scale EMP strike, it happened. Now they're ready to do it themselves against the southern United States. Why?"

"A message to the Chinese, for one," Bob said softly. "If we're now willing to do such against our own territory still in rebellion against them as they see it, the message would be clear. They're so desperate that they will order the same against everyone else in this world if they think they're about to go under. Second, it was to knock out people like you who were beginning to rise back up and put things together and who at some point would look at Bluemont and start asking questions."

"Therefore?" John asked.

"We have to hold to our oaths to protect the Constitution against enemies foreign and domestic," Bob replied, strength returning to his voice. "Yes, I took over what they called Eastern Command. I actually believed restoring order using our traditional military had to be done, but the ones I was first fighting against were barbarians like that Posse you wiped out. But then you were in front of me, John. That is when the inner questions started for me. I was ordered to bring you in. I tried to reason back that you had been provoked into that fight with Fredericks because you had no alternative but to fight.

"It didn't fly. I thought I could work my way around it, get you to cooperate peacefully, which you did order, and then they tried to kill you anyhow. That assassination attempt was of course to kill you and your family as vengeance for your defiance, but it was a message to me as well that I was being watched and to toe the line. And thus the questions began to hit at last on my part in all of this." He looked over at John. "Forgive me for not protecting you better."

"Nothing to forgive now, sir," John replied, but in his heart he knew if Makala had been killed that would have taken him beyond any forgiveness.

"When they ordered me to pull back to Roanoke, I knew I had to act, but how? Then your friend Linda handed me the deepest paradox of all. Did at least some of them know what was about to happen before the Day, protected themselves and their own, and left the rest of our country wide open for what then followed? That finally tipped it. That is why I had to come here and settle for myself what had to be done." He forced a weary smile. "What I have to do now."

Bob turned away from John and lowered his head. John knew what he was doing; he had seen it just days before in the chapel at Montreat. He remained thus for several minutes.

John heard him whisper, "Thy will be done." Bob made the sign of the cross and then leaned back in his chair and looked over at John.

"Get that administrator or whatever he is back in here," Bob said, and his voice was firm.

John opened the door, pointed at Pelligrino, and nodded to the guards, who shoved the trembling man back into the room.

"Again, I must protest this kind of treatment," Pelligrino started, but an icy glance from Bob silenced him.

Bob pointed to the control booth in the far corner of the room. "Do you know how to operate the equipment in there?" Bob asked.

Pelligrino shook his head.

"Find someone who can do so now."

Pelligrino hesitated.

"Now!"

"Phyllis is our communications person," Pelligrino blurted out.

"Get her in here," Bob snapped.

John opened the door, pointed at Phyllis, and beckoned for her to enter, which she did reluctantly.

"First of all, get me on the phone with Bluemont again, and put it on speaker. I want you and Colonel Matherson to hear it."

Pelligrino did as ordered, pulling over the red phone on the desk Bob was sitting at and pushing a single button that lit up on the face of the phone. Bob picked up the receiver.

"Who is this?" a woman's voice answered on the other side.

Bob looked over his shoulder at Pelligrino. "I said I want this on speaker."

Pelligrino looked to Phyllis, who switched on a speaker mounted above the desk.

"This is General Robert Scales here."

There was a pause.

"We demand that you put Mr. Pelligrino on the phone now," the woman replied.

"It's the other way around," Bob replied. "Whoever calls themselves president where you are, you put that person on the phone."

"Just who do you think you are?" came the sharp reply. "General, you have been stripped of rank effective immediately. You are to turn yourself over to Mr. Pelligrino and the head of security where you are. Any who continue to obey your orders will face the severest consequences. You will be escorted to a secured area where you wait until our forces arrive."

Bob actually smiled at that. "Go to hell."

"What?" Her voice was almost a shriek, and as it rose in volume, John found himself looking at the loudspeaker with surprise. He recognized who she was.

"Madam. You are to recall your forces now. Immediately."

"Mr. Scales, it's the other way around."

"I hold the trump card; you do not."

"You're an egotistical fool. You have fewer than eighty with you. We realize that now. You've undoubtedly learned by now there are additional security forces within the site. Whatever chance you had is finished. If you surrender yourself, I promise leniency for all those deluded into following you, and that is our only offer."

Bob cupped his hand over the receiver and looked at John and the two guards.

"Tell her to kiss our asses," one of the troopers replied. "Every man and woman under your command is with you, sir."

Bob nodded his thanks and then looked at Phyllis. "I want you to turn those cameras on and set up an uplink."

"To what?" she asked nervously.

"BBC, for starters. China, the whole damn world."

"I will not."

"I can have one of my tech people in here in less than five minutes and do your job for you," Bob replied coolly.

She did not move.

"Get someone. Sergeant McCloskey can handle it," Bob snapped to the two guards in the room, and one set off at a run, but the other guard came up close to John.

"McCloskey's dead," the guard whispered to John.

He could see Bob hesitating, such a rare sight, but all of it had become all so overwhelming. Every second that passed raised the chance that a counterstrike could hit them, and as if in answer, he could hear what sounded like gunfire from outside the command bunker. Chances were they were about to be overrun.

What had to be done, he knew Bob most likely was contemplating, but the moment dragged out, gunfire growing louder, and for John, it came down to Lee, Grace, Jennifer, all those who died. All those who would continue to die.

"Sir," John snapped, and he extended his hand out, indicating he wanted the phone.

Bob looked at him in surprise but then handed the phone up.

"This is John Matherson. You might not know who I am, but I know who you are."

There was a pause from the other end. "The terrorist from Carolina?" It was more a question than a reply.

"A citizen from Carolina who knows that you plan to take down the entire southeast region of the United States with another EMP burst within the next few days."

"What difference does it make that I'm talking to you instead of a general now formally stripped of command?" she snapped.

"I'll tell you the difference, ma'am."

There was no reply, but over the loudspeaker, John could hear whispering from those who were most likely in the same room with the woman
on the phone.

"I want all of you to listen closely. General Scales might not be comfortable with ordering this, but I no longer have a problem after everything you
bastards have done to us, to our country."

"How dare you!"

"I dare because I can destroy this place in a matter of minutes."

Another pause, whispered voices, and finally a reply, as if she were trying
to laugh his words off as an idle threat. "It was built to withstand a direct hit
on the surface from a nuclear weapon. Unless you have one with you, John
Matherson, your words are just that—words."

"But we are inside. This place has a central ventilation system. I have
enough of my people here that we will blow that, for starters. There is fuel
storage, gasoline and diesel; we will dump it and light it off. The barracks
are made of wood; after sixty-plus years down here, they'll burn like torches.
Your food supply is centrally stored; we already know where that is. A hundred gallons of gasoline tossed in there and lit and the life of luxury in here
turns into the way people like my family have been living for over two years
while your families are fat, warm, well-fed, and safe.

"Your water cisterns. I'll blow them, and while everything burns at this
level, we'll flood out any lower levels beneath this one as well. We will blow
this place, and in one hour, every single person in here will be standing out
in the freezing cold. And let me guess—do you have grandchildren in
here?"

"How dare you threaten them, you son of a bitch!" she shrieked.

"So you do have them here. So let's make this clear. I bet there are a couple
of dozen in that room with you, and all of you have families here. And by
the way, if your so-called secretary of state is there, tell him his wife knows
about Alicia and is waiting to discuss his mistress. I offered to loan her my
gun, and I think she's eager to use it."

He could hear loud cursing and then the voice of someone being muffled.

"Don't you dare try to play a blame game with me. We are not terrorists
who will kill children. But you most certainly are a terrorist. My daughter

died because of people like you. So the choice is yours: call your attack dogs off both inside here and any coming from the outside, and we continue to talk. Otherwise, I'm handing the phone back to General Scales, we start smashing this damn hiding hole, and you figure out what to do with everyone in here when they're standing outside tonight in two feet of snow and another storm is rolling in.

"I am a man of faith, and I swear to you before God I will not harm a single innocent person in this place. But I also swear to you that unless you back off now, every person in this place will be living like the rest of America in another hour. At least I'll give your people time to get into warm clothes if they have any and one pouch of an MRE each, but that is it. And that is a damn sight more than you and yours ever gave to the rest of this country two and a half years ago. I've said my piece. It is now you who have one minute to decide."

John tossed the phone down on the desk and looked over at Pelligrino. "Get on there and tell her I'm not bluffing!" John shouted.

Bob sat in perfect silence, looking up at John in surprise.

John drew out his Glock and pointed it at Pelligrino. "Tell her I'm not bluffing!" John shouted.

"John?" It was Bob speaking, but John did not look at him.

"Tell her."

Hands shaking, Pelligrino needed both to pick the phone up. "He has a gun to my head. He's just crazy enough to do it."

"One minute for the shooting in here to stop and for you to halt whoever is preparing to hit us, or this place starts coming down!" John shouted.

"He means it!" Pelligrino cried.

A pause, more arguing from the other end, and someone sobbing their kids were in the middle of it and to back down.

"Thirty seconds!" John shouted.

"All right! All right!" she cried.

It sounded like she was muffling the mouthpiece of the phone, but all could hear her shouting to get on a comm link to the security team in Sector Alpha and order them to cease fire and withdraw.

"Tell her she just bought herself a few more minutes," John said, looking at Pelligrino, who nodded and gasped out the message.

John stepped to the door into the room, telling the one remaining member of their team standing watch to go out to the gate and report back whether all was secure.

The distant sound of gunfire finally ceased. Two minutes turned to three and then four.

The guard, breathless, ran back into the cavernous main hall and then up to the communications center. "Whoever they are, they've apparently pulled back, sir."

John nodded and lowered his weapon away from Pelligrino, and the man visibly shuddered and sighed with relief.

"How bad was it?" Bob asked.

"Two of our people at the gate are down. I think one is dead."

John wanted to ask if his own friends were safe but knew he could not do so now.

Bob nodded and took the phone from Pelligrino. "Every death now is on your head," he said. "I'll call you back in five minutes. But if any moves are made, if anyone tries to approach from outside, what Matherson said will come to pass."

He hung up without waiting for her reply and looked back at Phyllis, who, though obviously frightened, was displaying more nerve than Pelligrino.

"You and I need to talk, and I promise you, either way you answer, no harm will come to you. You have my word of honor on that."

She nodded but did not reply.

Bob spared a sharp glance toward Pelligrino and motioned to the door, and the breathless trooper hustled him out of the room, closing the door.

"Sit down, Phyllis." Bob offered her a chair.

She did as requested, and Bob motioned toward the pack of cigarettes. She shook her head, but he drew one out for himself, as did John.

"Phyllis, how long have you been here?"

"Since the morning of the day the war started."

"Why you? Are you a family member of someone in Bluemont?"

"No, sir."

"Then why?"

"I'd rather not say."

That could mean a lot, but John sensed what it might be and did not press the question.

"And you being in here in this room when I came in?" Bob continued.

"I was assigned to work communications here. I used to be a producer and sometimes anchored for a television station in D.C."

For John, that seemed to fall a bit into place. She was tall, highly attractive, the type that would be pushed in front of a camera to interview some government official. It was easy enough to see that had developed out and why she was alive here rather than long ago dead back in Washington.

"I think you know that outside of here, Bluemont, and I can only assume now a few other places, our country has gone to hell."

She just nodded, head lowered.

"It could have been you out there, Phyllis."

"My parents, a sister"   she paused—"a guy who was once my boyfriend."

"Phyllis, do you know that Bluemont is preparing to launch an EMP strike against our own country?"

She hesitated. "There have been rumors," she whispered.

"And your thoughts on that?"

She did not reply.

John could see what Bob was trying to do and gently moved in on the conversation. "Phyllis, there are hundreds of communities like mine that just barely managed to survive. Barely. We're starting to crawl out of the dust, basic things, get at least a trickle of electricity up and running. From that, the chemistry lab in the college where I teach is again making anesthesia and antibiotics, things we once took for granted. Phyllis, have you ever witnessed an amputation with the victim wide awake, no pain pills afterward, no way to stop infection once it set in?"

She stared at him wide-eyed and then lowered her gaze and shook her head.

"How about watching a diabetic child die because her frantic parent could not find a single vial of insulin?"

Another shake of her head, but her glance turned back up to him.

"Yes, that was me. My daughter was twelve, and I held her as she died. Even with just a few extra hours' warning, so much could have been different. Phyllis, those of us left are trying to crawl out of the hellhole of what happened, and those people in Bluemont are about to hit us, to push us back down into that hole. Bluemont is going to smash all that within the next two to three days because it doesn't fit what they see as their plan.

"Look at me, please," John said, and she raised her head.

"How old was your sister?"

"Fourteen."

"My daughter was twelve when she died for want of a vial of insulin."

He held the eye contact, and this time she did not break away.

"What do you want me to do?" she finally whispered.

John stood just behind Phyllis, who was at the control board. It was lit up. She had indicated to him and Bob that the uplink was hot and also being fed to Bluemont as well.

If she was bluffing, she was being damned good at it, and he could only hope for the best and that she had made a moral choice—or, as Bob had interjected, a penance—and it was time for her to set her own moral choices straight.

Bob was sitting behind the desk at the far end of the room.

Phyllis looked over at John. "He's on," she announced, and she turned her attention back to the display board.

John wasn't quite sure what to do other than just hold his hand up and wave.

Bob nodded and looked at the camera, and John could see the image on a small screen in the control room. Certainly not the professional quality the world had once grown all so used to, but it would have to do.

There was no makeup, no smile, just a firm determined look.

"My name is Robert Scales. Until an hour ago, I was a serving major general in the United States Army and in command of all army operations in what was defined as the Eastern Mid-Atlantic Command Zone.

"My task, as assigned to me by an entity located in Bluemont, Virginia, claiming that it was the reconstituted government of the United States of America, was, and I quote from the orders I was operating under, 'to return to federal control all territory from Charlottesville and Richmond, Virginia, to the north, the Appalachian Mountains to the west, and the border with Florida to the south.'

"Until two days ago, I diligently followed those orders, believing that the entity located in Bluemont that claimed it was the government of the United States was a legitimate government. I no longer believe so, and that is why I am making this broadcast now.

"Several days ago, I was made aware of two actions by those who claim to be the government—one a crime of unsurpassed magnitude on what so many of us now call 'the Day,' the other a crime of nearly equal magnitude that same government was planning to commit within the next forty-eight hours.

"I shall review those crimes shortly. But before doing so, I am making the following statement and then demand. An hour ago, I wrote out my letter of resignation as a serving officer in the United States Army so that it can never be stated that one following a tradition going back to General Washington and those who served with him rebelled against his government. I therefore resigned and now have the freedom to act as a private citizen. Bear that in mind as I now make this demand. I demand that the criminal entity that claims to be the federal government based in Bluemont resign from office. That applies to the so-called president and every other official there.

"All of you who resign will stand trial by a duly created civilian court, for your crimes are of such magnitude you must face juries of your peers. Do not resign and you shall be construed as in rebellion against those who defend the Constitution of the United States and dealt with accordingly."

He paused and looked over at John for a few seconds, who had been carefully watching Phyllis's actions. Nothing seemed amiss. She had claimed to be linking the signal not just to Bluemont but also to several frequencies commonly monitored by ham operators, the frequency of America's Voice of Victory, as it was now called, and, even more important, the BBC. Her hands were shaking, and he looked over at her.

She was in tears but then whispered. "I'm with you on this now."

John gave a reassuring look back to Bob.

"I shall now review in detail my charges against those in Bluemont, an explanation of where I am now, and all that this place called Site R, from where I am broadcasting, symbolizes."

He spoke for nearly a half hour, amazing John with his ability to have thus organized his thoughts, laying it all out clearly with no teleprompter, relying on nothing more than a few sheets of paper with notes scribbled on them with a Sharpie.

John continued to watch Phyllis's actions. She stuck to her post, not making any attempts to shut things down. Bob had run down the list of events going all the way back to the Day and how it was now clearly evident that a very select few in the government, and beyond them political leaders and high-level economic leaders not directly in government, had word of the impending attack; conspired to conceal it while ensuring the safety of themselves, their families, friends, and allies; and ensured as well their seizing dictatorial power afterward. This cabal, as he called it, had ceded more than half of what had been America to other nations in order to ensure their continued hold on power and finally had plotted an EMP strike as a means of suppressing those attempting to rebuild and as a dangerous political ploy against the rest of the world.

"Why did they sink to this lowest of moral crimes?" Bob finally asked. "I don't know for certain. The warning about the threat of an EMP attack has been out there for years, decades, and yet no one acted on it. Was it ignorance or was it simple dumb disbelief? Perhaps for many, yes. But I recall all too well an interview with someone who was fully aware of the threat long before it hit. When he was asked why there was no action to prepare, his reply was, 'Don't we, the ordinary citizens of our country who are aware of the threat, realize the elites will take care of their own no matter what happens?'

"This day I have found that those who claim to be our government based in Bluemont did take care of their own while the rest of us faced the Day without warning, and hundreds of millions died. Every one of their deaths rests on those who knew and said nothing while looking out for themselves.

"I must add that I believe that some, for perverted reasons, saw this as a means of seizing power, no matter what the ebb and flow of politics, fearing perhaps they would soon be voted out of office. And the sickest crime of all is that—to paraphrase Milton, who in *Paradise Lost* once wrote of Satan—they felt it was better to reign in the hell they created than to serve in heaven. To a world, to Americans who lost so much but still survive, to personal friends, I must ask you: Should such as they be allowed to continue on in power? I point no finger at one political view or another; our petty arguments of left or right, liberal or conservative, seem so inane now in contrast to what we endured together. Regardless of what we once felt on such things, I believe we are united with these revelations that we must stand together to ensure that government of, by, and for the people shall not perish from this earth.

"In conclusion," Bob finally said, "I can only speak now as a private citizen, having resigned my commission in order to be free of what any might construe as a military coup. All men and women in uniform must now make a choice. If you are an officer, remember your oath is to protect and defend the Constitution against all enemies, foreign and domestic. It is your choice to decide if those in Bluemont are enemies of our Constitution and then act accordingly.

"I am asking that any force commanders in possession of nuclear weapons go to a full lockdown and vow that under no circumstance whatsoever will they deploy or launch such a weapon, except in response to nuclear weapons launched by another country against what is left of the United States, until a properly constituted government formed within the original guidelines of our Constitution has been re-created. Only after that takes place with a duly elected and morally guided government in place will those in direct charge of such weapons unlock them, strictly to ensure the defense of our country against outside threats.

"I am asking that those military forces directly attached to Bluemont, either defensively or currently moving toward offensive action to retake Site R, go to a full stand-down. I no longer have such power to order you to do so, but your unit commanders can.

"I am asking that any civilian-based military units within a hundred-mile radius of Bluemont move upon it now. I pray that there shall be no violence offered from our regular armed forces, who will instead join you in occupying Bluemont and placing under arrest any who are still there.

"Where I am located now, near Gettysburg, Pennsylvania, is the underground shelter I spoke to you about earlier. Having resigned my commission, I have no power to act here, but I am requesting of the officer who is taking over in my place to ensure that the civilians who have lived here safely for two and a half years shall be protected. Our own Constitution makes clear that no family member can be punished for the crimes of a parent or spouse. However, if those in Bluemont do resist or attempt to seize this place by force, all civilians within Site R will be ordered to evacuate and find whatever shelter and sustenance they can in the outside world all the rest of us have resided in for the last two years. If that is indeed the tragic result, I ask that you show them more compassion than their leaders have shown to us.

"So what is next?" Bob asked, and he looked at the camera for a moment as if almost expecting to hear tens of millions of replies.

"I leave that to you, my fellow citizens. Our once proud cities and our once beautiful capital have been reduced to ruin and ashes. I see the land around Bluemont to somehow be accursed. I will therefore close with a suggestion. I ask that thirty days hence, five representatives from each of the surviving states come to meet here at this place. I ask that you good citizens decide how they shall be selected, as it was once done when the founders met to frame our Constitution. I ask that we reaffirm that Constitution and create a reunited Union of States.

"Why here?" He paused for a moment. "Within sight of this place I am now broadcasting from, our nation, once divided, fought the bitterest battle of a bitter war. And yet, fifty years later and again seventy-five years later, former enemies met as friends, standing on opposite sides of a stone wall on a place called Cemetery Ridge and shook hands in friendship. But a few hundred yards from that wall, President Lincoln stood before the newly made graves of those who gave the last full measure of devotion and proclaimed that 'this nation, under God, shall have a new birth of freedom— and that government of the people, by the people, and for the people shall not perish from this earth.'"

There was another long pause.

"In your hands, my fellow citizens, and not mine, now rests the fate of this nation. I ask that Almighty God grants us his peace and guidance in the days to come."

He sat back in his chair, eyes still on the camera.

Phyllis waited for some sort of signal, but he gave none, and finally John whispered.

"That's it."

She reached across the board and threw a number of switches off and then looked over at John and began to cry. "I'm sorry I was ever here," she whispered.

"Consider what you just did as atonement," John replied. He stepped out from the narrow confines of the control booth and walked up to where Bob remained motionless.

"I guess all we can do now is wait and see what happens." Bob sighed.

" 'We shall nobly save, or meanly lose, the last best hope of earth,' " he said as if to himself.

CHAPTER NINETEEN

"If I could order you to stay, I would," Bob said, extending his hand.

John could only smile and shake his head. "I've had enough of it all, sir."

"Come back as a delegate?"

"What was it that Sherman said?"

"'If nominated, I will not run; if elected, I will not serve,'" Bob replied.

"Something like that."

"They're coming," Sergeant Major, now Colonel Bentley, announced.

John looked back behind Bentley. A half dozen men and women of what had once been Bob's command, which he had turned over to Bentley after promoting him to the rank of colonel before resigning his commission, came out of the tunnel bearing a flag-draped coffin. All came to attention, and even though Bob was no longer serving in the military, old instincts were still within him as he came to attention and saluted as Grace's coffin was respectfully loaded into the Black Hawk.

Maury followed, limping and helped by Forrest, along with Kevin and Reverend Black. Earlier in the day, in honor of his friend's request, Lee Robinson's mortal remains were lifted by helicopter to what was truly hallowed ground in front of the iconic statue dedicated to the men of North Carolina who had advanced across a sun-drenched field in what would forever be remembered as Pickett's Charge. Reverend Black had read from the

Ninety-First Psalm, Lee's favorite, and with full military honors, he was
laid to rest in the ground he had often said, quoting Joshua Chamberlain,
that here indeed was the vision place of souls.

It was hard for John to imagine life ahead without his stoic friend by his
side. Together they had often joked if they had indeed lived 150 years ago,
they would have faced each other as honor and duty demanded, but their
bonds of friendship would have endured. John wished that a photograph
taken of the two of them together had survived, but it was lost when his
house burned in the war against the Posse. They had attended a historical
event together and there posed for an authentic ambrotype, Lee in gray
uniform, John in blue, Lee's hand resting on John's shoulder in a gesture of
friendship and love.

So much was still in doubt. All thanked God that the military garrison
at Bluemont had not tried to attack Site R. They had all gone to their barracks to wait it out. As to the elite located in a highly secured reserve area at
the far end of the cavern? It was apparent that some attempted to flee via
a hidden exit. They were met by a hovering Apache and fled back inside.

Some had urged Bob to personally lead a move either to arrest those
within that special compound or to execute them summarily, but he announced he would not do either once it was learned that a missile that was
indeed nuclear tipped and had been moved into position at Wallops Island,
Virginia, had been rendered inactive by troops there. The warhead atop the
missile was seized and impounded by a team of Navy SEALs operating
from a carrier off the coast, whose commander announced he would no
longer accept orders from Bluemont, would remain in stand-down, and
would await orders from whatever government in compliance with the
Constitution was created.

Global reaction was compounding by the hour, some announcing that
Bob should act as temporary dictator, president, or whatever he wished to
call himself. China made clear it was occupying up to the Mississippi and
again issued the threat that any action against their humanitarian aid being
offered to the "stricken former United States" would be construed as an attack upon their mainland. But just this morning, word had come in via the
ambassador in China—who had served under the Bluemont government
but after Bob's broadcast announced his allegiance to a properly formed

government—that the Chinese foreign minister had informed him that as long as no action was taken against their occupation forces or their homeland, China would recognize the new government.

If anything at this moment, rather than a help, John saw himself as a liability for what Bob was attempting. In its dying gasps, Bluemont had played a recording of his conversation, heavily edited, to make it sound like he was indeed threatening to murder everyone inside of Site R. Unfortunately, no one had thought to record the conversation from their end, and John realized the best thing now was to distance himself from Bob until everything settled down.

But beyond that, he was weary and exhausted from all that had transpired, and the thought of yet more years of struggle to come had become overwhelming.

The turbines of the Black Hawk started up, and Bob motioned for John to step away for a moment. Bob reached into his breast pocket, pulled out a nearly empty pack of cigarettes, and offered one to John, who accepted, and Bob lit John's and then his.

"Thanks for getting me hooked on these damn things again," Bob said.

"Sorry, sir."

"I might have to call on you, John. But for now, maybe it is wise you just head back home for a while. That doctored recording does make you seem like a hard-ass."

"I saw it had to be done, sir, and I didn't want you in that role. Better me than you."

"Thank you, John."

They both stood silent for a moment.

"A question, John."

"Anything."

"Would you have done it?"

"What?"

"Smashed the place apart and driven those thousands out into the cold to starve?"

John looked past him, gaze lingering on the distant hills of Gettysburg. All the sacrifice that happened there. All the sacrifice endured there and up now to this moment.

"Sir, don't ever ask me that question again," John whispered.

Bob nodded. "Understood, my friend."

The helicopter rotor began to turn. The two dropped their cigarettes, John grinding his into the snow to put it out.

Bob held out the pack, offering the rest to him. John smiled sadly and shook his head.

"I once made a promise, sir."

Bob looked at him quizzically and then seemed to understand and nodded.

"I'm quit now, quit forever. This is the final day."

EPILOGUE

"May the peace of the Lord be with all of you on this most blessed of days of renewal and beginnings. I hereby declare the academic semester to be open."

There was a scattering of applause as Reverend Black, newly appointed president of the college, stepped away from the lectern of restored Graham Chapel of Gaither Hall, the name having been changed in memory of an honored couple who had resided in Montreat for most of their lives and actually been married in the chapel in a long-ago age.

There was the traditional closing hymn, the school song, led by the choir, and as they finished, the congregation started to leave. But then a lone voice from the choir began to sing a song that struck John to the very core for all its symbolism. The lone female voice echoed in the restored chapel.

"Try to remember the kind of September when life was slow and oh so mellow."

All stood frozen in place, and more than a few began to weep. John looked over at Makala, remembering the first time he had brought her to this chapel. A student up on the stage, unaware that she had an audience, had started to sing that song from *The Fantasticks*. It had become something of a theme of the time they had been through, a song of remembrance and loss.

Young Jennie was nestled in against her mother, having fallen asleep through most of the service, but was now stirring, looking up sleepy eyed at her father and smiling.

He put his arm protectively around Makala's shoulder and walked with her out of the chapel into what was proving to be a glorious early May morning, the date symbolically chosen since it was exactly three years ago that the Day had struck them all. And now, phoenixlike, the school was again stirring to life.

Following old tradition, John gathered with the other faculty at the base of the stairs to shake hands with the students leaving and heading to class. Mixed in were members of the community. Maury was still a bit ungainly with crutches as Forrest helped him down the steps. Maury's leg wound had become infected; Makala had struggled with it for over a month before finally conceding it had gone gangrenous and amputating it.

As he was helped down the steps by Forrest, who had become a dedicated friend to Maury during his long months of recovery, the two together reminded John of old photographs of Civil War veterans minus a limb helping each other along, sharing a bond that someone who had not been through their fiery trial could never understand.

Most of the students who shook John's hand were "the survivors" as they called themselves, their features hard, wiry, hands gnarled from an early spring of putting in crops. Most had already put in several hours of labor in the fields before returning to campus. Until the harvest was in, there would be but three hours of class a day near noontime and then back out later in the day to resume work.

His daughter Elizabeth was mixed in with the crowd. Now the mother of two, she was not attending classes but had come for the ceremony honoring all those who had fallen with the reading of the names of all students, staff, and faculty who had given the last full measure of devotion. As "Lee Robinson, killed in action, Gettysburg," was read off, John saw her lean in closer to her husband, Seth, Lee's son, who bowed his head as she held him close. For John, the fact that his comrade's son was registered in his class filled him with happiness and poignant memories as well. In a long-ago time, Lee would visit his class as a Civil War reenactor to talk about the equipment, uniform, and life of the troops. Seth, even as a ten-year-old, would proudly attend wearing a uniform handmade by his loving mother. He looked so much like his father and would forever be a reminder of one of the closest of friends.

John saw a man coming down the stairs who but a few years ago must have been full of the vigor of life, but on this day looked broken. He had arrived on campus only the day before. He was one of several dozen parents who across the months since the onset of a relative semblance of peace had made the journey to discover the fate of a son or daughter sent to this quiet, peaceful campus before the coming of the Day.

"We want you to stay with us for several days," John said as he grasped the man's hand. "There is so much to share with you about Grace, to tell you all that she meant to us, all that she did."

John's voice filled up. He had once thought of himself as being so stoic, able to contain his emotions, only letting them release when alone. Perhaps it was Jennifer that broke that in him. He had lost Jennifer; this man had lost Grace.

Grace's father smiled but offered no reply either way. "I think I'll go and sit with my girl for a while," he whispered and then continued on. John watched the man walk down across the front lawn of the campus for the long trek to the military cemetery at the edge of town. John had taken him there the day before and was touched to see that someone was still thoughtfully putting flowers on her grave, suspecting it was Kevin, who had taken her loss in such a way that it was obvious that he had been deeply in love with her.

"You'll be late, Professor," Makala announced, and John looked over at her, smiled, kissed her lightly, bent over to kiss Jennie, who stretched up to him with chubby arms for a "smoochie" and laughed as he mussed her hair, blond like her mother's.

He left his family and started on the short walk to his classroom. Then, as he so often used to, he stepped into a tiny octagon-shaped building just ten feet across, three of its eight sides open to face on to the bubbling creek that flowed down through the middle of the campus. It was the campus "Prayer Porch," a favorite place where he used to often come to sit, to listen to the creek tumbling by, at times to pray, at times to just soak up a moment of peace and solitude before the start of a class.

The walls were covered in graffiti, without exception all of them touching, a brief quote of scripture, a "Thank you, God," a heart with initials in it, but so many now "RIP, my love," "I miss you, sweetheart," and "I'll see you in heaven."

Several hundred names were written on the walls in long, orderly rows, the names of all those from the college who had died in the war.

Too many, far too many.

He sat in silence, looking at them. As years would pass, as it did with all wars, the pain would lessen, the aura and legends would grow as was so with nearly all wars, and memory of the names would drift into history.

The issues of this war were still in doubt. The day of the reopening of the school had been chosen because of all that was symbolized by this day in May, three years to the day since the start of the war.

Some things that John had said to the man who this day would be sworn in as a duly elected president must have stuck, and though John did not remember it, the new president did. That there was a final day and what John had learned was to be the theme of his inaugural address to be delivered at the hallowed resting place of Gettysburg. That the war had reached its final day. Perhaps it was just rhetoric. Half the country was still occupied by foreign powers.

As for those who once ruled from Bluemont, some had indeed met their fate at the hands of angry mobs that eventually stormed the facility while their "Praetorian Guard" had shown the wisdom of standing aside, in the same way the original Praetorians would do at times with an unpopular emperor when a mob stormed the imperial compound.

Many, though, had managed to disappear, John musing that such was often the case with people like that, a few cropping up as far away as South America and Africa, though one such nation thinking it would be a friendly gesture publicly hanged several of them.

Within Site R, there had actually been a standoff for several weeks between the guards and dwellers in what was actually known as Section Alpha and the troops under Colonel Bentley. The guards of that section finally agreed to disarm and for those within to face the same fate as the rest of the dwellers of Site R.

As for those elsewhere in the facility, it was a profound moral question for the nation as to what should be done with them. The majority favored just driving them out into the snow where more than a few waited just beyond the fence that encircled the compound to loot them at best or deliver far worse punishment. Many, therefore, still resided there after Bob, citing the example of Lincoln, appealed that to take vengeance on them was not in the spirit of what the country should again aspire to and that it was accepted that the statement against "attainder of blood" meant that no person could be punished for the crime of another family member.

The consensus was growing to let each of them take two to four weeks' worth of rations and find transport back to wherever they originally lived, though many now pleaded there was no place for them to go, that their spouses and parents were dead or had fled from Bluemont and disappeared.

Upon the revelation that Bluemont had indeed planned to loft an EMP over the southeastern United States, nearly every officer in the military had refused to accept further orders and within days declared that their oath was to the Constitution; as such, they would follow legal orders from a higher commander who had not been tainted by direct association with Bluemont and waited for such a person to be chosen. It was finally agreed that an admiral aboard one of the surviving carriers, who had ordered his SEAL team to seize the nuclear-tipped weapon at Wallops Island and was clearly untainted by any direct association with Bluemont, would serve as chief of all military operations until a new president was in place.

Bob's appeal for the beginning of a convention to reestablish a federal government had gotten off to a rocky start, ironically nearly identical to an argument when the original Constitutional Convention was held. Why were certain delegates sent rather than others? Who had the power to choose the delegates or even issue such a call for a meeting? Some states, particularly high food-production states, had experienced far fewer casualties than small urbanized states, such as New Jersey, which was all but depopulated, as was Rhode Island. There was also the question of whether delegates of states west of the Mississippi would be admitted. Texas, which was fighting what was nearly a full-scale war against Chinese and Mexican incursions, flat out said it was quit with the Union and wanted to proclaim that its boundaries should be what they had been when it was an independent republic, which had once included most of the southwest clear to California and parts of Colorado and Utah.

A smart compromise had actually been suggested by a history professor out of Purdue who specialized in the pre–Civil War South, suggesting that the thirteen original states should send the original number of delegates, and once a quorum was convened, delegates from states, in order of their admission into the original Union, would be greeted once the Constitution was reaffirmed. The idea, of course, was immediately seized on by those within the original states. It was seen as a way out of an impasse that threatened to cripple Bob's hopes before they were even remotely attempted.

And therefore, this day—what Bob at his inauguration as president called the Final Day—marked the beginning of a restored United States of America. Henceforth, this day in May would be observed with the same reverence as July 4, but also as a day of reflection as December 7 and September 11 were once observed.

The ringing of the campus bell stirred John from his musings. It was time.

He stood up, leaning over the railing. A blossom in the thicket of rhododendron that all but engulfed the small building was beginning to bloom. He gently plucked it free, held it for a moment, and then let it drop into the stream.

"Jennifer, sleep in peace, my little angel," he whispered.

He reached into his jacket pocket and drew out Rabs, flame scorched but still intact. The house next to where he had buried Jennifer and her grandmother was gone. There was no longer a windowsill for Rabs to rest upon and keep watch. But here, he realized, was a sacred place as well, where the names of so many others who had been lost were engraved. His gaze lingered on Grace's name, recognizing Kevin's handwriting. Picking up a pencil from the small table in the room, he wrote Jennifer's name beneath Grace's and placed Rabs on the table.

"Keep watch over all of them now, my little friend," he whispered, patting Rabs affectionately, eyes clouding with tears as he finally let go of the pain. All on this campus knew who Rabs was, and all would keep watch over him as well, and he would remain in the chapel as days, months, and eventually years slipped by.

John left the peaceful chapel, entered Belk Hall, and climbed the three flights of steps to the third floor to what he had once considered to be his classroom.

Of the thirty-five seats in the room, only a dozen were filled. He paused for a brief instant, taking that in, and he could not help but think that so much had been lost. Could they ever truly hope to recover?

One of the students, face creased by an ugly wound from the battle with the Posse, instinctively stood up and came to attention, the others following his lead. The man, for he was a man who was not even twenty yet, his childhood from a world that used to say, "Twenty-five is the new eighteen," had been robbed of adolescence forever. Would there ever again be a childhood for this generation? He looked at the old-style mechanical clock on the classroom wall. It was noon. Three hundred and fifty miles away, a friend of his—some hailing him as a George Washington reborn, others denouncing him as nothing better than a dictator—was being sworn in as president of the United States.

But then again, had not the same been said of Washington in his day, the legend not yet formed and ahead yet more wars, strife, a civil war that came close to forever rendering the Union apart, and from there global wars and finally the war of this generation?

Such had it been, and whether with hope or fear, such it would always be. There had been a chance to have prevented it all, but all the voices who had warned of its coming had been ignored, the mute testament of that folly the fact that two out of every three chairs in this room were empty. So many ghosts he could see hovering about those chairs—not just Grace, who, at least for a while, would be remembered, until, like all heroes, memory would fade even for her. So many others already half-forgotten. Their memories for him the ultimate price of the folly of letting those who let the nightmare unfold so easily take power and wield it while with honeyed words dripped lies of assurance and reassurance that they would all be taken care of. Forgotten the prophetic words that the price of freedom is eternal vigilance.

He realized that he had been standing before the class for several minutes gazing at the room in silence. Several were in tears as they looked upon him, and he felt his throat tighten.

"Stand at ease and be seated, please,"

He looked around the room, smiled, and then as he once used to do at the start of every class, John Matherson asked a question:

"Now, where did we leave off?"